RECLAMATION

A NOVEL

LISA CLONCH TSCHAUNER

North Carolina

Published in the United States by BQB Publishing
(an imprint of Boutique of Quality Books Publishing, Inc.)
www.bqbpublishing.com

Printed in the United States of America

978-1-952782-02-2 (p)
978-1-952782-03-9 (e)

Library of Congress Control Number: 2021932880

Book design by Robin Krauss, www.bookformatters.com
Cover design by Rebecca Lown, www.rebeccalowndesign.com
First editor: Andrea Vande Vorde
Second editor: Allison Itterly

PRAISE FOR RECLAMATION

"I've been in a relatively unique position of dealing with the counselors, social workers, and to a lesser degree, the actual victims . . . and even through various stories I've heard, I've *never* felt the panic, the horrors, and the relentlessness that victims feel of being held and trafficked and sexually assaulted like I did while reading [this] book. This story needs to be told to a wide audience!"

—Karen Marks, Agape International Mission Volunteer

"It's beyond my ability to understand how [the author] could be in the skin and souls of these victims and their families. But she DID. She took experiences that [we] have heard about for years and brought them to life. The author got into the heads and hearts of those who live this nightmare every day of their lives. I have no clue how she did it, but she did. This book stays with you. It does. From all the work we did on the ground in Cambodia, I can say that this book is profoundly moving in a much different way."

—Diane Blalock, Agape International Mission Volunteer

For Wyatt and Madison

PROLOGUE

June 26, 2012

Jenna

I enter my credit card number and the amount of five hundred dollars. In the memo section on the screen, I type, "This donation is made in the name of Mallory Shields, my best friend." I have twenty dollars taken out of each paycheck to make this donation every year. In my government job, it is all I can afford, but it's something, and I hope it makes a difference for someone even if it is too late for Mallory. The unimaginable happened on this date. The day the nightmare began for us both. She has been gone for five years. I vowed to never give up hope that she would safely return home to us someday, but the likelihood of that happening is next to impossible.

I realize I've been blankly staring at the screen noting my completed transaction for several minutes. With a deep breath, I log out of the donation portal and open up the spreadsheet to prepare for our quarterly budget meeting.

August 2, 2014

Ryan

A rabbit emerges from under the tree and I pull Carter's leash. He tenses up when he notices the rabbit, but he doesn't seem to want to go after it. I take a sip from the hot caramel drink I ordered from the local barista in the coffee cart on South Elm near my old apartment. *Our old apartment.* I lick my lips from the sugary taste. I only drink this sweet treat once a year on this day; it was her regular order.

I walk over to a bench near the lake and sit down. The breeze is cool for summer, but it is early in the day and the humidity will soon be overwhelming. This spot was always a favorite of ours. We would bring Carter here when he was a puppy, grabbing cappuccinos on the way. I scroll through the photos on my phone, stopping on the one of us together on the beach. Looking at it for several moments, I breathe deeply and then finally put my phone back in my pocket.

Today would have been our wedding anniversary. Mallory has been gone for seven years. We talked about having the wedding in this park. Her being gone is getting easier for me, especially now that I have a family of my own, but on certain days like today and her birthday, Mallory occupies my thoughts. I allow myself to relax into the bench and just take in the space around me. Her memory gets more distant each year, but it just feels right to acknowledge her on this day. Eventually, I rise up and Carter follows me back through the park as I exit the past and focus on the day ahead of me.

January 21, 2016
Renee

I look across the table at the empty plate. My eyes well with emotion and I almost can't swallow. I am pathetic, but celebrating her birthday allows me to remain hopeful. I push the food around on my plate, not feeling hungry. She loved my homemade macaroni and cheese. Each year on her birthday, we would do a special meal where she could pick anything she wanted for dinner and we would eat in the dining room rather than around the kitchen island. She had different themed parties with friends growing up and then later in college she would have gatherings with more mature celebrations, but no matter what, we would always do dinner together on her birthday. I've kept the tradition going even without her.

I fold my hands and rest my forehead on top. Tears trickle down my cheeks as I stare at the plate of macaroni pasta shells. My cell phone rings from the other room, startling me.

"Hey, Renee." My sister's voice brings me some comfort. She always calls me on Mallory's birthday.

"Hi there, Joanie," I choke out.

"How are you doing?"

"Okay. Okay, I guess." I wipe the tears and inhale, pushing my shoulders back.

Last year on this day, by the end of our conversation she thought she had convinced me to give in and hold a memorial service for Mallory. She wasn't the only one with that idea. The last time Jenna stopped by to see me, she had inquired about the same thing. I know everyone thinks a funeral will bring me closure and help me to move on, but I just can't. I'm still not ready to let her go.

I put my phone on speaker and begin to clear away the dishes from the table.

"Well, I just wanted to call. Been thinking about you all day . . . and Mallory." Hearing my sister say her name sends a wave of sadness through me that actually makes me ache.

"She would have been thirty today," is all I can say.

CHAPTER ONE

Mallory

June 26, 2007 – Dusk

I knew something felt wrong as soon as we got into the car at the temple, but I ignored it. I wanted to show Jenna how easy it could be to just go with the flow and let things happen.

Why did I ever keep going with that charade?

My head throbs where I must have fallen against the side of the van. I open my eyes to see one of the men standing above me, shouting in a foreign language. He's holding Jenna's phone and is shaking it at me.

Oh Fuck! Are they going to kill me for trying to keep the phone with me?

The man pulls me up by my arm and my legs feel like they are going to collapse. My wrists are still bound by the plastic ties. I look around for Jenna. Maybe she's still in the van, but I can't see through tinted windows. All I see is another man pacing in front of the van and talking on a phone. Then a large delivery truck comes over the small hill in the road and slows down.

Oh God, please let this be someone to rescue us.

The truck starts to turn around in the middle of the road and then backs up behind the van. Two larger men get out and yell something at the man on the phone.

I scream from behind the tape that muffles my mouth.

They talk harshly to the man grasping my arm. I wish I could understand what they are saying. One of them walks up to me and stands very close. He looks at me with dark eyes and a sour look on his face. He pulls me away, dragging me toward the large truck. *Is he saving me? Is he taking me? What is happening?*

My mouth is on fire under the tape. Tears and sweat sting my eyes. I kick my feet, trying to grip the ground and attempt to run, but this strange man is pulling me too fast. The gravel scrapes my legs. Then he stops and hoists me up, making me balance upright. He shakes me by the shoulders and yells something at me. My body trembles, and my esophagus burns like I might vomit.

I shift my focus to regain control of my legs so I might be able to run. I look at the man who keeps yelling at me and then, almost by reflex, my knee hits him right in the groin. He bends over in pain. He says something while almost laughing, and then his face works its way into a sneer with sharp eyes, and his hand strikes my cheek. My head is ringing, and I swear I just lost my sense of hearing in my right ear. Stumbling backwards, I fall to the ground only for the wind to be knocked out of me as the man kicks me in the stomach. My body folds in on itself with agony and shock.

Breathing heavily through my nose with mucus and tears covering my face, I manage to loosen the tape enough to gasp for more air. As I look up from the ground, a hazy fog clouds my vision. *Am I passing out?*

Another man comes over and grabs my arms, yanking me toward the larger truck. With a chain in his hands, he loops the zip ties on my wrists and then hooks me to a large bar on the side of the delivery truck. He pushes the tape back around my mouth with his dirty hand and then says something under his breath as he walks back to the van.

My hearing returns quickly as the screeching sound of the door slides opens to the back of the truck. To my horror, two of the men start pulling the women out the side door of the van. The women are still unconscious. One man takes the feet and another takes their shoulders, and they lift the women up and into the back of the delivery truck. The larger man who hit me is able to carry a woman over his shoulders and load her into the truck like a sack of grain, ready for delivery. There is shuffling inside the back of the truck, but I can't see anything.

Then they pull Jenna out of the van. Her body looks lifeless as they carry her. Her reddish-blonde hair drags on the dirt road. The two smaller men toss her up to the back of the truck. I hear her body hit the metal floor, and it makes me yell under the tape.

No! No! No! I wonder if they will kill me instead of putting me in the truck too.

A hand grabs my shoulder, and I can't turn around all the way. I try to pull myself away from his grasp, but there is no possibility of getting loose. He rips my head back by my hair and then something cold grazes my neck, maybe a knife.

This is the end.

I squeeze my eyes shut. Images of my mom and dad flash in my mind. I see myself with Jenna boarding a plane just days ago, full of excitement and anticipation. I see Ryan's face, his kind face with his trusting heart, as I wait for the worst.

I scream under the tape again. I'm sure I'm dying right here, right now. But I have to find a way to save Jenna. I can't let them kill me.

The sun has almost set, and I'm unable to make out much on the road. Only a few moments have passed even though it has seemed like an entire lifetime in those horrific seconds. Someone tugs on my hair and shoves a cloth in my face. In a breath, everything goes black.

CHAPTER TWO

Mallory

June 26, 2007: Time Unknown

Lying in my own sweat and stench, I try opening my eyes. Darkness fills the space, but I can sense other people nearby. Trying to steady myself, I move my arm and it's met with resistance. I am restrained to something above and behind me. Using my legs, as weak as they are, I push back against the wall to sit up. Squinting, I make out the shapes of other people squatting or lying near me. We are moving. I realize we are in the back of the delivery truck. I can hear the tires whistling beneath the floor.

With as much strength as I can muster, I lift my hands to pull the tape off my mouth. There are deep marks on my wrists where the plastic ties have dug into my skin. Using my numb fingers to try to grab the corner of the tape, I begin to pull. It stings as the tape rips away at my skin, but I gradually turn my head the opposite direction to help it along.

I hear a familiar voice in the distance questioning with a hushed urgency

"Jenna?" I whisper.

Pain shoots up from my lower back, and I squirm to situate myself to accommodate the discomfort. *How can this be? Is this just a nightmare, the worst possible nightmare?* A sickening feeling comes over me. I have no idea where I am or how far we are from the city. The hopelessness is overwhelming. I slow my breathing down and resist the tears welling up inside. *Focus, Mallory, stay calm.* The skin around my mouth pulsates from removing the tape. It feels a lot like when Jenna and I waxed our faces and eyebrows before graduation day.

College graduation. Christ. It was only a month ago. Just a month ago when I still thought my entire future was in front of me.

Hundreds of white chairs were lined up in rows filled with students and family, the scent of freshly cut grass lingered in the cool spring air. I remember the distant whistle of a train carrying coal to the east across the plains of the Midwest.

Ryan and I sat in front of the stage. I squeezed his hand and smiled as I felt the new ring on my finger. We hadn't told anyone but Jenna. Keeping it from her was impossible when we met up that morning to decorate our caps before the graduation lineup. We planned to tell everyone, including our families, that night at the big graduation celebration.

The ensemble finished singing, and the crowd applauded. Chancellor Richter stepped up to the podium.

"This year's graduation speaker is a shining example of what a Goodwin scholar can be. She is at the top of her class, has led her peers through countless hours of making positive change as the president of student government, and has received numerous scholarships because of her exemplary academic performance while at Goodwin. Not only is she an incredible student, but she is also a steward of her community. She serves as a volunteer counselor at the Everly Falls Crisis Center, and has organized the area celebration of veterans for the past six years and counting. She is a delight to work with and will be what we consider one of our elite alumni in about . . . " Chancellor Richter looked at his watch, ". . . twenty minutes." The crowd chuckled. "It is my pleasure to introduce Ms. Jenna Marquette as the graduation speaker for the 2007 graduating class of Goodwin College."

We all rose to our feet to applaud my best friend as she walked to the stage and positioned herself behind the podium. There was a slight ache in my cheeks from smiling so hard. Everyone around me had already sat down, but I stood, continuing to applaud. I winked at Jenna and then took my seat. Her speech was familiar. She had practiced it several times in front of me to get it just right. When Jenna neared the end of her address, her words went in a different direction than what she had practiced.

"And with that, I encourage each of you to find your passion and seize each opportunity to learn something new, to impact those around you, and to be the best version of yourself. Many of you came to this community to attend Goodwin College. I have been lucky to grow up in Everly Falls, and I always dreamed of going to Goodwin College. Shout out to my best friend, Mallory Shields, who has been with me every step of the way. She helped me face many challenges growing up, and in college, she taught me that it isn't just about the grades and achievements but about taking risks to do things without knowing the outcome and being okay with that. She has given me the courage to be real and to focus on making memories and creating happiness, not just making money and professional success."

Happy tears flowed as she made this public declaration of the importance of our friendship. Jenna was like my sister, and we had been through thick and thin. She was raised by a single mom after her father was killed during a deployment to the Middle East when Jenna was just a toddler. She had always worked harder than anyone else and met the mark with all of her goals. Jenna inspired me to be better.

Jenna looked so professional on stage with her strawberry-blonde hair straightened and framing her freckled face. Usually, her hair fell in waves and slight curls, which was perfect for her fiery green eyes and clever smile. She was a few inches shorter than I was, but her confidence always made her seem taller.

Jenna pulled out a piece of paper. "Mal, you know how special you are to me, and I wanted to share a poem to let everyone else know." She recited a poem about friendship, and the crowd let out ooh's and *ah*'s. I laughed uncontrollably. Most people probably thought it was Jenna's cheesy attempt at a heartfelt poem, but it was the theme song to *The Golden Girls*, our favorite rerun sitcom.

Jenna laughed, as she looked right at me. "Girl . . . I can't wait to leave for Thailand with you next week and spend the next year exploring the world and creating new memories. I would have never had the confidence to do this without you." She dramatically blew a kiss to me. "Class of 2007, congratulations to you all, and let's make it count!"

The crowd rose to their feet again and cheered. Jenna took a bow, halfway sincere and halfway sarcastic, as it turned into more of a curtsy.

Being selected as the graduation speaker was a great way for Jenna to really cap off and celebrate her achievements through college. She was always good at focusing and staying on course when it came to projects and homework. She was determined to graduate at the top of the class and to land a great job. Nobody was surprised when Jenna was offered a position with Jacobson Fielder, a local PR firm as the regional communications coordinator making close to six figures.

When I told Jenna about my desire to take a gap year before graduate school to travel and see different parts of the world, I expected her to disapprove. She would never do anything so frivolous and non-progressive to her career. If anything, I thought she would tell me it was going to be detrimental to my future when it came to getting into a good graduate program.

But she didn't.

It was early in the fall semester of our senior year, and I was lying on a blanket on the quad. I had just finished my Psychology of the Family class and was thumbing through a Southeast Asia travel guide my advisor had given me. Her sister had spent several years there as an English instructor in a small village near Bangkok. When I told my advisor I wanted to take a year off and travel to Thailand and explore other countries before going to grad school, she gave me her sister's email address and the paperback guide. It was almost overwhelming how many people had connections to Thailand once I told them I planned to travel there.

Jenna plopped down next to me, and I could tell there was something on her mind because she didn't lead with something funny. She had a serious look on her face, and she fussed with the hem of her shirt, a nervous habit of hers.

"Hey, you . . ." I sat up to face her. "This is a nice surprise. You hate sitting on the quad. What if you get wrinkled and dirty?" I chuckled.

"Exactly! The old Jenna would have cared about wrinkles and dirt," she announced. "But you're looking at the new Jenna who is more relaxed about such things."

"Oh, exciting. Tell me more." I sat up even straighter.

"Well, I just had coffee with Sebastian," she said in a serious tone.

She dated Sebastian Manns on and off during our junior year, and then they got more serious over the summer. She crushed on him the first two years of college. Bash, as we all called him, came to Goodwin from Hawaii to play football. When Jenna first saw him during orientation, she reacted so "girly," which was very unlike her. She wasn't one to giggle or blush. Granted, Bash was possibly the most beautiful person to walk the earth. His giant smile was a brilliant contrast to his smooth, caramel skin that highlights his buff and contoured athletic frame. He could capture anyone's attention with his confident swagger and long, wild black locks that always fell in just the right places, complementing his undeniable hotness.

At first, Bash and Jenna were friendly to each other, but he didn't seem to have any interest in dating. He was focused on football. Bash was also not the best student, which surprised me even more that Jenna would find him attractive. She usually went for the intellectual types. At the end of our sophomore year, Bash needed to raise his GPA, otherwise academic probation would result, which could prevent him from playing football. Bash was convinced he had a future as a professional player, so this shook him into getting some tutoring. It was the perfect time for Jenna to step in, and she did.

In his junior year, Bash was doing a lot better in school and somehow he and Jenna started spending more time together outside of the library. We were all surprised when Bash invited us to go to Hawaii and stay with his family over spring break that year. There were twenty-four of us; Bash invited some of his teammates and their girlfriends, as well as Jenna, me, and Ryan. Bash's family owned a chain of high-end hotels and resorts in Hawaii, and we were treated like royalty. Our entire group took up the top floor of one of his father's best hotels.

On the second to last day of our stay in Hawaii, we were all on the beach, and some of us were still trying to learn to surf before the trip ended. I had just fallen off my board and taken in a bunch of salt water, so I was lying on the beach catching my breath. Jenna was next to me slathered in sunscreen wearing a large floppy hat and reading *Anna Karenina* under her umbrella. In my opinion, she was being a bit overly cautious.

Suddenly, a man approached us and tried persuading us to walk down the beach to a party with him. He was dressed in board shorts and a faded Budweiser T-shirt. His hair was unkempt and his skin was sun-weathered. His voice was raspy and rushed, and I thought he was under some type of influence because he seemed off balance. We declined politely, but he lingered, continuing to ask. We kept saying no, but he wouldn't leave. Then Bash showed up and was in full-on active duty mode.

"Dude, get out of here," Bash said, keeping his aggression at bay.

The guy half-turned in Bash's direction and just blew him off. "Fuck off," he said, then took a step toward Jenna.

"All right, buddy," Bash said, stepping toward him. "If you don't leave my girlfriend and her friend alone, I have an army of Goodwin Gladiators who I guarantee live up to the name. Your choice, dude."

By that time, several of the guys had rolled up behind Bash.

The man's eyes grew wide as he realized he was drastically outnumbered and was by far the least athletic of them all. Surprisingly, he turned to Jenna and winked. "Well, if you get bored with these bottom-feeders, you know where to find me." Then he gave us the "hang loose" shaka hand gesture and scurried off down the beach.

There were chuckles, fist bumps, and grunting as Bash's crew slowly retreated back to the water or up to the bar on the beach. Bash knelt down next to Jenna. Her mouth was gaping open, completely smitten.

"Hey, sorry about that jerk. Are you okay?" Bash asked.

"Uh . . . sure. I mean, thanks. Yeah, he was kind of a jerk," she said, fumbling for composure. Now it was my turn to retreat and leave the two of them alone. I went to find Ryan, who was engrossed in a game of sand volleyball.

That night, after going to a luau hosted by Bash's family, Ryan and I were in our room packing up our stuff when I picked up a skirt I had borrowed from Jenna earlier in the week. I headed down the hall to her room to give it back to her, but there was no answer. I smiled, thinking about Jenna and Bash, together on our last night in Hawaii.

The next morning, they showed up in the lobby holding hands.

When I looked at Jenna, it was written all over her face. With a nudge, I gave her a slight smirk.

"Good morning. How was your night last night? Did you two have fun?"

"Oh, yeah. We were pretty tired, so we just crashed in my room. Right, babe?" Bash looked at Jenna for confirmation. Her cheeks blushed and she giggled.

From that point on, Bash referred to Jenna as "babe." It was cute at first, but it became increasingly annoying as time went on, at least to some of us. But Jenna never seemed to mind. She caught me up on all the gushy details during the plane ride home, and I couldn't have been happier for her to finally have the romance she wanted with Bash.

So when she approached me that day in the quad with her fast talking and wide eyes, I didn't know what to think.

"It's . . . over," Jenna finally said.

"What's over?" I said.

She looked out past the lawn. "Bash said he wasn't ever going to be what I wanted in life. He heard back from the arena football organization and was put on a waitlist. He doesn't think professional football is in his future."

"Damn," I said, knowing this must have been a blow to Bash.

"So, he's pretty sure he's going with plan B: go back to Hawaii to work for his father until he can get his teaching certificate, then hopefully find a school there to teach and coach."

She didn't seem as upset as I thought this might make her. Bash was her first love. Well, first real love. We didn't count the obsession she had with George Stephanopoulos during high school. She always joked about how he was going to be her future husband and they would co-anchor their own news program, ultimately becoming the world's next power couple.

We were sitting cross-legged, facing each other. I took Jenna's hands in mine and pressed our palms together, bringing them upwards and looking in her eyes.

"How does plan B sound to you?" I asked, pressing forward a bit.

"Bash told me how he would create a life of disappointment for me. He said I would never be satisfied with him just teaching and coaching. He tried to tell me how perfect my life was going to be and how successful I was going to be. He said he felt pressured to achieve as much as me, and eventually I would end up resenting him or leave him for someone better. Then I realized he was worried about our relationship based on how much disapproval or disappointment I would have with him."

She sighed. "I don't want to be that person, Mal. I need to relax and enjoy life more. I will never be happy if I keep expecting people to live up to my standards." Her eyes were pleading, as if I should understand the deeper meaning of this statement.

I smiled, giving her a questioning stare, and finally said, "Okay, brainy Jenna, I'm clueless. What do you mean?"

She pushed her hands against my palms and raised herself up. "Long story short, I want to go with you for a gap year."

"What?" I was bewildered. I stood up.

"I want to go." Jenna smiled. "Can I go with you?"

"But your job—"

"Yeah, I already thought of that. I talked to Jacobson Fielder, and they're okay with it. I mean, they're not thrilled, but they seemed to be receptive. The HR manager said unless the entire economy tanks, they will still hire me after a gap year. Besides, I have interest from some other companies too."

"What?" I repeated.

"Serious, Mal. I want to do something unexpected. I want to see what it's like to live day by day. I need to make some memories of this time in my life besides just going to college and then to work."

My face broke into a huge smile. The idea of having her by my side as we explored the world made me excited and also a bit apprehensive. My gaze followed a man across the lawn blowing leaves off the sidewalk. The smell of fall was sweet, and even though the air was cool, a feeling of warmness like standing too close to a bonfire came over me.

"Jenna, don't tease me like this. You know I would love for you to go with me. I can't think of anything I would want more, but I just can't believe you want to go."

"Yes, you do know me well." She put on her serious face, then smiled slightly. "But you also know how much I think and overthink and contemplate before doing something or even telling anyone about it."

"Exactly."

"So if I tell you I actually want to do this, you know I've thought this through." She smiled. "Mallory, I want to go with you to Thailand."

"Yes! Yes! Yes!" I exclaimed. "We're going to the other side of the world after graduation, and we're going together! But you have to promise you won't change your mind. Because you know me just as much as I know you. I will be crushed if you change your mind." I put on my best mock pout, dramatically clenching my hands to my heart.

"Promise." She stuck out her finger to pinky swear.

"I'm so excited." I bypassed the pinky swear and went for the hug. "We're going to have so much fun and see the world!"

Jenna helped me pick up my things. We headed toward Copeland Hall for my next class. Our pace was light as the leaves crunched under our feet. In another month, there would be snow on the ground.

"I want to know everything you've planned so far. Every detail," Jenna said as she looped her arm through mine.

"Jenna." I stopped and looked at her. We both burst into laughter. Jenna knew me better than anyone else. She knew I hadn't started any planning.

"Well, what I meant to say is that I can't wait for the two of us to plan this amazing adventure together," Jenna said and, arm in arm, we skipped across the quad together towards an unknown future.

Our friendship has always had a balance. I am the laid-back, laissez-faire part of the duo and Jenna is the one who is organized and structured. If only I could have been more like Jenna and mapped out a better plan for this trip, we might not be in the situation we are now.

There is a bump, jostling everyone in the back of the truck, and I'm jolted out of my memories. I try to swallow, to get a grip on my surroundings, but all I can think about is how it's my fault we are kidnapped.

Kidnapped. It's strange how I haven't put a word to what is happening to us until just now.

CHAPTER THREE

RYAN

June 26, 2007

"I know, Mom. I will. Yes, August second of next year." I balance the receiver of my phone between my chin and shoulder as I walk over to the thermostat on the wall, still pulling my luggage behind me. "Well, of course it's a Saturday, Mom. We did look at the calendar . . . not just randomly pick a day," I chuckle.

"Okay, well, I just was checking to see if you made it back," Mom says. "Are you tired?"

"I'm . . . beat, actually. Long flight." I sit down on the sofa and kick off my shoes. "Tell Lily to just keep Carter over there tonight, and I will pick him up in the morning. Is that okay?"

"Of course, son." Mom sighs. "Well, I'm glad Mallory liked the resort and that you joined them."

"They really loved it, Mom. It was beautiful. She said to tell you and Dad 'thank you.'" I lean my head back and hold the receiver in my hand. The clock on the wall says 8:30 p.m.

"Well, get some rest and we'll see you tomorrow," she says. "Love you."

"Love you too." I slowly lean forward and hang up the phone. The cool air from the vent blows down on me and I lay my head back again. The flight home from Thailand seemed to take much longer than on my way there.

It has been almost twenty-seven hours since I left my fiancée in what she called "paradise." Aside from lightly sleeping during the long legs of the flight, I feel exhausted and already miss her. I'm sure she and Jenna are already in route to Bangkok to start the adventure of their gap year.

I had surprised Mallory with an impromptu visit at the resort where she and Jenna were staying, courtesy of my parents as a graduation gift. On my last day there, the three of us were hanging out by the resort pool and drinking beer from a large bottle after the evening's festivities on the beach.

"This is paradise," Mallory said as she leaned back in the chaise lounge. Her demeanor was relaxed, partly because of the late hour and mostly because of the Singha beer.

"It's pretty good, but for the record, it's just as hot as it is back home." I walked around the edge of the pool, carefully balancing myself. We were the only ones at the pool, and the sultry night air made it seem like our own private retreat.

"We have to come here every year, Mal," Jenna said with the thrill of a new idea. "Let's agree now that we will come here every year for New Year's!"

"Agreed," Mallory said. She waved her hand for me to bring her the bottle of beer.

She took a swig, then handed it to Jenna.

"New Year's. Thailand. This resort. Every year." Jenna tipped the bottle back, but I noticed she only took a small sip. She was trying so hard to relax and have fun, but there was still a bit of her trying to stay on top of everything, and getting drunk wasn't on her to-do list. "Or every other year, at least."

They giggled at their own compromising skills.

I couldn't help but laugh with them. I was glad I had the chance to visit them on their journey before starting my new job. It hadn't been the plan, but when the new boss called and told me they were going to delay my start date because of office renovation, I decided to take advantage of the situation. I already missed Mallory even though she'd only been gone a few days. I knew I wouldn't have any other chance to visit during her year-long trip exploring, so I acted impulsively and booked a flight. My youngest sister Lily was happy to housesit and take care of Carter, our puppy, while I was gone.

"Okay." Jenna rose to her feet. "I have one more pact, and then I'm going to leave you two lovebirds alone."

"Let's hear it." Mallory faced her.

"If we somehow get lost on this adventure, or if anything happens, we meet back here. Like, we do whatever we have to do to get back here, you know?" Her face was more serious now.

"Jesus, Jenna." Mallory seemed deflated. "Why would you say something like that?"

"I mean, it's just smart to have some sort of central meet-up place, right?"

"Whatever," Mallory said. "It makes it sound like you think we're going to get lost or abducted or something."

"No, just in case we lose track of each other or something weird happens, we have to do what we can to get back to the . . ." She looked up at the sign above the building. "Garden Sea View Resort in Pattaya, Thailand."

Mallory stared at Jenna with a disappointed look.

"Come on, Mal." Jenna smiled at her. "It's just a backup plan. An easy way we can find each other."

"Whatever, Miss Paranoid." Mallory took the bottle from Jenna's hand and took a long swig. "Agreed," she said and handed the beer back.

Jenna sat the bottle down on the table. "Agreed. It's a pact." She grabbed her shoes and purse off the lounge chair. "And now, I bid you farewell." She reached over to hug Mallory. Then she gave me a hug.

She looked at me squarely. "Oh my gosh. I won't see you before you leave, will I?"

"Probably not, unless you want to get up at four in the morning." I smiled.

Then she leaned in and gave me another hug.

"Safe travels, Ry." She put her hands on my shoulders. "I promise, Mal and I will be very careful, and I will take care of her for you."

Mallory was still eyeing Jenna with a look of impatience.

"Also, please tell your folks thank you so much for the graduation gift," Jenna said. "The resort is beautiful." She smiled and kissed me on the cheek.

"For sure, Jenna," I replied.

"Love you guys," she said as she walked up the path to the hotel.

I looked at Mallory. "You know she means well, Mal."

"Yeah, you're right." She walked over and put her arms around me. "Besides, I don't want to let anything spoil our last night together on this magical island."

The next morning, I slipped out of the hotel room without waking Mallory, leaving her a note on the bedside table. It was out of character for me to write love notes, so I hoped she appreciated the sentiment. The shuttle picked me up and drove me to the small island airport, and I flew back to the US via connections in Bangkok, Beijing, and Houston. When I landed in Omaha, I contemplated staying the night at a buddy's, but then decided to just get back home.

The two-hour drive back to Everly Falls was rough. Every song on the radio reminded me of Mallory. Just a little over a month ago on the night of our graduation, we were together with our friends and classmates celebrating the big day, but I would have been just as happy if it were only the two of us, alone and unconcerned with the rest of the world.

The memory of her on graduation night immediately made my chest warm, and I felt a catch in my breath. Mallory's eyes had never sparkled so bright. She laughed as we moved closer on the patio that was being used as the dance floor. I loved her smile and her laugh; it might have been one of my favorite things about her. Justin Timberlake's synthesized voice was blaring with "SexyBack," and the energy at the after-party was incredible. Mallory has always given me a hard time because she couldn't believe I loved to dance. She loved it too, but while she had many skills, dancing was not one of them. But she didn't care, and that's what made it even better.

We were carefree and relieved at the end of such an important day as we danced and celebrated. This woman was going to be my wife, and it made me happier than I had ever been. I couldn't imagine my future without her. The music changed to Shakira and the song about her hips. We kept dancing, and Mallory busted out some really spazzy moves. I laughed and tried to make up for it with my smooth skills. I wasn't a superstar athlete, but I did have physical coordination. It's probably attributed to my mom, who's a dance instructor. Even though I've never taken a dance class, I think my mom and two sisters' skills must have rubbed off on me.

Even with her awkward dancing, Mallory radiated confidence and beauty. As I watched her have fun and let loose, a warmness filled me. Her tall, slender figure kept with the beat in a clumsy but endearing way. Her dark hair fell over her shoulders. Mallory had intense, beautiful eyes, but when she smiled—really smiled—her entire face lit up and anyone around her couldn't help but feel genuinely allured by her. She had a way of pulling people in and creating a sense of acceptance and encouragement. Mallory made me want to be my true self, and I loved her deeply for that. I wasn't always comfortable feeling vulnerable or out of my element, but with her by my side, facing life's uncertainties seemed doable. Graduation was a milestone for me, and it couldn't have come fast enough.

I pulled Mallory close to me. "I love you so much," I whispered in her ear. "Wife-to-be," I added.

She squeezed me tight.

Then I felt someone else's arms wrap around both of us.

"Okay, you two . . . help me." Jenna giggled. "Bash is looking for me and thinks we should have one last night together before he moves back to Hawaii." I could tell she'd actually been drinking. Jenna was pretty much in control all the time, so this was strange.

"Come with me," Mallory grabbed Jenna's hand and gave me a look that said *sorry* and *thank you* all at the same time, and they hurried off together to the bar.

After mingling with some people, I eventually made my way over to the bar area where Mallory and Jenna were talking with Sarah McAllister, who also graduated with us. She and I both majored in accounting and had several classes together. There was a man with her who I assumed was a boyfriend. He handed Jenna his phone and she was typing something into it.

"There he is!" Mallory shouted. "Hey, Ry, this is Seni. He's from Thailand, can you believe it?" She tossed her hand up and smiled at me. "He still has a lot of family who live there. He's offered to give us his aunt's number in case we need a ride or anything. She has a taxi service. Isn't that great?"

"Nice to meet you." I shook his hand and smiled. It was somewhat of a relief to know Mallory and Jenna would have a local contact. I looked over at Sarah, who seemed half in the conversation and half looking for someone else in the crowd.

"Saaarrraaahh," I said, drawing it out for comedic effect. "Congrats. Looks like we finally made it, huh?"

"Yeah." She shifted her focus back to me. "Now, for all those student loans." She seemed distracted and fidgety.

Seni handed a card to Mallory, who handed it to Jenna. I was happy Jenna was going with Mallory. Jenna was certainly a planner and would be sure they were safe and aware of where they were. I would've loved to have been the one going with her, but I understood why Mallory wanted to go on the adventure on her own. We both knew this time apart would only make us stronger.

I took a step closer to Mallory and slid my hand into hers. Her soft, warm fingers intertwined with mine and when I felt the ring on her finger, a smile washed over me.

"You ready?" I asked.

"Yeah, I'm wiped out. Is it okay if we give Jenna a ride home?" she asked as we headed toward the exit.

"Of course," I said.

"Nice to meet you," Jenna said to Seni, followed by a loud hiccup. She walked over to us as we headed through the gate to my car.

After we dropped Jenna off at her apartment, I took Mallory to her parents' house. She was staying there for a few days with some of her extended family who came in for her graduation. We kissed goodnight, and I watched Mallory walk to the door.

I drove around for a short time before heading home. Catching a glimpse of myself in the rearview mirror, I noticed I was smiling when I pulled up to the apartment and turned off the car. This stuck with me because it seemed different. Whenever I pictured myself in my mind, it was never with a smile, so it caught me off guard a bit, almost like I was looking at another person. I hadn't even been aware that I was smiling, but it made sense. College was over, my girlfriend said yes to becoming my wife, I was starting a great job the next week . . . life was good. So good that I didn't even make it to bed; instead I plopped onto the couch after feeding Carter, the Golden Retriever Mallory and I adopted together. I wanted to name him Bruce after Bruce Wayne to commemorate my love of Batman. Mallory rallied to name him Odinson after Thor, her favorite superhero. She said we could call him Odi for short.

But then we remembered a class we had together sophomore year at Goodwin. It was a history class taught by an eccentric professor who praised President Jimmy Carter every chance he could. I could always make Mallory laugh with my impressions of this particular professor. Just the passionate enunciation of "Cah-tah!" would have her rolling. Then we both knew the only solution was to name our dog Carter. And, as it turns out, Jimmy Carter was kind of a superhero in his own right.

Carter nuzzled on my lap. My eyes grew heavy, and then I fell asleep listening to Chuck Norris talk about fluctuating workouts in an infomercial. As I drifted off, I was still consciously aware of the campy smile that stayed with me into my dreams.

Now I long for that feeling that went with that smile, but as I roll over, the reality of not seeing Mallory for a year sets in and there is an awkward emptiness lingering inside of me. I close my eyes and hope for dreams of her.

CHAPTER FOUR

Jenna

June 26, 2007: Time Unknown

My body is shaking with pain. My eyes slowly open under the heaviness from the drug-induced sleep and I see several other people lying on the floor around me. My shoulder is on fire, and when I move, pain shoots up my arm because my right hand is tied to a metal bar on the wall.

I look around in the dark, squinting, trying to find Mallory. I feel the sticky residue on my face from where the tape had covered my mouth. Then it hits me, the smell of urine, sweat, and mildew. My reaction is to gag, but then I hear a noise next to me, a whispering voice.

A young girl, also restrained, is crouched down next to me. As I turn toward her, she says something in a different language but with a tone of warning.

"Where am I?" I ask her. "What is this place? Were you in a blue van too?"

She shakes her head. She doesn't understand what I'm saying. Her face is dirty, and she seems frail and unstable. She has long, dark hair and is wearing torn jean shorts and a dirty T-shirt that has an anime figure on the front. Her tennis shoes are untied, and the tube socks are filthy around the lower part of her legs. She looks young, maybe fifteen or sixteen. She doesn't look local; maybe she's a tourist too.

"Jenna," I say as I place my unrestrained hand to my chest, taking the risk of sharing my name with her.

"Olivia," she whispers after a long pause. It's hard to tell, but she says her name in a thick but slight voice. She might be German. "*Lastbil*," she says.

The word is familiar, but I don't think it's German. I try to remember my humanities class where we learned conversational German and several other European languages.

Then Olivia makes a motion with her free hand as if she is driving.

"Oh my god," I gasp as I realize we're inside the trailer of a delivery truck. But it isn't moving. It's so dark, it's hard to tell. I can only see the outline of the other people.

"Mallory," I say loudly. I hear moans and then several people shushing me, but Mallory doesn't answer me.

The soreness in my body is overpowering, especially on my right side where my arm is restrained. I am groggy and shaky as if I drank too much. My mind is swarming with thoughts. *How did this happen? Am I being kidnapped? Why am I here?* I've heard about women disappearing when traveling, like the Holloway girl from the US who visited Aruba. When we left for our trip a few weeks ago, I never imagined something like that would happen to us.

When I think back to this morning—*my god, it was only this morning*—my only worry was surviving the heat and the cramped hostels where we spent our nights. The hostel was much less extravagant than the resort. I remember feeling overwhelmed at the sight of my personal belongings spread out on the bed at the hostel we'd been staying at for the last couple days. It was the third place we stayed in the last few weeks, and each time I packed up, the piles of stuff seemed to multiply.

Two people had moved into the hostel the day before, so the

room seemed much smaller. I found it difficult to sleep in a room with strangers and the time change between Everly Falls and Thailand had been hard to adjust to. Mallory didn't seem to be affected by any of it. Maybe I was just feeling a bit homesick.

As I struggled to put most of my clothes in the space-saver bag and squish them down to compress everything, Mallory hopped up on the bunk above me. She used to hate sleeping on the top bunk when we were younger. She finally did it one time on a dare at a sleepover. She always used her fears and hesitation as fuel to face what scared her and to overcome it. I admired that about her.

"Well, off we go," Mallory said with a smile. "I'm excited to see Chiang Mai. Do you still have that map?"

I unzipped the pocket on the outside of my backpack and pulled out the map my aunt gave to me at graduation. It showed all the roads and routes for the different types of transportation in Southeast Asia. Her neighbor traveled the area a few years ago and gave it to her when she told him about our upcoming trip.

Mallory unfolded it, and I could feel her looking at me even though she was trying to make it seem like she was looking at the map.

"How are you doing?" she asked.

"I'm feeling better." I had felt queasy the night before. We both were trying to adjust to the heat in Thailand. I knew it was going to be hot, but I didn't realize how intense it would be.

"I think it's cooler in Chiang Mai. Thank god," she said with another smile.

"Yes, thank god."

We had flown into Bangkok and stayed the first two nights in a hotel. Then we took a shuttle to Pattaya and stayed in a resort on the beach for five days. The resort stay was a gift from Ryan's parents to Mallory for graduation. Not only did it offer a beautiful landscape, but the rooms had air-conditioning. Ryan even flew in and joined us for the last three days, which made Mallory super happy.

Pattaya was tropical, such a contrast to Bangkok. The beaches were similar to those in the movies with tranquil, aqua waters on white-sand beaches. There were lush, green mountains wrapped around the beach areas.

It was serene and I was happy to be there, but it did remind me a lot of Hawaii, which made me think of Bash. I would never tell Mallory this because I didn't want her to think I wasn't over him, but I often wondered how he was doing.

Mallory and I joked about it being paradise. The other tourists we met were fun, and I started to really relax. Mallory had finally agreed to plan out our next few destinations with me. Some of the people we met recommended that we travel north and check out the more rural locations. When we left the resort, we took the shuttle back to Bangkok.

I let out a sigh as I zipped up my backpack and slipped on my shoes.

"Hey, do you want me to help you pack up?" I asked Mallory.

"Um, sure, if you want to." She climbed down from the bed and grabbed her backpack from the floor. As she started putting her stuff in, she was looking around the room. "Damn it. I can't find my headphones." She climbed back up on the bunk.

I spotted them hanging out from under her pillow on the other side of the bunk. "Aha!" I grabbed her headphones and handed them to her.

"Thanks!" Mallory laughed and looked at me with a direct and sweet expression. "I'm so glad you're here, Jenna."

Mallory had a way of making me feel better. I think part of it was her ability to rally or persuade people and the other part was her evident love for the people who were important to her.

We took one more look around the room, and then stepped outside under the awning. The sun was intense, and sweat dripped down the middle of my back. Mallory and I walked toward the 7-Eleven we had been to the day before. It was easier to get a ride to Hua Lamphong, the train station, from there. I also wanted to get some postcards to write out on the long train ride.

At the counter, I tried to do the conversion of the baht in my head but ended up letting it slide. Every time we purchased something, it seemed impossible for it to be so inexpensive. After I paid for my postcards, I handed my backpack to Mallory and went to use the restroom. I lingered a bit, considering the purchase of an umbrella to provide some shade, and also to take advantage of the cool air in the 7-Eleven from the air-conditioning that was evident from the mechanical rattling throughout the store. I decided to forgo the umbrella. I saw many locals walking around with them, but I didn't want to add more items to my backpack. When I returned, Mallory was sitting on a bench just outside the door talking with a woman. She didn't look Thai.

"This is Ruth," Mallory said. "She's a teacher in Bangkok and said she has been to Chiang Mai several times."

The woman smiled at me.

"Hi," I said. "Do you like Chiang Mai?"

"Oh yes. It's beautiful there," Ruth replied. "I was telling your friend that you may want to travel by bus to save some money. There's an overnight bus that will take you directly there."

"Oh, okay," I said. Mallory had a convinced look on her face, and I could tell she was entertaining the idea of taking a bus instead.

My shoulders tensed at the thought. I always stuck to a plan if there was one, but I was trying to be more flexible.

Mallory thanked the woman, and then we headed down the street.

"Well, what do you think?" she asked.

"It might be nice to have the day here in the city," I said, pleased with my adventurous response.

"Cool." She smiled. "We might even have time to go see Wat Suthat, the temple you mentioned wanting to see."

The Wat Suthat temple was one of the oldest in Bangkok. It was the one with a large red swing in front.

"Well, let's go over to the market and look at our map," Mallory said, and we were off.

The streets in Bangkok were bustling, and we stopped at several shops, eventually making our way to a small café for lunch. At one point, I realized I wasn't as overwhelmed by the heat as I had been earlier. This was a good sign. Maybe I was starting to acclimate.

The city was full of noises and activity. We weaved our way down the sidewalks, going around stands, people, and the occasional trash dumpster. In the streets, the tuk-tuks, scooters, buses, and regular vehicles all commingled, following some strangely understood pattern and rules of the street. We passed by small markets and groups of people gathered around food stands. The smell of grilled meat permeated through the salty air, settling my stomach until it rumbled with hunger. All throughout our walk, we encountered different smells of food, trash, exhaust, and incense.

As we passed by people, I smiled and tried to look friendly. I was surprised by the amount of eye contact or staring people did when they saw us. There was a difference in cultural norms, and I was very aware of being an outsider just by being white. People smiled, but it was different from the Midwestern hospitality or connection I was used to. With my hair stuffed up under a cap, I felt less self-conscious. From our first step off the plane at the airport, I could tell I would always be identified as a tourist. Mallory blended in a bit more with her dark hair and strong features, but I stuck out with my fair skin and unruly, blondish-red hair.

Rommaninat Park was beautiful with lush lawns, large statues, and vibrant fountains. It was much quieter in the park than on the street. There was a group of teenagers walking around, and we asked one of them take our photo next to an elephant statue.

Mallory and I finally made it to the temple and entered through an archway. The monk standing near the entrance nodded toward several signs on the wall. We weren't properly dressed. After covering our sleeveless arms with scarves, pulling skirts over our shorts, and removing our shoes, we entered the temple and walked along the wall of golden Buddhas.

The building was serene and peaceful with the essence of sacredness, making it easy to relax and take in the Zen vibes around us. As we took our time walking through the structure, admiring the shiny, ornate walls, I noticed a lightness to our steps, a sense of etherealness.

We finally exited and took a moment to reassemble our attire, stuffing the scarves and skirts in our packs and putting our shoes back on. I pulled out my phone and realized we had lost track of time. Increasing our pace, we walked back toward the park.

"Do you think we should try to get a ride to the bus depot?" Mallory asked.

"Maybe," I said, looking around for a taxi or tuk-tuk, but not seeing anything close by. We kept walking the way we had come, but we were going to have to find some mode of transportation sooner rather than later if we were going to get to the bus station for the overnight ride to Chiang Mai.

I browsed through the numbers on my phone of key places and contacts I had programmed in before we left. As I scrolled through the list, I saw one for a shuttle service run by the aunt of the man we met at our graduation party.

"Hey, remember that guy we met at the party? I think his name was San ... or Seni. He was with Sarah McAllister. He said his aunt lives here and works for a shuttle service. Should we call her for a ride to Chatuchak station?"

"Sure," Mallory said. "I mean, why not, I'm not sure how else we can get a ride."

Just then, we saw two men in a car driving toward us. They slowed down and finally came to a stop. Then one of them motioned for us to come over.

Mallory looked at me, then took a step toward the car, but I put my hand on her shoulder. "No," I said. "I don't think that's a good idea. I'm going to call this shuttle place now."

Mallory paused and then waved off the car. As they slowly drove away, we walked back toward the temple to wait.

I reached the shuttle service and was surprised someone answered who spoke English. I explained we were at the temple and the woman on the phone said someone would be there to pick us up as soon as possible.

We waited outside for about thirty minutes. I started to get anxious. We needed to be at the station in less than an hour. Then a car pulled up with a woman driving.

"Jenna?" she said out the window. She introduced herself, but I didn't catch her name.

"Yes." We walked toward the car.

"You can put your bags in the boot, if you want." She looked like she was from Thailand, but she spoke with a British accent.

The woman parked the car and then got out to unlock the trunk for us to store our big backpacks. She was a petite woman, almost tiny in a sense. Her long hair was pulled back into a tight ponytail at the base of her neck and pulled over her shoulder. She wore an old pair of Adidas tennis shoes that looked too big for her with skinny jeans and a tank top underneath an oversized shirt that seemed to be part of a uniform for a fast food or service type of business.

Riding in the air-conditioned car felt good. It was nice to have cool air circulating around us. The drive took a long time, and the stop-and-go of the traffic was starting to make me a bit nauseous. Or maybe I was just hungry because I hadn't been eating well. I wasn't as adventurous as Mallory when trying different foods, but I also knew it would be something I needed to ease into.

"Are you enjoying your time so far?" the woman asked. She looked back at us in the rearview mirror. I noticed something uneasy in her eyes.

"Yes, it's fabulous," Mallory said. "The temple was amazing."

"So, is it just the two of you traveling on holiday?"

"Yes, we're just taking some time to see the world before we have to actually be responsible adults," Mallory chuckled. She seemed eager to talk with someone else who spoke English besides me.

"That's a good idea," the woman said. "You said you're going to Chiang Mai today? Will you be meeting friends there, or is it just the two of you?"

"We don't have any plans yet, but we do hope to meet new people while we're there."

"Have you been to Chiang Mai?" I asked the woman.

"Oh yes. Many times." She smiled as she looked back. Her eyes seemed to soften, and I felt a sense of relief. As she swerved around a slower vehicle, her horn sounded, and she said something in a different language at the driver of the other car.

"Yes, yes . . . Chiang Mai," she said as she refocused on us. "There are lots of places to explore like waterfalls, temples, night life. Do you plan to stay anywhere specific?"

"Yes, we have a reservation at a hostel there," Mallory said.

"Very well." She seemed to be impressed with our planning.

I saw the tall clock tower a few blocks away, and soon we pulled up to the Chatuchak Park station.

"Did you say your bus leaves at two p.m.?" the woman asked.

"Yes," I replied.

"I don't think you will make it in time." She gave me a deflated look. "I can phone the number and check for you."

"That would be great, thank you," said Mallory.

The woman dialed a number on her cell phone. I thought she was speaking in Thai, but we didn't understand. She talked for at least two minutes.

"No, I'm sorry it took so long to get here. You will have to take the bus later tonight." She was shaking her head.

"Oh well, that's okay," Mallory said. "We can just wait here. Maybe we can just hang outside in that park by the clock tower."

"Okay," the woman said in a hesitant way.

"Do you think it is safe?" I asked.

"Um . . . I mean yes, but I have a friend who drives a different, smaller bus. He could get you to the next stop on the main bus line, and you could meet your bus there," she said.

Mallory and I looked at each other, not sure what to say.

"I think it's okay for us to just wait," I said.

"Sure, sure. But we can help you make it so you can stay on time with your trip." She smiled again. "Would you like me to check and see?"

"Well, okay," Mallory said. "We really appreciate your help."

"Oh yes." The woman did seem very helpful.

While she was talking on the phone, I looked around the car. It was not a new car, but it seemed to be in good shape. I noticed some papers on the seat next to her that looked like tracking sheets, maybe for mileage or her fees.

Again, she called a number and spoke in Thai. I really needed to start learning more of this language. I didn't like feeling inept and left in the dark.

"Okay, ladies." She turned to look at us. "He can get you there. I'll drop you off a few blocks up. There is a market you can wait at, and he will be there in about twenty minutes. He said he can get you to the next stop on the bus route, and you should actually be there before the bus arrives."

"That sounds great!" Mallory said, looking at me. She must have noticed the look of hesitation on my face. "I mean, is that okay with you, Jenna?"

I wanted to scream, *No! None of this is okay!* But I knew that was just my worrisome side coming out, and the whole purpose of this trip was to do the unexpected and go with the flow. I felt uneasy deep down and wanted to trust my gut, but I stifled these feelings.

"Okay," I said.

The woman had us back in motion and we headed north. Five minutes later, she stopped and we all got out. She seemed a bit rushed as she helped us unload our packs from the trunk and put them on our backs.

"The driver's name is Prem, and he will be here soon. He will be driving a large blue van and will probably have about six to ten other people in the van too." She smiled again. "Have a great trip!" Then she got in her car and drove off.

"Wait!" I shouted, but she was already gone, her car disappearing into the traffic. "Mal, we didn't even pay her."

"Oh my god," Mallory said. "Should we call her again?"

"Probably. Maybe she'll come back before the van gets here. I hope this is cool . . . taking this van."

"Yeah, it should be all right. I mean, this way we can still travel through the night and arrive in the daylight." Mallory sat down on a bench outside the market.

We waited a few minutes, expecting the woman to come back for her money, but she didn't. I called her back, but there was no answer. Just as I was hanging up, the blue van arrived.

Thinking back to those hours earlier, shame emanates and starts to grow inside of me as I play this back in my mind. I should have known better than to get in that blue van. The moment seems surreal or like I'm in a movie and I become confused at how I went from that van to this vehicle. I squint my eyes and try to follow the rays of floating lights as they pass by to see the faces of the other people restrained with me. Where were the other women from the van?

If we had only stuck with our plan and taken the train. If I could have just been true to my gut and not try to impress Mallory with my faux chill response to catching the overnight bus when that woman at the 7-Eleven suggested it.

That woman. What was her name? Ruth?

My thoughts are multiplying now, and my anger spikes. Did she have anything to do with what happened to us? Was it just a coincidence she was outside of the market, or did she have an ill motive? I should have asked her for her full name or found out where she was a teacher. Closing my eyes, I try to make a mental picture of the woman so I can later describe her to authorities.

I sit down next to Olivia, who is sobbing quietly. Tears well up in my eyes, but I want to keep my wits about me. There has to be a solution here.

"Does anyone speak English?" I whisper loudly.

"Shhh, be quiet," someone says. The accent is British or Australian. I squint my eyes and see the silhouette of the woman speaking to me. "Don't talk or they'll come in here again."

"I'm sorry," I whisper. "Do you know where we are?"

"No," she says bluntly.

"Who did this?"

She doesn't answer. I hear her sigh. I take this as enough of a warning to stop talking. I lean against the wall and close my eyes. *How can we get out of this situation?* My thoughts go to my mom. Then I wonder about Mallory and where she is. What if she escaped from the blue van? Maybe she is in contact with the police and will come find me. Every breath hurts my ribs, and my heart is racing. I'm completely drenched in sweat, and then I realize I probably also urinated on myself. I have no idea how long I have been in the truck.

A screeching sound rings out and the back of the truck opens up halfway. As the light enters the rectangular space, my eyes make out the others: women and girls, probably twelve of them, and they are restrained. Most of them are still lying unconscious on the floor of the truck. I look at the woman sitting in front of me, and she shakes her head with a very serious expression on her face. She slumps forward to act like she's not coherent. I think it's a signal for me to do the same, but I need to see what's happening.

A man crawls into the back of the truck and then two women are pushed inside with him. He is carrying a gun and wearing military-style boots. I can only see the outline of him against the light. I can see other people moving about outside of the truck.

"Hey!" I yell. "Let us go."

The man marches over to me. "Shut up," he says in a thick, demanding voice.

"Sir, please." I try to stand up to reason with him. As I wobble to my feet, still hunched over with my arm restrained to the wall, the man pushes me down with the butt of his rifle.

"Shut up," he says again and then stands over me.

My insides explode with pain as he kicks me in the stomach. Then the gagging comes on again, and my throat burns as I dry heave. I can't breathe.

The man leans down over me and smiles, as if he's proud of himself. He isn't one of the men from the van. He pulls out a brown prescription bottle from his pocket, opens it, puts a pill between his fingers, and then opens his mouth while nodding at me to do the same.

No, no, no. I can't take anything they give me. It will hurt or kill me.

Then he shoves his fingers with the pill into my mouth and

pushes it back into my throat, making me choke. He yells in Thai toward the open door. Then a bottle of water is tossed in by someone from the outside. He opens it and motions for me to open my mouth again. This time, I slowly do as he tells me. He pours water into my mouth and he watches me as I swallow the pill. The water gives me slight relief. I didn't realize how thirsty I am.

He hands Oliva the water, and she drinks from the bottle. With the barrel of the gun, he makes a circular motion to tell Olivia to pass around the water bottle. She passes it to the person next to her.

Another man climbs into the trailer, and the two of them pull the woman who is lying in the entryway of the truck back toward the wall and bind her wrist. She is a black woman, possibly still just a girl. She looks so young and tiny, wearing a dress with bright colors that is ripped and torn. She isn't wearing any shoes.

They pull another woman back toward the other side of the truck. She has long, dark hair and Converse tennis shoes on her feet. My heart races at the sight. It's Mallory.

"Ma . . ." my voice trails off. If I speak, it will be worse than a kick in the stomach. My adrenaline becomes even more intense. I've quickly learned not to yell or even talk with the guards.

Mallory is unconscious. Her body is limp, and they don't seem to care as they push her against the wall of the truck. She is still wearing her Wonder Woman T-shirt and her hoodie is tied around her, but she's wearing sweats instead of her shorts, and there's dried blood around her ankles. My eyes fill with tears. What have they done to Mallory?

After cuffing Mallory's wrist to the wall of the trailer, the two men climb out of the truck and pull the door shut.

"Mallory," I whisper. "Can you hear me?"

She doesn't answer. I hear a few shushes from the others.

After several minutes of sitting in silence and listening to mumbled voices outside the truck, I hear an engine start. We are moving slowly. There are small holes where light streams through the truck box, but not enough to see the others.

I stand up and try to get my eye level with one of the holes, but the view outside is passing by too fast to focus. So I slide back down to the floor. A grogginess is beginning to overtake me. The pill the man gave me is working. With all the energy I can muster, I cough and gag to try to make myself throw it up.

Olivia nudges me with her foot, and I look over at her. She is shaking her head again.

I stop gagging and feel exhausted. I focus on my breathing to try to calm down, but it's not easy. The metal of the floor and walls of the truck against my skin almost sting. Swallowing hard to keep from crying, I finally let my eyes close.

CHAPTER FIVE

Mallory

June 27, 2007: Time Unknown

When I come to, I glance down to the end of the trailer, and through the darkness I can see flecks of light roll over Jenna's hair and pale skin as the truck moves. I try to capture her gaze, but her eyes are closed and I think maybe she's unconscious. I want to yell out to her, but it's dark and I don't know if the men with guns are in the back of the trailer with us or not.

Only hours ago, we were free. This happened so fast and I am trying to understand where we misstepped. What mistake did I make landing us in such danger? I just wanted us to get to a place where we could explore, see the beautiful landscapes of Thailand, and take in the sites and culture. I am groggy, and I let my eyes close again as I replay the events of the day and how we ended up from the taxi to the van. I realize I didn't even get the name of the taxi or the van drivers. I force myself to remember back to when the van arrived at the bus station where we were waiting.

The driver pulled up and hopped out. I was still trying to get used to the drivers being on the opposite side of the cars.

"Jenna?" he asked, and she nodded. He smiled and motioned for us to take our backpacks off. He seemed to be in a hurry as we slowly slid our arms from the straps of our packs. As soon as we had them off, he grabbed them and walked to the back of the vehicle.

"Wait, Prem, right?" Jenna asked as he opened the back of the van. "Sir, wait." She followed him. She reached for her pack and then unzipped it, pulling out a smaller cross-body purse with her phone and other items before zipping it back up. He lifted the pack into the luggage space.

He looked at me. I hesitated, but then opened my pack and pulled out a small bag that held my wallet, phone, an address book, and my journal. I also grabbed my hoodie with the Goodwin College crest on the front. I knew I wouldn't need it for warmth, but it could serve as a pillow for the ride in case it took longer to get to the main bus.

Prem led us to the side of the van. Jenna and I climbed in and found seats next to each other all the way in the back. There were four other passengers, and we made quick eye contact as we got in. They were all women. Two of them looked about our age or maybe a little younger and were speaking a different language, Swedish maybe. The two others were likely a mother-daughter duo. They looked to be Thai or of Asian descent. I smiled and the older of the two smiled back at me.

The van took off, and there was a small pop of backfire and the smell of diesel fuel. I leaned my head back on the headrest and put the hoodie between the wall of the van and myself. Jenna sat up straight and looked out the windshield up front. She likely would not sleep or rest. That was just Jenna, and I'd learned a long time ago that she just needed space and time to find her rhythm. She had a hard time relaxing, but I hoped she would find a way once we got the hang of this international travel thing. Jenna was the type of person who really shined but needed to gather as much information as possible to create a strategy to control what happened around her. I knew she often saw this as a fault, but to me it was somewhat comforting.

When we were in the sixth grade, Jenna and I had taken a trip to the mountains when we were in the Girl Scouts. We had never been that far away from home without our parents. Our small group of eight girls was very excited and ready for a new adventure. Two of the mothers volunteered to take us. We all loaded into two vehicles and headed west toward the mountains. Jenna and I sat next to each other in the back seat. We had gone to preschool together and had been best friends ever since. We were both only children and somehow seemed to connect in a very sisterly way.

Jenna was the golden Girl Scout. In true form, she was always the overachiever: selling the most cookies, earning her badges before everyone else, and being the first to memorize all the pledges and songs. Her uniform was always pristine and perfect.

Once we arrived at the camp up in the mountains, we joined about two hundred other Scouts from surrounding states. We had to stay in cabins with girls we didn't know, and Jenna and I were separated. I felt self-conscious. The girls in my cabin were older than me by a year or two and seemed very serious about Scouting. They looked at me in my wrinkled uniform with the duffel bag my mom made out of my favorite superhero insignias rather than the official Girl Scout–issued bag they all had. They told me to take a top bunk, which also made me feel weird, having never slept in a top bunk before. I tried to talk with them, but they ignored me. I sat cross-legged on the top bunk and pretended to read a book while the girls chatted and laughed about how many points they earned at camp last year, and how they were from the best troop or had the cutest boyfriend or the richest parents. When I couldn't handle it anymore, I pulled out my Walkman, put on the headphones, and was quickly transported to my happy place through songs by Tom Petty, the Clash, Patti Smith, and the Ramones.

Then someone entered the cabin and I leaned over my bunk. My heart leapt when I saw Jenna. I pulled the headphones off and watched as the mood in the room quickly changed.

"Hi, there. My name is Jenna Marie Marquette," she announced. "My cabin was full, and they asked for volunteers to move cabins, so here I am."

Jenna stood tall in her perfect uniform, bag, shiny shoes, and well-groomed braids. She was even wearing the stupid beret that I never could get to stay on my head.

"I am in the lead now with at least fifty points just for volunteering to move." She smiled.

The girls looked Jenna up and down. The tension was apparent, and I felt a sense of excitement building inside of me, like when the underdog scored the point that tied the game.

Finally, one of the girls took a step toward Jenna. "You can take the bunk next to me if you want," she said, sizing Jenna up.

"Thanks." Jenna sat her bag down on the bunk and then shook the girl's hand. "You can call me Jenna."

"Okay." The girl awkwardly shook Jenna's hand. "I'm Felicity." She then sat down on the bed opposite Jenna.

"You know what?" Jenna said. "I really would rather be in a top bunk." Then she looked up at me. "Oh hi, Mallory. Would you like to trade with me?" She winked.

Jenna never ceased to amaze me with her ability to hold court, even as a headstrong sixth grader. And just like that, the underdogs won the game.

But we were in a situation that not even Jenna could control.

The van hit a bump with a loud thud. We came to a stop. Jenna was looking straight ahead.

"Something's wrong," she whispered without taking her eyes off the road.

"Oh, we probably just ran over something," I said, stretching my back.

Just then, a black sedan pulled up in front of the van, blocking the road so we couldn't move. The van stopped. Prem got out and walked over to the vehicle. From my vantage point, I could see at least two people get out of the other car. Then Prem got in.

"What the hell?" Jenna said. "Hey." She gestured to the Swedish girl sitting next to the sliding door in front of us. "Open the door."

The girl looked confused as she grabbed the handle and tried to open it, but it was locked.

Two men were coming toward our van, then they got into the front seat. The black sedan drove off, and our new driver put the vehicle in gear and sped away. The smell of fuel was strong and my head started to ache near my temples.

"Sir," Jenna yelled. "I'm sorry, but what just happened?"

The men acted as if they didn't even hear her. The two women in the front seat of the van turned to look at Jenna. They didn't seem alarmed, or maybe they understood what was happening. The older woman pulled the younger one close while shaking her head.

My stomach grew tight and queasy. Sensing the danger of what was happening, the hair on my arms stood up, and there was a dull buzzing in my ears.

I watched as the landscape moved faster as the van gained speed. My heartbeat started to relax. Maybe I was just being paranoid. I took some deep breaths. I decided to try to calm down, so I laid my head on my hoodie against the side of the van.

"It's okay," I whispered to Jenna. "Looks like some type of shift change or driver switch." I forced a smile.

Jenna's eyes were focused forward and I could see the tenseness of her jaw. Perhaps seeing me relax would help her do the same.

We drove ten minutes before I felt Jenna's hand squeeze my forearm, and I sat straight up.

The man in the passenger seat rose up and crawled between the two seats to sit between the mother and daughter. He spoke to them in Thai. The older woman was pleading with him, almost crying. The younger girl looked back at us, but then he grabbed her hair and made her face forward. He had a black plastic bag in his hand, and they reluctantly put their small handbags inside of it. The mother put her arm around her daughter and pulled her close again. They were both crying.

He then crawled over the seat to the Swedish girls. As he knelt down, I saw a gun in his hand.

The first girl screamed something that sounded like a question. He didn't answer, just grabbed their purses and phones. The other pleaded with him, and then the first girl tried to kick the man away from her.

I was frozen in place. I heard Jenna's heavy breathing among the crying women. I felt like I was watching a television show in slow motion. What was happening?

Instinctively, I reached for Jenna's hand, but her hand was in her bag. She pulled out her phone and fumbled with it. Just then, the Swedish girl yelled and the man hit her on the side of the head with the handle of his pistol. She slumped forward. The other girl screamed and the noise bounced off the sides of the van, and the buzzing in my head became more oppressive.

The man held the gun up to the screaming girl. She stopped but was red in the face and crying as she looked down at her friend. He sat the bag down and pulled something from his back pocket. It was a zip tie. He put the gun into the back of his pants and grabbed the girl's ankles. He tightened the plastic tie around her feet so she couldn't kick him.

Then he leaned toward us, and I wanted to scream but was so afraid.

"Sir. Hello. Do you speak English?" Jenna's voice was remarkably calm and strong. But I knew when she started to speak it was a mistake.

He pointed to our bags and motioned for us to give them to

him. I reached across Jenna with mine and dropped it into the black plastic bag. Jenna hesitated but then cautiously gave him her bag.

Sweat dripped down my forehead and onto my cheek but I didn't dare move to wipe it away. The man said something to the driver who then tossed a roll of duct tape back to him. He caught it and then tossed it onto Jenna's lap. He pointed the gun at us and motioned for us to put the tape on our mouths. With shaking hands, we each ripped a piece off and fearfully complied. It was stifling, and my mouth was already so dry. Then he pressed his hand over the tape on Jenna's mouth. She was shaking with fear and anger, trying to pull away. He grabbed her face and sunk his fingers into her soft cheeks. Jenna moaned. He looked her in the eyes and kept squeezing her face until she looked away from him. When he finally let go of her face, he ordered her to press the tape onto my mouth. Jenna, her cheeks red and already bruising, softly pushed the tape over my mouth with a shaky hand.

The man barked a harsh word and then leaned over and pressed his hand hard onto my mouth. His hand smelled of metal and glue from the tape. Just the feel of his fingers on my face made me feel like passing out. The gun in his other hand was pressed up against the head of the Swedish girl in the seat in front of me.

She started to cry even louder.

The man shouted a response and then threw zip ties at us, making us tie each other around our ankles and our wrists with our arms behind our backs. We had to pull tight on the restraints while he watched. Terrified, I looked at Jenna through watery eyes. She wasn't crying, but I could see the terror in her expression. Her pale white neck had turned red with blotches. *I am so sorry, Jenna. I am so sorry. What is happening? Why?*

The man moved to the Swedish girls and did the same drill with the tape and ties. When he moved up to the front seat with the

Thai women, Jenna looked at me and then down toward the seat. I looked down at where she was looking and saw her cell phone wedged under her knee toward the edge of the seat. She couldn't reach it, but maybe I could—if I turned my back toward her and grabbed it with my hands.

While I tried to retrieve Jenna's cell phone, I was startled by an agonizing scream from the woman in the front seat. The man ripped the younger girl from her mother and pushed her into the middle row between the two Swedish girls. He then slapped a piece of tape onto the woman's mouth and slammed her head against the window. She was breathing so heavily I thought she might faint.

My attention returned to the phone. I didn't even know what I would do once I had the phone in my hands. Would I try to dial 911? Did 911 even work in this country like it did in the US?

It was starting to get dark outside and the sun would set soon. My mind was racing. I glanced at Jenna, wondering what was going through her mind. Was she devising a plan or figuring out a way to take back control? Her eyes were darting around as if she was creating an inventory. I decided to follow her lead. I took mental photographs of everything in the van, making sure I could describe it all if I needed to. Both men looked Thai and were wearing dark jeans. The driver had on a white button-up shirt with the sleeves rolled up. He seemed a bit younger and shorter, but it was hard to tell. He didn't look back at us; he just kept his eyes on the road. The driver spoke softly to the other man when he went up to the front seat between each task. The other man had on a dark gray T-shirt. His shoes looked like Sperry knockoffs and were old and worn in. He wore a thick gold chain around his neck. He seemed fairly tall because he had to crouch down a lot as he maneuvered through the van.

The van was a Toyota. The interior was made of gray cloth. There was another gun laying on the dash.

The woman in the front turned to look at her daughter behind her. Her hair was pulled back in a ribbon and she was wearing a light-colored canvas blouse with a high collar. She had dark eyes. I couldn't really see what the Swedish girls were wearing, but I thought I remembered them wearing shorts and T-shirts.

Jenna looked at me again and then down to the phone. I knew I would disappoint her if I messed this up. I had no idea what I could do with the phone if I got it. But then I decided I'd better try. She risked keeping it with her, so I needed to do my part.

I tried to subtly lean forward and twist my hands around to reach it. Jenna also wiggled enough to push the phone back and out from under her leg. I grabbed it quickly and took a deep breath. I sat back again and then looked at her with a questioning glance.

Then the man in the gray shirt turned and started to come to the back again. This time he was holding a cloth or towel. I didn't see the gun, but I was sure he probably had it on him somewhere. Jenna and I glanced at each other in fear.

The man grabbed the mother's head and held the cloth over her nose and mouth. She slumped down in the seat. He did the same with the Swedish girl he'd hit in the head and then the younger Thai girl. As he leaned over them and reached for the other Swedish girl, she pulled away. Her screams were muffled under the tape. With the rag over her face, her head fell backward against the window with a loud thud.

My heart seemed like it was pounding outside of my body, and my legs and arms had become numb. I was drenched in sweat and could no longer control my crying. *What was happening? Is he going to kill us?* I tried to stop crying long enough to hear if the other women were breathing, but I couldn't tell with the road noise and the buzzing in my head.

Was this how I would die? I pictured my parents and Ryan. *What will they do? How will they know this happened?* Regret paralyzed me. I should have never left the States. I should have never said yes to Jenna when she asked if she could come with me.

The man moved toward us, and Jenna fell onto the seat sideways to try to avoid smelling whatever was on the cloth in his hand. But he grabbed Jenna's head and pressed her face into the wadded up rag. She slumped over onto the seat.

The man pushed past Jenna and lunged at me. I felt the phone in my hand behind my back and squeezed it as tightly as I could. I kept thinking that when I woke up from this nightmare, I would find a way to call somewhere and save us somehow. As the man pressed the cloth over my mouth and nose, I tried not to inhale, but the scent was so strong, pungent, burning my nostrils. All I could think was *please, no, please, please no, no, no . . .*

I have no memory after that. It seems as if I am losing consciousness again, but then I am suddenly aware of my eyes clenched shut, not wanting to open them and be kidnapped anymore. I am unsure of how much time has passed. I am confused of whether I had been sleeping or not. Everything feels disorienting. I squeeze all of my muscles and hope with every ounce of my energy that when I open my eyes, I am sitting next to Jenna on a bus or a train or somewhere safe and that this is all a very bad dream. I inhale after internalizing all I can for as long as I can in some sort of prayer or wish for this to be over. The odor from the trailer hits me fiercely and I open my eyes to the same horrific reality as before. But this time, Jenna is looking directly at me.

CHAPTER SIX

Jenna

June 27, 2007: Time Unknown

We seem to have been moving for hours. My stomach hurts, and the constant pounding of my head is agonizing. My right arm is cold and numb. At the other end of the trailer, Mallory is sitting upright. We stare at each other, not breaking eye contact. Despair fills her eyes.

The vehicle has slowed down and is making multiple turns. Most of the others are awake and crouched down near the wall that restrains them. Many of them are sobbing. The back of the truck is so hot and stuffy. My mouth is dry, and my salty lips crack every time I try to move them. The dirt underneath me is sticking to my legs and makes a horrible scratching sound every time the truck turns and my body slides against the floor.

We come to a stop and my heart rate increases. As the back door of the truck screeches open, I try to see as much as I can outside. We are inside a building. It looks like some type of warehouse. There are concrete block walls, no windows, and a dirty floor with lots of tire tracks. Three men climb up into the truck. They are carrying rifles and dressed in some type of uniform.

They walk to the back of the truck. My eyes meet Mallory's again and stay there. One of the men approaches her and releases her wrist, yanking her to her feet. She tries to wriggle from his grasp, but he pulls her hands behind her and binds her wrists again with a zip tie. He pushes her forward with the rest of the women he's gathered. We're ordered to stand up. Then we're released from the wall and shuffled to the end of the truck where two large men are standing on the ground. Each woman kneels down and then one of the men lifts them from the edge of the truck to the ground.

Once everyone has been lifted off the truck, we are pushed into a different area. Concrete blocks and a couple of hoses are on the wall next to a box. There is a drain on the floor, like in a car wash.

Before I know what's happening, I am drenched with cold water. Two men are spraying our group of fifteen women with hoses. Several are screaming as the piercing water stings our skin. Some of the younger girls are pushed to the floor by the power of the water hoses. They are coughing and choking as the water hits them in the face.

When the water stops, we all gather close to one another and stand there, dripping for several minutes. One of the men stands guard and points a rifle in our direction. I try to get as close to Mallory as I can, but I don't want to move too much in fear of what might happen.

Then we are herded into a line up against the wall like farm animals. I look down the line. I don't see the other women from the van in the room with us. *What happened to them?*

We are all dripping and shaking. The men who sprayed us pull the hoses over to the back of the truck and spray the sides. The sound of water hitting steel echoes inside the building.

There are three other men standing in front of us with rifles in their hands. They aren't pointed toward us, but downward. They look at each of us up and down, laughing, and making comments that I don't understand, but from their tone I can tell their remarks are lewd.

One man walks over to a young girl standing at the far end of the line. He motions for her to turn around and face the wall. She just cries while looking at the ground. She is an Asian girl about fourteen years old.

He slings his gun around his shoulder and puts his hands on her shoulders, barking an order harshly, and then whips her around to face the wall. The other two men start toward us, so we scramble to turn ourselves around and face the wall.

I'm trying to take in as much of my surroundings as I can. The truck is plain without any writing on the side of the trailer. The cab looks older. The building has nothing special about it, just a concrete floor and block walls. It's dark. There's one table with some chairs around it. There are two men sitting at the table in addition to the other five. There are guns on the table, and I can smell cigarette smoke coming from where they are sitting.

The door on the back of the truck screeches and then slams shut. There is some dialogue between the men and then another door shuts. The truck starts, and the garage door lifts. We hear the truck start to move. In an attempt to look over my shoulder, I can only see the shadow of the truck leaving my peripheral vision.

The three men are walking close to us against the wall. I'm not sure what's happening, and I'm afraid to look. Then I feel something over my head and press against my eyes. I am being blindfolded.

I stand like that, slowly counting in my mind. I count up to one thousand at least four times. I know there are thirty-six hundred seconds in an hour thanks to being the news producer at our college radio station.

During this time, I can sense that people are walking around and some of the women are being removed from the wall. A door opens and closes several times, and I hear muffled voices from the other side.

Someone approaches me and puts a hand on my arm. I gasp. I am being led somewhere. My breathing is shallow and quick, and I try to calm down. *If I show them how scared I am, they win whatever sick and messed-up game this is.*

"Hello," I say softly, knowing it's a risk. Then I feel a hand over my mouth. I try to wriggle away, but there is a tight grip on my arm and fingers pressing hard into my skin.

There are two male voices speaking words I don't understand. I feel the warmth of sunlight on my face as I'm led outside. The person guiding me walks about twenty feet. I can see we're walking on concrete. I can smell the outdoors, and it is dusty. I am led into another room, and then the door shuts behind me.

I am not alone.

I sense the other person, and then I see boots from underneath the blindfold as they come closer to me. There is the hot breath of someone close to me.

The blindfold is pulled off, along with a clump of my hair. A man is standing next to me. He is also dressed in the same uniform as the men in the warehouse. His dark skin reminds me of Bash, but I doubt this man is Hawaiian. I can't decipher his nationality; maybe he's from Thailand.

He says something to me I don't understand. Then he pulls out a pocketknife. Gasping, I try to move away. He reaches behind me, then slides the knife under the black zip tie around my wrists and cuts it off. My hands fall to my sides. He grabs my hand and then pulls it onto his pelvic area.

No. No. No. This isn't happening. I realize this man is alone with me. I look around the small room. There are no windows. It's lit by a flickering fluorescent light. There is a desk with a chair and a cot in the corner.

I retreat from him and go to the door, banging my fist against it. "Help me!" I yell. Then he yanks my hair back and pulls me away from the door. He pushes me down on the cot face first. He takes the blindfold and wraps it around my mouth to keep me from screaming. The adrenaline rushes through me as I anticipate what I fear comes next.

His hand lands on my backside and then he tears off my shorts from behind, the button pulling open and the zipper coming undone just from his force. He does the same with my underwear. I try to wriggle away from him, but he's too big, too strong.

My left arm is pinned under my body as he presses himself down to me. My right arm is so weak and can't reach around to push him. Then he shoves himself into me, and sharp pain shoots throughout my body. All I keep thinking is *no, no, no*. I'm still squirming and moving, trying to keep him away, and he's getting angry. I can hear him grunting from behind me. Nausea and a strange taste like a chemical or toxic element overwhelms me.

Then he stops for a moment. Maybe he realizes this is wrong and he is going to let me go. I hear him shuffling around. I realize I'm completely exposed from the waist down. I'm trembling. I don't know what's going on behind me.

"Please . . . no . . ." My voice is muffled from behind the gag in my mouth.

The sharp slap against my backside rings in the stagnant air, the first of many hits onto my skin. This makes me gasp and choke from the gag even more. He is whipping me with a belt, grunting with each swing. Each time the belt makes contact with my skin, the sound rings louder in my ears. I try to hold my breath but then gasp again, the odor of leather and salt suffocating me to the point of dizziness. After ten lashes, I quit counting. My skin is pulsating.

Finally, he stops hitting me. My legs feel like jelly and tingle with numbness. Just as I start to feel the heat return to my skin with a burning sensation, he climbs on top of my backside and continues to force himself into me. Within minutes, he is done. His heavy body lies on top of mine. He smells of body odor and cheap cologne. I feel as if I have been smothered. My eyes sting from the tears.

After a few moments, he pushes himself up and stands above me. I can feel him looking down at my backside. He says something to me in Thai. He rolls me over and looks down at my face. I am crying through the gag. He begins to grope and stroke himself while looking down at me. I become aware of being naked from the waist down and curl into myself.

Angrily, he reaches over and pulls up my shirt and bra to expose my breasts. He pulls my left hand up and onto my breast and then steps back to watch me. I realize he wants to see me touch myself.

My backside becomes itchy, and my skin grows hot. I am lying on a dirty wool blanket on top of the cot. Where he has beaten me, I may be bleeding. I try to focus on this instead of the fact that this man is satisfying himself in front of me while watching me fondle myself.

Just then, there is a knock on the door. He seems startled and quickly pulls on his pants. I wrap my arms around myself, covering my nakedness in embarrassment.

He yells something through the doorway, then looks back at me.

I'm not sure what to do. I try to raise myself up. I pull my shirt down and pull the dirty wool blanket over my legs and bottom half.

The man opens the door and a young Asian woman enters the room. She's carrying a bottle of water. The man pulls her in and shuts the door. She doesn't look at me, keeping her gaze downward. She shakily opens her hand toward me and there are three pills. I slowly pick them up from her palm. Again, I try to make eye contact with her, but she timidly looks away. She reaches up and pulls the gag down from my mouth. If I fight, he will hit me again, and maybe even this poor, innocent woman sent to do the dirty work of drugging me. I put the pills in my mouth. Deep down, I know I will eventually end up taking them anyway.

I am deflated. I don't want to lose my wits, but my backside burns harshly. Maybe the drugs will give me some relief from the pain. She opens the bottle of water, handing it to me, and I wash the pills back.

The woman waits until I drink all the water, then she takes the bottle from me. I notice her arms and see bruises. She leans over and ties the gag back in place around my mouth. It isn't as tight as it was before. The skin around my mouth is probably rubbed raw from the itchy material.

Several hours later, I wake when I hear a noise and see the door to the room open. I must have passed out after taking whatever it was that they gave me. My legs and back are throbbing.

Another man enters the room. He doesn't look native to the area. He is American or European.

"Hmm. Beautiful." He looks at me.

"Oh, sir," I start to say, and then realize I still have a gag in my mouth.

He pulls the gag down off my mouth. He makes a *shhh* sign with his finger in front of his mouth.

"No talk, promise?" I realize he's not American but speaks at least some English.

He pulls me up and sits next to me on the edge of the bed. He rubs my back, and then when his hand goes over one of the welts, I cringe. He is looking at me while I stare forward, unsure what to do at this point. I am groggy and out of it.

"Please," I whisper, wanting to beg him to tell me where I am and what is happening and if I am going to die. He puts his hand up to my mouth to hush me. I can smell his aftershave. It was strong, like patchouli.

"No." He gives me a drink of water from a cup on the desk. He must have brought it in with him because I don't remember it from before.

Then he stands with his pelvic area in front of my face. He pulls my hands up to the waist of his pants. I'm not sure what to do, but then he starts to unzip. He puts his hands over mine and places them on his genitals. Then he grabs my head and pushes me forward, but I pull away.

He roughly places his fingers under my chin and pushes hard to make me open my mouth. Immediately, he enters my mouth. I feel it in the back of my throat and have an instant gag reflex. In my limited experience, I have only done this a few times before on my own accord. I know I can't stop him by myself. So I close my eyes and he is groaning and keeps moving faster and pulls the hair on the back of my head tighter. I am sobbing and trying to do what he wants all at the same time. Then he stops and pulls me over to the other side of the room. He pushes the chair out of the way and positions me so that my backside is exposed again. It's really hard to stand upright; my legs hurt terribly and my muscles are weak.

He places the gag into my mouth again. I try to scream as his hand slaps my backside with force. He hits me directly on one of the welts. He grabs me by the waist and pulls me toward him. His hands slide down my backside, then push me apart. It's like he's ripping me. I'm crying now. Terror and shame overwhelm me.

Oh my god . . . I am ruined.

As he forces himself into me, I bite down on the gag in my mouth, hard. I'm sure I am dying. Each time I let out a cry of pain, he lunges himself into me harder, tearing away at my backside along with my dignity. Now my head is so fuzzy and my body becomes numb. Clenching my fists and holding my breath, I am quickly losing my focus and then I am gone into a state of oblivion.

CHAPTER SEVEN

Ryan

July 9, 2007

Two weeks pass before we realize that none of us have heard from Mallory or Jenna. Renee, Mallory's mother, calls me after work on a Monday.

"Ryan," she says. No "How are you?" or anything. Her call has a purpose. "I ran into Sandra Marquette at the grocery store on Elm. She said she hasn't heard from Jenna in over a week. Then I realized I haven't heard from Mallory either." There's angst in her voice.

"Oh, they're probably just exploring and haven't had time to call home," I say.

"When was the last time you talked to Mallory?" she asks.

"Oh, let's see . . . well, I got a postcard." My mind is reeling. "I called Mallory when I got home from Thailand and left a message. Then she called me back the next day, which was actually the same day to her . . ."

"Ryan, how long ago was that? Do you remember a date?" Her voice is slow and deliberate. She is pushing for a solid answer.

"Um, let me think."

I walk over to the calendar on the front of the refrigerator. Mallory bought it in January thinking we'd commit to using it every day, but it's been left unused since March. I flip the pages to June and follow the weeks down. It's been thirteen days since we last spoke.

I feel like I've just been punched in the gut. I've been busy with my new job, helping to move furniture into the new offices, starting a new softball league, and going to a family reunion. I didn't even realize how much time has passed since I've actually talked with Mallory. When we have talked, she uses a calling card, and she doesn't want to waste the minutes on it, so maybe that's just the case.

"The last we spoke was like June twenty-fourth. I'm sure she's okay. I'll try to call her."

I hang up and call the hostels and hotels where Mallory and Jenna have been staying. No luck. Then Renee, Sandra, and I find ourselves at the police station in Everly Falls. We explain our situation to the night shift deputy who starts to fill out some sort of report. He stops writing midway through and excuses himself to make a phone call. Fifteen minutes later, a man shows up in plain clothes, introduces himself as the chief of police, and motions for us to follow him down the hall to his office. We tell the story all over again to this man who doesn't write anything down but listens intently. Then he instructs us to wait outside his office while he makes some calls.

The three of us migrate to the hallway and sit in the white plastic chairs. Renee and Sandra discuss their concerns with one another, comparing their last conversations with their daughters. I try to imagine Mallory and Jenna walking through the bustling and confusing streets of Bangkok. If Mallory lost her sense of direction in a city like that, how would she handle it? Would she know how to find help or be careful about who she asked? She always seems so self-assured, but I know she's just really leading with the confidence that things will turn out as they are supposed to.

I fidget with the key fob in my hands and shift in the chair. Renee and Sandra's voices become subdued as I focus on the hum of the water cooler across the hall to calm myself down. The idea that she could be in any sort of danger is just too unbelievable. Thinking about it makes the skin on my neck itch, and I swallow hard. Our lives have been so impervious, so idealistic . . . I know this. Bad things don't happen in our small, protected world. Images of the two of us as kids, then adolescents, teenagers, and now young adults flood my consciousness. *This just can't be happening.*

I will never forget the day I met Mallory. My family moved to Everly Falls when I was seven because my father got a job as the chair of the Humanities Department at Goodwin. I remember the first day of school at Longfellow Elementary. I didn't know anyone in the second-grade class and felt like the outcast. My little sister was in kindergarten, and I saw my mom standing with her in line on the playground. She looked over at me, giving me an encouraging smile. My mom always tried to be the "softer" parent, and my father was rigid and quite strict.

When we got into the classroom, I found my name on the decorated sign framed in Popsicle sticks hanging from the front of a desk and sat down. The other kids were giggling and shifting around the room. The scent of bleach faintly hung in the air along with a slight aroma of crayons. As everyone milled about and found their seats, there was the sound of chairs and desks being pushed around on the tile floor.

We had to introduce ourselves to the class, and the teacher, Mrs. Phillips, made us say what we wanted to be when we grew up. The students went in order from the first row to the next with responses like racecar driver, doctor, veterinarian, teacher. When I said "investment banker," Mrs. Phillips gave me an odd look, and some of the other kids did too, but she moved on down the row.

Then the sweetest voice piped up. "I am going to be a time traveler. I will travel through time and learn all about the past and the future. Then, when I am done with that, I think I will be a real estate mogul." She said it with such determination. Mallory Shields was sitting at the desk behind me. She was wearing a T-shirt with the Beatles album cover of "Abbey Road." Long dark hair hung around her face, and her pretty blue eyes were electric.

There was a pause in the air, and Mrs. Phillips began to say something, but an obnoxious, nasally voice interrupted her. "Time travel isn't real, dummy," a boy across the room shouted.

"Oh yeah, how do you know?" Mallory glared at him and raised her pencil as if she were taking down his name.

"It just isn't." He started to retreat back in his tone.

"You just don't think it's real," she said, still very self-assured. "When we're grownups, I'm sure it will be possible. Besides, I'll be able to afford a time-traveling machine because he will be my banker and give me a loan." It took me a second to realize she was referring to me. I smiled at her.

Mallory had drawn a line in the sand, so to speak. From that day forward, Mallory Shields and I became great friends. We only lived a few blocks from each other, and our families were friendly. We hung out with the same groups in middle and high school. We were in many of the same activities and both enjoyed music and superhero movies.

I was probably secretly in love with Mallory even back then. We only had one fight and it was when she was dating Kyle Stormer, one of my best friends in high school. Even though I called him one of my friends, he wasn't someone I really liked. Kyle was cheating on Mallory, and I told her so. She blamed me for trying to ruin it for her because I had recently been dumped by my short-lived girlfriend, Josie. Josie was one of the "mean girls" in our school but very popular for some reason. She only dated me because she wanted to get my mom to choreograph a routine for the dance team of which she was the captain.

That first fight happened at a party at the beginning of our senior year. We both had too much to drink. She was out by the pool when I found her, sitting on the edge, dangling her feet in the water. The air was still warm with the humidity left over from summer.

"Hey," she said and looked up at me. She had a calm but distracted vibe about her.

"Hey," I said and stumbled over to sit next to her. "Where's Stormer?"

"I don't know." She smiled as she looked down at the water.

"Look, I should tell you, Mal . . . he's a jerk. You're better off without him."

She snapped her head up. "What the hell, Ryan? Why would you say that? Isn't he one of your best friends?"

"Yeah, but so are you," I said carefully. "I mean, I know he isn't being, you know . . . true to you."

"Who? Is it Leslie?" Mallory seethed. She already knew what I was telling her. I felt like a jerk for making her feel bad. The music from inside was so loud I could feel the bass vibrating on the concrete.

"I think so. And maybe Carissa Wheaton too." I had to be honest. "But you're too good for him anyway. He just doesn't know how to handle someone smarter and cooler than he is. He wants someone who follows him around and—"

"Someone who will fuck him is what he wants." She paused. "We never did it, and that was a big deal to him."

Relief washed over me when I heard this. The thought of her with anyone else was hard to take.

"Well, I hope you aren't sad about it."

"Ry, you know I'm not the sad type. He really was a tool anyway." Mallory leaned into me, and we bumped arms playfully.

Maybe it was the alcohol or maybe it was the opportunist part of me, but there was some strange force that took over. I leaned in and kissed Mallory. She quickly pulled away and stood up.

"Shit, Ryan." She put the back of her hand up to her mouth as if to wipe off my kiss. "Don't do that. Are you going to be just like those other guys who think they can get with a girl when she's down?"

Mallory grabbed her Doc Martens and sweater off the plastic pool chair and disappeared back into the party.

My head was spinning. Had I really just done that? I might have just blown my chance—or worse, ruined our friendship. I sat by myself near the pool for a while. After years of dreaming about kissing Mallory, I wondered why I'd chosen that moment to make a move.

For the next few months, we didn't really hang out. We were cordial when we bumped into each other or were in classes and activities, but we didn't talk about what happened. I found out Mallory broke up with Kyle, which made me happy. Then, one rainy day, she knocked on my door. It was the Saturday after Thanksgiving, and I was home alone. Mallory was standing on my porch distraught and red-faced. She walked in, and I instinctively hugged her.

"What's wrong, Mal?" I could feel her crumbling.

"Grandma Aggie died this morning," she choked out. "She had a stroke."

I knew her grandma was really important to her. When we would go to Mallory's house after school, sometimes Grandma Aggie would be visiting and would make us snacks and talk with us about our day. Mallory spent a lot of time with grandma since her mom was always busy with real estate. Grandma Aggie always encouraged Mallory's spirit and would tell her how proud she was of her for being a bright, shiny star.

"Mal, I'm so sorry."

"She didn't even make it until Christmas," Mallory said. "I can't believe she won't get to see me graduate from high school."

We just stood in the entryway and embraced for a long time, swaying back and forth. Mallory's hair smelled like the rain.

"What can I do? I'm here to help. I mean, you know, I'm always here for you." I sort of pulled away and looked at Mallory.

"Nothing." She let go of me and then I let go of her, and we were awkwardly standing, looking at each other. "I probably shouldn't have come here. I just needed to get away from my parents. My mom is a mess and my dad doesn't talk about it, so things are just weird. I went out for a run and ended up at your house."

"I'm glad you did." I tried to smile. "Do you want to talk about it?"

She shook her head.

"Do you want to get your mind off it?"

She grinned slightly and nodded.

"Cool." I led her to the family room. "Because I just rented these from Blockbuster." I held up two blue DVD boxes. "*Spider-Man* and *X-Men*. How about a movie marathon?"

She nodded again, this time with a bigger smile.

After popping some popcorn, I placed the big bowl on the coffee table. The warm, comforting aroma of butter filled the room. Mallory pulled the blanket from the back of the couch and draped it over herself while I set up the DVD.

"Where are your parents and sisters?" She looked around as if she just realized we were alone.

"They're actually gone until tomorrow. They drove my cousins home because they stayed after Thanksgiving to spend time with Lily and Moe. I have to usher at church tomorrow, so I stayed home."

I sat down next to Mallory, and we devoured the popcorn and watched the film in silence. As the credits rolled on the big screen, Mallory shifted on the couch. We were right next to each other and both under the blanket. I couldn't concentrate on the movie because

I was very distracted by the heat of her body. We were so close that I could feel her every breath. I couldn't ignore how attracted I was to her, but I didn't want to upset her by making any wrong moves.

Mallory turned her head. "Ry, I'm sorry I got so mad at you at Haley's party. I had too much to drink and was being dramatic." She almost looked ashamed.

"I'm sorry too. I shouldn't have told you about Stormer that way, and I definitely shouldn't have tried to kiss you." There, I had said it. Out loud. "But what I should have done—"

"No, I'm glad you tried to kiss me. I just wasn't ready . . . yet." Her deep blue eyes were so intense, and then she leaned in and kissed me. And we didn't stop. Before I knew it, she was straddling me, and we were deep into it. My heart was racing. It was a careful balance of pure bliss and enjoyment while also trying to be cautious.

Mallory stopped kissing me but didn't move. She rested her hands on my chest and gazed down at me with seriousness. "Ryan . . . I love you. You were my first real friend in Everly, and I can't imagine not having you in my life. You really mean a lot to me . . . I mean, you're my best friend, but like, there's more."

Her words were like truth serum. I pulled her closer to me.

"I love you too, Mallory," I said with breathless certainty. *Could this really be happening?*

Before I knew it, we were upstairs in my bed. We were both naked, and I felt more myself than I ever had in my life. That night, we fell into each other in ways we had been waiting to explore. We finally acted on what had been building for several years. Sharing this experience—the first for both of us—was more than I could have hoped for. Even with awkwardness and a few giggles, the deeper connection and trust took over and all was right with the world.

I woke up the next morning with a sense of peace. But then I noticed Mallory was gone. I wasn't sure if she'd left in the night or early in the morning. I rolled over and buried my head in the pillow that she had slept on and inhaled the raspberry and vanilla scent from her hair still with a slight hint of rain. I just lay there contemplating what had happened.

I called Mallory before going to church, but there wasn't an answer. Later that evening Mallory returned my call. We both agreed that what happened the night before was pretty spectacular. I was relieved to hear Mallory say it first. By the end of the conversation, we also agreed to keep things casual. I wasn't sure how I felt about it, but I was still so pleased with the progress we had made beyond friendship.

It was disappointing when Mallory told me later that spring that she was going to UCLA to study psychology. She explained she wanted to have new experiences and to not be tied to a long-distance relationship. Somehow, I was remarkably calm. There was a feeling in my gut that we would be together someday. And later that summer, when Mallory's dad was diagnosed with early onset Alzheimer's, she decided to stay close to home to support her mom. With this decision, Mallory stayed in Everly Falls to attend Goodwin.

We kept it very casual for the first two years of college. In fact, Mallory and I were so casual that we both dated other people yet still had a close relationship with one another. We were friends first, and I think that's what made it work. The summer before our junior year, Mallory and I went on an exchange program to Ireland along with a group of other students. We didn't know the other students very well, so we spent a lot of time together. During the trip, Mallory and I decided to become "us" and make our relationship exclusive. When it all fell into place, I was happy, but not surprised, as I had already somehow known that it was going to happen.

From that point on, everything seemed to follow the typical

schedule, right up to me proposing to Mallory the night before graduation. She seemed surprised, but I think a part of her was expecting it. Jenna promised to keep it a secret; she had gone to the jewelry store with me several times to pick out just the right ring. Mallory was not a flashy person, so it was a hard decision. But she seemed to love it, and she said yes. I found affirmation in how it all played out. Before she left on her trip, I told Mallory I wanted us to set a wedding date even though it would be over a year away. Being away from her would be hard, but I wanted to give her this time to have an adventure. Mallory was a free spirit, and staying in Everly Falls while her fiancé studied for his security licenses and took his first job at a local investment firm probably wasn't deemed an adventure in her mind. I knew Mallory wanted to experience life outside the Midwest. She was ready to see a world she had never experienced before.

My parents seemed very happy with our news. My mom knew of my plans to propose before Mallory left. In fact, I think that was why they insisted on gifting her a weekend resort excursion in Thailand as a graduation gift. They wanted to support Mallory on her journey, but to also remind her of the people who cared about her back home.

Mallory and I agreed that once she returned and we "got hitched," she would start applying to graduate programs. By that time, I would be pretty established in my career and could hopefully find a good position with a firm wherever we ended up for her school. Then someday I could start my own firm. Mallory made me try to push myself. Everything just made sense when we were together and she believed in me and what I could do, even when I wasn't so sure. Now I feel as if I have let her down somehow.

If I only knew more, could have prepared Mallory more, told her she needed to be careful and not to talk to strangers or be alone anywhere. Why didn't I do more research or convince her to have a better plan?

I sit up straight as the police chief walks out into the hall. The hair on my arms stands up. He tells us someone from Homeland Security will be in touch within the hour and they will assist in contacting the authorities in Thailand and the US Embassy. The three of us stand up and thank the officers. I feel a wave of sorrow with a prick of anxiety. I wish I could go back and live in the comfort and happiness of my memories instead of the anguish of this uncertainty.

CHAPTER EIGHT

Mallory

Approximately 45 days after capture

"I don't know how that would work," I whisper as I look across the table at Jenna.

"We just do it." She says and looks down at the dried-out bread on her pink melamine plate. She has just shared a plan to help us escape this hell we are in.

We have been held against our will for at least a month now, maybe more. I try to keep track, but whenever they drug me it's hard to determine how much time has passed. Sometimes the rooms we are in don't have windows, and it's hard to tell the time of day. We were moved to a different building about two weeks ago and have finally been allowed to interact with one another and the other women and girls being held here.

Prior to this recent move, I was locked in a room for days or maybe even weeks with different people coming in and raping me, beating me, or drugging me . . . sometimes all three, usually while blindfolded. There was a small bathroom we were allowed to use, but a guard was always watching us. They gave us food in our rooms.

In this new building, we all take showers together in a space resembling a locker room. Maybe it's an abandoned gym or school. The rooms are still small and locked on the outside, but we are allowed to leave our rooms to eat and shower.

The first time I saw Jenna was in this building, in the shower.

A surge of emotion took over. I had imagined the worst because I hadn't seen her since the day we were unloaded from the truck. My first instinct was to go to her, but we were still being watched by the guards. There were bruises and welts marking her body, and it made me wince. All the women were bruised and scarred. My body had been abused too, but Jenna seemed to be extremely hurt. I had a feeling she was putting up more of a fight than most and it wasn't working in her favor.

I just wanted to go to her and put my arm around her shoulders. Even though I was getting better at keeping my emotions at bay, everything rushed back when I saw my best friend. My skin was reeling with a slow itch and I hurt inside—not for myself, but for Jenna. She had come with me. She had wanted to push herself out of the comfort zone she had grown accustomed to, and now we were both living a nightmare. I tried to refocus and breathe in to keep from crying, wanting to be the strong one now. I needed to be there for her the way she was always there for me.

I got as close to her as I could. We were being watched by men with guns. I asked her if she was okay.

"Am I *okay?*" she snapped. Then her face softened and she whispered, "I'm sorry. I'm glad to see you."

"Me too," I said under my breath. "You look badly hurt."

"I am, but I'll be fine."

"Jenna, I am so sorry. I'm scared. You can't fight them or they will beat you worse." I started to cry. I couldn't help it.

The guard cleared his throat and Jenna and I quickly looked away from each other. If they saw us together a lot, we would be separated, and we needed to stay together. We needed to get out of this together and alive.

Sitting at the table now, she shares her idea with me to get every one of the women to scream as loudly as possible in the shower. She has noticed two small windows at the top of the wall in the shower. They are likely for ventilation, but if someone on the outside hears our screams, then maybe they will go to the authorities.

"We will be beaten, or even killed," I whisper. "The other women are just as scared."

"What are we supposed to do, Mallory? We have to try something."

We stand up and take our plates to the sink to wash them.

"Okay, I'll try," I say as I turn on the faucet. I owe this to her. It's my fault we're here in the first place.

"We'll have to just do it and hope the others will too," she says as she's washing her dish.

We go back to our rooms. If we linger too long at meals or during showers, we won't get the privilege the next time around. This is a lesson I learned early on.

Two days later, we are all gathered in the shower. Once we are done and drying off, Jenna looks at me and then up toward the windows.

"Help!" she screams, and then keeps screaming.

I scream with her.

Some of the women run out of the bathroom, but a few join us. They see what we are trying to do. We scream and scream toward the windows. We might as well keep doing it since it isn't going to change the fact that we will probably be beaten for this stunt.

A sharp pain on the right side of my lower back forces me to fall to the ground as a guard bludgeons me. Immediately, two guards pick me up and pull me out of the shower. They drag me down the hall and put me in a different room and lock the door. It is pitch-black. Running my hands along the walls, I search for a light switch and find one near the door, but nothing happens when I flip it on.

I try to keep track of the time by silently counting, but soon that becomes too difficult and I lose track of where I am. I am left all alone without any food or water for what seems like days. I drift in and out of consciousness, and sharp pains stab my stomach. My eyes slowly adjust to the darkness and can make out shapes of objects in the room as the light creeps in under the door. When one of the guards opens the door, I see a small light high on the wall with a chain to switch it on. I wonder if I'm getting moved, but he just tosses in two plastic bottles of water and shuts the door. When I'm certain he is gone, I find the chain and pull to turn the light on, but nothing happens.

Finally, they bring me some food, small things like granola bars or packaged crackers. Each day, I am brought something to eat but I'm still confined to the room. There's a bucket in the corner where I go to the bathroom. Every so often, a woman is brought to my room by a guard to bring a new bucket and a wet washcloth to wipe my body with. I assume Jenna is also in some extreme confinement elsewhere. The strange thing is, I haven't been raped during this time. Although the reprieve is a good thing, the solitude is almost unbearable.

My body reacts when I am first put in this room. The hot flashes consume me and then I get dreadfully cold as the drugs make their way out of my system. This only lasts a short time, maybe a few days . . . it's hard to tell. The light outside the doorway could be natural light or lighting from the hallway. Soon I find myself thinking more clearly and logically. In order to keep my mind from turning to mush, I try to keep moving.

There is a mat on the floor where I lie down to sleep. I stretch and do different types of physical exercises like push-ups, sit-ups, and jogging in place. Just doing a little of this tires me quickly, but it does get easier each time. I need to strengthen my body. I am weak, and I want to be strong enough to escape if the opportunity arises. Keeping my wits about me is challenging. I recite the lyrics to all the Beatles songs I can think of and commit them to memory. Then I move on to Bob Dylan songs, Tom Petty, Queen, and Elton John.

Singing reminds me of my father. He influenced my love of the classics. By day he is an insurance auditor, but his true love is music. I used to marvel at his record collection when I was young. Down in the basement he would tell me to pick out a record. Then he'd show me how to carefully put it on the turntable and we would hang out for hours listening to the entire album, both sides. I would plop down on my tie-dyed beanbag and Dad would sit at his desk, shuffling through papers, but eventually migrate over to the old sofa. Dad would tell me all about the first time he listened to the album, where he was, who he was with. He would reminisce about seeing a concert, or if his old college band covered one of the songs back in the day. He always wanted me to learn how to play an instrument, but after several piano lessons in elementary school, it was clear to him that my aptitude for music wasn't there. Every now and then he would break out his old guitar and strum along with the song. I would just watch, a bit awestruck by my father, soaking in every moment of his rock star replay.

Thinking about Dad brings tears to my eyes. I miss my parents terribly. Before this trip, I usually spoke to one or both of them every day. By now, my parents and Ryan must have figured out something was wrong. Surely, they would find a way to rescue us, wouldn't they? My mom is smart, a problem solver, and I know she will be able to get to us somehow. I just have to believe that. Are there search parties or investigators looking for us? Are they questioning people in Thailand? Do they know we went to the temple before we were kidnapped? Have they found our bags? Where are our passports and phones? Have they been calling us? Can they track our phones?

My body is changing and reacting in strange ways. I figure a lot of this is physical because of the lack of nutrition and clean water, but most of it is because of the mental anguish. I try to suppress the guilt and shame growing inside of me, but it's overwhelming. I run my hand over my naked ring finger. My engagement ring had disappeared the day we were abducted. Ryan will be so upset—not in an angry way, but in a hopeless way. That is his personality, and I know when he figures out what happened, he will blame himself somehow. I like to imagine him as a superhero breaking down the door with force and weapons, and then, after annihilating all the bad guys, he whisks me off to our life together and we are happily married. Such fantasies are easier on the soul, but eventually I find my way back to reality and swallow the truth of the situation.

After what seems like weeks, I am finally moved out of the dark room and back to my normal room. My privilege to shower returns, but this time only half of us are allowed to shower at the same time. Jenna is not in my shower group, and our shower groups are the same as our meal groups.

I now see very little of Jenna.

Hopelessness creeps in after several months of abuse. The rapes and beatings become my daily normal. Shutting down all emotions when this happens is getting easier for me. My body is not my own anymore, and it brings a sense of sadness and helplessness. The drugs just make the situation worse. I am always on something. This makes it easier for them to handle us, I think. I am not sure what pills they've been giving me, but addiction is setting in.

One day, they bring us all out to a big room in the building. It is similar to the first room we were in after they unloaded us from the truck, but there isn't a drain or a garage door. There are only ten women. I'm not sure what happened to the other five. Maybe they are still being held in the dark rooms. I try to avoid thinking about what could have happened to them.

They make us all take off our clothes. A year ago, this would have been so uncomfortable for me, but now it seems routine. I can understand their commands now, even if I don't understand the exact language they speak. They throw a bag at us and tell us to put on the clothes inside it. We each grab garments and hold them up. There are pairs of shorts, thin T-shirts, and flip-flops. We put on the skimpy clothing the best we can. Even though the clothing is very small and meant to be tight, most of us are rail-thin and the clothes don't fit like they should.

After we dress, one of the guards points to the wall and has us line up along it. I see Jenna three people down from me. We make eye contact, but she is really out of it. Her strawberry-blonde hair is tangled and her skin looks so pale. She is not well. The guard motions for us to put on blindfolds.

A door opens and someone enters. From what I can see under my blindfold, it is two men and a woman. They walk up and down in front of us. They speak quickly with the main guard, and then they walk out.

A hand grabs my arm. A guard is walking me toward the door. I realize there is another woman on his other side.

"Jenna," I yell out. "Where are you? I love you."

The guard yanks my arm hard to pull me toward the door, a warning for me to be quiet.

"Mallory." Jenna is crying. "Keep fighting."

The last thing I hear as I'm ushered away is a dull thud and Jenna's wail of agony.

CHAPTER NINE

Mallory

Approximately 150 days after capture

With my hands tied behind my back, I'm shoved into the back of a minivan. I sense the bodies of women around me. I lift my head to try to look under the blindfold. Two men are visible through the windshield. They are exchanging money. The man taking the money looks so familiar. I know I've seen him somewhere before. I don't see anyone else around.

I try to turn my body to jiggle the handle. It's locked.

I can't get the face of the man out of my mind. Maybe he is one of the rapists. I usually can't look too closely at them. I try to peek again from under my blindfold, but they are gone. I hear two people get into the car and start the engine. I can only see the back of the driver's head, and it doesn't look like the same man who took the money.

The vehicle is moving fast. I slouch down in my seat and think about Jenna. How will they find us now if we aren't together? How did this happen? Are they going to kill me now or, worse yet, is this how I will live the rest of my life?

Will Ryan ever want me again if I return home? I have become jaded, a different person physically and emotionally. He is still so pure and represents everything good in the world. I yearn for him and the sense of calm and security. I have been forced into sex and actions with countless strangers that I can't even explain. I could have all sorts of diseases from the disgusting men . . . the rapists.

A few weeks ago, we were stripped down and lined up. One by one, we were taken into this damp room where our blood was drawn and we were examined. I asked the man who seemed to be a doctor what was happening, but he didn't respond to me. I wondered if they were testing us for diseases. I doubt they would even tell us if anything was wrong. Terrible ideas raced through my mind about what would happen if we were sick or infected . . . would they sell us? Let us go? Or worse yet . . . kill us?

The car ride is jerky with sharp turns, and I can't help but bump into the women sitting next to me. We can't balance ourselves with our hands behind our backs. It is dreadfully hot and sweat pours from my body, even being scantily dressed. There's a sort of disconnection between my body and my mind. I feel like a stranger to myself. Aside from the physical abuse of the violent rapes and beatings that have left me marred and with scars I don't think will ever heal. I truly think the spirit inside of me has died.

When the van stops, we are brought to a room and the zip ties are removed. I hear the door lock from the outside. Slowly reaching up, I remove the blindfold.

There are three of us—me, Olivia, and CeCe. They are younger than I am. Though we are from different countries, we have learned a little of one another's language and can understand well enough to communicate.

The room looks more like a house now. There is a window, but it has a cage on the inside, so we can't reach the frosted glass. It's up high on the wall, which makes me think we're in a basement, but I don't recall going down any stairs.

There is a thin mattress on the floor and we all lie down next to each other. Other than sleepovers as a child or being around Jenna growing up, I have never been as close to other women physically as I have since being forced into this living hell. However, each day it has become less awkward and there is somehow a sense of comfort about it.

We all come from different lives and cultures, but being together in this one has created a bond somehow—one that will tie us together forever, I suspect. I would guess CeCe to be from the Thailand area or from somewhere in southeast Asia. She is a beautiful young woman, but the look in her eyes is empty a lot of the time. I have so many questions I want to ask her because I feel she knows more about what is going on than any of us. She has a slight build and warm, dark skin compared to mine which is pale and almost translucent without any exposure to the outside.

The sun is setting outside and it will be dark soon. The walls look concrete, or maybe stucco, with peeling white paint that had been put on thick. The floor is a vinyl tile and is dirty around the edges and corners. Olivia is quietly sobbing, and she eventually falls asleep, or maybe I do.

The next day we are instructed to change clothes. A guard has brought in a big cardboard box with clothes in it. They look like medical scrubs. We are blindfolded again and herded back into a vehicle. They drive us to another location and into a garage. We take off our blindfolds and leave them in the minivan.

The man in the passenger's seat gets out and opens our door. He cuts our hands free and then hands each of us a granola bar. We cautiously unwrap it and eat it while he watches.

There is an odd, overwhelming smell coming from the house. It's vaguely familiar, and it reminds me of concerts and college parties where people would smoke pot.

The driver of the van emerges and unlocks the door to the house while the other man with the gun motions for us to go in.

Inside the house is a long table. It looks like we are in a kitchen area, but the appliances are all missing. There is a sink. All the windows are boarded up from the inside, so we can't see out, but light shines through the cracks between the boards. There are several other women sitting at the table, working. They have buckets next to them, and there is a large pile of what looks like dried plants in the middle of the table. We are each taken to a seat next to someone working.

I am seated next to an older woman. Her hands move so fast it's hard to see what she's doing. I soon realize the green plant is marijuana. The woman looks down at me watching her and slows down a bit. I watch her for a long time. She is wearing blue latex gloves and using a weird, curved pair of scissors to cut the leaves off the plant. She puts the trimmed pieces in the bucket, and then the waste goes into a big trash bag sitting next to the table.

I'm given a pair of scissors and gloves. I repeat the process I just learned. After getting the hang of this new "job," I look down at the bucket and see that I've filled it halfway. The woman next to me has probably filled two buckets full in the same amount of time.

It occurs to me that we are sitting at a table without being restrained and we have scissors in our hands. I pause and look up to see a young boy watching us. He has a rifle in his hand pointed at the floor. About twenty feet away, there is another man sitting in a reclining chair. He is much older, but he has a pistol on the table next to him and a rifle across his lap. The rifles look like military or semi-automatic weapons. I have only come in contact with hunting rifles. I have never held a pistol or even seen any other type of gun in real life, only on television or in movies.

We work all day. Slowly, there are people who are instructed to leave the table. Some walk out the front door and some go through the garage. Pretty soon CeCe, Olivia, and I are told to stop. The young boy takes our scissors and gloves from us and follows us into the garage. The van we arrived in is sitting there with the garage door closed. We climb in and are told to put our blindfolds on. I hear the door lock on the van. We exit the garage and again are taken back to the room we have come from.

In the room, there is a bag with some random food items in it: an apple, a loaf of bread, and five small bags of chips. The three of us sit on the bed and share the food. We keep the more comfortable scrub-like clothing on, and we fall asleep on top of the bed.

The next day, we go through the same routine. I am now much faster at the work we do. I wonder if this is what I will be doing, and if I won't be raped or beaten anymore. Although I'm working faster, my hands are shaky, and I am having hot and cold flashes. At first I wonder if maybe I am really sick, but then I realize I haven't taken any pills for at least three days, and my body is detoxing.

This routine continues for several weeks. The same house, the same people. Granola bars in the morning and a bag of food at night. Sometimes we get more food than other times. There are meat sticks that look questionable, but we eat them anyway. We need all the energy we can get.

The three of us start to really connect. We are learning how to talk to each other, oddly enough, though we don't have much time to do it. We are watched all day and not allowed to talk to anyone. Then we work until late into the night. It's strange how I don't even notice the smell of weed anymore, though it probably wafts from our clothes. We only shower once a week, and we wear the same clothes for days at a time. I'm not even sure if the clothes are ever washed.

One day on our way to the weed house, I tilt my head back enough to see out the window from underneath the blindfold. At one point I'm sure I see a sign that says "Cambodia" on the bottom. *Are we in Cambodia? Were we brought to Cambodia in the back of that truck?* That night in our room, I try to share what I saw with Olivia and CeCe. They just shake their heads. They don't know either.

That night, I lie awake thinking about how I can escape. The drive between the houses is my window of opportunity. If I can somehow take the weed-trimming scissors with me, then I can cut my hands free on the ride and reach for one of the guns. CeCe and Olivia can cut their hands free too, maybe before I reach for the gun. If the scissors are free, we can use those as an extra weapon. If the three of us can take out the two men in the car, we can make an escape. This just might work. I will tell my companions about my plan tomorrow.

But I never do.

The next day, after we are done working, we return to our room but the men separate us. CeCe stays in our room, and Olivia and I are put into two different rooms. The man who always drives us comes into my room. There is something in his left hand, but I can't tell what it is. He says something to me in Thai, sounding impatient. Then he grabs my arm and inserts a needle. It's a cold burn.

This makes my focus go blurry, and I sit down. That night, I am raped several times. The guards have their way with each of us. When they are done, they put us back into our regular room and handcuff us to a bar jutting out from the wall.

The next day, the routine takes another turn. They make me put on the shorts and T-shirt I arrived in and leave the scrubs. I am blindfolded again and put into the back of the minivan with my hands tied. Even though my mind is still hazy from the rapes and drugs, I can tell the route is not the same and we are taken to a different house. I am no longer cutting marijuana but have returned to the original work detail of sex trafficking. I am defeated and begin to lose hope in a more profound way as the rapes increase, sometimes six or seven times a day.

Months pass with this routine, maybe even a year or more. I try to keep track of the days in my mind, but it is difficult to keep my thoughts straight between the rapes, the beatings, and the drugs.

I am addicted to whatever drug they continue to give me. I feel like a robot. It's as if I'm losing my mind. The drugs make it better, and I'm actually happy to have them in my system. I keep to myself, being alone in a room most of the time. I try to force myself to think of home, my parents, life in college, and when I was younger. If I would have just been satisfied enough without taking a gap year, staying in Everly and planning my wedding, none of this would be happening. Thinking about Ryan makes me long for the safety I felt in his presence. Just his smile brought me stability and always a sense of security.

Sometimes I make a deal with myself. If I can make it through the day without crying or wanting to hurt myself or someone else, at night I allow myself to imagine I'm with Ryan, just at home watching a movie or walking Carter in the park and teaching him to play fetch. But sometimes it's just too much. I am incapacitated by sadness and longing for my life. It makes me physically ill.

The loneliness is hard, and I sleep a lot. But then I have distorted dreams where things seem familiar but aren't quite right. Sometimes I dream I'm safe at my home, but then the familiar kitchen morphs into the weed house kitchen and I wake up sad and confused.

I'm afraid I might be losing those memories. When I do find myself feeling consoled by tranquil remembrances, I am overwhelmed by guilt of what has happened and shame of who or what I am now. Every moment is filled with despair. I actually want the pills and shots they force on me because at least that feeling subsides for a while. I don't fight. Jenna told me to fight. I know she's fighting, wherever she is, but I'm starting to fall into a state of depression. Even when I try, I'm so weak, there is no use. I do what I need to do to stay alive, even if it means barely so.

Today is different. They have put us into different rooms—sometimes different buildings—but I take off the blindfold and gasp. I'm in a hotel room. This has happened only a few times, and each time they bring me back to the house with the other girls, I regret not trying harder to escape or even yell for help. But in the hotel rooms, I am lethargic with drugs and usually tied down and gagged.

I've been in this room before. I've been raped on that bed. I recognize the abstract picture on the wall. I pull up my knees under my chin and balance myself on the metal folding chair. I'm nauseous because of the dank smell of mildew along with my empty stomach. The screams of anguish from the room next door cut through the thin walls, making my muscles contract with each piercing cry. This far into this shitty nightmare, I know exactly what is happening in that room and many others in this makeshift prison. The girl in the room next to me has only been here a week or so. She is young and the guards call her by name, Boupha. She is still fighting, and I tense up every time I hear the sound of a hand striking against her skin or her body being pushed to the floor.

Just let him do what he wants and get it over with.

A pang of remorse floats inside of me. But I know . . . I have experienced it firsthand, and it will only get worse for her if she pushes back.

Am I being poisoned by the evilness in the air around me? Is it making me crazy enough to just accept what is happening without at least trying to avoid the abuse? Sweat falls down the backs of my calves from the hot, dead air in the tiny, dirty room. It pools under my feet into the cheap rubber soles of the oversized flip-flops I am forced to wear. The tickle of this makes me shiver a bit and then feel the itch, the irritation all over my skin. It starts in the center of my body and radiates outward until everything itches, and I want to start peeling my skin away, layer by layer, to make myself disappear.

There is a loud banging noise in the next room, and I hear a harsh male voice yell out. I gasp when the wall shakes, and Boupha lets out a guttural cry as she's thrown against it. The wrestling of bodies continues until it doesn't. There was the sound of a knock and then steps toward the room. After the click of the door unlocking, there were two muffled male voices.

What happened? Was she unconscious, or even possibly dead?

No . . .

I can't breathe. I'm next and I know it. I have never wanted to disappear more than at that moment.

Did they kill the girl? Are they going to kill me? Do I want them to kill me?

My body tenses when the door handle turns and the squeak of the hinges sends a chill up my spine. A hazy light pours around the silhouette of a tall figure. A gruff sound of a man's voice rumbles in the small space. Tears fill my eyes and seem to fuel the burning in the front of my head. I want to turn away, to shake it off, and hope when I look up he will be gone, but he is coming toward me as the door shuts behind him and there is the click of the lock.

CHAPTER TEN

Jenna

Approximately 620 days after capture

The man in charge almost killed me for my behavior.

I attempted to scream for help again when we were in the shower, and the other women screamed with me. It's been a long time since Mallory and I were punished the first time for attempting this and she was taken away. I knew I would have serious consequences for doing this again, but it didn't matter... I had to try. When the guards barged into the shower room, the women stopped screaming. Some of them ran out. I was still looking up at the windows and screaming as loud as I could, determined despite being the only one left in the shower. The last thing I remember was being hit with something solid. And when I woke up, I was in a room by myself, the only light coming from a small window up high.

It feels like I've been here for several weeks, but I can't be sure. Maybe it's only been days.

The room has a metal bed frame like in a dorm room. There isn't a mattress, just a thin scratchy blanket. It is sweltering. The stench from the metal bucket where I've been relieving myself was terrible at first, but I've grown impervious to it. The floor is concrete with a layer of dirt and grime. I try to walk around as much as possible. My body is breaking down and I've lost weight, especially muscle. There is no energy in me. The food they bring consists of broth with bread or rice. Sometimes it's old raw vegetables, which I force myself to eat. I've never liked raw vegetables even in their best state, but I can't be picky.

At first I am hesitant to make noise, but eventually I start whispering to myself. I try to recall different things I have committed to memory like laws or lines from a play. Eventually, I realize I'm talking at normal volume most of the time. Sometimes I stop, but before I know it, I am whispering, which evolves into talking aloud again. I challenge myself with figuring out big math problems in my head or remembering all the US presidents.

"Washington, Adams, Jefferson, Madison . . ." bounce off the walls around me.

"The Fourteenth Amendment, section one: 'All persons born or naturalized in the United States, and subject to the jurisdiction thereof, are citizens of the US. No citizens of the US and of the State wherein they reside'—"

The door opens. This might be the end. The guard shines a light on me as another guard takes me by the arm and leads me toward him.

"No," he says, pointing up. Then he pulls the black rifle from over his shoulder. He points it at me. "No?"

I can tell he wants a response from me.

"No," I say in a small voice. I don't look at him. My inclination is to cry, but there aren't any tears in my eyes.

The guards take me up some stairs and then to the shower room where I stand alone. The water on my dry skin is welcomed, and I can see the dirt from my body washing down to the concrete floor and into the drain.

The guard stands with another man in the entryway of the shower and watches me. They talk to each other in surly voices. I don't understand what they are saying, but I am able to pick up one word: *American*.

After the guard shuts the water off, he motions for me to get out of the shower. I look to the bench where I'd put my clothes, but they are gone. The guard grabs my arm and pushes me out of the shower room down a dimly lit hallway. The other man unlocks a door and pushes me inside, locking it again behind me.

The room has some plastic chairs along the wall and a small table in the corner with clothes on it. There are nylon pants, like sports warmups, and an old shirt that buttons up the front. It is oddly shaped, like maybe for a child, but I manage to put it on enough to cover my wet body.

The door opens and another woman is pushed into the room. She is dressed in an equally odd-fitting shirt, a long black skirt, and plastic flip-flops.

"Hello," I say, trying to make eye contact.

She looks up at me. She has a bruise on her cheek and her hair is matted to her head.

"Hmm," she says lethargically, probably drugged.

I sit down next to her in the plastic chair. There are marks on her ankles where she has been restrained. She is hunched over. I sit there for a bit, and eventually she lays her head on my shoulder.

All I can do is cry. *This is a fucking nightmare.* That is all I can think of to justify this hell I'm in. How is it possible for people to be treated this way? Never could I have imagined something like this, especially happening to me. I've read about the sex trade and human slavery and all of this terrible shit in books and newspapers and watched it on the news programs. I even watched the documentary *Sex Slaves* for an assignment in a global issues course at Goodwin. I thought I understood. I was so naïve and so safe.

I don't want to die this way. I start to pray. I'm not sure who I'm praying to or even if I'm really praying, but I just can't imagine my life in this place anymore. I try to imagine myself in my old life. But I can't. I will never be the person I used to be even if I do make it back home.

Shaking my head, I start to reason with myself. I can't give into this sense of fragility. I need to find my strength and make a plan to escape. I close my eyes to picture the layout of the building—or as much as I know of it—mapping it out in my mind. I mentally measure the dimensions of the rooms and halls, the number of steps it takes to cross them, counting the number of guards based on the different faces I remember. Just when I think I have a good idea about what everything looks like, my brain conjures a memory of being isolated in a different room or restrained to a different bed or being raped in some other part of the building. My mind is so vulnerable and I can't keep it all straight.

I wake up when the door opens. The woman who was in the room with me is gone. Someone must have come to get her while I was sleeping. There isn't anyone in the doorway when I look up. I walk over and see daylight at the end of the hallway. I cautiously walk out of the room. My feet are shaking underneath me.

There are stairs leading up to another door, and I slowly walk up. Surprisingly, the door opens when I turn the handle, and I find myself in the kitchen area and the familiar space from before. Unsure of what to do at this point, I sit down at the table like I am supposed to be there.

A man comes into the kitchen and stares at me. Then he picks up an apple from a bag on the counter and hands it to me. I hold it in my hand for a minute, noticing the soft spots and bruising.

"Eat," he instructs.

I follow his orders and take a bite of the apple. The sweetness makes my teeth hurt. I haven't eaten fruit in so long. When I finish, he motions for me to get up, then he takes me back to the room where I was before I was sent to the solitary room. He takes out a set of keys and unlocks the door. He isn't forceful like many of the other guards. He just shuts the door behind me and locks it.

The room is big with three thin mattresses and a dirty rug on the floor. It's old and seems out of place, one of those braided rugs formed into a big oval. The place where I slept before is occupied with a woman sleeping with her back to me.

Another young girl I recognize is sitting against the wall on the mattress across the room. She was there a few days before they locked me away. She smiles at me and looks at the space next to her. I walk over and sit down. There is a jug of water on a desk with some cups, so I reach over and take a drink of water.

"Grace?" I say to the girl, trying to remember her name.

She nods.

"My name is Jenna."

She smiles again.

From that point on, business continues as usual. The rapes are becoming more frequent.

I've lost count of how many men have forced themselves on me. It's unbearable, but I have found a way to escape and not feel the agony when they do what they want with me. If I think too much about what's happening, a feeling of despair and nausea overwhelms me. The hard liquor and drugs they give me somehow allows my mind to become blank. If I am still somewhat coherent while being raped, I ball my hands up into fists and almost force my body to disengage from my brain. There are times I can completely block out the fact that I am being assaulted by these barbaric animals.

Sometimes, when forced into rooms with some of the men, they try to talk to me. Twice, I've been given money directly after being raped. I try to communicate with these men, thinking they might help me, but when they sense my desperation, they quickly leave the room. I always give the money to one of the men in the kitchen. I know not to keep it. One of the other girls got caught with money and was beaten so badly she limped for days after and within a week, she wasn't around anymore. Today, several of us eat together in the kitchen. As I look around the room, I begin to realize how vastly different we all are. At least half of the women seem to be of Southeast Asian descent. They sometimes speak to each other in very brief, hushed tones, but the rest of us seem to all be from different races, backgrounds, ages, and cultures. Although several of us have been here for some time, others are new and very standoffish. When we look at one another, we have an unspoken language in which we communicate the uncertainty and fear of our situation.

I stand and take my plate over to the counter. One of the newcomers is a tall, dark-skinned girl I would guess to be around eighteen years old. She has been standing in the corner of the kitchen, not attempting to get any food. I risk placing my hand on her shoulder and giving her a compassionate look. She flinches and steps away from me. I try to smile, but she scurries away and down the hall.

Afterward, I wash the dishes with the other women. I feel a different energy around me. Something is amiss. I try to look around without being noticed. There are men in the room next to the kitchen speaking into radios, probably three or four of them. I can hear them calibrating and cleaning their guns. I mentally count the women in the house. I think there are twenty, maybe a few more. Some of them are mean, some of them are sad. There are women of all different races and ages kept in this house.

A man enters the kitchen. He ignores me at the sink and walks into the room with the men. He says a few words to them and they scatter down the hallway.

Before I know it, we're all standing in the garage, facing the wall with our arms behind our backs and our hands bound with plastic zip ties. In a slight attempt to look over my shoulder, I see several vehicles in the garage, one of them a big truck. Some of the women resist by yelling and trying to turn around. They must know something bad is about to happen.

Grace is standing next to me, shaking, and I see her pants are wet. Her big eyes look up at me full of fear. I try to give her a consoling expression and hide my own confusion and apprehension. At the end of the wall, guards are slipping bags over the women's heads. This hasn't happened before.

Then it goes dark. A rope snakes around my back and through my arms. We are being pulled together toward the center of the room by the rope.

Peeking under the bag, all I can see is my feet. We scurry across the concrete floor and are led up a metal ramp that hurts my feet. We are being put into the back of a truck again, this time without being handcuffed. They tie the rope to the side of the truck and, as the rope pulls me down, I sit on the floor.

The door screeches shut. I want to shake my head and try to get the bag to fall off, but I'm not sure if a guard is in the truck with us.

The truck begins to move. I can hear women mumbling, some are talking, some are crying.

"No men?" I say quietly. I expect this might result in getting hit, but nothing happens.

"No men," I hear another voice say.

Fuck it. I have to do something. I shake my head, then lean against the wall and use that as leverage to pull the bag off. I'm in shock at what I see. Twenty or so women all tied to the wall of the trailer.

We all lose our balance when the truck makes a sharp turn. Most women still have the bags on their heads, but some have removed them. I wiggle my hands and wrists in the zip ties. Maybe I can find a small hole in the side of the truck to see through.

Then the vehicle stops abruptly. We collectively gasp. If they see we've removed the bags, we will be beaten for this. I'm already sweating. I have acclimated to the heat, but now I'm on fire. My skin is crawling and blood pumps through my veins with vigor.

The back door to the trailer lifts open and the sunlight pours in. Lights are flashing and people in uniform are looking into the back of the truck.

A woman in a brown uniform steps up into the truck. She looks around at first with an expression of shock. She is local, or at least looks that way. Then she realizes we are all staring at her in confusion. Immediately, the look on her face becomes that of extreme compassion, almost motherly. She says something I don't understand, but several of the women sigh at her words. She carefully begins to walk around us, removing the bags.

We are being rescued.

CHAPTER ELEVEN

Jenna

Rescue Day

It's like a dream. I sit alone in a small room in what looks like a police station or some kind of government building. Out in the hallway, people walk past in business clothes and uniforms. The authorities take my information and someone brings me a blanket, water, and a tray of food. I'm a bit queasy, so I can't eat much.

A small group stops outside my door to speak to one another. I can't understand them, but I hear my last name. The door opens and a woman comes in followed by two men. One is wearing a uniform, different from the guards I'm used to, but it looks familiar. The woman walks over to me.

"Ms. Marquette," she says. "My name is Anna Hamilton, and I am a consular advocate from the US Embassy here in Cambodia."

"Cambodia?" I ask. I'm not sure what else to say.

"I am here to help you get back home safely." She looks at me for a sign of understanding.

"Yes," I say. "Please, I want to go home."

"We need to ask you about where you have been. It is important that you tell these men everything you know, okay?"

I nod. I have to tell them about Mallory. They have to find her and save her too.

"My friend, Mallory Shields . . ." I start. "She was with me in that place. Has she been rescued too?"

"Ma'am," Anna says, "I need you to focus on the information at hand, and then we can discuss your friend. We plan to get the names of all the other women and children you know about."

I feel choked up and want to cry. This is strange and disorienting. Anna pushes the water bottle toward me, and I take a drink.

"We will try to go slow, but time is of the essence right now." She nods to the plainclothes man, and he sits down across the table from me. Just being in his presence gives me an uneasy feeling, like I'm being punished. Anna sits down next to me.

"How long?" I ask with a distinct hitch in my voice.

"I'm sorry?" Anna asks, a bit confused.

"I mean, what is the date? How long has it been?"

"Oh, I see." Anna shakes her head and glances at the plainclothes man. "It is Tuesday, March 3, 2009."

"My God . . ." I whisper.

Anna pulls up her chair, making a scraping noise on the floor, which startles me back from my state of shock. She looks at me with concern.

"Jenna, I know this part is hard. Let's move on and get this over with, okay?" she asks.

I nod, still trying to process that this is all happening.

The man pulls out a file with photos in it. He places headshots and photos of men next to each other on the table. Then he asks me something I can't understand.

"Do you recognize any of these people?" Anna interprets for him.

I take a breath and try to focus. I recognize several of the men in the photos and point to them. Most of them are guards. Others are drivers, and a few of them are men who raped me. As I identify them, the uniformed officer takes down the information and leaves the room.

They continue their questioning with Anna interpreting. They want to know how long I've been held there and how many other people were imprisoned with me. They ask me how I was abducted and from where. I tell them everything I can remember. I am so detailed about everything that I expect some parts to make them uncomfortable, but none of them seem surprised by the information I share with them.

I'm in this room with them for several hours. We take a few breaks, but I'm exhausted.

"You are doing very well. This information is going to be helpful." Anna tries to make eye contact with me. "I am sorry this experience is taking so long. We will be done soon."

"Please let me contact my mother," I urge. "I need to tell her I'm okay. Can I please call her?"

"Of course," Anna says. She continues to explain that the information we've just shared is for the Cambodia police. They were tipped off about the building we were kept in because many people heard screaming and saw strange activity around the area. They have been tracking this location for about a week before knowing for sure what was going on. Their goal is to arrest the person in charge and anyone involved in the human-trafficking ring.

"I will take you to the Embassy, and we have to file a report there as well, but it won't take as long," she explains. She asks me if I want to see a doctor before going to the Embassy.

"No." I shake my head. "I just want to call my mom and find Mallory."

"I know you have been through a terrible experience, and I am very sorry this happened to you." She's trying to be compassionate. "I do promise you it is over. I will make sure you get home. I won't leave you while you're here, okay?"

"Where am I?" I ask. "I'm not going anywhere until I call my mother and tell her I'm alive and where I am. I don't trust you or anyone." I begin to cry uncontrollably.

"Jenna, I know . . ." She reaches her hand across the table to comfort me, but I pull away.

"No." I slowly stand up. "I can't trust anyone. I mean, you seem for real and nice, but . . . no, just no. I have been kidnapped, pumped full of drugs, beaten and . . . raped repeatedly for almost two fucking years. How can anyone let that happen to a human?"

The blood is rushing to my head, and I'm getting agitated as tears stream down my face.

Anna looks up and says something to the man, and he leaves the room.

I wipe my eyes with the edge of the blanket. Anna takes the napkin from my food tray and hands it to me.

"If you call your mother, Jenna, will you promise to come with me to the Embassy?" She asks this as if I have an alternative plan or somewhere else to go.

The man returns to the room with a cordless phone that's large and clunky. Anna dials the number I give her and hands the phone to me.

"Hello." My mother's voice sounds so different than I remember. "Mom?"

There is silence. Then she gasps.

"Jenna. Jenna Marie," she says. "Oh my god, Jenna, is that you?"

"Mom, it is me," I say through my sobs. "I'm okay. I'm alive."

I explain to my mother where I am and that I had been kidnapped. I lie and tell her I haven't been hurt. I can't explain to her over the phone what happened. I give her Anna's name and the address of the building where I am. I tell her they are taking me to the US Embassy. I ask her about Mallory, but she says nobody has heard from her. I begin sobbing harder.

Anna asks to speak with her. She says there is a protocol to follow, but someone will be in touch with her within the hour to explain more and arrange for her to meet us in Cambodia to take me home.

"You are a very brave and smart young woman," Anna says. She stands, picking up her files. "Are you ready, Jenna?"

I nod as if in a trance, still processing that I just spoke with my mother. We leave the building, and Anna drives us to the Embassy herself. The passing landscape is mesmerizing, but it's hard to focus. The last time I was in a vehicle where I could see outside was the van when Mallory and I were abducted. At the thought of Mallory a shiver crawls down my spine and my eyes well up. *Mallory . . . where is Mallory?*

We arrive at the US Embassy and are led through a back door. I'm put into a room by myself, which leaves me with a sense of uneasiness.

Anna returns with another woman and a man who ask me more questions about what I have been through. They take down more of my personal information and then they ask about Mallory.

I explain as much as I can. I tell them Mallory had been taken from the house months ago and I haven't seen her since. I'm not sure where she was taken. They write down Mallory's information.

Anna says they have arranged for me to stay in a hotel across the street from the Embassy, and there will be guards outside my room for protection. "I'll be happy to stay with you . . . if you would be comfortable with that," she says.

I nod, knowing I don't want to be alone. When it's time to leave the Embassy, the sun is setting. Walking freely without a gun or restraint seems almost uncomfortable. I'm uneasy and unsure of everything happening. Anna stays close to my side, and although that makes me feel safe in the moment, there are fleeting thoughts of uncertainty I can't force out of my mind.

Anna is a tall woman with a stern demeanor. She keeps her

jet-black hair short and has a natural beauty to her. She seems well trained, but also someone who knows how to work the system. I can tell this is not the first time she has been an advocate. Although she seems very strong, every now and then I get a glimpse of her clenched jaw, and I know this work has taken a toll on her.

Once we're in the hotel, I shower and change into new clothing that Anna had brought up in a suitcase from the trunk of her car. The clothes are soft on my skin and everything smells different, almost sanitary like. I'm able to eat some food brought up by room service: a cup of soup and a sandwich, which I selected from the menu. Just choosing food is such an oddity. An overwhelming sense of relief mixed with shame churns deeply inside of me. Breathing deeply helps, but my appetite doesn't last long, and I only finish about half the food.

I sit in the club chair near the bed for at least fifteen minutes just rolling through the recent events, which are all at once blurry and distinctly clear. I am feeling a bit better and, with each breath, I start to calm down, but I still feel a sense of apprehension. My mind is like a metal ball in a pinball machine, bouncing from one thing to another, all to avoid being sucked down between the two flippers at the bottom where I convince myself that this is either a dream or a trap.

Anna booked the adjoining room, and I ask if she can leave the door open all night, which she does. Before going to bed, I plead with her to see if she can find any information about Mallory. She tells me she'll see what she can do. With that I'm able to fall asleep much easier than I anticipate.

The next morning, Anna sits with me while I eat breakfast in the room. She tells me again that she strongly recommends seeing a physician because I could have internal injuries I'm unaware of. When I hesitate, she assures me it's very safe.

I shake my head, and she doesn't pressure me. Her experience with situations like this is obvious. I will go to the doctor when I return home. Having strangers poking and prodding me is the last thing I want, and I don't trust anyone right now.

"Will you be able to find any information about Mallory today?" I ask.

"Yes. I'm going to work on that this morning while you continue to rest." She smiles. "Don't worry, I will be right next door in that room. If you need anything, you just say my name, okay?"

"Thank you," I say, realizing I have not said thank you to her until now.

"Of course," she says. "It is my job to protect you and help you."

She has some materials for me to look over about the legal system in Cambodia and how trafficking cases are processed. She lays it on the table and tells me to take my time reviewing it. She just wants me to be aware of my rights before leaving the country.

"Your mother is on her way here now," she says. "She will have a stop in Beijing before arriving and is supposed to call. I will wake you up if you're sleeping so you can talk to her, if you want."

"Yes, please," I say.

I spend the rest of the day in the hotel room, staring out the window for most of the time. The city is so big, and I look at it as much as I can. I hear Anna on the phone in the next room. She isn't speaking English.

Returning to the bed, I turn on the television but don't understand any of it, so I quickly turn it off. I must have fallen asleep again because the next thing I know, I wake up in a panic until I realize where I am.

Anna comes into my room. "Aha, you're awake," she says. "Are you hungry?"

"No. I'm still full from breakfast."

"It will take time, but you need to try to eat to get your strength back up." She smiles.

We both sit down at the table in my room.

"Jenna, I am very sorry, but there isn't anything in our system about your friend Mallory."

"So she's still out there somewhere?"

"I'm not sure," Anna says. "There is a missing person's report on her, and it has been sent to all embassies and authorities throughout Southeast Asia. There is also one for you. That's how we were able to confirm your identity."

"I can't believe this," I say. But I can believe it. I stopped using that expression months after we were abducted.

"Sometimes it's more difficult with foreign victims," she explains. "When these monsters kidnap a foreigner, they sometimes keep them more hidden because it's easier to identify someone who isn't local or part of the culture. They are able to charge more when they trade them or sell them for sex because there are fewer kidnapped than local women."

"What can I do? How can I help her?" I feel myself start to break down again.

"Right now there isn't anything you can do except to get healthy." She smiles. "It is an awful, vicious system of crime. You helped more than you can imagine by telling the authorities everything you did yesterday."

"Did they arrest those men?" I ask naively.

"They're working on it."

Her phone rings from the other room. It's a call from my mother in Beijing. She tells me she will be here before I wake up the next morning. Her voice sounds more familiar to me today, and I muster a smile when we end the call, feeling a bit more relieved knowing she is closer.

When I wake up the next morning, my mother is in my room with me. She is sitting in the chair close to the bed, watching me sleep. As I look up at her, our eyes exchange so much emotion, and we both break down in tears. I sit up in the bed, and she moves over to embrace me. We hold each other for a long time.

"Oh, my baby." She weeps as her arms create the safest place I've felt in so long. "I am so sorry. I am so sorry, Jenna."

"I'm sorry, Mom." In a moment, I'm a little girl finding solace in my mother's presence.

"Oh, how I love you, my dear." She puts her hands on the sides of my face and looks me in the eyes. "I'm so happy to have you back. Praise the Lord. I missed you so much, and I love you so much. We're going to get you home where it is safe."

"I love you too, Mom." I sit up straighter and put my feet over the side of the bed. "Mom, Mallory . . ."

"Shh. I know, baby. I know." The consolation in her voice doesn't match the doubt in her eyes.

I tell my mother that I can't go home without Mallory, and she doesn't argue with me.

But then as we sit across from each other eating breakfast, she begs me to come home for now and promises me she will come back with me to search for Mallory. "There are more things we can do if we were in the States to help search for Mallory," she says. I know she's probably right. To be honest, I don't have the energy to fight them on this subject anymore. The thought of going home is set in my mind.

We make a stop again at the US Embassy, and I say goodbye to Anna and thank her for everything. She promises she will continue the search for Mallory, and she will stay in touch with me. She gives me her direct phone number and e-mail.

Twenty-nine hours later, I walk through the front door of my childhood home. I go into my old bedroom and fall onto the bed. My bedroom is the best place for me right now. While I was in college, Mom took down the childhood posters and painted the walls a soft gray to tone down the obnoxious bright green I had painted in high school. The furniture is the same, minus the canopy attachment I loved as a little girl. The room brings me comfort. My mother brings in the quilt I've always loved. It was a gift made many years ago by my great-aunt on my father's side. As a child, I loved its softness and would wrap myself in it every day. It was getting worn out when my mother negotiated a takeover about the time I was going into sixth grade. I recall not being very happy about this until I realized she was trying to preserve it for me.

I spend the first few days sleeping a lot. My body is replenishing itself and replacing all the abuse and residual drugs with rest and recuperation. I haven't slept that well for years, at least without being under the influence of something. When I'm awake, I watch the news and read newspapers. So much has happened in my absence.

On day four, I finally go to the doctor. My mother has been briefed by Anna on what happened to me. We've spoken briefly about it, but I'm not ready to go into detail with her. She knows enough to know I need to see a doctor and have a thorough screening. I've waited as long as possible because I just want to be safe and the idea of having another stranger looking at my body or touching me makes my stomach turn.

As I sit in the room following the physical exam, Dr. Monroe, the general physician, asks me a series of questions. She then explains that there are some concerns she has in terms of my blood levels, and she will know more when she receives the labs back. Until then, she wants me to schedule a visit with a mental health practitioner and my OB/GYN.

"Jenna, do you know you are pregnant?" She gives me a consoling look.

I must not have heard her correctly.

"I'm sorry," I grimace. "Did you just say pregnant?"

"Yes, I did." She offers me a bottle of water. "That also explains the nausea. I am not sure how far along you are or the condition of the pregnancy, considering the ordeal you have been through. We would like to get you in as soon as possible so you can be aware of your own health and choices." She hands me some paperwork. "If you would like, we could call a referral and schedule an appointment for you."

I can only stare at her in a state of disbelief.

CHAPTER TWELVE

JENNA

March 20, 2009

I sit on the edge of the exam table in the OB/GYN office, waiting for the physician to return to the room. The test was simple, but having another person touch me and violate my privacy gives me such angst. I have quickly built up that barrier of never allowing myself to be abused or raped again, and this seems a bit too close to that line or parallel to it. I know it is procedural and completely legitimate, but it still makes me nervous.

The door opens and Dr. Ramirez enters, this time without the nurse. She is a short woman with a warm smile and I guess her to be in her mid-thirties. She sits back down on her stool and rolls over to me.

"Jenna," she says as she crosses her legs and folds her hands on top of the file on her lap. "As we anticipated, you are indeed pregnant."

I inhale deeply and nod slowly. I turn my head to look at the wall, which is adorned with diagrams of the female anatomy including the different stages of fetal development inside of a woman's womb. I feel emotional and somewhat expect a reaction of sadness, but it doesn't come.

"Jenna," Dr. Ramirez leans over to the side to get my attention again. She pulls the file out and opens it. "It says here that you are unsure of the date of your last menstrual cycle, is that correct?" She pauses, waiting for my response.

"Uh, yes," I look toward her, then to the floor. "Well, I mean, I haven't had a period in a very long time. You see . . ."

"It's okay, dear." Dr. Ramirez's expression becomes one of empathy as her nod matches mine from a moment ago. "I am aware of your circumstances. I wasn't going to discuss this with you, but as your doctor, I want to be honest and open. Is that all right?"

I nod and look directly at her with the relief of not having to explain the last eighteen months of my life to her.

She senses my conflict.

"Is your mother here with you, Jenna?" she asks.

"Yes, she is in the waiting room."

"Do you want me to go get her? It might be nice for you to have someone with you as we discuss the options you have going forward." Dr. Ramirez starts to rise up from her stool.

"No." I say immediately. "I mean, she doesn't know why I'm here. I told her I had to have a more extensive exam because of . . . because I have damage and the . . ."

"Oh," the doctor says with understanding, "I see. That's absolutely okay and makes sense."

She rises up and pulls open a drawer along the cabinet wall in the tiny room.

"Well, I do hope you share with her or with someone." She smiles at me and passes a pamphlet over to me. "The good news is that you are home now, Jenna, and you are in a safe and familiar environment. Along with that, I just want to be sure you know that you have options."

"Options . . ." I say in a whispered tone, half stating and half questioning.

"Pardon?" Dr. Ramirez asks.

"It's just interesting to think there are options . . . now . . . when I haven't had options for a very long time. Somehow, this doesn't seem like the type of option I want."

Dr. Ramirez continues to look at me with warmth and I begin to let my guard down a bit.

"I'm sorry," I say, knowing this probably isn't easy for her either.

"This must be a shocking and difficult position to be in." Her eye contact is drawing out my feelings, and I almost want to just let go and relinquish the control and composure I am hanging onto by the thinnest of threads. I haven't shared how I really feel or what thoughts have been going through my head with anyone for so long, I'm not sure I know how.

"This is fairly new territory for me too, Jenna." She smiles as if she knows exactly what I'm thinking. "I am here to support you and help you through the process. How do you feel about this pregnancy?"

"Feel? Like, am I happy?" I respond, confused by her question.

She shrugs her shoulders as she returns to the stool in front of me. "I don't want to assume anything. I'm just asking where your mind is so that I can give you the best guidance and resources possible."

The realization of my adulthood falls upon me in a heavy way. It may be the first time I have acknowledged my age and stage in life. The seriousness of the decision I have before me seems almost make believe.

"I can't have a baby," I blurt out after a moment of silence. "I can't have . . . this baby."

"Okay, well, it's good to understand what you're thinking." She points to the pamphlet in my hand. "There is a good deal of information you might want to read to be sure you understand all paths through the process."

I look down at the trifold paper in my hand, which I notice is trembling.

"Jenna," Dr. Ramirez says with a soft voice, scooting closer to me. "You don't have to make any decisions today. Based on the exam and the fact that you have been back in the US for a couple of weeks, I would suggest taking a little time. We can do an ultrasound of the fetus to get a more accurate estimation of the time in utero. If you decide to terminate—"

I inhale again at the mention of the word.

"I know," she continues. "It's a big decision, but if that's what you want to do, the sooner the better, but I do think you have some time. Your body has suffered a great deal of harsh conditions and your nutrition is lacking based on your bloodwork, but I am confident, with some dedication and implementation of a good diet and vitamins, we can get you back to a good foundation of health."

I look at her but can only imagine how pathetic I look at this moment.

"Take a few days, even a week or so, to evaluate your choices. I will help you in any way I can." She smiles again.

"I don't need a week," I say with a stern voice. "I don't want to be pregnant or to have a child. I can't." I push my shoulders back. "I have to get back to my life and focus on finding Mallory."

"Mallory?" she asks, then tilts her head back as if remembering. "Yes . . . I can imagine you are very concerned for her safety."

"I am," I say, stepping down from the table to look Dr. Ramirez squarely in the face. The examination gown flows around me and I hand the pamphlet back to her. "Can you do an abortion?"

"Well, if that's what you want, I can certainly refer you to a clinic in Omaha." She does not take the brochure.

"Please." My arm is still reaching out to give her the brochure.

"Jenna," she says with a bit more authority in her tone, "that information is for you to take. Regardless of what choice you make, it is important for you to have the facts. And yes, I can set up a referral to a colleague of mine at the Women's Center in the Omaha metro area. I will personally make the call and reach back out to you with the details."

"Thank you," I say, not expecting her to be so receptive to my resoluteness.

"Of course, dear." She smiles, and her kind eyes bring back a sense of comfort. "It will be a few days, and it will likely take a week or two to get an appointment, but I will do the best I can. Will you have someone who can take you and be with you?"

"Yes." I remember my mother, sitting in the waiting room for me. "I will have my mother with me. I just need to figure out how to explain it all. She's a pro-lifer, so this is not going to be easy."

"Oh, sweetie . . ." says Dr. Ramirez. "I think we are all pro-life and right now, that life is yours."

I appreciate Dr. Ramirez with her candidness and her compassion. She turns and pulls another paper from the brochure drawer.

"Jenna, I am sure this has been mentioned, but I want to share some information about a therapy group that meets across town once a week. It is for people who have experienced sexual trauma and abuse. A friend of mine offers the group to her patients, and there are several survivors of sex trafficking. I am sure she would be more than willing to take you on as a patient both privately and with the group if you would like."

She writes a number on the paper and holds it out to me. "I will let her know to expect your call?"

I take it. "Thank you. I . . ." I am not sure what to say. "I'll think about it."

"Fair." She stands and smiles again. "Well, I will let you get dressed. Please expect a call from my office in the next day or two. We will get everything set up for you."

That night, I join my mother in the living room and I tell her of my condition and my decision. I keep my emotions calm as I am expecting her to have a strong opinion. In the recent years, probably due to my abduction, she has found a renewed sense of faith. She was always a very Christian woman—I don't remember a time when my mother didn't attend church or the occasional bible study—but on our way home from Cambodia, she filled me in on her reconnection with her spirituality and how her pastor and church family have been so comforting. She attributes "Jesus Christ our Savior" with my rescue, and I honestly don't have the mental or emotional capacity to dive into this topic with her. I am happy she has had this support system, to be honest. I do know from growing up and her comments or various prayers she shared, she has always viewed abortion as wrong, and this conversation is going to be difficult.

Upon my news, her expression is very blank, though tears fill her eyes and roll down her face while I speak. I tell her of my pregnancy because of the rapes. I explain my decision to terminate the pregnancy. Avoiding the word "baby," I just put it all out there. I ask for her support and tell her how important it is for her to respect my decision even though I understand it might go against her beliefs.

After several moments, she rises and comes to me. Putting her arms around me, she tells me she will support any decision I make and is just happy to have me home. She agrees to be my person and to take me to Omaha for the appointment. She asks me how I am feeling, and if there is anything she can do for me at that moment. When I tell her I am okay, she wipes her eyes and says she is going to go to bed for the night. I look at her and ask if she is okay, and she nods, still with tears that don't seem to stop. I know she needs to think about this and, quite honestly, I know she wants to be alone with her thoughts and likely her prayers. She respects me and what I need and now I must respect her in the same way.

Dr. Ramirez set an appointment for the abortion at the end of the following week. She has been an incredible physician, going above and beyond the typical doctor-patient protocol to protect me and my privacy and out of understanding of the difficult situation I am in. She gives me specific instructions and assures me that I will have plenty of space and there will not be any media, protestors, or attention of any kind when I arrive at the clinic.

I try my best not to think about being pregnant or the procedure awaiting me. Emotions are running through me as expected for someone who was just rescued from the most terrifying and abusive experience and returned to their childhood home of safety and sanctuary. But there is a nagging pull on my soul. Everything just feels off, and it disturbs me. In the materials Dr. Ramirez gave me at the clinic, I read about the multitude of hormones running through my system which is also causing my mood to fluctuate. Nausea has started to come on a daily basis, and for a few days, it is a struggle just to get out of bed enough to make a cup of tea or read the newspaper. Some days I don't even do that. Exhaustion consumes me, but I never fully sleep, or at least that is how it feels. I startle at the slightest noise and often find my dreams to be unpleasant memories of the brothel and the abuse.

In one dream, Mallory is sitting next to me, holding my hand in the back of the truck where I was rescued. She is smiling at me and telling me she knows a secret. There is a calmness to this dream, a sense of peace, but then when I awake to realize it was a dream, sadness overtakes me. I can barely force myself to breathe.

Avoiding sleep, I think about the other women and girls who were held against their will alongside me the last eighteen months. When we first arrived, there was a pregnant woman named Safiya who slept in a different room. She was probably about my age and had the most beautiful complexion. I guessed her to be Mediterranean. The fact that she was still forced to have sex while pregnant was appalling to me. Then, three months into our capture, she went into labor and gave birth. None of us knew if it was a boy or girl because the baby was taken away from her. I can still hear her bawling and sobbing through the walls of the brothel. I saw her in the kitchen area a week or so after, and she looked very ill with dark ashen circles under her eyes. Men continued to rape her, and I couldn't imagine how much more difficult this was for her and the pain she must have felt physically and emotionally. I didn't see her again after that day in the kitchen. At the time, I had forced myself to stop thinking about Safiya because it broke my heart to even contemplate that situation; to be forced to have the baby and then have it taken from you without the slightest consideration, likely to be sold by the criminals who captured us. But now, this memory continues to resurface and I can't stop thinking about poor Safiya.

Dr. Ramirez comes to the front of my thoughts and I picture her face when she explained to me that I have choices. Safiya had no choice. She had no choice about getting pregnant and then no choice about having the child ripped from her arms. I was fortunate to have the choice at this stage and to be free to make the decision about my life and my body.

A surge of energy spreads through me and I roll to the side of the bed, pushing my legs over the edge. Sitting there for a moment, I feel lightheaded, but rise to stand. I pull on my robe and walk out from my bedroom into the kitchen. I am surprised to see my mother sitting at the kitchen table.

"Oh, you're up." She greets me and sips from her cup of tea.

"Yeah, I can't sleep."

"Probably just nervous for tomorrow." She takes her cup over to the sink. "We should be on the road by 7:00 a.m. Is there anything you want me to bring or anything you need before I head to bed?"

I glance down at the table and see an old photo album that my mother must have been looking through. I sit down and open it up to see the tattered photos of me as a baby. Seeing me with both of my parents is such an old image in my mind and the photos almost look unreal to me. It's hard to imagine my mother with my father when I don't have much memory of him.

"Did you always want to be a mother?" I ask, almost involuntarily.

"Oh Jenna, I never thought I would be married, let alone be a mother."

"Really?" I ask, surprised and suddenly aware that my mother and I have never had a conversation like this before.

She comes back over and sits down as I look through the album.

"Believe it or not, I was a lot like you. I was ambitious and driven by my work when I was young. I always wanted to go to law school. I met your dad my junior year of college. When he walked into the diner where I worked, everything changed."

I looked up at her, wanting her to continue. Her eyes were dreamy as she was reminiscing.

"He was wearing his uniform and was there to catch the bus back home to Lincoln. He had just graduated from his advanced training in the Army. He sat in my section and when I walked by, he asked if he could call me Sandy. That got my attention right away." She sort of giggles as she retells a story I know she has replayed in her mind a lot. I feel like I should know this story, but my mother didn't really talk a lot about my father after he died.

"He was so handsome, Jenna," she continues. "I realized he saw my nametag. I took his order and found any excuse to return to his table. He asked me to join him for a cup of coffee when my shift ended, and I did." She smiles and sits back in her chair. "We talked for hours. I had never had anyone show that much interest in me before. In fact, he missed his bus because we were so deep in conversation. He told me all about the service and how he wanted to open up his own auto repair shop when he finished his four years. We talked about family, school, and friends."

"How long was it before you saw him again?" I ask.

"I saw him the next day," she laughs. "He took the night bus to

Lincoln and then came back the next day and picked me up when I got out of class. Oh goodness, we were so young and so . . . "

"In love?" I ask.

"Oh boy, were we." She shakes her head and looks off across the room. "Well, you know the rest. He went back to Fort Sill in Oklahoma where he was stationed, and when he came home for Christmas we ran off and got married."

"Did you want children?" I ask again.

She pauses for a long time. "No. At least not at that time . . . yet." Her hand reaches out, and her long fingers brush over my hand. "You were a happy surprise to us. I just never really understood parenting since I was the youngest of a big family. My parents were so much older than the parents of my friends, and they always seemed tired to me. So I always felt that children were . . . I don't know, a hassle or trouble. I think that's why I focused on my education."

I nodded. The story seemed vaguely familiar to me, but I wanted her to keep sharing.

"Your dad knew that school was important to me, so after we married, he went back to the service to finish out his enlistment, and I stayed here and planned to finish college." She gives me a glossy look. "But a year later, you arrived. So I left school and we went to live on base with your father. He was over-the-moon in love with you, Jenna. We both were, but I was just out of my element. Eventually, I caught on. I got to be friends with several other wives of servicemen, and they helped me figure stuff out."

"He only had a year left, and we planned on moving back here to Everly. Your Uncle Denny had some money saved up, and he and your dad were going to open a shop. We never thought he would get deployed with only a year left." She starts to get emotional, and I can see this is still such a raw experience for her to revisit.

"I'm sorry, Mom."

"No, it's okay, sweetie," she wipes her eyes. "It actually feels good to talk about this with you."

"Yes."

"Anyway, there I was, my husband was gone and you were this headstrong little thing that became my everything in an instant." She looks at me. "So no, being a mother was not an easy thing for me, but somehow it became what I was, all that I was. I thank the Lord, the benefits from your father's death allowed me to work at the VA part-time while you were growing up so I could be there for all of those moments and events."

"You were, too." I smile at her and squeeze her hand. "You made the other moms look like amateurs."

My mother's eyes perked up at that comment.

"Seriously, Mom, thank you." I realize how little appreciation I have shown my mother throughout my life until just this moment.

"Oh, Jenna." She says as she blushes a bit. "You don't thank a parent, it's just what they do."

There is a long silence, but it isn't without meaning.

I know if we sit here any longer, we will begin to rehash my experience and my mother almost losing me too.

"Well, we'd better call it a night and try to sleep, Mom." I lean over and kiss her on the top of her head.

We don't go to Omaha the next morning.

I wake up with the word "choice" in the forefront of my thoughts. Something feels different inside of me. I contemplate my situation and actually having the choice to make about what my future looks like. I think about Mallory and her current reality. I think about my mother and her choice to dedicate her life to making mine the best she could. I suddenly realize I want to be a mother. In this moment, on this morning, I choose to become a mother.

CHAPTER THIRTEEN

Ryan

January 4, 2013

My legs are cramping from the long flight. I want to stand up, but I don't want to disturb Jenna, who is sleeping next to me. I have made this trip several times, and it never gets shorter. At least we're on our way home. The total flying time from Omaha to Thailand is about twenty-eight hours, but it usually takes around thirty-six with the layovers and connections. We are on the longest leg of the flight from Beijing to Houston. I push the tray table back into the upright position and try to stretch my legs forward a bit. After the flight attendant walks through the cabin with blankets, I lean my head back and reflect on the many trips and how we got to this point.

Jenna's rescue four years ago left me with mixed feelings. I was happy for her return, but I was angry and confused that Mallory was still missing. At first, I was hesitant to see Jenna because I was worried she would tell me something terrible happened to Mallory and that was why she hadn't been rescued.

Jenna had been very open about the conditions of her capture and explained the abuse, the drugs, the forced sex work, and the living conditions. It was like something from a movie when she said it aloud. I had to remind myself that this was true and real. It was very hard to think about Mallory in those conditions. Somewhere in my mind, I kept picturing Mallory and Jenna having a great time backpacking through these beautiful countries, taking pictures and meeting locals.

After Mallory and Jenna were confirmed missing late in the summer of 2007, I went back to Thailand with Mallory's parents, Ken and Renee. They had set up a meeting through the US Embassy with the authorities in Thailand to discuss action they could take to locate Mallory.

Renee was frustrated during that trip. Ken was not doing well with his memory from the early onset Alzheimer's, and she was trying to deal with that situation and also make some headway with the police.

Once we were able to sit down with the authorities and the investigation team, they were able to share information with us. They showed us footage from CCTV on the day Mallory and Jenna boarded a van. After that point, there was no other information. The driver was unidentifiable, and there was not a trace of the van. They did get the plate number, but in the last four months, it had not been located.

On the afternoon of our first day in Bangkok, I went for a walk around the area to get some space. The postcard I had gotten in the mail from Mallory had a picture of Wat Suthat, a Buddhist temple, so I headed there. It was sent over a week before we realized they were missing.

The thick, hot air made everything seem stagnant and polluted. The evident feeling of loss was amplified by the congestion and chaos, making the hurt worse. Everything I looked at or tried to connect with made me fall apart just a little more. It wasn't easy to shake it, but after walking for a while, I started to find more of a rhythm, darting around things on the sidewalks, weaving in and out of pedestrians, stands, and vehicles. Each time I looked up, I would see someone who seemed suspicious to me. The locals seemed to stare. Paranoia was to be expected, but it seemed to overtake me.

Stopping at a market stand, I bought a bottle of water and a pair of cheap sunglasses. The man took my money and said something

I didn't understand. I crossed the street and sat on a bench for a few moments in the searing sun that beat down onto the street. Moments later, the man from the stand was pointing across the street and talking to another man. Sweat formed on my forehead and I stood up. The man he was talking to crossed the street in my direction, making his way through the tuk-tuks and small cars.

"Hey. Hey," he said as he approached me. "You American businessman, yes?"

"Excuse me?" I asked.

"Here in Bangkok for fun? We have girls. You want a girl?" He came closer to me and stood directly in front of me.

"What?" There was a buzzing in my head from the heat and from this confusing man trying to talk to me.

He reached into his back pocket and pulled out a glossy trifold brochure. "We have girls you like . . . lots of girls." He tapped the brochure in the palm of his hand.

My stomach turned, and I felt a mix of rage and distress when I realized what was happening. I reached for the brochure, but he didn't hand it to me. Instead, he opened it and pointed to the pictures of women displayed inside.

"You want to buy? We have girls for good price. You with other businessmen? We come to you." He paused.

"What is your name? Who are you?" I asked, feeling dizzy, but realized this was the type of person who might be involved with Mallory and Jenna. I reached for my phone in my pocket to take a picture of him, but he quickly took off.

I rushed down the street but didn't see where he went. Returning to the stand where I bought the water, I thought I could ask the first man, but now there was a woman working there. I tried to ask the woman where the man had gone or what his name was, but she didn't understand me.

As I made my way back to the hotel, I tried to remember what the man looked like. My head was faint and I felt queasy. I stepped into a small alcove between two buildings and threw up. As I was heaving over, I realized I was also sobbing, and I wondered if Mallory's picture was in a brochure like that, or if she was a "girl for sale" as the man had said.

When we met later that day with the Thailand police officer, I shared this information. I tried to describe the man who had approached me, but this was not news to the authorities. The sense of frustration and helplessness was beyond measure. We had asked for all the information about car accidents or unidentified people who had been found. None of them were a match to Mallory or Jenna.

Something changed inside of me after that trip. On the flight home, I stared at the back of the seat in front of me, not even remembering the layovers. I'm sure I spoke to Renee and Ken, but it was all a blur. Perhaps it was simply shock and not wanting to believe this had happened. I think Renee cried all the way home, and Ken went in and out of it, sometimes emotional and sometimes oblivious. This was probably better for him. In fact, he really seemed to succumb to the Alzheimer's fast after that trip. Stress was found to accelerate the disease.

The entire trip was grueling. I felt a sense of guilt, and I knew Renee and Sandra, Jenna's mom, felt this as well. From that point on, there was no good news. I felt useless. Renee and Sandra had contacted a human rights activist who was also an attorney and they made another trip, but it didn't garner any additional leads or information.

Weeks and then months passed. Every time my phone rang, I thought for sure it would be Mallory. And every time I picked it up and didn't hear her voice, it crushed me just a little more. I kept to myself for about a year. I worked. I went home. I lay on the couch with Carter. That was my schedule on a loop. Somehow, Carter made me feel closer to Mallory. He was fully grown, and I knew he could feel my sadness.

When August 2, 2008 came and went, I had fallen into a state of depression. We would have been married on that day, and the thought of Mallory never returning to our life was almost too much to handle. I tried to appear strong on the outside, but each day I felt less and less. My mom came over at least once a week to check in on me, bringing me food stored in Tupperware containers and helping with light housework. Finally, one day she coerced me into seeing a therapist. This began to help bit by bit, and I seemed to become more comfortable "acting" as if things were getting better. The truth was, I would hear a song or see something that reminded me of Mallory and completely crumble inside.

I tried not to let it show at work or in public, but I knew my mom and sisters could see it. My dad just avoided me, which told me he probably knew it too but didn't know how to deal with it. I had simply given up. The golf with my coworkers stopped, and I no longer went out with friends the way I used to. I was just tired of trying. Every time I would try to distract myself from the situation, it would end with a friend or colleague asking how I was doing and offering "prayers" or advice about the situation. It was just easier to avoid it altogether. The real driver was when Pam, one of the partners in our firm, asked if she could set me up with her niece over the holidays. "My niece is visiting from Des Moines and thought you might be ready to get back into the game," Pam said. Just entertaining the thought of dating made me retreat into my solitude more.

After Jenna's rescue, it gradually became easier to talk to her because she understood. She helped me see things from a different perspective. It was hard, really hard. She shared information with me that made me sob, that made me furious. Hearing about the torture and abuse they both endured was awful and killed me a little whenever I thought of it. Instinctively, I found myself becoming overly protective of my sisters when we were in public places, once even threatening a bartender who kept hounding my youngest sister for her phone number at a cousin's wedding.

I eventually quit seeing the therapist. Jenna knew Mallory as well as I did, and we were able to console each other knowing what a fighter she was. Mallory also had an intelligence about her that was more street-smart than book-smart, and we agreed this would help her in any situation.

When Jenna first told me she was going to have a baby, I was shocked. It took me several moments to realize that meant she was pregnant from being raped. A wave of anger and sadness came over me, and I winced with repugnance just thinking about what had happened to her. Her situation made me achy and hollow inside, and I was at a loss as to what to say to her.

"I'm keeping the baby, Ryan," she said softly to me from across the table. We'd met for coffee down the street from my office at a local shop.

All I could do was nod.

"I know it seems crazy," she continued. "But what happened to me isn't this baby's fault. I know it will be hard, but I really think I can love this child."

"What if you can't?" I blurted out.

"I don't know." She smiled. She was so much calmer than she was before. That was a noticeable change in her. It was like she had a truer sense of life and reality. "I feel like this baby has been with me through this terrible and ugly journey, and it deserves the chance at happiness as much as I do."

I looked at her. I wasn't sure if it was my place to give advice or to just support her. I chose the latter.

"I get to make the choice," she continued. "I mean, I didn't get to choose what happened to me, but I get to choose how I am going to face the future and this is what I choose. If someone forced me to give this baby up or forced me to have this baby, I don't know how I would deal with that. I finally feel like I am getting back some of the control in my life."

"Well, I'm here, J," I said, and I put my hand on her forearm. I wasn't sure where the nickname "J" came from, or if that was the first time I'd used it, but from that point forward, it stuck. "I will help you any way I can," I continued. "I can be Uncle Ryan. If you need money or anything, just let me know and I'll try to help."

"Thanks, Ry," she said. "We'll be okay. I'm going to keep living with Mom for at least these next few years. That will make it all easier."

"That's good." I couldn't imagine what a hard decision it had to be for Jenna.

"This baby will be loved. I know it." She smiled and put her hand to her stomach.

"How long?" I asked. "When?"

"My doctor said around Thanksgiving, so just about four months away." She looked out the window of the coffee shop.

"How have you been feeling, like, physically?" I asked.

"Good, actually." She looked back at me. "In a weird way, it seems like being pregnant is actually helping me recover both my body and my mind. My heart might take a while." She was almost stoic, and I couldn't help but admire her courage at that moment. "But I want you to know," she started, "this doesn't mean I will give up on rescuing Mallory. I promise, Ryan, I am still dedicated to keeping on the Department of Homeland Security and the police over there. We can't give up."

Smiling and nodding, I took a drink of my coffee.

Jenna gave birth to Thomas on a snowy day in early December 2009. She was a week overdue, and it had really put her over the edge and worried us all. Her mom called me at work to let me know.

I went to the hospital after work, picking up my sister on the way. Moe helped me pick out the baby gift. When I entered the room, Jenna was lying in bed and she didn't look so well. There was a little brown bundle wrapped in a blue blanket in a clear basket next to the bed. Sandra got up and gave me a hug. She picked up the tiny baby and smiled down at him.

"Ryan, meet my new grandson, Thomas." She beamed. "He's named after his grandfather, Jenna's dad, who was so strong and brave. Isn't he just beautiful?"

"Hey there, little guy," I said with a smile.

"Oh my gosh. Can I hold him?" Moe asked.

"Sure." Sandra and Moe stepped away from the bed, and she put little Thomas into Moe's arms.

Jenna had tears in her eyes, but they didn't seem to be joyful tears.

"Hey, J." I put my hand on her shoulder. "Congrats. You did it. He looks perfect. How are you feeling?"

"Oh, Ryan." Then she began to weep. Her mom glanced over at us and took a few steps away with Moe and the baby.

"Hey there . . . what's wrong?" I tried to be as sympathetic as I could.

"I don't know. I thought I would be happier or feel better after he was born." She wiped her eyes. "I really miss Mallory right now. I wish she were here with me, Ryan. I need her."

"I'm sorry, J." I squeezed her shoulder. "She would be so excited for you though, wouldn't she?"

Jenna nodded.

"He looks very healthy." I looked over at my sister cooing at him.

"I'm just sad and angry," Jenna said. "You know, I wanted to go back to the resort on New Year's Eve to look for her, but I don't think I can now. Not with the baby . . . with Thomas. And I just can't . . . my mind is too mushy right now."

"Hey, I understand." I wasn't sure about going over there anyway. "What's important right now is for you to feel better and start a life for you and Thomas."

"But Mallory . . ." she choked.

"Mallory would want the same," I said. "When she comes home someday, she will be very proud of you for doing what you needed to do for yourself and your new son."

We decided that a year later, on New Year's Eve 2010, we would go to the Garden Sea View Resort just in case Mallory found her way back there. That was my third trip to Thailand. It was difficult and strange. Every person we saw, we would look twice. It was a challenging trip with a lot of false hopes. Jenna was feeling unsettled being back there and leaving Thomas at home with her mother. She was on edge and stayed very close to me. I remember when she called my room in the middle of the night because she was scared. I talked to her for at least an hour until she fell asleep.

It was hard being in such a beautiful place for such a dark and terrible reason. We would sit in the common areas of the resort or on the beach and see people full of joy while we were both in such a hopeless state. We were planning to fly to Cambodia from Bangkok and to show Mallory's picture to locals to see if anyone had come in contact with her, but we actually decided to come back on New Year's Day.

On that trip, I remember looking at the men who were at the airport, flying into and out of Thailand. Single men. There were many of them, and from the information Jenna had shared with me and all the research I had done, I knew many of them were coming to the area for the purpose of raping women or children who were being prostituted. It was sickening. I couldn't even sit down while waiting to board the plane.

For most of the next year, in 2011, Jenna and I would get together for lunch or dinner once a week. She had started a job working for the attorney general's office. This was very different from the communication's firm she planned to work for out of college. But it allowed her to be involved and advocate for trafficking victims in the US and all over the world. I was amazed and often inspired by Jenna's dedication. She was motivated to keep the search for Mallory active. She turned her frustration and fears into action. She was also dedicated to Thomas. Her new role as a mother was probably the most surprising part of Jenna's story.

Since Jenna's rescue, she and I have traveled back to the resort three times. The second time was easier, but still confusing, and it was still frustrating that there were no answers or even leads to finding Mallory. On that trip, we went to Bangkok, and Jenna showed me all the places they had visited together.

This last time was different. It's 2013, and throughout the past year, Jenna and I have gotten closer, and I've become involved in Thomas's life, spending more time with the two of them. He's a great kid. Jenna needs someone to help out when she travels for work every now and then. When she signed him up for tee ball, she asked if I would come to his games.

I've never missed one. He's pretty good, too. Thomas is super smart like Jenna, but he also has a great personality. He's funny, and it's great to hang out with a little person I can share things with. Just experiencing his "firsts" in life is kind of a cool opportunity and now makes me smile, something I've found hard to do. I could tell early on he would become a superhero movie fan.

At the resort this New Year's Eve, Jenna seemed to know more about what to expect. Last night, our final night there, we talked over dinner about how we needed to start expanding the search for Mallory. She discussed going to Cambodia, which finally seemed possible after years of doubting if she could handle it. She has been exposed to the realities of human trafficking all the time through her work and knows the likelihood for Mallory to be able to reach the resort was nearly impossible. Of course, what we didn't discuss was the likelihood of finding Mallory alive, which grew less and less with each passing day.

Last night, I returned to my room and started gathering up my stuff. I poured myself a drink and pulled out some papers I needed to review about a company we were auditing next week at work. There was a tap on my door.

"J," I said as she came into my room.

"Ryan." She stopped about halfway into the room. "Is this okay?"

Before I realized what was happening, Jenna and I were in each other's arms and kissing. I'd considered this possibility over the past year, but I had always pushed the idea aside, knowing it wasn't right. But right then, with Jenna there, somehow it didn't feel wrong. I realized I did feel attraction and love for Jenna. I had always felt love for her and then for Thomas, but now it seemed different, more intimate. It wasn't the same as how I felt for Mallory years ago, but I couldn't deny there were feelings there. With Mallory, it had been a process, and I'd had to think about it and anticipate how things might go in certain situations. With Jenna, it was easier. I didn't have to adjust who I was or what I did to accommodate her and Thomas in my life or to be a part of theirs. There seemed to be some sense of normalcy to what I was feeling. Relief.

The seatbelt signal blinks and brings me back from my thoughts. The lights in the plane are low. Jenna shifts and raises her head.

"Oh gosh." She smiles up at me. "Sorry. How long have I been sleeping?" She stretches her arms in front of her.

"Maybe an hour," I say. "Sleepyhead."

She bumps her shoulder against mine. I let my hand fall over hers, then bring it to my lips and kiss it, the comfort and desire from last night still lingering.

After a few moments, Jenna pulls her scarf from her neck, leans it against the wall of the plane, and once again closes her eyes.

CHAPTER FOURTEEN

JENNA

March 29, 2010

I hear Thomas crying from his crib. I roll over and the clock on the nightstand reads 6:30 a.m. I just got back to bed at five after the last time he woke up. Next to the alarm clock, I see the framed photo of me with Mallory at the waterpark when we were about ten years old. I squeeze my eyes shut as they fill with tears. I miss her so much. My emotions have been heightened the last few months with all the hormones and lack of sleep that comes with having a new baby.

My mother has been so helpful and even wakes up for those early morning feedings. I think she has bonded with Thomas more than I have, which leaves me happy but also a little jealous. But I honestly don't know what I would do without her. I've struggled with everything. Breastfeeding hasn't worked too well for me as Thomas isn't interested. This has left me feeling almost rejected and a bit depressed. I've been doing the best I can with pumping and supplementing with formula for the first few months.

I knew what to expect, and I almost feel like I anticipated this. I have been going to therapy since early in the pregnancy and also the support group for survivors of sexual assault that Dr. Ramirez had recommended. From that counseling and learning from the experience of others, I was ready for the flood of uncertainty and mixed feelings, but some days have still been harder than others.

Today, Mom had to leave early for some insurance training for work. So now I lie in bed and know that I am the only option. I get up and toss on my robe. I go into the nursery and look down at Thomas and his tiny little body vibrating with each outcry. He seems so strange to me still, and I am trying to feel that magic connection that mothers talk about. It has been almost four months and I am still waiting for that moment. I reach down and pick him up.

We walk into the kitchen and I grab a bottle to warm on the stovetop. I bounce him over my shoulder while we are waiting, but he continues to scream. My head is pounding.

"Come on, Thomas," I plead with him. "Just today, can we just try a little harder to get past this?"

I start to hum, hoping it will relax him and make the crying stop. Instead, he seems even more angry at the sound of my voice. Maybe he has gotten too used to my mother and prefers her in the morning. I sit him down in his baby carrier on the counter and fasten him in while I test the temperature of the bottle.

"Here, how about some music, Thomas?" I say, looking around for the radio Mom usually has on the shelf, but I see that it is gone. In its place is an older mini cassette player I recognize as Mallory's. Renee, Mallory's mom, had brought over some things a couple of months ago when she visited me to meet Thomas. Most of them were toys or stuffed animals that belonged to Mallory when she was little, but I remember seeing this tape player in the box. Again, a flood of emotion runs through me. I press play on the cassette deck and immediately hear the guitar of John Fogerty followed by his raspy voice as the song, "Have you Ever Seen the Rain," plays from the tiny speakers.

"There we go . . . maybe a little CCR will help." I say as I turn it up to drown out Thomas's wailing. I walk over to the refrigerator and fill a glass of water for myself. The cool water feels good on my scratchy throat and wakes me up a little more. I take a breath and return to the bottle cooling on the counter and then turn to pick up Thomas. He is sleeping.

I smile and somehow, it feels like Mallory is there in the room with me. I carefully unfasten Thomas, pick him up, and hold him close to me. His soft breath tickles my neck and he nuzzles into me. I think about her and how when we were kids she would play all of this older music and school me about the artist and where the music originated. Swaying back and forth in the kitchen, I am reduced to sorrow and satisfaction all at once. I feel more connected to my son than I have before and I am more distanced from my best friend, but her spirit is with me. We dance to the end of the song and then I take Thomas back to his nursery and gently lay him back down in his crib. He sleeps until noon, giving me some much-needed rest.

At the end of the week, I share this with my therapist. She tells me that it makes sense that I am missing and possibly grieving for my best friend. She suggests continuing to keep her in my thoughts and to share parts of her with my son, or as she says it, "my new family."

I continue to attend therapy and find that it does help to connect with other survivors. Then one day I sit down in the community room for our group session and words escape me. Across the room are two young women, teenagers actually, who are introduced as sisters. They have been brought to the area through a refugee mission at the church and have escaped a sex trafficking ring in Laos. After the session, I introduce myself to the sisters. They only speak a few words and phrases of English, but we are communicating through our eyes and expressions.

Over the next year, I spend a lot of time with Dara and Keo and eventually start volunteering with the refugee mission group through their church. I help both of them learn how to speak English and communicate better. They visit our home and love to spend time playing with Thomas. We prepare meals together, and I learn about their lives and culture as they open up and share. I teach Dara how to drive and she is able to get a driver's license, which makes her incredibly proud.

As we continue to attend the group therapy session together, we begin to share our experiences in Southeast Asia and being held captive. I start to learn more about that way of life and why it is such a common crime in their land. With my mother's help, we work with some local businesses to help Dara and Keo get jobs in Lincoln. The church helps them with finding a place to live and moving them to their new home as well as getting set up with furnishings and work attire. Thomas and I visit them often and sometimes they come back to Everly Falls to visit our group therapy. I miss them and find myself longing to help more survivors.

My therapist must have noticed this change and renewed energy in me because she asks if I would be willing to serve on a congressional committee that was addressing issues of sex crimes and trafficking. I've been working part-time with the state Attorney General's office in the communications department. This allows me some flexibility with Thomas who is growing fast. He is learning new things every week, it seems, and loves going to daycare. My job eventually turns into a full-time position, which coincides with Thomas's enrollment in preschool.

Along with making several trips back to Thailand and staying in contact with Anna Hamilton at the embassy in Cambodia, I continue to search for Mallory. I feel good about the work I am doing and hope to make a difference not just for her, but other women and children who fall victim to these monstrous criminals. Some days it is a heartbreaking process, but I am dedicated.

In the summer of 2011, Thomas and I move into a townhome in a newer development close to the college. It is a change to not have Mom there all the time, but I also want her to get the chance to be a grandmother, not to always feel so responsible to take care of us. Ryan and I have forged a friendship that I cherish, and he is very involved with Thomas. I think it has been good for Ryan, and I have noticed his spirits have lifted and even the presence of happiness on occasion. I know it was very hard for him at first. He misses Mallory as much as I do.

My work keeps me busy and preoccupied. With Thomas to focus on, it is easy to dismiss depression or anxiety when it sneaks up on me. I have continued therapy, but cut back to only once per month. Sometimes, if I stop or think too much, I get a sense of paralysis thinking about Mallory. The guilt of my own happiness starts to overwhelm me, and I take on a new project or focus on a current trafficking case.

There is a multistate trafficking case that breaks open in the fall of 2012 and the perpetrators are apprehended. The authorities find victims and survivors across the Interstate 80 corridor spanning from Wyoming into Illinois. Through our mission group, several of the surviving young women and girls are placed in homes throughout the Midwest. There are three women in their twenties that come to the Everly Falls area. I form a strong bond with one in particular, Diana. I learn that she was lured into trafficking through a scumbag boyfriend who got her addicted to drugs first and then eventually led her to selling herself for sex to get more drug money for him. She was only fifteen years old when she got involved with him.

She begins to come to the group therapy session that I now sometimes facilitate. I can tell she is still a bit shaky in this world that is not familiar to her. The fact that she has so little regard for herself cuts deep for me and reminds me of the way many of the women in Cambodia were. Slowly, she begins to speak up and share her story with the group. I start to see her dress nicer and sit up straighter. These are all good signs. I help her complete some paperwork to get financial assistance for dental work she needs and to apply for a couple of jobs online.

When I arrive at the community center one day, Diana is waiting for me outside in the hallway. She is very agitated and I ask what is bothering her. She tells me she was turned down for a job and is very upset about it. I assure her that there are many other opportunities and something will work out. Throughout the session, I see her slowly disengage. When the meeting ends, I ask if we can go get coffee. I know she is feeling low and I want to help her so badly.

When I walk out to my car to meet Diana, she is nowhere to be found. I try calling her number, but there is no answer. The next morning, I get a call from the office at the church where the mission group is headquartered. Barbara, the office manager, asks if I have seen or talked to Diana. I explain the situation from the day before. Then I learn that she cashed the check she received for the dental work, but the dentist has no record of payment. My heart sinks.

We learned in our training and with experience that the likelihood of survivors falling back into drug use and even trafficking is very high. I keep going over everything with Diana in my mind, trying to figure out what I could have done differently. Then it hits me, the paralysis.

I call my mom and ask her to pick Thomas up from school that day and if he can stay with her for the night. I only need a night to let myself recover from this blow. But a night turns into a week and before I know it, I am in a full-on state of depression. Finally, my mom comes over and helps me out of bed. I shower and she gives me a ride to my therapist's office.

It takes several meetings over the next couple of weeks to understand what is happening to me. My therapist asks me some difficult questions, which ultimately lead me to accept that my feelings about Diana directly relate to my sense of loss with Mallory.

"Loss of Mallory." These words play repeatedly in my mind and I try to push them away.

It has been almost five years since I last saw Mallory. The images and construed nightmares of what has happened to her are too much to keep dismissing. Each passing moment I lose her more and more. The sorrow I feel is impacting my ability to live and it is suffocating me. What else can I do? How can I accept that she is gone?

I return to work and decide that I have to make at least one more attempt to see if any more information has been found or any action has taken place. I call Anna in Cambodia, who has stayed in touch, but she does not have any news. She almost seems annoyed at my call. I call several other numbers to different agencies tracking information, but again, nothing. I pace the floor in my office, knowing deep inside the pivotal moment I am reaching. The conflict grows along with the impulse to avoid it, but then there is the presence of something else, a coercion of sorts pulling me in and forcing my hand.

Some days I feel like I am the only one trying. I think of Renee and Ryan. I know they have not given up hope and maybe I could match their unwavering faith that someday she will be found if only I didn't know what I know. If I could erase my experience of being beaten, raped, drugged, traded, and treated less than human, then maybe I could also live in the world of hopefulness. The struggle between hope and reality is too much to bear.

I stand at my desk and look down at the files and notes strewn about. There is a framed photo of Thomas. Next to it is a framed picture of Mallory and myself on the day we boarded the plane to Thailand. Our stupid smiling faces and naivety is too much to look at. With all the force I have inside myself, I strike my desk and push everything onto the floor with a guttural noise registering somewhere between a growl and a scream.

I fall to the floor and sob.

Lydia, our receptionist, opens the door to my office.

"Jenna?" she says softly.

I look up at her and know she is startled by my behavior. I keep sobbing uncontrollably.

"Are you okay?"

"She is gone, Lydia. She is gone and I can't do anything to bring her back." The tears continue.

Lydia comes over to me and gently kneels down to sit next to me. I lean toward her, burying my face into her shoulder and I keep sobbing.

"She is gone. She is gone." I repeat this over and over to Lydia, someone I barely know. Each time I say it, it becomes more real and, somehow, more relieving.

CHAPTER FIFTEEN

Mallory

May 5, 2016

I walk along the path between the buildings, the sun beating down on me. I long to remove the cover from my head and face and let the sunlight hit my skin. I've just finished working with some young boys in the village. Today was difficult; they weren't very focused on learning English. From what I can gather, it's toward the end of a Muslim holiday or some day of celebration. It sounds like they are all leaving to go to a feast this evening in a different village. Confused by the different traditions and rituals practiced in this place, it's hard to understand what's really happening. This distraction kept the boys from staying on task in the lessons I was trying to teach them. I was distracted too. It filled me with relief to know most of the men would be leaving the village soon. We would still be guarded, but I always feel less afraid when the men are gone.

I stop between two buildings, looking to the fence that surrounds the village. There isn't anyone in sight, and I can't see any windows in the buildings from where I stand. A sliver of sunlight falls on me. I slowly pull back the cover from my head and raise my face up to the sky. Even though it's hot out, it feels good to have the direct sunlight on my skin. I am taking a risk being outdoors without having my head and face covered, but it's just for a second. A year ago, I would have never tried this. Since I've been in this village, I have been less afraid of my captor. He isn't mean or cruel the way the last men in charge have been. He also has a different level of power with the people in the village. He may be a general or sheikh. I never talk to him or address him directly, so I'm not sure what to call him. In my mind, I just refer to him as "the Commander." He doesn't beat me very often, and when he forces himself on me, he isn't as violent as some of the other men. In fact, he didn't even restrain me at first. It was clear early on when I arrived that he had purchased me because I'm American. He wanted me to teach the boys in the village how to speak English. The other women didn't like me at first, and some of them still don't. They think I'm treated better than they are because I'm American. I try to be as kind to them as I can. I know they are not any better off than I am.

When I'm not teaching, I am working, and the other women always leave the worst chores to me. I have to clean out the latrines and burn our trash, which often leads me to getting sick. My immune system is weak. I have been stung several times by some type of spider or insect, and it seems to drain me each time. My body is taking its toll. Some days, I wish I had the pills or drugs like before, but then I realize that was probably why I seemed so tired and lethargic.

When I walk through the back door of the house, I shiver just from no longer having the sunlight. I put the box of food that I brought from the classroom on the counter. The older boys didn't eat lunch that day because of the impending feast. The younger boys were allowed to eat, but there were still some leftovers, so I brought it to the house to share with the other women.

Suddenly, I hear a voice from the room behind me. I turn to see one of the head guards rifling through the metal cabinet in the corner. My heart races. For the most part, he is not mean to me, but I still don't trust him . . . or anyone. It's also strange that he's in our quarters.

He looks at me as if he is wanting my help. Then I realize he is looking through the box where our fake identification books are kept. They use these when they trade women between villages or brothels. Sensing his urgency, I walk over to him. He must see the fear in my eyes.

"Fahima. German." He says, handing me the box. I look at the books one by one and find the one for Fahima. They look like passports but without the nice cover. I remember when they took my picture for the book. The name they gave me was Tayla, but nobody ever calls me that. They all refer to me as "White" or "America."

I can't find one for Anke, the young German girl who arrived a few months earlier. I assume that's who he meant by "German." I have to look at each photo because I'm not sure what fake name they gave her in the identification book. I look through them a second time. Suddenly, he grabs the box from my hands and slaps me across the face, and I fall backward onto the floor. The box of identification books falls to the ground, and he storms out of the front entrance.

As I stand up, Fahima enters the concrete house. She looks at me with tear-filled eyes as she passes by to go to the bedroom where we all sleep. I quickly get up and follow her. There's a chest where we all keep anything we consider our own. She pulls out a drawer she shares with another woman and places items inside a small bag: a set of clothes, a brush, and a small bag that holds some hygiene products. I put my hand on her shoulder. She looks back, and we quickly embrace.

Even though it's just a second, I can feel her trembling. She is scared, and with good reason. They are taking her with them wherever they are going tonight. It's likely I will never see her again. She will be sold to someone else. The process is familiar, having happened to me several times before coming to this village.

As Fahima leaves the room, the young German girl is led in by a guard. She is so young and scared to death. However, she keeps raising her voice to the guard. She hasn't learned how to work the system yet to keep herself from being beaten. He pushes her down to the ground with the butt of his rifle. She scoots across the floor to the old chest and only takes a small bag that has some toiletries in it. As she lifts herself up, she reaches over to her bed, pulls the sheet off the thin mattress, and wads it up under her arm. The guard barks an order to her that I can't understand. As she is led out of the house, my heart hurts for her. She is clearly considered a bad trade by the men and will likely go to a different village where she is not treated well.

I hear the truck drive off and feel a sense of relief, although I still keep my guard up. I don't think I can ever feel comfortable or safe like I did in my previous life. Of course, back then I was oblivious to it, taking my simple, stable little life for granted. I took my own worth for granted. Back then, I never realized what being female meant in other parts of the world, how women were considered chattel or less by men.

This place is a little more tolerable, but not much. The other camps—or better yet, prisons—where I had been kept were un-imaginable. So far, I have been in seven different places that I can recall. I often think about how I would describe them if I ever returned home. I think I'm in the Middle East somewhere now, far from where Jenna and I were taken. I do know that the first few locations are not far in proximity because we were always driven by truck, but it seemed as though we were taken overseas by barge to get to this village. I was with sixteen other women, and we were cramped into the space. Some had luggage, but I only had the clothes on my back. We were all restrained and tied together. They covered our heads completely as they loaded us. We were on that ship where it was dark and sweltering for what seemed like days before we were released. In the beginning, nausea consumed me and I lay in the corner on some old furniture cushions that had been tossed in when they loaded us. We removed the coverings from our heads, but there was little light. A few holes in the top of the container seemed to provide some airflow, but not much. Every so often, someone would drop in bags of packaged food and bottles of water in the top of the trailer. I barely ate anything. Finally, we were unloaded, separated into different trucks and, with our eyes or heads covered, driven for several hours until arriving at a different village. I was forced to remove my clothing and stand for what seemed to be an hour or so. Beneath the cover on my head, I could see the boots of the people walking all around us. Then I was covered with a long shirt, loaded into a smaller vehicle of some sort with another woman and brought to this village. The other woman was older and of Middle Eastern descent. She was only in this village for about a month and then she was gone. I still don't know what happened to her, whether she was traded or killed.

There are so many other women, many just girls whom I have crossed paths with in this world. I squeeze my eyes tight just picturing the many faces and truly hoping they are still alive or have found peace in some way. Then I picture Jenna. I have not seen Jenna for years. Every time she comes to mind, I dismiss the weight of the possibilities. Is she still fighting? Is she still being held captive and tortured? Or did she somehow escape? Where is she now? I can only hope that she's still alive. Her strength was always such an asset to her. Responsibility overwhelms me as I allow myself to think about her. I miss her so much. Grief and sorrow gnaw at my soul.

I sit down on the bunk for just a moment and begin to wonder how much longer I will be kept in this place. The sense of relief from the men's absence is turning into something else, and I begin weeping. The tears are of solace. I am glad to not have been one of the girls traded again. I try to keep track of the days, but it is difficult. Because I teach in the classroom, I have access to paper and pencils. In the back of the old notebook I use to write out my lessons, I keep track of days. I have to be careful because it can't look like this is what I'm doing. I make a dot-by-dot picture of cherry blossoms, my favorite, and I keep adding to it. For each day I am here, I add another dot. So far, I have 497 dots, so I estimate that I have been in this village for about a year and a half. Of all the women held with me, I have been here longer than all but four. There are always about twelve to fifteen women in total. In the room where we sleep there are only twelve metal-frame beds, so if there are more women, the newer ones will have to sleep on the floor or in bed with another woman.

I stare down at the cement floor. We try to sweep it several times a day, but it's always covered with a layer of dirt. It's actually a very fine layer of sand that always gets into the house even though we wipe our feet. The walls of the house are stacked concrete blocks, equally as dirty, and there is a metal roof. The room we sleep in doesn't have any windows, and it grows hot during the summer months.

I always feel filthy. Even after bathing, I immediately feel dust on my skin. The only time I have a truly clean feeling is on the nights I am brought to the Commander in his house. Before I'm with him, I am made to shower. The bathroom in the main house is much more modern than that of any other house or bathroom in the village. I am able to dry off with clean towels that are soft. For the few minutes before I am taken to the Commander's quarters, I feel my skin breathe. I have become so immune to the rapes that I actually look forward to the nights when I get to shower in the main house. One time early in my stay, I let my shower last too long. We only are given about ten minutes to clean ourselves. I remember how long it took to get used to this new arid climate. For the first several months, I itched all the time. The water felt soothing on my irritated skin. When I was restrained right after, I knew I was in trouble. The guard brought me into the Commander's room and whipped me while the Commander watched. I wasn't sure exactly what was wrong, but the next several times I was brought to the main house, a guard was in the bathroom with me while I showered and turned the water off in a matter of minutes. I learned to make this process brief and eventually was allowed to shower alone again.

A scorpion scurries across the floor and into the other room, catching my attention. I look down at my forearm at the welt from some type of bite or sting. When I first arrived, I would get very ill from these bites, resulting in terrible stomach cramps along with diarrhea and vomiting. My head would throb, and I would feel like I was suffocating. Often, I would be afraid to go back to sleep. I now only have red welts on my arms, legs, and sometimes my torso. Usually they go away in a few days. But I know something has been feasting on me as I sleep. I wake up with a shortness of breath often, but after drinking some water, I can usually manage my normal daily duties.

With the men gone from the village, the other women will want to bathe and wash their clothes in the main house. Whether or not this is possible will depend on who is guarding us. Sometimes the men with guns let us have certain privileges when the Commander is gone, as long as we serve them in whatever way they want first. Often, one of us takes on this responsibility to make it possible for the other girls.

I walk into the other room that we use for cooking, eating, and just gathering. It is similar to the sleeping room with the concrete floor and walls, except there are two doors on opposite sides. They are wooden doors that don't really seal in any way but cover the opening and are locked from the outside. One faces the front of the village and one faces the back path that leads to the other buildings. There are two small windows, and on a few occasions, there is a bit of a breeze. In the scorching summer months, we often get up from bed and just sit in the bigger room so we can feel the cooler breeze.

The room is outfitted with some old, used furniture pieces. There is an old metal kitchen table that reminds me of my grandmother's kitchen table on the farm. Mismatched chairs and a stool are placed around it. This is where we eat. There aren't enough chairs for everyone, but the rest sit on the old sofa. There are also two old rocking chairs. They are strange and must have come from the main house because they look ornate and out of place, especially compared to the two other chairs that look like old office chairs. They are in terrible shape. The seats are torn, and the knobs to adjust the height are broken. These have been added to the collection within the last six months. There is a counter with cabinets on the far end where we keep some dishes and any food we can find. There is an old, blue cooler-like jug for our drinking water. We have to fill it up each day from the water pump in the middle of the village.

Our gathering together in the house is not social. We aren't allowed to talk to each other, and sometimes they even stage a guard in there, especially when new girls arrive. But usually we are left alone in the house. Even though we can't actually speak to one another because we aren't allowed to, and most of us speak different languages and can't easily communicate anyway, we are still able to communicate through our facial expressions and our actions. I can tell when the women are upset or don't like something just by their reactions. We can also support each other or give each other comfort by sitting close or allowing ourselves to stand together and lean on one another.

There's a rotation with the girls that can be anticipated. My turn is once every three weeks. A guard comes to our house and pulls one of us from the bedroom. We are usually in our room before the sun goes down, some of us even sleeping because most of the women work hard during the day. I'm actually one of the lucky ones because a good portion of my day is spent teaching the boys. The other women are responsible for cleaning the main house, the other buildings in the village, or vehicles, or unloading and reloading trucks with supplies or items that are sold and traded on a regular basis, and other difficult tasks. The two women who have been here the longest are responsible for cooking all of the food in the village for the Commander, the children, his men, and the guards. There are also two other women who are responsible for all of the children and looking after them. I haven't been here long enough to see a new child born yet, but I know it's going to happen soon because Tarana, a girl who has been there a little longer than me, is pregnant.

One night, after I had been with the Commander, a guard was walking me back to our building and instead of going directly back, he stopped along the way and shoved me to the ground behind a storage shed. It was dark and I couldn't see much. As I tried to get my bearings, I felt something strike my arm and back with such force it made me gasp. My instinct was to scream, but I knew I couldn't or it would be worse. I wasn't sure what he was hitting me with, but it whipped a terrible sting through my canvas gown, and I was sure I was bleeding. As I gasped, he pulled the hijab from my head and shoved part of it in my mouth. He pushed my head down into the dirt and then lifted my gown from behind. I knew what was coming, but I was not prepared for the torture I was about to endure.

Suddenly, an excruciating pain ripped through my lower half, too sharp to be a part of him, but felt more like a stick or tool. He pressed down with his arm onto the top of my back, pushing my chest and head further into the dirt. Gravel scraped the side of my face and filled my ear, causing the sounds to be muffled. He pushed and pulled on this object a few times, each time sending unbearable tremors through my body. It felt like I was being torn in two. I bit down on the hijab to keep from screaming. Then he pushed himself into my backside and the sting of it was too much. My body went numb and my vision went out of focus, but he didn't seem to notice as he continued on and on and on.

I remember coming back to reality when I heard the voice of another guard. He pulled the first guard off me and was speaking to him in a harsh whisper. I was lying there, not sure what might happen next. I didn't dare move because they could shoot me. I was lying in the dirt with my entire lower half exposed. I thought maybe the other guard would climb up next and also have his way with me, but instead he yanked me up by my arm. I rose to my feet. He walked me toward the house. We walked past the other guard, who was leaning against the shed with his head down. I could hardly move my legs, and he was walking so fast he was almost dragging me. When we got to the house about a hundred feet away from the shed, he unlocked the back door. He turned me around and said something in a language I didn't speak, but I knew the meaning. He was warning me to keep my mouth shut. He shoved me in and locked the door behind me.

It was dark inside the house. Lying on the dirty floor, I slowly pulled the hijab from my mouth and gasped for air. My face stung from the dirt and scrapes and I tried to shake the gravel from my ear and hair. I didn't want to wake any of the other women, and I didn't want them to know what had just happened to me. Maybe this happened to them too. Tears ran down my face. Using the table to pull myself up, I could feel the blood running down my legs. I felt my way around to a candle on the counter. I lit it to give myself enough light to try to wash my face and the throbbing areas the man violated. I was trembling so hard that it took me twice as long to clean myself. Once I had finally accomplished this, I hobbled back to the bedroom and slowly lay down onto the bed. I knew this would be a slow heal. I just hoped it would heal. I had been raped like that in other places, but never without being drugged. Now I understand why they drugged the girls they captured.

I was full of anger and despair, wanting it all to stop, but knowing it was likely not going to for a long time. Something had to happen. Living like this was not living. It was just waiting to be killed. Just as I was contemplating the worst option possible, I felt a hand on my head. It was from one of the other women. Her bed was adjacent to mine. I reached up and grabbed her hand, and she squeezed mine tight as I continued to sob. She knew. Her compassion and care that night was so consoling to me. Just her touch made me remember that I had to be strong and that I could make it through.

Over the next several days, I tried to keep my eye out for the guard who had assaulted me, but I didn't see him anywhere in the village. I did see the other guard who pulled him off me that night. I wanted to let him know I appreciated that he helped me, but he never made eye contact with me. I was convinced the guard who attacked me must have been sent away. I also know that if the Commander found out about it, I would be traded or even possibly . . . the thought of it shakes me to my core. Just knowing that I would be damaged goods in the eyes of the Commander, enough so that he would just have me killed was too real.

Sitting here now, watching the men leave the village, wondering about how I could ever be "thankful" to one of these guards for anything is such bullshit. This place is such a fucking terrible place, and this life is such a fucking terrible life. When I think of the truth of it, it makes my blood boil.

But I'm still alive. As long as I'm still alive, I must have hope.

CHAPTER SIXTEEN

Mallory

May 5, 2016 – Dusk

All the women come into the house late in the afternoon, calmer than usual because of the men's absence. Most of them gather clothing and personal items for bathing. As I walk into the bedroom, they turn to look at me, and I know they want me to distract or negotiate with the guards to let them have time in the main house to bathe and wash clothes. I know this because they have each put something on my bed. This is a way we communicate with each other. There are some small food items on my bed, as well as a scarf and piece of soap, and even a small bottle of lotion. I wonder where someone found that. Maybe she took it from the main house the last time she was there, or from the children's quarters.

With a squeamish feeling in my stomach, I undress and put my kaftan and pants into the pile of dirty laundry, and then put on a new set of clothes from the chest. Then we strip the sheets from the beds to wash as well. We pick up the items and, together, go to the door. Tarana knocks. She is able to be a bit more forward with the guards because she is pregnant. They wouldn't hurt her in fear of harming the baby. The guards know there will be consequences if something bad were to happen.

A young guard opens the door, and when he sees us holding laundry and clothing, he knows what we want. Another guard walks up, and they speak to each other. After a few moments, they lead us to the main house. I'm at the end of the line, and one of the guards takes my arm. Since I'm in the back and not carrying anything, I'm the "sacrifice" for the night.

When the women enter the main house, they all look back at me, and I recognize the appreciation in their eyes. Looking around, I realize there may be only two guards in the village tonight. The rest of the men must have gone with the group that left the village for the celebration feast. This surprises me. Other than the time I was attacked by the guard, I've only been with the guards by themselves a couple of times before, so I'm not sure what to expect. I don't remember much from those times because I've blocked a lot of it from my memory. I do remember there were only a few of them, and they weren't violent. I simply went to their quarters where they put me in a room by myself and gave me a strange liquor to drink. I was feeling lightheaded, and they each took their turn with me. When they were done, one of them walked me back to the main house where I helped the other women finish the washing. I don't remember it lasting very long.

The two guards lead me to their quarters, one older and one younger. They have a bottle of liquor, and I can tell they have already been drinking. The older guard hands me a full glass and motions for me to drink. It tastes awful and burns my throat, but it feels warm on the way down and immediately makes my stomach churn. He fills the glass again and makes me sit on a cushioned chair. I drink it as fast as I can without regurgitating it. I'm surprised when the younger guard stumbles toward the back of the house and into the bedroom. He doesn't close the door but just falls onto the bed as if he is not feeling well. The older man looks at me, motioning for me to take off my clothes. I try to neatly pile my clean clothing on the table next to the chair. He then pushes me down onto the chair sideways so my legs are hanging over the arm. He drops his pants. He grabs my breasts with his hands and squeezes them so tightly it makes me want to scream. He stops for a second, and then he puts something in my mouth to quiet me. I think it's a rope or maybe a handkerchief. Then he violently gropes, pulls, and bites, and it's absolutely agonizing. But soon he refocuses his attention and shoves into me. The force of being stretched and torn is even more grueling. I turn my head and stare at a small table in the corner of the room. The sounds he's making become background noise as I focus on the table and try to breathe, just wanting it to end.

It's over in a matter of seconds. He lifts himself off me and pulls up his pants. I'm lying there, drenched in his sweat and semen. The smell in the room makes me gag and I think I'm going to vomit. My breasts are sore and I'm numb between my legs.

The guard abruptly pulls me up by my arm. I remove the material from my mouth. He tosses my clothing to me, and I scurry to get dressed. He doesn't make eye contact with me but grabs the rifle leaning up against the wall and points it in my direction. My stomach suddenly drops, and I almost fall to the ground. But then he motions to the door with the rifle. I scramble to my feet and walk out. As I round the house, I fall to my knees and gag and heave. Nothing comes up, so I inhale deeply and rise to my feet, and then rush into the women's house. Surprisingly, the guard does not follow me.

The women are gone. I stand in the main room for a moment, but nobody comes into the house. I shuffle to the bedroom where I fall onto the bare mattress on my bed and cry. I lie there for a long time before I realize I have the house to myself.

I quickly get up and look out the back door, trying to spot the guards. There is no one in sight. Perhaps they are all at the main house, or possibly having dinner with the younger children. This is something we also do sometimes when the men leave the village.

In the other direction, I notice the gate to the village is not closed all the way. It must have stuck after they drove through earlier. I wonder if a guard is standing outside the big gate. My heart is pounding, the adrenaline pumping. I drink a glass of water while quickly pacing in the main room. Then a breeze comes through the window, shaking the back door, which is still unlocked.

I run into the bedroom and reach under the bed for the old pair of hiking boots I wear when it is muddy after a rain. They were there when I arrived and I inherited them, and they keep my feet dry. I adjust the hijab on my head. This is my chance. I bite my thumbnail as I pace, a nervous habit I've had since childhood when I am contemplating something.

I think of the woman who was hanged in the middle of the village, left there for weeks after she was shot trying to escape. The Commander wanted to be sure we all understood what would happen if we tried to get away. *No, no, I don't care if I get caught. I just have to try to escape, because to not try is just giving up. And knowing that is a worse reality.*

A spark has been ignited inside of me. If I don't act quickly, the opportunity might not ever come again. Cautiously, I walk outside and around to the front of the house. I think about the guards and the one who was passed out. I'm curious where the one who raped me went. When he ordered me out of his quarters, he seemed angry and flustered, almost embarrassed. Standing outside at the corner of the house, blocked from view of the main house and any other structure, I survey the gate, which is about a hundred yards away.

This is it.

All at once, my feet hit the ground and I feel like I'm flying. I run fast but on the tips of my toes so not to be heard. I keep my eyes ahead of me, letting the horizon pull me toward it. As I approach the gate, I know it's likely there's a guard on the other side and I might be shot, but it doesn't stop me. I simply slip through and keep running. Holding my breath, I wait to feel pain, to drop to the ground, to hear a shot in the air. But there is nothing. It's been years since energy has surged inside of me like it does in this moment.

My body keeps moving, fueled by a mix of fear, uncertainty, and anticipation—somehow without getting tired. Increasing my pace, I keep running and running. Leaping over rocks and dunes, never looking back, I run into a sandy field full of brush. I force myself to ignore the space directly around me because acknowledging it might slow me down. Instead, all I see are the mountains far ahead against the backdrop of a darkening lavender sky. I focus on the peaks in the distance and keep running. Each step is with intention, and the significance of it shifts the balance of being suffocated and stifled in captivity to the favor of freedom. Creating more and more distance, my emotions grow stronger and empowerment keeps pushing me forward. I'm oblivious to the tears streaming down my face until the sun starts to disappear behind me and the air grows cooler.

The terrain is getting rockier, and I start to climb into some foothills. I keep going, but I'm not able to go as fast. I want to scream out, *Help me!* But if the wrong person hears me or finds me, it will mean my death if they return me to the village. So I repeat it in my head—*help me, help me, help me*—and then eventually I whisper it, almost as a chant giving cadence to my feet moving upward.

Just before the sun is completely gone, I stop for a moment and crouch behind some bushes in the hills. The air is dry and getting cooler. It seems like there is a thin, smoky layer of sand hanging in the air. The smell of fuel, like at a gas station, lingers. Not seeing any vehicles, I wonder if maybe it's just the odor of the vegetation around me.

I finally look back and can't see the lights of the village. My body is aching, and my muscles are starting to clench. My feet are sliding inside of the boots, and I know I have to keep moving or I might pass out. The journey is arduous, but I can't risk stopping. My pace slows, but I keep moving forward. My legs are not on steady ground, slipping on the rocks and sticks underneath my steps. At one point, I fall and slide backward, realizing that I am climbing upward at a pretty steep incline. I pull myself up and start walking again, but continue to slide on the dry leaves and needles against the hard, dry earth. My feet are blistering from being bare in the boots, but I try to ignore the pain. My breathing is becoming labored, and I realize I can probably be heard if anyone is near. Then the thought enters my mind: *I don't know where I am or where I am going.* But it doesn't matter. I have to get as far away as I can. The farther away from the village I can get, the more likely I will eventually find someone who might help me.

I have been running away for hours and continue to climb higher and higher. The brush becomes denser, and it's harder to breathe. I decide I will go for another hour or so and then possibly stop to rest or even sleep for a couple of hours. I am thirsty and can feel the tightness of my skin and my lips chapping from breathing in so hard.

After more climbing, the brush starts to thin out, and I come to some type of clearing. It reminds me of when my dad and I would go camping in the summer. We used to make an annual trip to the Rocky Mountains in either Colorado or Wyoming to hike and camp. Sometimes my uncle and cousins would go with us, but my mom opted out, not being much of the outdoorsy type. Reminiscing about my family brings a tearful smile to my face and, for the first time in a long time, I feel the slightest chance of seeing them sooner than later.

I stand in the clearing and look ahead. There are lights far ahead in the distance. Maybe they are from another village or some type of camp. It doesn't look like a big place, but I can tell there are different structures and that means . . . people. *I have to get there. I have to keep moving and moving.*

When I step away from the clearing and move forward into the brush toward the lights, my foot slips and my ankle twists, and I fall to the ground and begin tumbling. I am falling, and I am falling hard. My body hits rocks and twigs as I roll and slide downward. *Is this how my story ends?* Gasping and reaching, I try to stop myself, but the momentum pulls me down even faster. My body is scraped and poked and then my head crushes into something solid.

CHAPTER SEVENTEEN

Cash

May 7, 2016

Ten miles from the COP, our combat outpost, my battle buddy
Sinclair and I have orders to scope out possible landmines in the
area. We're part of the Explosive Ordnance Disposal unit, or EOD.
The sergeant wanted to move the COP closer to the mountains to
help keep people healthy with the cooler temperatures. Sinclair and
I separate and move in opposite directions. A rustling noise in the
desert brush stops me in my tracks at first, then I follow the sound.
I see her curled up next to the tree covered in dust and sand. She is
wearing some kind of long canvas shirt and torn pants. It seems like
she has been there a while and looks as if she is dying, with pale skin
that has yellowed around her eyes. She is dirty and pretty banged up
and as I slowly get closer, I can see she is bleeding too.

I radio in to let my crew know my location and what I've found,
and in seconds, Sinclair is helping me. As he approaches, I start
walking toward the figure of the woman lying on the ground, but
he stops me.

"Wait," he says, and then approaches her with his mine detector.

"Seriously?" I ask, knowing in my gut that she isn't a decoy. But
Sinclair has seen more than I have when it comes to ambushes, so
I step aside.

He holds his detector near her body, circling her and the ground
around her, but there isn't any noise. Sinclair steps back and nods to

me, indicating that it's okay. We both set down our equipment and crouch down next to the injured woman.

"We need to get her back to the truck." He takes her pulse and then forces her eyes open to look at her pupils and responsiveness. "She's still alive, but barely. And she sure as hell doesn't look like she belongs here."

As I carefully pick her up, she starts to come to a bit, but her eyes remain closed. I carry her about five hundred feet back to the truck. We gently sit her on the back steps of the vehicle. Sinclair is our unofficial crew medic, and he quickly goes to work. He grabs the metal box with the first aid kit from one of the storage bins on the side.

While he starts to clean the wound on the side of her head, I hold her upright with one hand and hold her head in my other hand. She looks fairly young and is not Middle Eastern. She flinches when Sinclair uses antiseptic and gauze on her wound, then flickers her eyes open. There's a look of terror in her eyes when she sees us. She tries to stand up, lunging forward as if to take off running, almost falling to the ground.

"Easy, you're injured. Wait, wait, it's okay. We won't hurt you," I say, trying to use a soothing voice. I have no idea if she speaks English or where she might be from.

As I steady her, she pulls her arm away and it looks like she is trying to say something. She takes a few steps as if to take off running again, but her leg is injured and she collapses onto the step of the MRAP.

She is hurt and very weak. It is evident from the dirt all over her she has been out in the desert for days. Taking a wet wipe from the kit, I try to wipe some of the dust from her forehead and face. At first, she cringes and pulls away, but it seems as though she gives into the exhaustion.

"Hey there," I say softly. "It's okay. You're safe now. I'm Private Rigden from the US Army Squadron 5435."

She tries lifting her head slightly to look up at me. Her mouth looks incredibly dry, and she has probably seized from heat and dehydration. I offer her my canteen. She tries to reach for it, but she either doesn't have the strength or it's too painful. So I hold it up to her mouth, and she drinks until the water is gone.

Sinclair notices her leg bruising and unlaces then removes the hiking boots to see if her feet are okay. Her lower leg and ankle have a terrible bruise and immediately start to swell up. Her feet are mangled with blisters and are bleeding in spots.

She is more than just injured. This woman has clearly been abused or beaten and is almost dead. Something terrible has happened to her; I can see it not just in her physical condition but in her eyes. I've heard about the heinous treatment and dire living conditions of women who are taken captive. Even the treatment of women who are free is appalling. I have witnessed women being beaten in the streets and spit on by others. I am never sure about what they did, but it always strikes me as cruel and unnecessary. It's hard to see it happening and not be able to do anything about it most of the time. The thought of my sisters, my cousins, my friends being tortured and abused is enough to infuriate me.

Sinclair tries to wipe the wound on her head and clean out the rock and sand. He is getting ready to wrap her head with gauze when she leans forward slightly and vomits, probably because I let her drink too much water. She only spits up some of it, and then she's dry heaving. It's hard to watch.

"Hey, can we wait in wrapping it?" I ask Sinclair, putting my hand up to protect her from his over-doctoring approach. "I think we need to get her back to the FOB to the TMC and then to a hospital as soon as we can."

"Okay, let's hurry up then." He starts putting the items back into the kit.

I look down at her and wipe her chin. "My name is Cash." I make eye contact with her. She has such deep eyes that pull me in and make me want to know more about her.

She is still very out of it, frightened and disoriented, and just stares at me.

"We're going to take you to our FOB where we have a troop medical clinic and then try to get you on a chopper to a hospital. You're okay now, and you're safe." I grab the blanket from the storage box and carefully wrap it around her.

"Do you speak English?" I really hope she understands. "Just nod your head if you do."

She nods.

"Can you tell me your name?"

She whispers, "Mallory Sh . . ."

I can't understand the last part. Slouching over slowly, she seems to pass out.

I scoop up her frail body as quickly as I can while still being gentle. Sinclair opens the back doors to the MRAP, our mine-resistant vehicle, and he hops in. I carefully lift her up to him, and we situate her between us. I hold her upright, and both Sinclair and I try to keep her as still as possible. We cover her with another blanket we find in one of the storage compartments.

We certainly aren't used to this sort of an ordeal. One moment we're out on a mission locating possible landmines, and the next we find a woman. My mind is whirling, trying to imagine how she got here.

Sinclair reaches over to feel her pulse, then gives me a serious but confirming look. He hits the roof in the back of the truck to alert the soldier driving we are ready, and we begin moving over the sand at rapid speed. We ride in silence. I really hope she will wake up when we get her to the medic and her wounds can be treated. We need to learn more about who this mysterious woman is and what she was doing in the middle of nowhere at the bottom of the foothills in Iraq.

CHAPTER EIGHTEEN

Cash

May 9, 2016

". . . I made out at first sight to be a fine lady's dressing-table. Whether I should have made out this object so soon, if there had been no fine lady sitting at it, I cannot say. In an armchair, with an elbow resting on the table and her head leaning on that hand, sat the strangest lady I have ever seen, or shall ever see."

As I hear her shift in her hospital bed, I look up from the book.

"Two cities . . ." she whispers in a strained voice and opens her eyes.

"Hi there." Setting the book down on the chair, I walk over to her. The sun is setting and the soft light is coming in through the small window. It bounces off the light gray walls in the small room and creates a shadow, making her look almost like a mirage.

As I approach her, she studies me with her eyes. Remembering what the medic told me about moving slowly and using a soft tone of voice, I don't get too close to the bed.

"You're awake," I say. "I'm happy to see this." I gradually approach the side of her bed. "What did you say before? Sorry, I didn't hear it clearly."

She coughs and then attempts to straighten herself up. Her face grimaces; it's obvious she's in pain from her injuries. I restrain myself to help her because I don't want to cross the line or cause her any more discomfort.

"*A Tale of Two Cities,*" she says softly. "If you're going to read Dickens to me, I prefer that over *Great Expectations.*"

At first, I'm confused, but then look back at the book I've been reading from.

"Oh, that. Yeah, sorry. It was just one of the books in the donation box." I walk back to the chair, picking up the copy of *Great Expectations* and turning back to her. "Have you been listening to me read?"

"Yes." She nods her head, but winces from the pain. "It has been nice. Thank you."

"Ma'am, I am not sure if you remember me, but—"

"You found me." She looks straight up at me. "Private Rigden, US Army Squadron 5435, right?"

I smile, impressed she remembered. "Right."

"Thank you, Private Rigden." She seems stuck in a thought. "I probably would have died if you guys hadn't found me."

"Please, ma'am, call me Cash." I'm not sure why I said that. I haven't heard anyone call me by my first name since enlisting in the Army four years ago. I take another step toward her, but she flinches a bit as I approach.

"Oh damn, I mean . . . oh gosh, I'm sorry." I step back.

She takes a breath and pulls the blanket up with her free arm. "It's okay. I'm just, well . . ." Her voice trails off and she takes another deep breath, wincing a bit, probably from her broken ribs. "Thank you, Cash," she says with a friendly expression. "I know you don't mean any harm."

"Yes, ma'am. I mean, no. No harm, ma'am." I feel awkward and also comfortable, which makes me unsure, a sensation I haven't felt since my days in basic training. I self-consciously glance to the floor. Being in the military for the last four years, everything I do is based on an order or some procedure I have committed to memory.

I look at this waif of a woman in front of me. She's obviously been through hell, but she seems to be fighting through it. I'm curious about her and also feel almost proud of her endurance.

"I can go, if you want. I just wanted to make sure you were okay," I say.

There is a pause.

I turn to gather my things, but then she shifts and clears her throat.

"No, please . . . it's nice of you to check on me. Stay, please. It's just been a long time since I have actually been free . . . I mean, able to talk or communicate with anyone. I'm afraid I'm a bit out of practice."

I find myself almost relieved. I'm curious about her, and her story.

"I hope you're feeling better, or at least starting to," I say with a smile. "The medics said you are going to recover, but it might take some time."

"Ah, it's just a few scratches." She gives a small laugh as she raises her leg up a few inches from where it's propped up. "No, really. I am feeling better, thanks to you. I'm not exactly sure of all the details yet, but I know I'm on the mend . . . physically, at least." Suddenly her face falls, and she looks away.

"Hey . . . it's okay," I say. "I can go, really. I don't want to make you uncomfortable."

"No, Cash, no . . ." She gives me a strange look. "It's just so surreal, I guess. I had almost given up on ever returning to life." Her voice is scratchy with emotion. "It's hard to believe I'm here and I'm alive. It's good, really, just so crazy."

"Well, it might seem crazy, but you're right, it is good," I say. "They want to get you to the hospital at Camp Buehring in Kuwait, but they have to wait for the dust storm to clear before they can get the chopper here."

Honestly, I'm not sure of the details either, but the little bit of information my sergeant shared with me and Sinclair was that she claimed to have been taken from Thailand around nine years ago when she was backpacking with a friend. Since then, she has been held captive, traded, and abused terribly. I swallow hard just thinking about this, but try to keep a strong face.

"I know it's hard to think about." She smiles again as if she's reading my mind. "It's okay, Cash. I'm okay. I'm alive, and I'm going home very soon."

"Yes, ma'am."

"Okay. Well, you're the first friend I've made in a really long time, so if I have to call you by your name, you have to do the same, please." She holds out her hand. "It is nice to officially meet you, Cash. My name is Mallory Shields."

Scrambling to set the book down, I reach over to her and take her hand. I understand I'm supposed to keep my distance. The female guard outside the entrance to her room gave me all the rules before going in, but I also don't want to be rude. Her grip is surprisingly strong for someone so close to death a day ago. It's uncomfortable for her physically, but it's so incredible to see her trying to make light of the situation.

"Are you a Dickens fan?" she asks, looking at the book sitting in the chair.

"Oh gosh, ma'am . . . I mean Mallory, I'm not sure. I wasn't that far into it." I try to sound smart because I can tell she is smart, but I also feel compelled to just be really honest. "For reals, the main guy, Pip, he seems kinda like the world is against him so far."

She doesn't respond, just looks at me with her blue eyes, which look like they once must have shone brightly but are now shadowed by a certain darkness. She's seen some horrible things.

"I mean, I'm not really much of a reader." I glance down a bit. "I have read more since being over here. They send them to us . . . some group, I think they're called Operation Paperback or something. We don't have much else to do in our downtime."

Again, she is just listening intently.

"But you . . . you must be a reader, huh?" Then I realize how ridiculous this sounds.

"I was at one time," she says quietly. "If I had to recommend one to read for sure . . . you should really check out *A Tale of Two Cities* . . . it is by far Dickens's best work."

"I will add it to my TBR list, for sure."

She looks at me strangely. "Your what?"

"Oh, gosh, right." I shake my head, realizing she hasn't been around today's culture of acronyms. "To Be Read. It's like, your bucket list for books. I keep track of all the books I want to read on this website called Goodreads and then order them on Amazon."

"Amazon. Yeah . . . that kind of makes sense. I remember ordering some books off the Internet. I think it was Amazon, right." She blinks and looks at the water bottle on the stand next to her bed.

"Oh, sorry, here." I grab the bottle and hand it to her.

She takes a few sips of water and hands the bottle back to me, and then relaxes a bit in her bed. She carefully reaches around and adjusts her pillows to lay back a bit more. Maybe she's tired, and it's time for me to leave.

"Well, I'd better let you rest," I say. "I'm so glad you are recovering well, and . . ."

"No, please, stay."

"Are you sure? If you want to rest, I can go." I don't want to go.

"Yes, I'm sure. I mean, if you have the time. It's nice to not be alone. It's hard to explain, but . . ."

"No problem. I'm happy to keep reading, Mallory." I eagerly move back to the chair and pick up the book.

"Actually," she says. "Do you want to just . . . talk?"

I set down the book. "Uh, I mean . . . sure. What do you want to talk about?"

"Anything," she says. "Everything. Tell me why you're in the Army. Where are you from? What's your family like?"

I sit back down. "Yeah, sure. I mean, if you would like that."

She nods, leaning back and closing her eyes.

I tell her all about myself. I share with her what it was like to grow up in rural Virginia and how I was raised on a dairy farm where my parents and grandparents both lived and worked. I share how my father forced me to go to college to learn a trade so that I didn't have to work so hard farming because it was becoming less lucrative and more work.

I tell her about finding my way to the military after going to community college to become an electrician. I explain that my favorite uncle was killed in 9/11 and his son, Tanner, who was several years older than me, enlisted. He was on his third deployment when he was killed during an ambush in 2009. Tanner was like a brother to me; I struggled after his death and found myself very lost.

She's lying there with her eyes closed, maybe asleep, and I stop. Then she whispers for me to keep going.

I tell her the only logical thing I could think to do was to also enlist and honor my uncle and cousin by fighting for the freedom of others. I haven't talked this much to another person in a very long time. Talking to her, even when she's going in and out of consciousness, is very easy for me. This might be the first time I have really talked to anyone about my life, at least since college. I tell her that I had a girlfriend and we were planning to marry, but then when I enlisted in the Army she was so upset, she broke it off. Somehow, after thinking about it more, I realized that was for the best and that I wasn't in the state of mind to be anything to anyone at that time, let alone a husband.

"I like your story," she says as she slowly opens her eyes.

I realize I'm slouched back in the chair beside the bed. I started the story with my elbows on my knees and staring at the floor. Somehow, I became much more relaxed and leaned back.

"Well, it isn't much of a story." I chuckle softly, remembering how I used to think it was an interesting story until I actually did become part of the military and met so many others with similar stories.

One of the medics pops her head into the doorway and taps on her wristwatch indicating it's time for me to leave. Immediately, I sit up straight in my chair and hear Mallory let out a soft chuckle at seeing me come to attention so quickly.

"Visitation is over for today. We need to do a check on the patient before lights out. Please say your goodbyes."

"Yes, ma'am," I respond and rise to my feet.

"Cash?" Mallory says. "Thank you."

"Of course," I say, clearing my throat.

"I think I'll get to go home the day after tomorrow. Would you please come back and visit me again tomorrow? Will you still be here?"

"Yes, for sure." I say, knowing I'm scheduled to get back to the outpost at the end of the week.

"Okay, I'll look forward to it."

"Rest up, and I promise I'll be back tomorrow." I walk out of the room and down the hall. I'm about halfway to the elevator when I realize I left the book in the room. I think about going back to get it but decide against it.

Sinclair and I are staying in the temporary barracks at the FOB. Since we've been with Mallory since her rescue, we had to accompany her to the main base and give statements about how she was recovered.

Sinclair is excited to be at this base because he's able to call home and FaceTime with his family. He and his wife have just had their third child, and he's always been eager to have time and technology to communicate with them.

I lie in my bunk and think about the past few days. A sense of purpose brews inside of me. My mind keeps returning to Mallory Shields and her bravery. This experience has brought some closure to an unfinished feeling I've been harboring. Finally, I am a bit less empty and am aware of a connection forming inside, just realizing the magnitude of how we came to find her in the desert. In the short time I've been around her, I can sense that she is someone who is loved by many people and has a special force of nature about her. Eager to go back to see her tomorrow, I close my eyes and fall asleep.

The next morning, I finish giving my statement to the commanding agent at the head office on base. After that, I stop by the commissary and pick up a gift. I was hoping for some flowers, but that isn't an option, so I consider a stuffed animal and then decide that's too mushy of a gift, so I opt for a sweatshirt, knowing she doesn't have anything with her. I also grab a few magazines from the US. I believe Mallory would like to catch up on some of the things happening, and I know the flight back will be long.

When I arrive at the troop medical clinic, I walk down the hallway to her room. Surprisingly, there is no longer a soldier outside of the room. The Army posted a female soldier outside of her room since she arrived because of concerns they had about her and the criminals that had abducted her.

I open the door to find the bed empty. The small room is empty and sterile without a sign of her being there. Then out of the corner of my eye, I see *Great Expectations* lying on the tray table in the corner of the room. Inside the cover, she wrote a note.

Private Rigden, Thank you again for your kindness, bravery, and service. Thank you for sharing with me yesterday. Your story is very interesting and inspiring. You are now part of mine. Words can't describe how grateful I am. Be well and take care.

—*Mallory Shields*

I put the note in my pocket and make my way to the medic station. They explain that Mallory was transported to the base in Kuwait earlier this morning. The wind shifted and they were able to get a helicopter sooner than expected. Satisfied, but disappointed, I leave the magazines and sweatshirt at the clinic and return to the barracks.

CHAPTER NINETEEN

Mallory

May 14, 2016

Washington, DC has motion in all directions. I remember visiting DC several times as a child with my family and feeling so small, looking up at all the big, statuesque buildings and monuments. Now, as I look out the window of my hospital room, I feel somewhat uneasy about all that movement of people and cars below. Agent Sommers has just left, and I think about all the things she shared with me about reuniting with my family and friends from life before the abduction.

It actually surprised me to see Agent Sommers. When I first arrived back in the States, I spent the first few days with her, Captain Nattawly, and several other agents. It felt more like an interrogation, but as overwhelming as it was, I tried to remind myself that it was probably more my perspective since it had been so long since I'd spent time with people from my own culture who spoke English. They asked me to share as much detail as I could with them about the people and places I could remember from the last nine years. This was difficult for me, but it would have been even worse if it hadn't been for Dr. Kramer. She helped them handle the questioning in a way that was more sensitive to my boundaries and emotions.

Dr. Kramer had a sense of familiarity about her. She was a middle-aged woman with a stocky build, and her soothing voice matched her kind expressions. Her calming effect was that of a kindergarten teacher but with the savviness of a highly educated professor who could interest anyone in any subject. I liked how comfortable she seemed with herself; it even came through in her style. She wore a loose-fitting blouse and leggings with funky-colored boots. Her grayish-brown hair was pulled back in a messy bun, and she always nodded when she spoke. Dr. Kramer had a way of showing me that she was listening and that she understood and empathized with what I was saying. She was a protector, something I hadn't felt from another person in a long time.

The entire recovery team was concerned with how this happened to me and explained how *human trafficking* or *sex trafficking* had been a growing concern globally. This was the first time I had heard this terminology. I'd always heard it called *abduction* or *kidnapping*. They wanted me to describe as many people as possible and continued to ask me about names and places. I could sense they were growing frustrated when I would stumble over my words or pause to remember certain details.

I kept asking them about Jenna and her experience, wanting to talk to her and to see if she remembered the same things I did. They had told me in the hospital before leaving Iraq that Jenna had been rescued seven years earlier from Phnom Penh, Cambodia. When they told me this, my reaction startled me. There were many emotions and thoughts coming to the surface. Uncontrollably, I started to cry and to laugh at the same time, not knowing if this made me happy, angry, sad, resentful, or grateful. They were patient and gave me time to process what I had just learned.

They asked me about the places where Jenna and I were held together. A lot of questions were about the day in Bangkok when we were kidnapped. Most of their questions were about when I was traded and transported to another country, ending up in Iraq. I was sad to learn they didn't find anyone in the village after my escape and rescue. I had no idea where those women might be sent, and my empty answer was not helpful to them. I hoped that the other women would have been rescued and freed but was disappointed to learn that was not the case. I described each of them and what I thought to be their names and where they might be from. I thought of Tarana and wondered if she was okay and hoped she would have the chance to be with her baby and find freedom someday.

They showed me a few photos of different people, including other victims who had gone missing and had yet to be recovered. It was hard for me to look at the pictures and discuss these cases, which I imagine was unhelpful to them. They also showed me some suspect photos and other places where women had been held to see if I recognized anything. The most difficult were the photos in the Cambodian brothels. I felt sick looking at these images and thinking back to when I was held there and the awful things I did . . . and what was done to me. There were some familiar photos and I recalled a few names. I guessed as best as I could on timeframes and locations, but it wasn't as exact as I believe they were looking for. Dr. Kramer made them take several breaks to give me some space and time to process what was happening. Every time before we would resume, she would look at me and tell me we didn't have to keep going. Her support really did help, and knowing she was there made it possible for me to continue.

Before being brought back to the United States, the questioning while I was recovering on the Army base had been much more aggressive, but it didn't last as long. At first, I was isolated and questioned by someone trained to detect brainwashing or mind control. Later, I found out they had been unsure of my identity and thought my presence may have been an act of terrorism. This filled me with anger at first and then a bit of skepticism. I started to wonder if I could trust these strangers. But once they confirmed my identity and did a full medical exam, they became much more compassionate and willing to help me.

Today's meeting with Agent Sommers was different. Her visit was with a purpose. She was advocating for me, but she was also preparing me. Dr. Kramer was also there, and they both seemed to care about my well-being in a protective way.

"Mallory," Agent Sommers said, "tell me how you're feeling . . . physically, mentally, emotionally."

I gave her a half-hearted thumbs-up.

She smiled. "I just want to let you know things are going to move pretty fast for you. There will be a lot to take in and many people who want to see you. Are you ready for that?"

I nodded, and we all sat down at the table in my room.

"I have been doing this for a while, and I have learned it can be pretty hard to see people that you love and care about after an experience like yours," Agent Sommers said. "It can be difficult, and it will be challenging to see people from your life before captivity without being reminded of your recent past."

"That makes sense," I responded.

"Take it slow," Agent Sommers suggested. "You might be inclined to just share everything all at once, but maybe hold back a little . . . give it some time, and perhaps even try to eliminate parts of it from your memory."

"Okay." I wasn't sure what to say. I really couldn't imagine wanting to discuss any of what I had been through, but I knew people would be curious.

They had already connected me with a counselor in Nebraska and wanted me to start therapy as soon as possible to help with what they called *reentry*. Dr. Kramer asked if I would be comfortable journaling, believing it might help me to come to terms with some of the elements of my captivity and abuse. She also believed it might be a good way for me to identify the parts of my experience that changed me and the parts that made me stronger and more in touch with who I had become.

At first, I was a bit put off by her assumption that I was any different. But as I looked at both of them, I knew it wasn't worth the fight. I was different, and there just wasn't any way around it. Not only had this ordeal been my reality for almost a decade, but it impacted me in ways that I couldn't deny.

Understanding why they advised me this way, I knew it would be hard, but I also knew it was difficult for me to hold back, especially with emotion and even more so with the truth. Dr. Kramer explained how parents grapple with their own burden in these situations. How they blame themselves and deal with enormous amounts of guilt. She had some medical theory she attached to this, but I can't remember what it was.

Dr. Kramer did give me some good tips to use when dealing with people who are close to me. The one that stood out the most to me was to smile as much as I could. She explained how this can change the energy and help others feel more relaxed around me—something about dopamine and our brains and how we let down our defense mechanisms. She also suggested journaling about the people, situations, and feelings I encountered in the trafficking experience, as well as the people in my life before captivity: memories and lists of what I appreciate about them prior to visiting with them again.

Moving away from the window, I sit down at the table a few feet away. This isn't a typical hospital room, it's more like a fancy hotel. There are some common spaces I checked out earlier, like a lounge, a pool, a gym. There's also a cafeteria and coffee shop. I do appreciate the quietness in addition to the cleanliness and safety. Each time I leave my room to walk around the halls, one of the nurses or assistants go with me. I was nervous to walk around by myself at first, and I still avoid looking directly at other people as I pass them. I know it will take time to heal the emotional scars.

In a few hours I'm going to be reunited with my parents in this room. I had a choice where I wanted to see them, and this is where I've felt the most comfortable. The room is very neutral with white and beige linens on the bed, matching the draperies, and striped wallpaper. There's a round table by the window and a recliner in the corner. The neutral look of the room evokes a level of stability and safety. Just then, I'm overwhelmed with emotion and bite back tears. *Ryan.* I wonder if he knows yet. I want to ask Agent Sommers about Ryan Samuelson, my fiancé—or former fiancé—but I just can't bring myself to. He has probably moved on in life, and I can't imagine dealing with that news. Although I wouldn't blame him or have bad feelings toward him for it, I just don't want to know, at least not yet. I came to terms with this idea years ago.

Private Benson brings me some clothes. They are new with tags on them, and as I get dressed, I realize it's been so long since I've worn anything so clean and new. She also brings me some personal use items like lotion, shampoo, face wash, toothpaste, and a new electric toothbrush. I have to admit, brushing my teeth is one of the best feelings since I've escaped, with clean water and for as long as I want.

"Thank you," I say.

"Of course, ma'am." Private Benson stands there, and I can tell she wants me to look at what she has selected. "I wasn't sure on the size, and I tried to guess, so they may be a little big, but I wanted you to be comfortable."

"Oh, I'm sure it's all fine," I say with a slight smile. I pull out a couple of T-shirts and a hoodie. There are jeans, socks, underwear, and a couple of bras, as well as a pair of sandals and tennis shoes.

"Please let me know if you need anything special or want me to get a different size of anything." She smiles. "I can also get you anything specific like cosmetics or specialty items you prefer. I know you won't be here much longer, but maybe it will help you as you get ready to go home."

"Yes, home." I nod. "Well, thanks again. This will all make me feel better."

"Sure thing, ma'am." She nods and starts to leave my room.

"Wait," I stop her.

"Yes?"

"It's just Mallory . . . please, call me Mallory . . . no more ma'am." I smile. "And I have a weird question for you."

She stands there, waiting for me to reveal what I'm going to say as if I'm going to share a big secret, something riveting and something I haven't shared yet with anyone.

"Taco Bell," I blurt out. "Is there a Taco Bell near here?"

"Taco Bell, ma'am? I mean, Mallory?"

I smile and nod.

"Um, well . . . let me check. Would you like me to bring you something?" she asks.

I know Taco Bell is still around because I saw one on the drive from the air field. I pause for a moment as I try to read Private Benson's level of adventure.

"Can you take me there?" I ask. "I mean, I know you probably aren't supposed to, but I haven't left here since arriving two days ago, and I would just like to go for the ride. We can just do a drive-through, so I won't even get out of the vehicle."

"I will need to check with the captain first. I'll be back." She leaves the room.

Moments later, we are in her personal vehicle and pulling out of the parking garage.

CHAPTER TWENTY

Renee

May 14, 2016

The call comes early on Saturday morning. A gravelly male voice says, "Hello, is this Renee Shields, the mother of Mallory Shields?"

My stomach drops. The only reason I kept the old home phone after all these years was in case Mallory tried to call. I gasp and hold my breath for a few seconds, realizing the person on the other end of the phone is waiting for a response.

"Ah, yes, yes . . . I'm sorry. This is Renee. Mallory Shields is my daughter," I say. I'm shaking. I think he's going to confirm she's died, but a small part of my soul still hangs onto the possibility that she is still alive.

"Mrs. Shields, this is Captain Nattawly at the Department of Defense in Alexandria. Approximately ten days ago, your daughter was rescued near an FOB in northern Iraq. She was very weak and in bad health. She had taken a fall, and her ankle was broken along with several ribs, and she sustained other minor injuries."

I lean back on the wall and sink down to the floor. Tears stream down my face.

"She's alive?" I cautiously ask.

"Yes, Mrs. Shields. Your daughter was transported to a larger base where her immediate injuries were treated. She has been recovering since and was then flown out of Iraq back to the US. She is at our military hospital in Washington, DC."

"Oh my god." I'm not sure what to say next. My mind is spinning. I somehow feel detached from my own body. *Am I dreaming?*

"Ma'am, are you still there? Mrs. Shields?"

The authoritative tone of his voice startles me back to reality, and I clear my throat. "Yes, yes . . . I will be there as soon as I can. I will get to the airport and on the first flight." I begin to shake uncontrollably.

"Do you have something to write with?" the captain asks. "I can give you some instructions on how to get here."

I quickly rush over to the desk. There's a framed photo of Ken and Mallory I had taken at Disney World when she was five years old, and a sudden emotion ignites inside of me. *My daughter is alive. My daughter is alive.* These words run through my mind.

I grab a pen and paper. "Okay, okay." My voice is unsteady. "Please go ahead."

He gives me the information for the hospital and offers to fly me to Washington, DC on a military plane if I'm not able to get a commercial flight. He gives me his personal number as well.

"Mrs. Shields, will you be traveling with your husband or other family members?"

"Um, well, no. It will be . . . I think it will just be me." My mind went to Ken. He's not healthy enough to travel. Then I think about Jenna. I haven't talked to her much in the last couple of years, but I know she'll want to know.

"Should I bring anyone with me?" I ask.

"No, ma'am. I just want to know what to expect and what to tell your daughter." He then instructs me to call him back with my travel plans. He explains there's a hotel next to the hospital and they can reserve a room for me. He will arrange to meet me or have someone meet me when I land to take me to Mallory.

We say our goodbyes, and before I know it, I spring into action. I quickly book a flight for this afternoon from Omaha. On my drive to the airport, I call and leave a message for Captain Nattawly with the details of my flight. I hardly remember driving or boarding the plane. I didn't call Jenna because I'm not sure what to tell her. I finally decide to wait to call her until after I see Mallory. I need time and space to process all of this. I want to have as many details as possible to share with Jenna when she asks.

The flight is a blur. I'm amped up, shaking, resisting the urge to cry, in shock. I don't know what to think. So many images of Mallory flood my mind and I catch myself forgetting to breathe every so often.

I can't help but be apprehensive and still have a slight sense of doubt that Mallory has actually been found. There were too many failed attempts.

I think back to how full of hope we all were the first time the FBI had a lead on locating her. Mallory and Jenna had been missing for a year, and we were finally getting some response from Homeland Security and the FBI. The FBI had agents stationed throughout Southeast Asia, and they were working all of their contacts to find Mallory and Jenna.

That was the first time we met Agent Stevens. He came to Everly Falls to meet with me, Ken, Ryan, and Sandra. He assured us that the agency was doing all it could. Pictures and profiles of our daughters had circulated from the inside agents in Thailand to their local connections with police and authorities. We learned that when a US citizen is abducted overseas, it really disrupts the trafficking operations because they know the FBI will get involved and police activity will increase. He was certain they were close to finding them.

Two weeks later, we were all sitting in a room in the FBI building near downtown Kansas City. Agent Stevens had summoned us there because they were going to be raiding a location where they believed Mallory and Jenna were likely being held.

The room was like any conference room in a large commercial building. It smelled of new paint, and the furniture seemed to be fairly new as the leather chairs were stiff and not worn in. The five of us—me, Ken, Ryan, Sandra, and Agent Stevens—sat around a table with a conference phone in the middle. There were windows high up on the wall, and the sun was shining onto the table.

Agent Stevens laid pages out on the table. He also unfolded a large map that showed several of the countries near Thailand.

"Here was the location where they were last seen." Agent Stevens pointed at a location that looked like the entire city of Bangkok. "Our sources say they were taken from there by the traffickers hours later to the north of the city." His finger moved about an inch on the map.

"And?" Ken was getting very impatient. The stress of our daughter's disappearance was a lot for him to handle. Every time I looked at him, his eyes were filled with tears.

"According to the source, the operation in charge of kidnapping these victims usually had the MO of taking them to Cambodia." He slid his finger down and across to the next country on the map. "The laws are really messed up here, and this crime is more a way of life."

Ken sunk down into his chair. Ryan, who had never sat down, paced the room. Sandra and I leaned in over the map. Sandra had not been very talkative and seemed scared. She felt alone. I knew this from our one-on-one conversations, and I could tell she was having a very hard time. Jenna had been her world and was almost more of a companion than a daughter. After Sandra's husband was killed in the service, she said Jenna was her only reason for living. From our friendship over the years, I knew that Jenna took care of Sandra as much as the other way around. I reached over and gently took her hand in mine.

"So, Agent Stevens, have they located Mallory and Jenna in Cambodia?" I asked.

"Our reports show that they have identified a crime ring with several foreign women who are being held and," he cleared his throat, "they are being sold in the sex trafficking business."

I diverted my attention to Ken, who had a blank look on his face. I knew he would not be up for processing this.

"And that is where the girls are?" Sandra asked.

"We don't have an actual confirmation that they are at this location, but the inside source says there were two American women who were brought in months ago." He could tell we were on the edge. "We have been watching and learning each step of the way. The brothels with foreign women are easier to find because most of them are full of young women and children from Cambodia. So, American girls would stick out more, but this also means they try harder to hide them too."

"Brothels?" Ryan asked as more of a statement. He shook his head. "How can they do this?"

Agent Stevens explained that the local police were forced to deal with the private militia and criminal network that allowed the human trafficking and sex trade to take place in these countries. They all wanted to make money for their information and, when a raid was planned, often an inside cop would tip off the brothel owners and they abandoned their location or sold all the girls to another crime group.

"I know this is all hard to hear, but I need you to stay strong." Agent Stevens pulled out his phone and looked at something on the screen. "We are very confident that this could be the rescue of Mallory and Jenna."

Finally, I exhaled. I think I had been holding my breath the entire time he was talking.

"Okay," I said. "So what's happening right now?"

He looked at his watch. "Well, it's eleven-thirty here, which means its one-thirty in the morning there. The local police in Phnom Penh have a task force on the ground and are ready to raid and rescue. They should be going in within the hour, and we will hear as soon as they recover the victims."

Ken's skin had paled, and I could tell he was zoning out.

It seemed Sandra could sense my stress. "Agent, if you think it will be a while before we hear anything, would it be okay if we left for a bit?"

He looked at Sandra strangely.

"I mean, maybe we could go grab a quick snack or coffee." She smiled at me.

"Uh, sure. I mean, yes, that might be a good idea," he responded.

Ryan walked over to the table and put his hand on Ken's shoulder. "Hey, why don't I go get us all something for lunch and bring it back. You guys get up and walk around a little, and hopefully we'll hear something soon." He forced a smile.

"That would be great, Ryan," I said, grabbing my purse to give him some money.

"No, Renee, it's okay. I saw a cafeteria on our way in. Is that okay with everyone?" He didn't wait for an answer as he grabbed his jacket and left the conference room.

Ryan brought back sandwiches. We all sat around the table and tried to pretend we were interested in eating. It was impossible—we were all on the edge of our seats. Agent Stevens ate about half of his sandwich and then started looking through more papers. Ken was the only one who ate his entire sandwich. I remember this moment well because he even asked me if I was done with mine. I pushed it toward him and he ate it. The sound of him chewing was nerve-racking. He didn't say anything, but I could tell his Alzheimer's was in full force at that moment. In a way, I wished I could just vanish to a place where I couldn't remember that this terrible situation was our reality. Realizing how awful it was to have that thought, I patted Ken's arm while he finished his sandwich.

The agent's phone dinged.

"Okay," he said, "here we go. They're getting ready to go in." He pulled the phone console from the middle of the table and dialed a number. It rang several times, then someone picked up.

"Reeves here."

"This is Agent Stevens, and I have the victims' families with me. Do you have eyes?" He stood up and leaned over the phone console with both hands pressed down on the table.

"Yes, Agent. They just went in."

"Okay. We will be here on the line. Let us know."

Agent Stevens pressed the mute button and remained standing.

"So, our agent is standing by. The local police are raiding the building where we believe they are holding the victims . . . and hopefully Jenna and Mallory." He sighed. "Once they confirm the rescue, Agent Reeves will let us know."

"How soon will it be? Can we go over there, or will you immediately send our daughters back home?" I asked.

"Ma'am, it will be a process, but first we will need to confirm the rescue and then identify each victim."

He sensed my displeasure with his answer.

"I know this is difficult," he said. "We appreciate that you're here, and we appreciate your patience. I didn't even want to tell you about this at first, but when we got the reports . . ." He pulled out a sheet from the pile of papers and pushed it across to me. "The source identified two American girls matching the descriptions of your daughters."

I picked up the paper and glanced at it.

"I think this could be it, and I wanted you to be here when we got the call," he said with compassion and also a tone of wanting us to know they were doing all they could.

"This could be a win for all of us."

Just then, a scratchy sound came from the conference phone speaker and Agent Stevens unmuted the phone.

"We're here. What's happening?" Agent Stevens said.

We lean forward in our seats, hanging on to every millisecond in the brief pause that followed.

"Empty, sir." The agent's voice was very matter-of-fact.

Sandra let out a sound somewhere between a sigh and a sob.

"It was close. There was still warm water in the sink . . ."

Agent Stevens sunk down into his chair. "Damn it," he said in a loud whisper, cupping his hand over the top of his face in frustration. "Thank you, Reeves."

"Sorry, sir. We will be in touch after our debrief."

Agent Stevens disconnected the call.

The silence that followed was like a graveyard. Nobody moved. Finally, I dropped my face into my hands and sobbed. I remember it took a long time to reel myself back from that day and all the hope we had all had.

That was the first of many failed rescue attempts. After that day, we learned there were several other close calls. But we never went back to the Kansas City field office or met Agent Stevens in person when a possible rescue mission was happening. He would e-mail or call to let us know they had some promising news, but time after time, it was never successful. After Jenna was rescued, we learned that there had been several instances where the authorities were only hours away from possibly finding them. Just thinking about it knots my stomach with remorse.

The pilot's voice announcing our landing brings me back to the moment. As I step off the plane with my carry-on, there's a young woman in a military uniform waiting at the gate. "Mrs. Shields?" she says with her hand extended.

"Yes." I step toward her and gently shake her hand.

"Nice to meet you, ma'am. I am Private Benson, and I will take you to Captain Nattawly and Agent Sommers from Homeland Security."

She takes my carry-on and starts to walk away from the terminal. It's obvious she is acting on orders, moving through procedure with a rapid pace.

Outside of the airport there's an SUV with flashing lights parked by the curb. We get into the back seat. There's another soldier driving.

"Hello, Mrs. Shields," he says with a strong, deep voice. "I hope your flight was okay."

"Uh, yes," I say. "Thank you."

And we're off. It's all so overwhelming. "Private Benson," I ask after a moment, "when do I get to see my daughter? Are you taking me to the hospital now?"

"Yes, ma'am."

We sit in silence for the rest of the drive. Realizing I must be a mess, I pull out my compact and comb from my purse and try to smooth out my skin and run the comb through my hair. My heart is racing as I wonder what Mallory will look like after all this time. Will she recognize me? People change . . . I've changed.

There's a buzzing inside my purse, and when I pull my phone out, I see Richard's name. *Richard.*

"Hello," I say softly. "I'm sorry, I meant to call you."

"Are you okay?" His voice calms me immediately.

"Oh yes. Oh my goodness, I am so thoughtless." Tears form in my eyes. I didn't even consider calling Richard to tell him what happened. Rushing to get to Mallory, my mind was going a hundred different directions, imagining what the reunion would be like.

"Mallory. It's Mallory," I continue. "She's alive. I'm in DC right now."

"What?" He seems shocked. "Do you need me? Are you okay? Uh . . . is she okay? Have you seen her?"

"I will call you back as soon as I can. I don't know much yet."

"Yes, let me know when you can. This is amazing news, Renee. I am so happy for you . . . and her. I love you, dear." Then he hangs up.

Richard didn't even cross my mind in all of this excitement and confusion. This fills me with guilt, but I decide to tuck that away and out of my mind for now. I know I will figure it all out. Right now, I need to focus on Mallory and getting to her as soon as possible.

The driver pulls up in the drive of the Hilton. Private Benson and I get out. She takes my carry-on from the back, and we walk in. A man and a woman are sitting in the lobby; they get up when they see us enter.

Private Benson salutes them. "Sir, I will take care of the check in." Then she walks over to the guest desk.

The man extends his hand. "Mrs. Shields." We shake hands. "We are very happy to see you. We spoke on the phone. I'm Captain Nattawly." He pauses for a second and stares at me. Then he starts to introduce the woman with him, but she interrupts.

"Hello, Mrs. Shields," she says, shaking my hand. There's a sense of warmth from her. "I am Agent Sommers with Homeland Security. We have been working in liaison with the FBI, and I have been briefed by Agent Stevens from the Bureau. We want to discuss Mallory with you before you see her."

"When can I see her?" I blurt out.

"Soon. Is it okay if we sit over here and visit first?" She motions to a small alcove in the lobby with three chairs positioned around a small table near a fireplace.

"Yes," I respond, and we walk over to sit down.

"Mrs. Shields, when I told you we rescued your daughter over the phone, I didn't tell you much. We are simply here to share what we know about her state of mind, her current physical condition, and to prepare you before you see her." He looks over at Agent Sommers.

"What's wrong?" I ask in an urgent tone. "Is she hurting now? I want to see my baby." My throat tightens as my emotions escalate.

"Yes, Mrs. Shields . . . we're getting to all of that." Agent Sommers gently places her hand on my shoulder.

"Renee, please call me Renee. And I'm sorry." I take in a deep breath. "You don't know what this feels like. I just want to hold her in my arms."

"Let me go get you some water." The captain quickly walks over to the front desk.

Agent Sommers gives me a sympathetic look. "Mrs. Shields . . . Renee. You're right, I don't know what this feels like. We want to reunite you with your daughter as soon as we can." Her voice is soothing. "There are some circumstances we want you to be aware of, and we want you to know what to expect when you see Mallory."

"Okay. But please know, I understand she has probably been to hell and back. I know what condition she was in right after she was taken. Her best friend Jenna was with her for the first two years. Jenna was rescued in Cambodia in 2009." I reach into my purse and pull out a tissue to wipe my eyes.

"Yes, so you know how human trafficking works and how horrible the conditions can be to the survivors." She nods her head as she tries to maintain eye contact with me. "We're not sure, but at some point during Mallory's captivity, she was traded to a Middle Eastern group." She pulls out a file from her purse and places it on the table. "We think she was held here for the last couple of years." She pulls out a map of Iraq and points to an area.

"I don't understand why you're showing me this." I know she's trying to be informative, but all I can think about is Mallory.

"I know this is hard right now. It's late, almost nine o'clock. I'm not sure that seeing Mallory tonight will be the best course of action."

I clench my jaw. "No. I want to see my daughter."

Agent Sommers pulls a photo from the file and hands it to me. It's a picture of a woman lying in a hospital bed with her leg in a cast. There is some type of wrapping around her chest and an IV is hooked up to her arm. Her head is wrapped in bandages, her face is sunk in with deep, glossy eyes, and the side of her face is bruised.

Mallory . . . it's Mallory.

She looks like a shell of the person that I used to know . . . my daughter, my baby girl.

My mind flashes to the day when we said goodbye at the airport when she left for Thailand. She was carrying a giant hiking pack and looked so strong and grown up. Now she looks like a defenseless and abandoned victim. Tears burn my eyes and trickle down my cheeks.

Agent Sommers scoots her chair closer to mine. As I stare at the picture, I hurt inside, aching so terribly.

Captain Nattawly returns with three bottles of water. I guzzle almost an entire bottle, feeling the water wash down my throat and stagnate my crying. I need to see my daughter, but I need the full story. I've waited long enough—almost nine agonizing years—so one more night is doable.

"Okay," I say with strength. "Promise me I can see my daughter the first thing tomorrow."

She nods. "Of course."

"Okay." I sit up straight and push my shoulders back. "Tell me everything."

CHAPTER TWENTY-ONE

Renee

May 15, 2016

I lie in the hotel bed unable to sleep. The glowing red numbers on the alarm clock read 12:15 a.m. The information Agent Sommers and Captain Nattawly shared with me is replaying in my mind. The photos of the village from where Mallory escaped were vivid, but all still seems so unreal. The thought of my daughter living in those filthy conditions makes me sick to my stomach.

After Mallory was treated at the base camp, they moved her to a bigger Army base. They said she was aware of everything happening and was very cooperative and very informative. She told them about how she escaped and for how long she thought she had been gone. A shiver runs through me just thinking about how scared she must have been.

Even so, Captain Nattawly and Agent Sommers were impressed with Mallory's ability to remember details of this experience. Agent Sommers explained that everyone who encountered her since the rescue could not believe she had survived the ordeal and could actually speak about it. They all agreed she was incredibly strong. Thinking about Mallory's bravery makes me feel proud, but then I feel guilty. I knew this day would come, but I vow to try to be as positive as I can for when I see her tomorrow.

I can't wait to put my arms around my dear Mallory and hear her voice and look into her beautiful eyes. I can't wait for her to say the word *Mom*. So many times over the years, I've woken up startled in the middle of the night because I heard someone say "Mom," and I could swear she was in the room with me. Then I would realize it was my mind playing tricks on me or the end of a dream.

Four hours later, I awaken and robotically shower and dress. After getting ready and heading down to the lobby thirty minutes earlier than instructed, I leap to my feet when I see Private Benson come in. She sees me and nods. And then I follow her to the SUV parked outside, at last ready to see my daughter.

The lounge area in the hospital isn't like a typical waiting room. There are different areas of arranged chairs and tables, all with nicely upholstered material or leather. The lighting is subtle and soft, and there is a large sofa in front of a beautiful marble fireplace. The rugs are soft and complement the furniture and hardwood floors that gleam with polish. Along one wall is a bar with different coffees, teas, and fruit baskets for the taking.

Agent Sommers is waiting for me. She is standing with a woman who is a bit shorter and looks to be about my age. The woman has wild hair pulled back and exudes a vibrant energy. She smiles at me with a warm expression that seems open and friendly.

"Good morning, Mrs. Shields," Agent Sommers says. "I hope you got a good night's sleep."

I nod. She motions for me to have a seat in one of the chairs.

"Mrs. Shields, I'm Dr. Kramer." The woman extends her hand. She isn't dressed like a typical doctor. Her attire is much more casual, but there is an air of expertise in her style. She's holding a notebook and some files.

"Nice to meet you," I manage to say. My heart is thumping with eagerness but also nervousness.

"We just wanted to give you a quick moment to ask any questions before seeing Mallory." Agent Sommers has that look of empathy on her face again. She has a way of looking into me and understanding where my mind is. "Dr. Kramer has been treating your daughter and wanted to give you some information from her perspective on Mallory's condition."

I look to the doctor. She emanates a feeling of warmth, and there's kindness in her eyes as she smiles.

"We do everything according to the law and protocol," Dr. Kramer says. "I have a copy of the HIPAA agreement Mallory signed. She did give us permission to share information with you and her father about her medical status."

Dr. Kramer pushes a form across the table. I fold it in half without even looking at it and slide it into my purse.

"Okay, Mrs. Shields," she continues. "First, I have to tell you Mallory is doing remarkably well." She pauses to make sure I'm *really* listening. Feeling her connection—or whatever it is—I slowly exhale and relax just a bit.

"You did an incredible job raising a strong daughter who is determined and honest. We have a system of rating trafficked patients in different areas, like how well they are able to talk with people, how uncomfortable they are when around people or when they are alone, how forthcoming they are with sharing their experience, whether they avoid eye contact or being approached, what they do when they are touched, how reality-based their questions or responses are when we visit with them . . . There are more, but what I am trying to say is that Mallory has rated very high. We always start with a baseline of somewhere between one as the lowest rating and ten as the highest. A typical victim of human trafficking comes in at about a two and a half or three. Mallory's baseline is around six."

I smile and tears come to my eyes. *Yes, that is my daughter.*

"Quite frankly, this was very astonishing to all of us," she exclaims. "My colleagues even spent extra time evaluating Mallory and reviewing her case. Each individual is different, but we think her time during the last part of her captivity allowed her to process some of the trauma from the earlier abuse she experienced. Although," she says, "it is possible that there may also be some regression. Her situation is unique, so we don't have a lot of prior research to compare this to. The reality of the situation, as you may know, is that survivors like Mallory are very uncommon. Being held captive for almost nine years and discovered alive . . . well, Mrs. Shields, you know where I am going with this."

I nod, trying to process what Dr. Kramer is communicating.

"Sex trafficking is a harrowing road. It is possible that Mallory has been broken in many ways and partially recovered in her experience. We see this sometimes with transitional survivors, or women who have been traded and relocated multiple times."

My head is spinning as I try to process the vastness of the nightmarish journey Mallory has endured.

"She has likely acquired a skill set that has allowed her to adapt, but has also guarded her from showing certain emotions. It is a way of self-protecting or coping. It is also a way of compartmentalizing the trauma she has experienced. On the surface, it may seem to be gone, but it is still there deep under the surface."

Again, I nod, my heart wrenching. Mallory had always been so expressive and shared her feelings freely with those around her.

"What this means, Mrs. Shields," Dr. Kramer continues, "is that Mallory's transition should go smoothly if we can all be aware and help her acclimate. She is going to need your patience and understanding as well as others she interacts with regularly. We want you to be aware of how deep her trauma may be. The process of recovery may be messy and difficult."

"Yes. I am ready to do anything necessary," I say.

Agent Sommers hands me a box of tissues from the side table.

"I just want to see my daughter. I want to get her back home where she is safe and with her family."

"That is our goal too, Mrs. Shields." She smiles and then opens the notebook. "Mallory is going to really need your help. We have arranged for her to see a therapist back home." She hands me a yellow card.

"Dr. Patricia Drake is an incredible therapist who is renowned in her field. We actually did our residency together at UCSD. I think Mallory will really like her." She leans forward, interlacing her fingers.

"Mrs. Shields," she says softly, "I know you are experiencing some extreme emotions right now, and it will likely continue. We highly recommend that perhaps you see a professional during this time to help yourself too." She smiles. "I am happy to recommend a therapist in your area if you would like."

"Thank you," I say and sort of chuckle. "I'm all set. I've actually been in therapy for the last eight years."

"Oh, wonderful." The doctor sits back in her chair. "This will be a good foundation for you. If you need any additional assistance, please don't hesitate to contact me. We also can recommend some support groups and online resources for families of victims."

"With Mallory's situation and Ken's Alzheimer's, I was pretty lost for a long time." I feel the need to explain my counseling. "A good friend recommended seeing Ramona, a therapist in Lincoln. She has been a godsend in my world."

"Good, good," Agent Sommers says with empathy.

"I will definitely be making an appointment soon, I imagine." There will be so much for me to unpack in my next session with Ramona.

Dr. Kramer smiles as she writes something down. "As far as Mallory's physical condition, she seems to be recovering well from her injuries during the escape. I think Agent Sommers has explained that to you." She looks over at the agent.

"Yes," I say, nodding.

"There are some other physical concerns we want you to be

aware of," Dr. Kramer says in a gentle tone. "Mallory has suffered many years of abuse. Considering the situations she has been in, her body has done well to repair itself and heal."

She pulls a paper from her file and quickly reads it.

"There are a few things to be aware of and perhaps address with Mallory as the two of you begin to reconnect," the doctor continues. "First, Mallory endured harsh conditions in the Middle East, and these included being stung by scorpions, which has put her at risk of allergic reactions to insect bites and venoms. She will be more vulnerable than the average person. I suggest that she keep an epinephrine injector or EpiPen with her and those around her should as well."

Scorpions? My throat is dry and I take a sip of water.

"Mallory's diet is going to be key to her recovery. She has been malnourished for a long time. It will take some time for her to be able to eat like we do, so I encourage you to be patient with her. We have already discussed this with her, and she agrees to work on taking supplemental nutrients through vitamins and drinks. She also needs to stay hydrated."

I nod, soaking in all of this information.

"The more sensitive topic is Mallory's reproductive capacity." She looks at me, her eyes showing sympathy. "It is unlikely that your daughter will have biological children of her own, Mrs. Shields."

Tears burn my eyes. I want to say something, but the words won't come out. My heart aches for Mallory to not have the opportunity to become a mother herself.

"When examined, they found scarring on Mallory's reproductive organs that has led to damage. This is not uncommon for victims with this type of sexual assault and abuse. We can talk later about what to expect in the future and possible things that can be done to remedy any discomfort she has as she ages. We have had this discussion with Mallory, but we also want you to be aware."

My cheeks are burning from anger.

"My recommendation is to take it slow. Don't force any conversations with her, and let her bring up questions she has or suggest things that she wants. I know this sounds counterproductive, but I also suggest lowering your expectations and exercising patience. When Mallory is going to see someone from her past for the first time, you can help by explaining they need to approach her a bit slower, let her make the first moves and guide the conversation. This will be frustrating at first because she has been conditioned to not speak or take action. It is a way for her to take back that control without pressure. Listening is one of the best ways we can create comfort for abuse victims. There will be a lot of silence."

I haven't even thought of this. I knew it would be overwhelming at first, but I just thought being there for her would be enough.

Dr. Kramer explains what the protocol should be when Mallory comes home. I am her guardian, so I need to set some ground rules. Many people will want to see her, but large gatherings or welcome-home type of events are discouraged. Anyone who spends time with her, especially those who are seeing her for the first time, are to keep things calm. They have to ask Mallory before hugging her. We must take things in small steps, and less is more in this case. Mallory will not always speak up because she wants to make things seem normal and please everyone. I have to be the filter for this. It all feels overwhelming, but I will do whatever it takes to make sure that my daughter is home and feels safe.

Dr. Kramer leans forward. "An important thing to keep in mind is that Mallory was the victim . . . although we try not to refer to her as that. But rather a survivor. This, again, seems unrealistic considering the torture and abuse she endured. In addition, we know that everyone who loves her and cares about her were also victims and suffered because of her abduction, especially you as her mother. I'm sure your therapist has discussed the vicarious trauma you have experienced." So much trauma. Years and years of trauma, of guilt, of loss, of anger, of depression. Of holding out hope only for my world to come crashing down over and over. To be so helpless. I know all of this all too well.

"As Mallory begins to share details with you, or if she does, this may trigger that vicarious trauma for you." She then hands me a brochure, which I glance at and then put into my purse. "Sometimes the things you learn will be very hard to hear and understand. Anger can often be a response, but you have to find a way to hold that in and just listen."

Dr. Kramer's genuine concern is apparent. Agent Sommers continues to nod and is a stoic symbol of support in the situation. I'm grateful for these women.

"However," Dr. Kramer continues, "if you can put those feelings aside when you're with Mallory—and there will be many emotions of guilt, shame, sadness, regret, and more—but put these aside and save them for when you talk with your therapist or other support people in your life. It will allow you to just be present and consider Mallory. She already has these same types of feelings, and we don't want to burden her with more."

My throat tightens and I can feel the emptiness burn inside of me as Dr. Kramer describes the guilt that I am truly feeling. After a moment, I look up at her and know my expression tells all.

Dr. Kramer gives me a consoling look. "This can be a tricky balance because you don't want to outwardly treat her like a victim. That is why it is important to use the word *survivor*. Your daughter is very smart, and she seems emotionally aware, which is very surprising considering what she has endured. She can tell if someone is treating her special or different because of her situation. This can cause very conflicting feelings for her and often have a negative impact on the relationship. And remember . . . this is going to be a process."

Agent Sommers nods in agreement.

"There isn't a tried and true method," Dr. Kramer continues. "Each person's recovery will be different, and there will be mistakes, but there will also be progress. Time and forgiveness is the best remedy here."

"Thank you," I say.

Dr. Kramer gives me more paperwork with additional resources. "And please be sure to take care of yourself too," she says." Find a way to relax and give yourself time in all of this. Do you have any additional questions for me?"

I shake my head. I know I will have a million questions later, but all I can think about right now is being with my daughter.

Agent Sommers rises to her feet and sort of slaps her hands together. "Well, Mrs. Shields, are you ready to see Mallory?" she asks.

We all stand up. Dr. Kramer takes my hands in hers. She has such kind eyes, and I can tell she is really rooting for us and for our situation.

"Mrs. Shields, I want the best for you and your daughter. Please don't hesitate to reach out to me if you need anything. You are one of the lucky ones, always know that. It can seem that it is not that way, but most of these cases don't turn out with a reunion. Cherish one another and bless you both."

They walk me down the hall and to the elevator. We go up a few floors and down a corridor. Agent Sommers gives me her card and then takes a step back. Dr. Kramer shakes my hand. They smile at me and then turn to walk down the hallway.

Taking a deep breath, I stand at the door for a moment. I put my hands on my cheeks and smile. Finally, I knock on the door.

CHAPTER TWENTY-TWO

Mallory

May 15, 2016

There's a knock on the door.

My nerves have been building up all morning. I stop pacing and slowly fill my lungs with several deep breaths. This is such a different kind of anxiety than any I have experienced. I've had weeks to prepare for this moment, and I don't want to be uneasy, but I am. It doesn't make sense.

Calm down, calm down, it's just Mom.

I'm not sure what to expect, and I'm not sure how to act.

Will my mom be scared or disappointed? Will she be ashamed of me or accept what happened to me? I have so many questions.

Another knock on the door. My emotions are on the ready. I want to try my best to contain myself and hold back, but I know it will be out of my control soon. I haven't felt this way in a long time even though I've played out this reunion in my mind hundreds of times.

I open the door and there she is. *Mom.* She is so beautiful.

My mother has always had the most natural and contagious smile and eyes that sparkle with love. She's always had a big personality and always saw the best in others. However, now she seems smaller and more reserved. Although her elegance and beauty still show, she has a look of worry about her. She looks a lot like how I remembered Grandma Aggie.

"Hi, Mom." I begin to cry.

"Oh, Mallory," she says, exhaling, and instinctively we are embracing. We hug for so long, and I crumble in her arms as we both sob. Her purse drops to the floor and I can feel her knees almost buckle.

"I love you so much, my darling daughter. I love you, I love you," she says over and over.

As we embrace, I can feel her strength, but I can also feel her fragility. For the first time since my escape, I am experiencing a very new but somehow familiar emotion. It's hard to describe except to say it must be love, that unconditional love we always take for granted. The realization of this and of the fact that this is the first time I've been hugged in nine years makes me melt into her shoulder.

She continues to repeat how much she loves me, and I can't imagine what it's like for her to see me again and to know the world I've escaped from. Dr. Kramer tells me this will be difficult and to take it slow.

Finally, we release each other and just look at one another. We are both still trembling, taking a step back to really see one another.

"Mom," I say softly, "you look beautiful."

"Oh, my love . . ." She smiles, then gently places her hand on my face the way she used to do when I was a little girl, tucking my hair behind my ear.

Before I know it, we are embracing again. I feel like the nine-year-old girl who has just crashed her bike down the street and raced home to my mother to comfort me.

She holds me in her tiny frame as I nearly collapse. We are both a mess, but it is a joyful mess. Regaining my composure after a few moments, I wipe my eyes.

"Please, come in." I move out of her way and shut the door. She picks up her purse and walks in, and we sit down at the table.

"How . . . how are you doing, Mom?" I'm not sure what to say, knowing I want to keep it light and not have to unpack everything at this moment.

"Sweetie . . . I am doing fine. I am just so happy to see you right now, I can't even think of anything else." Her hands are shaking.

"I'm happy to see you too. Dad . . . is he okay? They said he didn't come with you." I know I'm probably not going to like the news she gives me about my father.

"Mallory, your father is actually doing well. He didn't come with me because I came so quickly after they called me, and I didn't have time to figure everything out. I know he will be happy to see you."

"What about his Alzheimer's? Has anything happened? Is it worse?" I want her to be honest with me.

"It was very hard, dear," she says. "There are a lot of details we can get to later, but after you . . . well, I mean . . ." I sense her hesitation.

"Okay, I know the doctor recommends we don't dive right into everything, Mom," I say frankly, "but I really just need to be okay talking to you. Can we please do that?"

"Oh, Mallory. Yes, whatever you need," Mom replies.

"Okay, good." I exhale and she smiles. "So, let's just say it . . . I was taken. I was kidnapped. I was addicted to drugs. I was abused. I was raped." I can see her tense up as I say all of this. "I was trafficked, I was sold and traded to really bad people."

Tears are streaming down Mom's face.

"We have to be able to say it," I say. In fact, I don't think I've actually said it that way yet, not out loud anyway. "We can call it something different, just to get through conversation if that helps."

"I am so sorry, Mallory."

I instantly feel the guilt stirring within me for making my mom feel this way.

"Mom. I'm okay." I keep my game face on and want to be proactive in how we deal with the undercurrent of the situation. "I. Am. Okay."

She grabs a tissue from the box on the table and wipes her eyes. "I know, and I'm so thankful."

"I realize you are sorry and that everyone will probably feel sorry in some way for what happened to me, but I can't dwell on it. We can't dwell on it. I want to move forward, so please be honest with me." I hold out my hands and she places her hands in mine.

"Okay. Well, after you were . . . taken," she looks at me, and I nod to show it's okay for her to say it, "your father's health continued to decline. It became so much work to keep up with him and the disease. In 2012, I moved him into the Arbor Ridge facility where they could care for him much better than I could."

"Oh, Mom," I exclaim. "I am sure that was a hard decision for you. And you were all alone, I'm sorry."

She shakes her head. "It was hard. I had lost you, and then I lost your dad bit by bit each day." She was looking down at the table. "I visit him, but he only knows who I am about twenty percent of the time."

"Do they think there is any hope of a cure or recovery?" I ask.

"Not at this time." She wipes her eyes again. "But, Mallory, he is doing better. That part is true. He wasn't happy the last few years at home, and neither was I. I didn't know how to help him or give him the attention he needed. There are trained professionals at Arbor Ridge, and he is in a community where things are set up to accommodate him and others suffering from this awful condition. His physical health and disposition have greatly improved."

I am eager to see my father, and I want to see for myself.

"Are you still working?" I ask.

"Oh yes. I gave up real estate right after your dad went into the home. It had become very difficult to care for him and still be able to manage the crazy schedule. I took a position at a title company and now just do the behind-the-scenes work. It also helps to have a more stable income."

"That makes sense," I say, letting the information sit for a moment.

"Are you feeling better?" she asks with a concerned look. "The agent and captain explained what had happened to you when you escaped. They said you were pretty hurt." She makes a strange face, as if she said something she wasn't supposed to. "I mean, I'm sorry . . . we don't have to talk about that if you don't want to."

"It's okay, Mom. Yes, I am feeling better. My ankle still hurts a bit, and when I breathe in deeply, my ribs are painful. But I'm eager to get out of here and go home."

"Of course," she says. "Do you think it will be soon?"

"I'm hoping to go home with you, if that's okay?"

"Absolutely. Of course, I mean yes, that's what I was hoping," she says. "Whenever you're ready. We can stay here as long as you need to."

We sit for a few moments in silence, and it's comfortable. It's obvious we both have a lot on our minds.

"Mom."

She looks up at me.

"They told me Jenna had been rescued in 2009."

"Yes," she says, taking a deep breath.

"How is she? Is she okay? I thought maybe she would come with you. I really want to see her."

"She is going to be so happy to see you, Mallory." Mom smiles, but looks down at the table. "That girl has never given up on finding you."

"Really?"

"Jenna has been so involved in fighting for you and other victims . . . I mean, people who have been taken and abused like this." Mom quickly stands up. "I'm sorry, I just need to walk around a bit."

"It's okay," I say. "Are you feeling all right?"

"Oh, I'm fine, dear." She walks over by the window and looks out. "It's just that . . . well . . ." She takes another deep breath. "Okay, you want honesty, and I am afraid of too much too soon."

"Mom," I say, concerned. "What is it? Just tell me."

"It's better for you to see Jenna. This is her story to share." She turns to look at me. "But you're my daughter, and I know you should know this before seeing her—"

"What is it?" I'm not sure where this is going, but it feels like something bad is coming.

"Jenna is married now, Mallory."

"Well, that isn't terrible, is it? Is she happy? Does she still live in Everly Falls?"

"Jenna is married to Ryan."

The weight of her words are heavy in the silence.

"Ryan?" I ask. "You mean, my Ryan?"

She continues to look at me, and the implication is there. He's not my Ryan anymore.

I stand up and walk toward the window. All those times I've considered the possibility of Ryan being married when I returned home, I've been able to accept it. I didn't expect him to still be waiting for me after all these years. But I never dreamed he would be married to Jenna.

It's starting to rain outside. I bite my thumbnail, my mind is moving in all directions. I stare out the window and focus on the dome of the Capitol building in the distance. I'm not sure how to feel about what my mother just told me, but I want to be positive about it. In time, it will make more sense to me, and I know after

I see Jenna and Ryan again, and together, I can come to grips with it all.

"Thank you for telling me," I say, still looking out the window. "Do they have a family?"

"Yes." She pauses. "They . . . they have a son. I'm sure Jenna will want to see you and introduce you to him herself."

Feeling lightheaded, I take a few deep breaths, then walk back to the table and sit down.

"Yeah. Of course. I want to see her and Ryan and meet their . . . their son too," I say, smiling weakly.

"Well, I will call Jenna tonight if you would like," Mom says hesitantly.

Agent Sommers told me the only person contacted was my mom. Over the last week, I imagined making that phone call and hearing Jenna's reaction to my voice, but now . . . I can't. Not yet.

"Sure, that would be good," I say, grateful she offered. "I want Jenna and Ryan to know I'm safe and tell them I will reach out to them when I get back to Everly Falls." I look at her, and we both sigh.

"Mallory . . ." She tears up again. "I'm just so happy to have you back."

There is a slow humming in my mind. The lump in my throat has grown to a steady ache deep inside of me. I swallow it down and put on my best smile.

"Are you hungry? How about we go to the cafeteria and have lunch?" I say. I want to get out of this room. The still air has grown heavier somehow.

"Yes. That would be nice."

Mom and I eat lunch, and then she spends the afternoon helping me pack up the few items I've accumulated throughout the past two weeks. It seems strange to have "belongings" after only having what was on my body for the last decade. Relaxing on the bed for a few moments, I decide to take a nap. A headache has emerged as Mom updates me on the last nine years while we were packing.

She tells me of the hard things like Grandpa George passing away. He was my father's father and my only grandparent left. She shares information about other family members, marriages, kids born, new neighbors, and other newsworthy information. Mom tries to explain some bigger things like the economic recession and Barack Obama as the president, but it's all starting to seem like a lot.

She asks if it's okay for her to stay in the room while I nap. As she lies down next to me, it feels good to have her close and to have someone nearby who loves me and cares for me. I know she doesn't want to leave me, and I understand why she feels this way. When I wake up, she is sitting at the table in my room and reading on her iPad.

There is a knock at the door. Mom walks over and opens it.

"Dr. Kramer is here, Mallory." She looks at me as I sit up in bed, and she waits for me to nod before letting her in.

The doctor walks into the room. "Hello," she addresses us both. "How are we doing?"

"Wonderful." My mother sits with me on the edge of the bed.

Dr. Kramer smiles. "How are you feeling, Mallory? Do you think you're ready to leave and go home?"

"Yes," I say even though inside I am unsettled.

"Good," she says. "Well, I would like to have you stay one more night and then in the morning we will do one more exam, if that's okay?"

"Okay," I say.

"Can I stay here with her?" Mom asks. I know she doesn't want to let me out of her sight, but I need to have some time to myself in order to think.

Dr. Kramer looks at me and seems to read my thoughts. In a soft but stern voice, she says, "Mrs. Shields, I think it's a good idea for Mallory to have some time to herself tonight. I do promise she's safe and secure here at the hospital."

"Yes, Mom," I say. "It's okay, I'll be fine. I also want you to get some rest. You can stay in your hotel, and I'll call you after my exam tomorrow morning. Is that okay?"

"Of course," Mom says with a smile.

"Well, then it's settled," Dr. Kramer says. "I will let Agent Sommers know, and I'm sure Private Benson will arrange for transportation."

After saying goodbye to the doctor, my mom gathers her purse. She hugs me for a long time. I know saying goodbye right now is hard for her, even though she knows I'm okay and she will see me in less than twelve hours.

I'm exhausted and want to shower and do some journaling about the day. Dr. Kramer was right about journaling in that it helps me process what I'm thinking. Also, I really like the feeling of writing again. It's been so long since I've been free to write in this way.

I sleep very soundly and feel rested when I wake up. This is probably the first time since my escape that I've felt so rested. It's true what they say about the connection between a mother and daughter. Seeing my mother and feeling her love has brought me a sense of peace.

After my exam the next day, Private Benson arrives and drives us to the Bolling Air Force Base. Captain Nattawly insisted that the military fly us home, so Private Benson boards the plane with us and we fly to Offut Air Force Base in Omaha. As we unload, she walks us through the base and out to the front of the terminal where a cab is waiting. She gives me her card, instructing me to call her if I ever need anything, even if it's a quick trip to Taco Bell. We both chuckle about this and say goodbye.

My mother and I are now on our own. The taxi takes us to the parking garage of the Eppley airport on the east side of Omaha where she parked her car.

On the way, I feel my mom reach for my hand, startling me at first, but then realize I've been fidgeting and breathing strangely. Her caring touch instantly calms me down.

"It's okay, sweetie." She smiles. "I am here and we are okay. I understand."

I believe it will get better each day.

CHAPTER TWENTY-THREE

Ryan

May 15, 2016

"Hey J," I yell out as we walk through the door. Thomas races past me and almost trips on Carter's dog leash. I drop the mail on the table in the entryway and unhook the leash from his collar.

"J?" I call out. "Jenna, are you here?"

When I enter the kitchen, I see my wife hanging up the phone, and there is a strange energy lingering in the air. On the kitchen table is the folder—the one full of news clippings and printouts of stories from when Jenna and Mallory disappeared. I haven't seen that folder for years.

Jenna is crying and holding onto the counter.

"What's wrong?" I rush over to her.

"Mommy, look, look . . ." Thomas runs into the kitchen and pulls on Jenna's shirt. "Daddy and I found these at the park." He is holding two rocks in his hand. "Fossies," he exclaims.

Thomas is beaming as he shows Jenna. She kneels down to his level, looking directly at him. His wide, dark eyes watch her to see if she likes what he is showing her.

"Thomas, these are wonderful," she says, sniffling and running her fingers over the rocks in his hand. "Fossils are special because they tell us about our history."

"You're crying, Mommy. Why are you crying?" Thomas asks with a concerned, almost scared look on his face.

"It's okay, sweetie. I am very happy." She looks up at me and reaches for my hand.

"I want to show them to Aunt Moe," he says. "Will she like them, Mommy?"

Jenna nods and stands back up.

"Thomas, you'd better go put those fossils in the bathroom sink so we can clean them," I say.

He rushes off down the hall to his bathroom with his contagious enthusiasm. I can't believe how much he has grown in the last year and that he is going to be in kindergarten in a few weeks. We decided to hold him back last year because Jenna thought he was a lot smaller than the other kids, and she wanted him to grow into his mind a bit more. He is super smart. I used to laugh because he seemed like he was a genius child with the questions and conversations he would have, and his little body would just vibrate with excitement when he wanted to share or learn.

Thomas is very shy around new people, probably because he is usually with us or with his grandma, Sandra. We don't like to leave him with people he doesn't know, so it was an easy decision for us to wait a year before school.

It even took Jenna a while before she would leave him with my family. My parents adore Thomas, and so do my sisters, especially Moe. She is one of the head curators and educators at the Denver Museum of Nature and Science. She is single and doesn't have children of her own, so she tends to spoil Thomas. He loves when we go see her or when she visits. He also enjoys playing with his cousins, my sister Lily's two girls, but I've been happy to see him have a special bond with Moe.

My father really warmed up to Thomas in a grandfatherly way, even though he and I never did find that father-son connection. In fact, it surprised me at first, but then I decided to just accept it and be glad for it. He often takes Thomas to campus with him. They will talk about so many different things. Although my relationship with my father might not have been what I wanted, I am happy he and Thomas have a strong kinship.

Jenna is wiping her face with the back of her hand. Then she takes a drink of water.

"What is it?" I ask.

"Mallory." She leans back against the counter. "She's alive, Ryan."

"Wait, what?" I ask, believing I might not have heard correctly.

"Renee is with her now in DC." She looks at me. I can tell she is searching my face for some type of reaction.

"Mallory is alive?"

Jenna nods. She then abruptly puts her arms around me.

"Isn't this the best news ever?" she asks. Her tone sounds forced, like she is convincing herself.

I stand in that spot with a million different feelings running through me. Then I realize Jenna is hugging me, and I slowly put my arms around her.

"Renee said she is bringing her home tomorrow." Jenna backs up and looks out the window over the sink into the backyard. "She was in Iraq when she was rescued."

I sit down at the table in the kitchen, not sure what words or response to use. I need to think.

"Ryan," Jenna says with a sharpness, "what are you thinking?"

"I think, I uh . . . I mean," I stammer. "This is wonderful news . . . amazing news. Is she okay? How?"

"I don't know a lot of details yet, but Renee said she is doing as well as could be expected."

"What does that mean?" I ask, knowing that Jenna probably can't answer that.

"Well, Renee said she was sort of sick and had been hurt but was recovering." Jenna moves over to the table and sits across from me. "'As well as can be expected' means she has endured this nightmare for the last nine years, Ryan. Nine. Fucking. Years."

Jenna bursts into tears again, and she gets up and goes to the refrigerator. She takes out two bottles of beer, opens them, and hands me one. She sits down and takes a large gulp from the bottle.

I look at her strangely. She's never been much of a drinker. The only reason we have beer on hand is because of our monthly progressive dinner party from a few weeks ago. We were the first stop on the tour with appetizers and drinks, so Jenna thought having some nice craft beer on hand was a good idea.

"Jenna, this is good news." I reach across the table for her hand.

"I know, but I can't help feeling like the worst right now." She looks down at the Jurassic Park placemat where Thomas eats his breakfast each morning.

"In what way?" I ask, needing her to say out loud what I believe we're both thinking.

She immediately backtracks. "Not because she's alive. It's great news. It's the best news." She bends the corner of the placemat back and fidgets with it. "It just means that I didn't look hard enough or fight enough to search for her." Her next words are weighted with meaning. Even the way she sits at the table is different, more collected or drawn inward. "We failed her . . . I failed her."

There's a defeated look in her eyes, and I know she's addressing the real, unspoken situation. She married her best friend's fiancé. And I, Mallory's fiancé, married her best friend. Regardless of how many times the slight possibility entered our minds about Mallory still being alive and returning someday, nothing could ever truly prepare us for the uncertainty we feel right now.

I stand up and pace between the table and the sink. "J, we can't think like that. You have dedicated your career to help fight trafficking. We went over there so many times and never got any answers." I try to rationalize it in my head, but it all comes up short.

Jenna looks at me intently. "I'm afraid it will break her," she says softly.

I don't have a response to this.

I grab the beer and walk over to the sink, then take a big swig. "How about we just try to relax," I say. "Mallory would want us to be happy knowing she is coming home."

"Do you mind if I go lie down for a bit?" Jenna says. "My head is killing me, and I don't want to end up with a migraine."

"Of course, you go rest," I say.

Ever since Jenna was rescued, she gets migraines under especially stressful situations. She doesn't get them often, but when she does, they can make her very sick. Besides, I need time to think and figure out how I'm feeling about all of this. I realize I'm imagining different scenarios in my mind again.

"Can you get Thomas dinner?" she asks. "I already boiled the noodles, and the sauce is in the refrigerator."

"Sure." I walk over to her and pull her close to me as I can feel her starting to weep.

"I know. It will be hard," I say.

"Ryan . . ." Jenna pulls away from me a bit.

"No." I pull her closer. "Mallory will understand this, J. You know she will."

"It just feels so wrong now," she says, and she is right. There is a feeling of guilt or weird responsibility to justify the love Jenna and I have for each other.

"Please don't make assumptions," I say. I frequently say this to Jenna; her mind tends to go to the worst-case scenario when unexpected things happen.

"She was my best friend, Ryan. She is my best friend."

"Mine too."

She pulls away, and I let her go as she slowly retreats down the hall to our bedroom.

"I love you, J. We will take this one step at a time," I say as she closes the door behind her, knowing full well that I'm saying it for my benefit as much as hers.

Thomas is in the kitchen when I walk back in. He is trying to fill Carter's water dish from the sink. I turn on the faucet for him, and the water splashes up and into his face.

"Ahhh, Dad," Thomas says.

Grabbing the dishtowel, I kneel down to wipe his face. I look into Thomas's eyes. He brings me clarity whenever I doubt things in life. I pull him in for a tight hug. His arms go around my neck, and he squeezes me.

"I like *o*'s." He giggles. Then I remember how he and Jenna call hugs *o*'s and kisses *x*'s. This started last year when Thomas was learning to read. It was Valentine's Day, and Thomas asked what *x*'s and *o*'s meant when he was trying to read the card I gave Jenna.

After putting Thomas to bed, I grab another beer from the fridge and go outside and sit on the deck. The locusts are buzzing and the humidity hangs in the evening air. I look out toward the horizon, facing east. The sun had set about an hour ago and the night sky is sparkling with stars.

Breathing in deeply, I wonder what Mallory is thinking in this moment. I used to do this often when I missed her, but that was years ago. I haven't thought about this in a long time. I try to picture her in my mind, and all I can see is what she looked like as a young girl. I even try to hear the sound of her voice in my head. I always thought this was strange, but our family therapist told me this was normal. This was how I was moving on and getting past the feelings I had for Mallory.

The sliding doors behind me open and Jenna comes out. With her sitting softly beside me, I can feel her warmth against my arm.

Her vulnerability is evident. She may be more vulnerable than I have ever witnessed. This is a fleeting moment between us, and I know by tomorrow Jenna will have a plan put together. She will armor herself and identify the steps she needs to take to handle this situation.

Wrapping my arm around her shoulders, I feel her shiver. The energy between us is different somehow. Learning about Mallory is a game-changer, but I also know we can handle it. Jenna and I are together because we work together when things are difficult. This will be another challenge, but I know we will get past it.

Time has a way of changing a situation without anyone noticing. It can smooth out the rough edges; it can reposition people and opinions. Mallory will be a very different person, and knowing and accepting that has given me the confidence that we will all make it through this and someday look back in retrospect.

"Hey, you feeling better?" I ask.

"I guess," she replies softly in the slight night breeze. She is wearing one of my old T-shirts, and she pulls it over her knees. I stare down at her toes peeking out.

"We're going to make it through this, J."

I take a deep breath and pull her closer. I reach over and lift her chin so she is looking at me. Her eyes are glossy and she looks worried. In all honesty, this is the Jenna I love the most, probably because this is when she needs me the most.

I lean down and kiss her. Her soft lips are salty from the tears and worry. She doesn't reach for me, but I can sense the longing in her just from the way she kisses me back. Our kiss lingers, almost like we are sealing a deal or coming to an agreement. She eventually pulls away and stares out into the night sky.

We stay out there for a long time in the heavy night air, sitting next to each other without words.

CHAPTER TWENTY-FOUR

Renee

May 16, 2016

I find myself unable to stop from glancing over at my daughter in the passenger seat. It all still seems so surreal. Her energy is different to me, not how I remember. I try to remind myself that she is different. She is so quiet, almost tranquil, as she watches the landscape pass by with each mile as we make our way home on the interstate. I see her watch the large trucks with curiosity and distain.

"It was like that, Mom," she says softly, pointing to a semi-truck with an enclosed trailer.

"What's that, honey?" I ask, not sure what she means.

"When they first took us." She watches as different vehicles pass by. "We were in the trailer of a truck just like that."

"Oh, baby . . ." I'm not sure how to respond. I have a million questions, but I don't want to overwhelm her. "Do you want to stop for a bit? We can get some fresh air, walk around a little, if that would help."

"No . . . it's okay." She adjusts in her seat and turns to look at me. "Sorry, I'm just thinking out loud, I guess."

"Well, you think out loud or inside or however you want. We can talk about whatever is on your mind whenever you are ready." My words feel forced and contrite, but I just don't know how to make this better.

Just then, a loud ring interrupts the quiet classical music playing on NPR. The screen on the dash reads: "Incoming call: Richard."

I hurry to press the button on the control panel to decline. I look over at Mallory, holding my breath. I exhale when I notice that she hasn't flinched as she gazes out the window.

I turn off the stereo and disconnect the Bluetooth to avoid another disruption. I'm not ready to tell her about Richard or explain our relationship.

I signal and exit off the interstate onto the highway that leads into Everly Falls.

"Ten miles to go," says Mallory.

"Yes. Are you okay?"

"Mom, I'm fine. You don't have to keep asking or worry," Mallory says with a bit of exhaustion but also in a dismissive way.

She shifts in her seat and seems to notice familiar things.

"Oh, right . . . the old wildlife preserve is near here, isn't it?"

"That's right. They have actually built it up even more with an educational building and some camping spots, I believe." I'm eager to have some dialogue. "Do you remember when we would picnic there when you were little?"

"Sure. Of course, I remember. Dad would always bring out the old kites, and Jenna and I would see which one of us could get the highest."

I chuckle, but the way she said this tugs hard inside of me. I wish I could just erase the past twenty years and be in the very moment she just described.

"Look, the ice cream cabin is gone." Mallory points to a flashy green convenience store along the highway.

"Yes, they put that new station in about six years ago when they redid the on-ramp to the interstate. They tore down that old cabin."

"Pistachio was Dad's favorite, do you remember?" she asks.

"Yes, and you would always ask for extra sprinkles." I smile, watching her take in each roadside structure and sign as we begin to enter the suburbs of Everly Falls.

"Jimmies."

"What's that, dear?" I ask.

"They were called Jimmies, right? The sprinkles? Wasn't that what Aunt Joan always told us?"

"Oh yeah, that's right," I reply.

Mallory rubs the palms of her hands on the top of her knees. She seems a bit nervous. She is making a light humming noise.

As we approach Everly Falls, we drive past the Safeway market on our way into town. Mallory is looking intently at the buildings that are new to her. Several people are milling about the parking lot with carts and kids, loading groceries and waving hello or gathering for quick chats.

"Wow," she exclaims. "So many new buildings. This was just an open field . . ."

"Yes, a lot of this has come up in the last five years or so," I say. "Maybe once you're settled, we can come over to the grocery store. I know we could use a few things at home."

Thinking to my sparse refrigerator at home, I really want to stop on our way into town, but I know that will be a bad idea. I remember what Dr. Kramer told me about limiting Mallory's exposure to outside triggers and taking things slow.

There is a dull buzzing sound coming from the center console. Mallory picks up my cell phone from the top of my purse and looks at the screen. "It says 'Richard,'" she reports.

"Oh, geesh," I say, taking the phone and pressing the side button to decline the call.

"He's called you a couple of times now, Mom. Go ahead and take it if you need to," she says as she continues to look out at the suburban sprawl.

"Oh, no need," I respond. "He is just . . . an old client. I think he wants me to look up some title information or something. It can wait." I'm satisfied with my ability to come up with a fake reason for him calling, but I'm also feeling a bit ashamed for not being honest. It's just too soon.

Mallory continues looking about, still rubbing her palms on her knees and humming softly. I want to feel the joy of having her back and alive before I have to deal with her resentment toward me for seeing another man. I fear that Mallory will see this as a betrayal of her father on my part. She was always very defensive when it came to Ken and how he was treated, especially with his disease. I hope in time she will understand and see things from my perspective, but I'm just not even close to broaching that topic yet. I have no idea where to start and hope time will be on my side.

I turn off the bypass and go by the city park. In a matter of minutes, I am pulling into our neighborhood. There are a couple of strange vehicles outside the house. They look like media vans. I was hoping to get home before this happened. I go around the block and then decide to just make the best of having an attached garage by pulling in and pushing the remote button in the car to shut the door before we get out.

As I turn off the car, Mallory takes a deep breath. She is looking around the garage as if she feels the presence of someone else or is hesitant to get out.

"It's okay, Mallory. We're home now. The media won't bother us inside the house," I say, trying to ease her mind.

She hesitantly opens the car door.

As we enter the house, Mallory moves very slowly into the kitchen. Her hands follow along the countertop, across the appliances, and then finally she stops at the end of the island. She looks around in awe, as if she is in a place she has never seen before.

"Are you okay?" I ask, a bit confused. I thought she would have been so happy to walk through that door, but she seems lost or confused.

"Mom," she says, and I notice she's trembling. "Am I really

home? This seems so unreal. Like I'm dreaming. It seems like I've made it up in my mind."

"Honey . . ." I say, trying to hold back tears. Seeing her struggle with this is almost unbearable. "You are home. It's okay to take your time getting used to everything again."

A tear falls down her cheek as she slowly steps toward the eating area. I walk over and put my arm around her shoulders. I can't help but join Mallory in having mixed emotions. It does seem unreal, like a fantasy. I just keep reminding myself this actually happened. *She's home, she's really home.* Several times on the drive home, I'd put my arm on hers just to be certain it was real.

Mallory stands and holds herself up at the counter. Her gaze scans the kitchen and dining area. It's as if she is waiting to remember something or to make some sort of connection.

"Not much has changed, has it?" I look at her with hope for some recognition.

"I have just pictured this for so long in my mind, it started to seem more like a painting or a drawing, you know?" she replies softly.

She walks around the kitchen island into the living area. Picking up a photograph from the desk, her hands are shaking as she looks down at it and then wipes tears from her eyes.

"Mals, how about if you go lie down for a bit and rest. I will make us some tea and bring it in to you," I say.

"That sounds nice. Thanks, Mom." She smiles and slowly makes her way across the room and down the hall.

I head into the garage and grab the few bags we have and my purse. Glancing at my phone, I see another missed call from Richard and a text message with a question mark.

"Sorry, I just got home. Busy getting her settled. Will call later," I text.

He replies within a few seconds. "Understandable. Please let me know if you need anything."

A streak of guilt hits me as I realize how rude it has been to not communicate with him.

Just then, the doorbell rings and someone bangs on the front door. It startles me and I almost drop my phone in the sink. I'm not ready to talk to reporters or the news. Of all the things the authorities discussed with me in DC, preparing me to face the media was not one of them.

When I look through the window, I'm relieved to see it's Mrs. Campbell from next door and not a reporter. She has a beaming smile as I open the door. I usher her in as several people from different directions start toward the door with cameras and microphones.

"Hello," I say, noticing she's carrying a large casserole dish covered in aluminum foil.

"I thought you and your daughter might like some of my eggplant parmesan. It will last for days in the refrigerator, and it freezes well too." Mrs. Campbell's eyes are looking around for a sign of Mallory.

"Oh, that is so thoughtful of you." I take the dish from her and smile. "Mallory is resting now, but maybe in a week or so she will be up for some company."

"Oh . . . yes, of course," she says. "Well, please let me know if there is anything you need. I am so happy you have your girl back, Renee. It is a blessed turn of events, for sure."

"Yes," I say, nodding in agreement. "And thank you so much. This will be wonderful, I'm sure." I set the casserole on the sofa table.

The teakettle whistles, almost as if to summon me back to the kitchen area, giving me a good reason to say goodbye to Mrs. Campbell.

"Well, I'd better get that," I say, opening the door to usher her out.

She leans in and puts her hands on mine, like a double handshake.

"Please, anything you or darling Mallory need, okay?" She smiles and slips out the door. I watch through the sheer drapes covering the picture window as she moves across the lawn, putting her hand up to reporters approaching her. Relief washes over me, and I realize the kettle is still whistling.

When I go into Mallory's room, she's standing by her old desk and looking at the photos on the wall above. Her emotions seem right on the surface, almost as if she has been holding them back until walking through the door of her home. I expected tears, but instead, there's a strange, contorted look on her face as she focuses on the picture of her and Ryan from their time abroad in college.

"Here's some tea, Mallory." I set the cup on the desk.

"Mom," she says brokenly.

"I know, honey." Her hurt from knowing that Jenna and Ryan are now married is evident.

Her fingers outline Ryan's face in the photo. "So many days, I imagined him. I imagined us . . . together, and what our lives would have been like. There were actually times those pictures in my mind kept me sane and probably alive."

Then her gaze moves to a picture of her and Jenna with their arms around each other, standing in their softball jerseys from middle school.

"Who is this?" Mallory whispers partly to me and partly to herself.

I walk over and look at the photo. "Oh, you two were something, huh?" I chuckle a bit to lighten the mood. "Jenna is going to be so happy to see you."

"It is so strange, but I don't even recognize myself in these photos." She seems a bit frustrated with herself.

"Oh Mal, it's just going to take some time. Be patient with

yourself." I try to console her, but I can tell she needs to do this in her own way. She takes a few steps toward the window and looks out through the blinds.

"As time went on, I figured Ryan had probably found someone else and moved on . . . but somewhere, deep down, I still hoped maybe he was waiting for me, you know?" She turns and looks at me.

"Oh sweetie, I am so sorry." I wish I could take on this hurt for her. "This has to be hard, and I wish I could change it for you."

"It is what it is. I just never imagined him and Jenna . . . married." She chokes on the word.

Then her posture changes, and she pulls her shoulders back, inhaling deeply. She shakes out her arms, wiggling her fingers.

"No," she says, her voice stronger. "I can't do this. I have to find a way to accept this and be happy for both of them. They're my best friends. They're my people."

She looks at me for confirmation.

I embrace my daughter. She is stiff at first but starts to soften a bit. Still, I am confused by her lack of emotion, but I am sure her reactions are going to be much different after everything now.

Finally, we sit down on the bed, and I just brush my hand over her hair to try to soothe her. I look at this girl—now woman—this brave, damaged, but resilient woman who is my daughter. I can only imagine the mix of emotions flowing through her. She has never been good at hiding her feelings, even as a little girl. Her expressions speak louder than any words she could ever use. Right now, she is incredibly vulnerable in a way I have never seen her before, and justifiably so. Her bravery is valiant, but she also has some hesitation packed alongside.

I have to do everything I can to help her now. I am playing both mother and father, even though I know coming into her home, back to where she grew up, is bringing up some deep feelings, and she is likely missing her father. He was her go-to problem-solver. Ken was always the one who could take a serious situation and make it lighter, easier, and eventually manageable, but yet with that bit of tenderness that Mallory required. I really need to do my best to channel some of those traits, or at least hope they've rubbed off on me over the years. I can try my best, but nothing I do will ever fill the void of Ken.

As she lies back on the bed, Mallory closes her eyes and finally lets the weight of this transition go a little bit. Staying next to her, I continue to brush my hand over the top of her hair and over her shoulder. This time I am the one humming while I watch her slowly fall asleep.

CHAPTER TWENTY-FIVE

Mallory

May 24, 2016

"In the past two years, the work we have done in the AG's office has led to significant policy change, increasing the sentencing for trafficking criminals. The punishment is now 75 percent more severe than it was just ten years ago. Most of this has been attributed to raising awareness around this crime and bringing it to the attention of the public. Although the work I do seems more focused on criminal justice and political science fields, I am very grateful for the communications degree I earned at Goodwin. I encourage you to step outside of your studies and gain skills that will help you prepare for your future. I appreciate the opportunity to share with you today. I think we are out of time, but please feel free to reach out via email with any questions you might have. Thank you."

From down the hall, I can see into the classroom just enough to watch Jenna standing in the front and speaking to the students. She is guest lecturing to a political science class at Goodwin College and has no idea I'm here. Her navy suit contrasts with all the old wood paneling in the lecture hall and her now amber-colored hair. She's a natural and speaks with an ease and smoothness that would never lead someone to know of her past. Jenna has always been most comfortable speaking to groups, delivering well-thought-out messages.

This is part of the reason I want to catch her off guard. I need to connect with the real Jenna today, to feel the true best friend I've missed so much. If my visit is unexpected, she won't have time to prepare a conversation for us. It can just be the real her and the real me.

We have plans to meet at my mom's house for dinner tonight. Ryan is coming too. My mom is trying to take things slow when it comes to me seeing people, not wanting to overwhelm me. I initially thought seeing Jenna and Ryan together for the first time would be best, but after giving it more consideration and wanting it to seem like a success for my mom and her efforts, I know I have to see each of them alone.

The class applauds Jenna, and the students file out of the room. A few must have lingered because it takes some time before she and the professor walk out.

"Anytime," Jenna says. She shakes the man's hand and he leaves. She swings her satchel over her shoulder and walks down the hall.

Jenna is coming toward me, and she's smiling as she reaches into her bag and pulls out her keys. I'm standing about ten feet from her, and she looks up just in time to make eye contact.

I smile, and she smiles back as if I'm just another student or faculty in the hallway. Then she stops. The corners of her smile turn up, showing her bright white teeth in contrast to the dark lipstick she is wearing, her eyebrows raising and her cheeks flushing: authentic Jenna.

"Oh my God, Mallory." She rushes over to me and starts to give me a hug but stops. "Can I hug you?" she asks.

"Jenna," I say, embracing her. She's going to be on high-alert around me. Remembering Jenna and her structured ways, as well as the fact that she has been working with survivors of trafficking ever since her return, I know she'll want to do things according to an advised method.

"This is unexpected," she says into my ear as we are still embracing.

Students walk by and give us strange looks, but it doesn't matter. It's as if magnetism is pulling us together, and I don't think the jaws of life could tear us apart.

We are both completely lost in our sobbing and uncontrollable shaking. Her heartbeat vibrates through her entire body as we embrace, and memories of Jenna and I when we were younger are playing through my head. She really is my balance, and I've missed her so much throughout these years. I didn't fully realize it until this moment.

Finally, we each take a step back.

"I love you so much, Jenna," I blurt out.

"Mallory," she says my name, but then stops.

"It's okay," I say to her, "I just wanted to see you before tonight, and I hope it's all right showing up here. I called your mom, and she told me you were on campus today for this."

She nods her head, tears still falling from her cheeks.

We walk down the hall to the front entrance of the building. Outside, we make our way to the bell tower and sit on the stone bench. The afternoon is beautiful with the sun high in the sky. The semester has just started, and everything around us smells like a new book. The marching band plays in the distance as they practice on the football field.

She takes my hand in hers.

"Mallory, I am so happy you're here and you're—"

"Alive?" I finish her sentence. She looks down. "Sorry, but you don't have to hold back, Jenna."

"I know." She looks back up at me. "You were always better at sharing your feelings."

"You're better than you know, my friend." I squeeze her hand and I'm glad she squeezes back.

"I'm sorry."

There is a long pause, and I'm not sure how to respond. Jenna had to say it, and I know she had to say it. I didn't need to hear it, but I also can't make her understand it's unnecessary, and I really don't have the energy to try. All I want is my friend back.

"I know," I finally say, realizing she needs me to give her some type of response.

"There is so much . . . so much I want to share with you." She looks out across the green campus.

"Well, there isn't any rush," I say. "We have the rest of our lives, right?"

She reaches into her purse, and as she pulls out a packet of tissues, an action figure falls to the ground. When I pick it up, I smile as I realize it's Thor. I move his arm up and down, then giggle as I imagine Jenna with a little boy.

"Jenna, you're a mom." I hand her the small figure. "I'm so proud of you."

"Thomas is special," she says with a smile. She hands me the tissue packet. "I can't imagine our lives without him."

I can feel her tense up after saying that.

"Yeah, so I hear you married my fiancé?" I say with what I hope comes across as a comical depiction of disapproval.

She looks genuinely apologetic. "Mallory, I want to—"

"You know I'm joking," I interrupt with exaggerated lightness. "That's what I do." I swallow all the things I want to say. "You and Ryan completely make sense to me, Jenna," I say instead. "I am very happy for the both of you."

"Really?" She sounds doubtful. "I know you're saying that, but I feel so weird about it all now."

"I know, but it's okay." I sit back down, then speak the truth of my heart. "The two of you were my world before this shit happened to us. I love both of you and can't imagine not having you in my life now."

"I'm not sure how to feel about it all," she says. This is the real Jenna talking. She seems to have a more candid feel about her, but I guess we all have changed.

"Listen, I know you have spent all your time since you were rescued trying to fight this awful system and this crime from growing. Jenna, you are the only person I know who could take what happened to you—to us—and turn it into a powerful tool to help others and to make a difference."

"I had to, Mallory. I hated to think of you still trapped in that awful world." I can tell she's thinking about the abuse, terror, and helplessness from her own experience. "I just wish I could have helped you."

"You did help me, Jenna. Thinking about you and our families back here was what kept me alive and fighting."

"We went back several times," she says. "Remember the resort?"

I nod, remembering how naïve and clueless we both were at that resort.

"Ryan and I went back on New Year's Eve for several years, and I traveled to Cambodia, with my mom and your mom to talk with the Embassy again. Your parents also looked for you, Mallory."

"Jenna . . . I know. Please, you don't need to say any of this."

"Mallory, we all thought you were gone forever."

"But I am not gone forever, and I plan to live the rest of my life the best way I can," I say for my own benefit more than hers. Then I speak the truth again: "To do that, I need you in my life, Jenna. I need you and Ryan. I need you both in my life . . . as my friends. And sure, it's different than how I imagined years ago, but I'm good with that. The last thing on my mind is rekindling a romance with Ryan or trying to be a wedge in your relationship or marriage. But I still need you both as friends in my life. Is that possible?" It's almost as convincing as when I rehearsed it in my mind.

"Of course it's possible," Jenna whispers.

"Okay, it's settled then," I say softly. I stand up, then grab her hand and pull her up too. I want to tell Jenna that my heart is a little broken, that I do feel betrayal on some level, but I can't. I just can't. I figure in time it will be something I can let go.

"From this point forward," I continue, "we are here for each other. We are honest with each other and we cherish every moment we have with each other."

"Deal," says Jenna.

I hold out my pinky for a pinky-swear. Then she interlocks her pinky with mine. We burst into giggles.

Jenna gives me a ride back to my mom's house.

"Thank you," she says as I reach for the door handle. "I needed this time with you, Mal."

"Yes." I smile. "We both did."

"I love you," she says, teary-eyed again.

"I know. See you tonight."

I go inside and can smell the lasagna baking in the oven. Mom is in the kitchen chopping a red onion for the salad, and I go over to give her a hug.

"How was your walk?" she asks.

"Good." There is a tiny sting of guilt for not telling her that I saw both Ryan and Jenna, the real reason for my walk.

"Why don't you go relax and freshen up before dinner?" she says with a smile.

I quickly jump in the shower. I want to be reenergized for dinner. Seeing the two of them was emotional, as I knew it would be, but the other, more confusing, emotions I felt were exhausting.

Ryan was surprised when I showed up with coffee at his office this morning. The receptionist called him, and he greeted me in the lobby.

"Are you still a fan of a strong Americano?" I asked.

"Oh, Mal," he responded, and immediately hugged me without thinking twice. The memories of a decade ago came rushing back so fast I almost dropped the coffee. Ryan's presence was still anchoring. His smell, his demeanor struck a chord I wasn't expecting. I wanted to scream out to him how much I missed him and how sorry I was to have worried him, but I knew I just couldn't do that, not anymore.

"Surprise," I said.

"Come in, come in."

We entered the office. "Oh, Elaine, do you mind rescheduling my eleven o'clock?" he said.

"Sure, Ryan," she said, and smiled at me. I think she was aware of who I was. I've started to sense this when I go places in town with my mom. People are catching bits and pieces of my story and my return to the US on the news.

Ryan's office was very modern and seemed rather cold to me. The desk was metal and the accompanying furniture was sleek black leather. He didn't have any photos or personal items in the office. Sitting in one of the chairs, I hoped he would sit next to me or near me, but he took his seat behind his desk as if I were a client.

His familiar eyes and stoic resolute demeanor were still in place, but I could see more than nine years of time when I looked at him. He actually looked like a very attractive man in his early mid-forties. His hairline had receded a bit and he somehow seemed a bit shorter. Aside from those slight changes, he still had that all-American, Midwestern charm and dashing good looks.

"How are you feeling?" he asked.

"It will take some time," I said. "But despite everything . . . surprisingly well."

"Good, good." He was playing the part, and that was fair. I did catch him at work where it was probably easier for him to put up a wall or hide his feelings. It was going to take some effort to get past this exterior. I thought catching him unexpectedly might work, but it was going to be more difficult than I anticipated.

As I looked across the desk at him in that moment, he reminded me of Jenna, emotions at bay and solid in his reaction. I knew then that I had to be candid and acknowledge the elephant in the room or it would continue to be awkward and superficial between us.

"Ryan," I sighed.

Nodding, he smiled in a strange robotic way.

"Let's cut through the awkwardness here." I smiled artificially as I searched his face to find a connection. "I wanted to see you before dinner tonight to be sure we understand each other."

"Of course," he said, still with the half-pre-programmed smile on his face. "But what do you mean?"

I looked at him straight in the eye. "Now that I'm back, I need you to leave Jenna. You have to remember that we were engaged first, and it doesn't matter to me that you two have been married now for several years. And I understand you two have a son. Well, I would prefer if you didn't have anything to do with him either."

He just stared at me dumbfounded.

"I mean, I am the one who suffered the longest, and now that I'm back, it is only fair that we go back to things exactly the way they were before. You know, like a decade ago."

His eyes grew wide, and I could see the wheels spinning in his head.

"What do you think? Can I move in soon?" I leaned forward, raising a mischievous eyebrow. Then I smiled.

"Mallory," he said, and then he laughed a deep belly laugh. I remembered that laugh, and I knew I had the original Ryan back in the room. "Jesus, Mal, you had me there for a second."

I laughed too. "Sorry, but I had to do something."

He stood up and came around the desk, then he sat in the chair next to me. He leaned forward with his elbows on his knees, staring down at the floor. Here he was. Finally, he was processing some of this, and I could feel the emotion building. His eyes were red, and he looked up at me.

"I am so sorry." He shook his head and looked down again. "I thought about this moment for so long and I wanted to be ready. But I don't think I could ever be ready for this. I guess I just sort of blew it, huh?"

"It's a tough moment to be ready for, clearly." I put my hand on his shoulder. "And I know you're sorry. I know you wish you would have looked harder, fought harder, tried harder, and I sincerely appreciate it. But we both know enough now that we know it wouldn't have mattered. Nobody was going to 'find' me, and it wasn't for lack of trying."

He looked up at me.

"Ryan, I'm so happy you and Jenna are married to each other and have started a family," I said, forcing my words to sound as authentic as possible.

His body relaxes at this statement.

"I want you to know that I don't hold any anger toward either of you," I continued, which was true. "The situation sucks, but I won't let this get in the way of my friendship with you or Jenna."

There were a few moments of silence.

"So please, let's move forward," I said. "Can we do that and still be friends? All of us?"

"I would really like that, Mallory." He nodded.

"Good, because I'm going to need you both." I smiled and rose to my feet.

"You don't have to rush off," he said.

"I do, actually. I have some other stops today." I got up. "Can we keep this visit between us?" I asked, then realized how shady that sounded. "I mean, don't tell my mother . . . act surprised. She wants tonight to be really special." This much, at least, was true.

"Of course," he said and smiled.

"Great, I will see you and Jenna tonight."

I rinse my hair out and stand under the running water for a long time, replaying the conversation in my head. Today was hard, but necessary. Seeing them both really tapped my energy, and my emotions are close to the surface right now. I need to find a way to stifle them down to make it through the night. The water turns cool and I end my shower. I dry off, dress, and purge my emotions into my journal so I have a clean slate before everyone arrives.

CHAPTER TWENTY-SIX

Mallory

May 24, 2016

Jenna and Ryan arrive on time. While having already seen them individually lessens the shock, I'm unprepared for the strike of reality that hits me when I see them together. I hide this thought with a smile as we all hug, acting as if it's the first time we are seeing each other the best we can. I assume by now they've probably told each other about my surprise visits, but I still want to let my mom feel she was in control of how I'm acclimating with being back home.

"Oh, Renee," Jenna says. "It smells incredible in here."

"Thank you, dear." She smiles and brings a bottle of wine to the table. "Mallory always loved my lasagna, and I haven't made it since . . ." She almost seems to catch herself, then rights her smile. "Well, for years."

"Can I help you with anything?" Jenna asks after an uncomfortable pause.

"No, no . . . you all sit and visit while I go pour some wine," Mom says, recovering quickly. "Who would like a glass?"

Jenna and Ryan eagerly say yes. I wouldn't mind a glass either, but I'm trying to get on track with my food intake. Since returning, it's been an adjustment. Everywhere I go, all they want to do is feed me, and it's going to take a while for me to eat American food again. I've actually considered becoming vegetarian because it might be an easier transition.

As we sit down at the table, I look at Jenna and Ryan. I've noticed since they arrived that they have a sense of unity, like they belong together. I want to be okay with this, I really do, but something inside of me is just unsettled. I've noticed little details like when Ryan helped Jenna out of her jacket and then hung it up for her. He was always attentive that way, but I can't help but feel strange about it. I shift my attention to my smile again, maybe forcing it a little because I don't want them to feel awkward. Taking a deep breath, I dive right in, trying to make things as normal as possible.

"So, I was disappointed when Mom said you weren't bringing your son to dinner tonight," I say.

"He's at home with Moe," Jenna says. "She's visiting this week, and he needs to get to bed early with his last day of preschool tomorrow morning."

"When can I meet him?" I ask.

"Soon," Ryan replies. "He has a tee ball game this weekend. Maybe you can come to that."

Jenna nudges Ryan. Knowing I wasn't supposed to see this, I pretend not to notice.

"Well, that sounds fun," I say.

The doorbell rings, and it's Sandra, Jenna's mother. Mom invited her, wanting to include her in this reunion. Sandra reaches out and cups my face in her hands.

"Oh, you beautiful girl." We embrace, and she squeezes me tightly, almost taking my breath away.

"Hello, Sandra," I say, stepping back and taking her jacket. "I'm so glad to see you."

"Mallory, we are so glad to see you, my dear." She has tears in her eyes.

For some reason this throws me off guard. She seems overdressed for a casual dinner with friends and her perfume is very evident. Not to mention, she was the first one to break the unspoken rule and draw attention to the situation everyone else seems to be avoiding.

My mother steps in, bringing Sandra a glass of wine.

They lean in and kiss each other on the cheek. Sandra and my mother forged a closer relationship early on in our disappearance, which I think helped both of them. Mom told me they haven't seen much of each other in the last few years, but I know they have a strong bond because of what they have been through.

Sandra hangs her purse on the coat tree next to her jacket, then takes the wine glass and sits next to Jenna at the table.

"Renee, I have always loved your home. It is so . . . cozy and welcoming," Sandra says, but in a way that sounds like she's using more forgiving words than what she means.

"Thank you," Mom says politely, placing a basket of garlic bread on the table. I can tell she caught Sandra's tone but masks it with a smile. "I have always wanted to remodel and update my style, but just never seem to get around to it. Maybe it would be a good project for Mallory and I this winter." She turns to me with a raised eyebrow and a grin.

"Sure," I respond. "But I don't think I'm going to be much help when it comes to what's in style." I chuckle at my own expense.

No one else joins in.

"Well, it seems to change so fast these days," Jenna says reasonably.

"Yes, who would have ever thought high-waisted jeans would be back in style?" Mom says, and it seems to lighten the mood a bit.

"I am glad it is getting warmer, but I do miss my boots and scarves," says Jenna. "Mallory, maybe we can go shopping one of these weekends." Then her tone softens and grows concerned. "I mean . . . when you're feeling up to it."

She's trying to be sensitive to my needs, but I just want to talk to my best friend. Still, at least she's acknowledging what happened.

"I would like that," I say, telling her with my eyes that I'm just the same old Mallory. "I'm sure I have a lot to catch up with. I mean, when it comes to clothes."

Mom places the lasagna on the table and then takes off her apron to sit down.

"Dinner is ready if you all are," she announces.

"Oh, I remember this lasagna," says Ryan. "I always loved lasagna night when Mallory and I . . ." He looks at me, his voice trailing off, and there is a perplexing moment of silence.

"Italian is my favorite," Jenna steps in, dramatically. There is a rustle, and I know she nudged Ryan's leg under the table, but she hides it by shaking out her napkin and putting it on her lap.

I catch my mom giving a sympathetic smile to Ryan.

We pass dishes around the table, and once everyone was served, Sandra asks if she can say a blessing.

"Of course," says Mom, giving me a puzzled look.

Following Sandra's lead, we all join hands and slowly bow our heads.

"Our Heavenly Father," she starts, "thank you for bringing us all together again. Thank you for watching over Mallory as you did with my Jenna."

I look up to see my mother glance in my direction.

"We ask that you bless this food so that it brings nourishment to all of us so we can be stewards of your good work in the world. Please keep us safe and out of harm's way for all the days to come. Please watch over my dear Thomas as he finishes preschool and help him to find friendly faces and kind children to accept him and include him in kindergarten. Thank you, dear Lord, for returning Mallory to us. In his name we pray, amen."

"Amen," repeats Ryan.

When I let go of my mother's hand, I realize I've been clenching my grip while listening to Sandra's prayer. It's unsettling how casually she mentioned my return home. I swallow and take a breath, knowing I need to relax and try to focus on the positive this evening. My mom wraps her hand over mine after letting go and gives a little squeeze. Her acknowledgement relaxes me.

"Thank you, Sandra," Mom says. "That was . . . nice."

Throughout dinner, we chat idly about the new library they are building in town and how it's going to be full of leading-edge technology and great maker-space equipment. We discuss the increase in the speed limit on the highway south of Everly Falls. Easy topics. I'm out of practice with everyday conversation, so I spend most of the time just listening and observing everyone's faces. If I were a stranger walking in on this conversation, it would seem like a pleasant dinner—at surface level, at least. But I see Ryan has been refilling his wine glass several times, and every once in a while he would meet Jenna's eyes, which were slipping him looks that were less than cordial. I try to keep my foot from tapping rhythmically on the floor, and stifle the urge to hum aloud with nerves.

As my mom starts to clear away the dishes from the table, she says, "You have to save room for dessert."

"Oh, Renee," exclaims Sandra, who seems oblivious to the tension around her. "What did you do?"

"It's a surprise," Mom says.

Jenna looks at me from across the table. "Mallory," she starts, and I can tell she's serious. "What can I do to help you transition back home?"

It's still sinking in that she's addressing the situation. "What do you mean?" I ask.

"I mean"—she leans forward—"I know it's a lot to think about now, but I want to help you if you plan to work or go back to school or whatever it is you decide to do."

"Oh. Thanks." Honestly, I hadn't thought about it. I was still trying to convince myself that this all wasn't just a dream and that I was going to wake up back in the village. "I'm not sure what I plan to do. I can't imagine going into psychology like I'd planned to do before. Just thinking about what happened to me—and you— might make me less equipped to handle certain situations . . . you know, triggers and that kind of thing."

"I can understand that," Jenna says. "With my job, I work with a lot of tough situations involving kidnappings, human trafficking, and mistreated women and children."

I take a deep breath. The terms she used just rolled off her tongue so easily. Of course, Jenna is exactly the type of person to overcome her struggles and help others who are in the same situation. That's strong-willed Jenna.

"But I have to say, seeing a therapist was the best thing I ever did . . . the best thing *we* ever did." Jenna motions to include Ryan.

There's the sense of unity, that sense of being a team that for some reason cuts me deep. I realize I'm not sure which bothers me most, seeing them together or their level of comfort with the entire situation.

"Yeah, totally," I reply, trying to be casual. "I have actually been seeing a counselor as well. I'm just not sure I can ever be on the other side of it like I had planned to do before."

"Well, I want you to take your time, but I would really like to help you as you decide what the future holds." She smiles.

"Do you like your job, Jenna?" I ask, hearing my tone grow cold.

"I do," she says. Then she sighs. "I mean, it is a lot. And yes, there are certain triggers, you are right there. But there are also times when the reward of helping someone or getting someone out of a bad situation can be worth all the hard times."

"Well," I say calmly, fighting the storm that's rising in me. "I think it is admirable for you to be dedicated to that type of work."

"She is dedicated," Ryan says, looking at Jenna.

She smiles back at him.

I want to scream.

"All right," my mother says with forced zeal, passing out plates for dessert. She must have overheard our conversation. "Who wants a piece of tiramisu?"

I look up at her in surprise. Dad was always the dessert baker in our family, and his tiramisu recipe was my favorite. My dad . . . I missed him so much. To say I was grieving for him doesn't even begin to express it. When I was in the village, I thought of him a lot because it brought me strength, but then I thought about how proud he would have been of me making the best of a really shitty situation. He was always finding the positive or trying to see the unseen benefit when bad things would happen.

"Wow, Renee, that looks amazing," says Ryan.

My mom has too cheesy of a smile on her face as she pulls the cover off the large dessert dish. "Well, I'm not sure it'll be as good as Ken's, but I followed his recipe the best I could."

"It looks wonderful," Sandra says. "And I'm sure there are not any calories, right?"

There is uncomfortable laughter. Mom dishes out the dessert. I take a bite. It's not nearly as good as I remember it—when Dad made it—but I put on a smile and say, "Wow, Mom. Tastes perfect, just like when Dad made it."

"Renee, how is Ken?" asks Sandra.

"He's . . . getting along," Mom replies through a tight smile. I can tell she's the one who is starting to feel awkward, especially now that the topic changed to my dad.

"Mallory, have you been able to see your dad?" Jenna asks.

Thinking back to a few days ago when I arrived at Arbor Ridge, the home where my dad now lives, I tried to visit. I walked up to the counter to check in, but as I started to write my name, I froze. I slowly retreated and walked outside. I went around to the side yard to a small pond with a fountain and sat on a bench. I watched some of the residents through the window. Then I spotted him. My dad was sitting at a table on the patio with five other men. It looked like they were playing cribbage or some card game with a board. One of the men said something and tossed his cards down on the table. Then I heard it, the deep, bellowing laugh that could only belong to my father. My heart felt as if it flipped inside my chest. Watching him converse and interact with these people made me tear up.

I knew I needed to figure out how to fit myself back into his life, a life that had changed drastically. Visiting him turned out to be more difficult than I imagined. It was good to see him doing well and enjoying things like playing cards and being with others, but how do I come back into a world where he might not even remember me? What if forgetting about me brought him that joy? Knowing what I had endured would have been so hard for my father in his right mind. Maybe being without his mind or his memory was a better place to leave it. I was so torn. At the very least, it was good to see him from afar and know he is in good spirits. It might take some time, but I knew I would figure out how to visit him.

"I'm going to see him soon, maybe later this week," I say.

"You haven't seen him yet?" Sandra asks, and I avoid her judgmental stare.

"Do you need a ride, Mallory?" Ryan asks, sensing my anxiety.

"Thanks, but Mom is going to take me. Or I can walk too," I add, realizing how childish I sounded. "I just think it's good for me to see him alone."

"That makes sense," says Jenna, ever the reasonable accommodator. "There are so many strides in Alzheimer's research. I hope they can help your father, Mallory."

I give a small sigh. "Me too."

The phone rings. We all seem to sit up a bit straighter at the sound. Mom answers it from the kitchen, and Sandra begins taking the dishes to the sink.

"Yes. Well, this isn't a good time," my mom whispers loudly into the receiver. "She isn't doing interviews right now." My mother has been fielding calls from different media outlets, and I appreciate her for it. The reporters and news stations don't seem to understand what it means to give someone space.

Ryan, Jenna, and I all look at each other.

"Oh yes, I remember what that is like." Jenna looks at me with an empathetic gaze. "It does eventually stop."

"I hope so," I smile at her, happy we're on the same side again. "I mean, I know they have an agenda and probably mean no harm, but I just need some time."

"Of course you do, Mal." She grins and stands up.

We move into the living room to sit. My mom still has the sage green furniture she had before I went to college. I sit in the chair adjacent to Ryan and Jenna on the sofa.

"Do you think you would ever be interested in volunteering?" Jenna asks me suddenly.

"Volunteering?" I repeat.

"I mean, when you're ready, of course, but talking with other survivors of trafficking or abuse." She pauses. "I know you want to keep yourself away from certain triggers, but maybe it could also be therapeutic for you."

"Oh Jesus, Jenna," I rub my eyes, exhausted by the constant questions about pursuing education or a job, or volunteering when I'm not even used to having my life back. And even then, it's not exactly the same. Not really. "I don't know. It's going to take some time for me to get to that point."

"Of course. Sure," she says. "Well, whenever you're ready and whatever you need."

I softly sigh. "I would really like to just spend some time with *you.*" Not problem-solving Jenna. Not polite and professional Jenna. But my best friend Jenna. "I would love to see your house and meet Thomas."

"Yes, let's plan it." She looks over at Ryan with a smile.

"And Ryan," I say pointedly, "I need your help too."

"Sure, whatever I can do," he says.

I sigh. "I have to get my driver's license again, and since it's been so long, I have to take the test."

"Oh man, that sucks," he says. "But yes, I'll help you however I can."

"Cool. It will be a while, but I hate having Mom drive me everywhere," I say, lowering my voice.

When Mom and Sandra come into the living room, Jenna and Ryan stand up.

"We'd better get home to make sure that Thomas is ready for bed," Jenna says. She leans over and hugs me, then goes to hug my mother.

We all embrace and say good night.

As they walk out to their cars, I stand at the screen door, watching Ryan and Jenna get in their car. I smile and wave mechanically as they pull away from the curb, and then let the sweeping sadness come over me. Wanting to stifle it, my throat tightens and there is a hitch in my breathing. I want to cry but feel like I shouldn't, like I don't have the right to feel this way.

I feel Mom walk up behind me and her soft hand rubs my back. Her compassionate touch releases the floodgates, and I stand there crying in the doorway, looking out, imagining what could or should have been.

CHAPTER TWENTY-SEVEN

Mallory

July 11, 2016

The noise outside the door makes my heart leap out of my chest. Sweat forms on my palms and the soles of my feet. I pull the covers over my head, but it doesn't get any quieter. Muffled voices of men are getting nearer. Deep tones converse outside my door, but I can't understand the words. I don't want to draw any attention to myself. My stillness is almost paralyzing.

Anxiety courses through me while I try to stay still and hold my breath. I peek out from under the blanket, seeing the glow of daylight outlining a tattered window shade. I turn to face the door in the other direction where the voices are coming from. A bar of light flows from underneath the door, but not enough to see clearly around the room.

I shift in my bed and pull the blanket up again. There is a rattle at the door handle as someone unlocks it from the other side. Quickly, I slip down to the end of the bed and try to roll between the wall and the mattress; maybe I can even slip underneath. But then a sharp pain shoots up my calf. There is a chain around my leg. The cold, hard link of metal presses into my anklebone. As I twist my foot, the sharpness takes my breath away and I almost scream but cover my own mouth.

The door creaks open and I can see the outline of a large figure through the thin sheet covering my eyes.

A gruff male speaks in a foreign language. His voice is rumbling and familiar and has a cut to it.

My eyes squeeze shut and I try to disappear so the man might not know I'm there.

"No!" I cry as the blankets are ripped from me.

I gasp for air as the man's body lands on top of mine. He is grotesquely heavy, and the smell coming from him is pungent with a hint of onions and gasoline. My gag reflex kicks in but then halts as he grabs the back of my neck and pulls me over to the edge of the bed. His strength is massive, and I am defenseless, knowing I can't fight him but still wanting to.

My eyes are open but can't focus. I am sure my foot or ankle is broken from the force he has put on my body when he pulls me across the bed. My ankle throbs with the exaggerated beat of my heart. His hand strikes my face as he pulls my nightgown over my head, and I can't see.

I continue to scream *No! No! No!* but there is no sound. My voice is gone. I wriggle beneath the man, kicking with my free leg and hitting him with my arms, but it doesn't seem to affect him at all. Then I feel his knee lunge into my stomach and the pain is so shockingly harsh that my consciousness begins to fade.

This can't be happening again.

Then I feel ten thousand needles enter my body through my pelvis. I know what is happening. I am being raped. The torture is beyond anything I have felt before. The agony is worse than ever before. Somehow, it's even different. I try to make my body go numb . . . I know how to do this. I have done it many times before. But it isn't working. I can still feel the torment and pressure of my body being abused.

"Let me go," I scream. I pull my foot up. I try to loosen the chain around my ankle even though the agony rips through me. I have to try something.

Then he abruptly stops and the room is silent for just a moment. I pull my nightgown back down and I can see him in the shadows, standing over me with a gun. In the semi-darkness, his eyes have a deep red look, the way a monster's eyes glow just before it attacks.

The silence is broken by the sounds of cries beyond my door. Walking to the door, he puts his head to it, listening.

It's the voices of little girls begging for help in the distance, maybe just down the hallway. Surprisingly, my foot slides from the constraint of the chain and a surge of energy fills my body. I pull the chain around my hands and slowly make my way off the bed to stand behind the man.

Something is not right. The feeling of carpet beneath my feet isn't right. Through the darkness, I can make out stuffed animals—*my* stuffed animals—lining the shelves in the room, and my childhood posters hang on the shadowed walls.

"Mallory!" a voice screams in the distance from the other side of the door. "Help me, Mallory!"

I know that voice. It's Jenna.

The man turns and is startled to not see me in the bed. As he spins around, I use all of my strength to swing the chain and hit him across the face with it.

He yells and drops the gun, then he scrambles to grab at the chain as it falls to the floor.

I try to reach for the gun, but it's too far away. As he bends over to grasp the gun, I quickly open the door and slip out. Jenna's voice is coming from down the hallway in my mother's room. I try to run to her, but my legs are so weak and I am going too slow.

"I'm coming, Jenna," I shout.

As I move past the study and look in, there are several young girls tied up. They are just children and have a look of terror in their eyes. They are crying and begging me to save them without even speaking. I begin to cry. I know they don't understand why they are being hurt like this. They are so frightened and ashamed.

"I will come back for you, I promise," I whisper loudly to them as I keep walking toward the end of the hall. I focus on the closed door, from where Jenna's voice was coming. My legs don't seem to work as I try moving faster. Everything is in slow motion.

Behind me, the man's grunting and his footsteps are getting nearer. Fire shoots up my legs as I push to move forward, too scared to look back to see how far behind he is. I have to get to Jenna and save her.

As I pass the linen closet, I look at my reflection in the full-length mirror that hangs on the outside of the door. Perplexed, I stop immediately. How can this be? My reflection is of me when I was seven years old, and I'm wearing my favorite *Little Mermaid* nightgown. How am I only a child?

Jenna. Oh my god, is Jenna only a little girl too?

"I'm coming, Jenna!" I scream out again, resuming my walk down the hall.

As I reach the doorway to the bedroom, I open it slowly, and what I see inside isn't my parents' room. It's the room where I was first imprisoned after my abduction. The dirty room in the dirty house in Cambodia.

Then the man's footsteps are right behind me. He is barking short, angry words. Jenna is lying on the floor with her hands and feet tied behind her to the metal frame of a bed. She is blindfolded. It's the same bed that was in the room where I was locked up for so many months. I run toward Jenna, but the man grabs me by my nightgown and pulls me away.

"No. No. No!" I scream, still trying to crawl into the room to help Jenna.

A loud, piercing sound rings through the air and the entire house shakes. He has aimed the gun at Jenna and fired.

I open my eyes.

I'm staring at the ceiling fan in my bedroom. I sit up as I hear the gunshot sound again and realize it's the garbage truck outside. The ground shakes slightly as they lower the trash receptacles and drive down the street. I am in my bed. I am in my room. I am safe.

The room is filled with early morning light. I reach over to the nightstand to grab my water bottle. My mouth is so dry, my body is still shaking. I gasp for air, realizing I have been holding my breath, and bury my face in my hands as tears stream down my cheeks. I pull my legs up with my knees to my chest. My muscles ping with angst from being so tense.

The nightmares are terrible. They have been getting less frequent, but each time I seem paralyzed by the way my mind creates these vignettes of horror. I have learned from Patricia, my therapist, that the way my body and brain balances these memories is part of the process. But knowing why it works this way doesn't make it any less intense. She has prescribed something for me to take before bed to help with the night terrors, but I am trying to get off medication as quickly as possible. Maybe it's too soon.

Once I catch my breath and my heart rate recedes, I look around at the room and its simplicity. The "childness" of it is gone, but evidently still very present in my mind.

I head down the hall to the bathroom to brush my teeth. I grab the toothpaste and my toothbrush, but my hands are shaking uncontrollably. I can't connect the two things together and stand there, staring at the SonicCare in my right hand and the tube of Crest in my left.

"Jesus, *I hate this!*" I scream. I drop the toothbrush and toothpaste onto the vanity and fall to my knees in front of the sink on the bathroom rug. I lean up against the cabinet while I try to quiet my mind and reconnect with the logical side of myself. I'm really good at hiding my trauma from others, but when I'm alone and things are slow and quiet, I can't hide it from myself. When it's just me, I can be undone by the most unexpected things.

Slumping over to my side, I curl into the fetal position while I focus on the black rubber end of the door stop a few feet from my head. *Breathe, breathe, breathe.* I can hear Patricia's voice on repeat. I picture my breathing in my mind—making its way in, holding it, and slowly exhaling. I repeat this several times and each time, my body and mind comes back to me a little more.

Recognizing this has been a full-on panic attack—one of the symptoms of trauma—I know what to do. I'm getting a little better each time at bringing myself back to a normal breathing pattern and slowing everything down, or at least trying.

Slowly, I sit back up and lean against the cabinet. Taking a deep breath, I rise to my feet after several moments have passed. I pull my robe from the hook on the back of the door and slip it on while making my way into the kitchen for a cup of tea, knowing that I have to keep moving forward.

My mother is already gone. I can't remember if she was going to her office for work or had an appointment to go to for my father. I'm glad to be alone, though. She already has a lot to deal with, so my continuous nightmares are not something she needs to know about.

I hate these dreams. They take me back to when I had no control, remind me of all the young girls who were captured and raped. It makes me mad and angry, but also helpless and weak. Thinking about the young girls I encountered during my captivity breaks my heart. They were completely terrified and unaware of what was even happening. At least I knew I was being violated, but they just thought it was what happened. They thought being abused and treated in a subhuman manner was the life they deserved because it was so normalized in their culture.

I enter the kitchen still frustrated about the nightmare. But, somewhere, I feel a shred of hope because this time, in the dream, I did take some control. I decide to move on and keep this in the back of my mind to discuss in my next therapy session.

Patricia has talked through the feelings with me and says it will get better. She refers to it as *survivor's guilt* and explains how powerful it can be on a person's psyche, especially with PTSD. If I can try to journal about the dreams, writing down all the details, it can help me process and maybe someday I will be more comfortable talking to others about my experience.

As the kettle is brewing, I walk into the living room. I look out the window and see the neighbors getting into their car to start their day. The woman is telling her daughters to put on their seatbelts as they pile in with their swimming bags. They are elementary aged, about the same age as the girls in my nightmare. For a fleeting moment I think, *What if it were them?*

The kettle whistles, jolting me from my thoughts. I pour the boiling water over the lemon ginger tea bag in the cup and take a deep breath of the steam. There is something therapeutic about a cup of tea in the morning.

I carry my tea to my bedroom to grab my journal, then head toward the study. I need to look in and remind myself it's just my mom's office. There are no young girls being enslaved there. I don't want the nightmares to have power over me.

The sun shines in through the window and around the slats of the wooden blinds as I slowly walk into my mother's office. Being in the actual room helps push the nightmare from my mind, or at least makes it less vivid. Framed pictures from when I was young line the shelf. Each year my father and I took a photo of us camping with my cousins. There is also a photo of my parents and I at the Grand Ole Opry when I was about twelve years old.

The room smells like my mother. It's a blend of a Clinique's *Happy* perfume and fabric softener with the slight sweetness of coconut. Somehow, it makes me feel closer to her, and helps settle me.

I sit down behind the desk in my mother's old Stickley office chair that creaks and spins around. It is beautifully made of wood with burgundy leather insets. She's always loved this chair, and I remember when we brought it home from the auction. It was a warm fall day. My dad had to remove the chair from the pedestal to get it to fit in the back seat. I was being bratty and complained about riding in the back of the car with the chair. I must have been about nine or ten.

My dad kept begging me to quit complaining. "Come on, Malsy." He looked at me from the rearview mirror and winked. "After we unload the chair, you and I can go and get some ice cream."

"Dad," I said in a low voice, full of attitude, "I won't be able to lift my arm to eat the ice cream because this dumb chair keeps hitting me."

"Don't be so dramatic, Mallory," Mom said over her shoulder while thumbing through a magazine in the passenger seat. I remember how loudly she chewed her gum.

Rolling my eyes, I tried to push the base of the chair away from me. I vividly recall that I did, in fact, have a bruise from the chair continuously hitting my upper arm each time we went over a bump or took a left turn. I showed it to my mom every time I had the opportunity and demanded to wear a short-sleeve shirt to school to draw some attention.

Now, exasperated, I sigh and shake my head at the thought of being such a dramatic child and complaining about something so small.

The tea feels good on my throat. It must be sore from crying in my sleep.

Spinning around in the chair to face my mom's desk, I bump the mouse and her monitor lights up. When I wiggle the mouse, the password box pops up. I lean forward, feeling compelled to accept the challenge of guessing her password. I type in "MalloryAgnes."

"No kidding," I say to myself and smile in a satisfied way as her desktop appears. There are a ton of files and folders showing on the screen. Most of them have names, numbers, or both underneath. A lot are addresses for properties she has been researching for the title company she works for.

Then I spot the folder titled, "MALLORY."

I double-click the icon; there are hundreds of files and folders. As I begin clicking and reading, I quickly realize that this is an archive of all the information my mother had gathered about my abduction. There are scanned articles, maps, and thousands of e-mails copied into folders labeled for each year. There are files with resources listed and documents sent to her by the FBI and Homeland Security.

There is a folder titled "GROUP." As I open it, I read correspondence messages between my mother and other women, and even a few men. It becomes clear that these are letters between the parents of trafficked victims.

September 8, 2014

Dear Joni,

I was so happy to hear about your reunion with your beautiful daughter, Lindsey. I know it has been a long and tough road to finding her and getting her back home. Your story is very inspiring. You and your family are strong and have been so important to our support group. You are loved. We are here to help you in any way we can. You have given me another wave of hope to keep looking and fighting for my sweet daughter.

Please let me know if we can help in any way.

Love,

Your friend, Renee Shields

I read through many similar notes and messages. Some are just to encourage others to not give up and to thank them for their continued support. There are emails to and from Ryan, Sandra, and Jenna. There are articles about other victims and other rescues.

In one folder, there are pictures of the brothels and vehicles that were discovered when raids occurred. In one photo, I recognize the rooms where we had been kept. They were so close to finding us, but they never did. *How could they be so close?* It brings a queasiness to my stomach, and I quickly close out the image.

One folder contains all of the messages from my mother to Agent Stevens of the FBI. I think there was one every month, sometimes more than one per month.

Then a folder catches my attention that is titled, "TO YOU." I open it to find hundreds of documents. Tears stream down my face as I read the first few.

August 1, 2010

My Darling Daughter,

Today, I thought I saw you in the grocery store. I was shopping in the produce aisle and caught a glimpse of you peeking over the potatoes at me. Do you remember when you were little and would play with the potatoes while I shopped? You would create these little plays or musicals, naming them and making each of them dance about. Then I realized it was just an illusion. It must have seemed very real though because Mrs. Banner, your fourth-grade teacher, noticed me just standing there with the door to the lettuce cooler open and staring off into space.

I miss you more and more each day. I won't ever give up on finding you, Mallory. I know you are out there. I can feel it. I know that signs like seeing you in the grocery store are there for a reason. Your father knows it too. Each night we set a place for you at dinner. Sometimes this makes us sad, but other times it makes us talk about you, think about you, and laugh about all of the wonderful times we had when you were younger.

Wherever you are, please know we are doing everything we can to find you and we love you.

Mom

File after file, I open and read documents, letters, reports, debriefs with traffickers who had been apprehended, other parents, and on and on. I know my mother was never going to share this file with me, and part of me feels guilty for continuing to read everything, but then it also gives me a sense of justice somehow.

My mother was always my biggest advocate. She truly never stopped believing I was alive and out there. How could she have ever possibly found me? She must have felt so alone and helpless. At this moment, I realize she has been through her own trauma. I knew this on some level, but really haven't let it sink in.

The garage door growls, and I know that means my mother is pulling in. I look up at the time on the computer screen and realize it is two o'clock in the afternoon. I quickly close the files and turn off the monitor.

My mother enters the house through the kitchen side door, and I greet her with tear-stained cheeks.

"Honey, are you okay?" she asks as she sits her purse down and hangs up her jacket on the coat rack.

"No, Mom, I'm not okay. But I'm getting there." I reach out and pull her to me. I feel her body close to mine, and we hug for a long time.

We both have changed because of this awful experience. Things will never be as they were before, and this is okay. As we embrace, I find myself at a place of acceptance and somehow . . . gratitude. We are a little damaged and we are a little bent, maybe more than a little, but we aren't broken. Not totally, anyway. My mother never gave up on me, so I can't give up either. We are alive and together. We will make it.

CHAPTER TWENTY-EIGHT

Jenna

August 5, 2016

I have never been in the "back side" of a shopping mall. As I stand next to the desk of the property manager for the Central Plaza Shopping Center, my stomach is twisting and turning.

"She is just a little taller than I am, with long dark hair. Her name is Mallory Shields and she is my best friend and she has . . ." Through my sniffles, I describe Mallory to the security guards standing in the office.

Gus, the property manager, stands up from his desk and puts his hand on my shoulder. I immediately pull away, feeling nauseous.

"Ma'am, it's okay. We will find your friend." I sense his concern but then also his feeling of me being overly dramatic. "Which store were you last in when you saw her?"

"We were in Famous Footwear." I take a tissue from the box he'd given me and wipe my eyes. "I was going to go down to the LadyBoss Boutique to look at suits and told Mallory I would meet her in Bath & Body Works, but when I went there, I couldn't find her anywhere in the store."

"Okay, ma'am."

"'Okay'?" I ask. "Wait, what do you mean by 'okay'?"

"We have a system for finding lost people in the mall, ma'am." He walks over to the front desk and says something to the woman who had originally helped me. "You e-mailed the photo you showed me?" he asks me.

"Um, yes, to the address you gave me." I look down at my phone and open up my e-mail.

The woman types something on her keyboard, and then she stops as she notices something on her screen. She then whispers something to Gus, and he walks behind her desk to look at the screen. I'm guessing they recognize Mallory's photo and now understand why I'm so upset that we have lost each other in the mall.

Gus picks up a receiver, and I hear his voice amplified by the sound system.

"Attention Central Plaza customers, be sure to visit the food court today for the best selection of eateries and options. And don't miss the feature film starting soon in the Central Plaza Cinema."

I'm concerned by this. It seems like a strange time for him to make such an announcement.

"Okay, I sent the e-mail," says the woman sitting at the front desk. She looks up at Gus. I see her screen and the photo of Mallory I had sent.

The security guards all file out of the office and into the main hallway of the shopping mall and then divide into different directions.

"Okay, ma'am," Gus says. He looks at me with kindness. "All employees working in the stores here at Central Plaza know there is a missing person alert. We use the code about a feature film starting so that we don't set off too many alarms." He is looking at me weird, and I can tell he needs me to show him I'm tracking and understand what he is saying, so I nod in understanding.

"Janet just sent each store the picture and description of your friend, and the security guards have already started the search around the mall. The best thing you can do is to go look for your friend and keep trying to call her cell phone so that it is pinging towers near her location. I will start looking over the security camera footage for the last hour or so." He looks down at his watch. "Can you please keep me up to date when you do find her?" He reaches across the desk and hands me his card. "Call that number and Janet or I will answer, and we can let security know. What's your number?"

I put his card into my pocket and then give him my number. "I'll keep looking in the stores on this side of the mall and check back in when I find her, or in thirty minutes, whichever comes first," I say.

As I'm leaving, I hear the phone at the front desk ring and Janet answer.

"Oh good. What? Okay, I will tell Gus." She is nodding and I can hear a deep voice through the receiver. "Really? Yeah, she's still here."

"Ma'am, they found your friend." Janet writes something on a yellow sticky note, then hands it to me.

"Roger, the head of security, is with her now but she won't go with him."

I look down at the note. It says aisle two in Best Buy.

"He said she is really upset and won't talk to anyone."

"Oh no," I say, and rush through the doors and down the hallway toward the bright yellow sign of Best Buy. As I run into the store and look up to find aisle two, I see the security guard standing in front of the aisle with the manager next to him.

"I'm with her," I say to them, and they move to let me into the aisle.

Mallory is crouched down in front of a shelf of print cartridges. Her eyes are closed and her arms are wrapped around her knees, which are pulled up to her chest. She is rocking back and forth, humming to herself with a look of emptiness in her eyes.

"Hey . . . what are you doing down here?" I ask as I gently kneel down to sit next to her.

She looks up, a bit startled at first to see me, but then she seems to sigh with relief.

"I'm sorry, I couldn't find you in Bath & Body Works, and so I started looking in other stores. What happened?" I ask.

Mallory just leans into me. Tears glisten on her face. I put my arm around her and can feel her body shaking.

"It's okay, Mals. I'm here now, and you're okay." I know exactly how she feels right now. Several times right after I was rescued, I would get spooked when I found myself in a strange place or large crowds.

"Jesus, Jenna . . . I feel like an idiot." She rests her forehead on her knees.

The security guard walks toward us, and I can feel Mallory tense up when she sees him.

"I'm sorry, sir." She looks up at him. "I didn't realize you were trying to help me."

"Ma'am, can I escort you and your friend back to the property office?" He stands above us, holding a box of tissues for Mallory.

"Thank you, sir," I say. "Can you please just give us a moment?"

He pauses and thinks about this. Then he walks back to the end of the aisle to keep customers from coming into the space.

Mallory is all disheveled, and her skin is red from being so worked up. I reach into my purse and pull out a tissue to give her.

"Do you want to talk about what happened?" I ask.

"I just freaked, Jenna." She sits up straighter and drops her legs into a cross pattern as if she is meditating.

"I left the shoe store and started to walk to the bath store, but then I saw these two men coming toward me. They were wearing business suits and, I don't know, but they seemed to be coming right for me."

I stay silent, not wanting to interrupt her.

"Anyway, I slid into some bookstore and waited for them to pass by me. When I felt like they were gone, I realized it was silly, but it still made me so anxious. I don't know if it was because they were men or in suits or what, but I just kept thinking they were there to take me or something."

I pivot my body to face her and let her know I'm listening.

"I started to walk back toward the bath shop to find you," she continues, "but I had this weird feeling they were following me. I kept looking back, but then I started walking faster, almost running. I panicked and then I came in here to hide."

"Mallory, I'm sorry. We should have just stayed together in the mall. I forgot how crazy it is getting used to all of this." I motion to the mall and shopping and people in general. "I tried to call you," I say, "do you have your phone?"

"Oh crap, yes." She grabs her purse from the floor next to her. "Jenna, I'm sorry. I forget about this thing all the time. I know I need to get better at looking at it and using it."

"It's okay." I smile and rub Mallory's back. "I get it, and you are just fine. The most important part is that you're okay."

We sit there in aisle two of Best Buy for another thirty minutes. Gus, the mall manager, walks by and looks down the aisle. I smile at him, and he says something to the guard and then leaves. The guard stands up a little straighter and keeps the aisle safe and off limits to shoppers.

While Mallory and I sit here, I tell her of several instances where I got really nervous or felt like I was being followed or stalked, explaining how eventually these situations lessen over time, but how hard it is to feel comfortable being alone or around strangers.

Mallory shares with me how she felt like she couldn't breathe and how she began to feel pain all over her body when she thought the men were following her. She remembers the images of men in suits who would come into the room when she was in Cambodia and rape her or beat her or how she would have to stand with other girls in front of different men to be selected and then taken to a room to be abused. She explains how she felt dizzy and helpless not knowing where I was or what direction to go. She says she felt incredibly lost, almost paralyzed, and that was when she found herself in this aisle, and she just stopped and closed her eyes. She just waited there until I found her.

"Will this feeling always be there?" she asks.

"Which feeling?" I say, knowing there are a lot of emotions for Mallory right now.

"The feeling that this isn't real. The feeling that I'm going to wake up and be back in that shithole village with the other women being held against our will. The feeling of being insignificant or just a piece of property?"

I really want to tell her about how sometimes, in the middle of the night, I wake up because I feel Ryan next to me and I think he is one of the monsters in my bed to hurt me like so many years ago. I still haven't escaped that feeling or those episodes where I am full of fear or shame. Sometimes, I wake up with Ryan consoling me because in my sleep I am screaming and thrashing, trying to get away from a rapist in my nightmares. But I don't want Mallory to lose hope. And I don't think she will want to be reminded of my marriage to Ryan right now. She says she's "okay" with Ryan and I being married, but I wonder if the situation is more difficult for her than she lets on.

All I say is, "It does get better eventually."

She seems relieved.

"Don't be so hard on yourself, Mals. It takes time. I'm surprised you were even ready to get out and explore shopping or being in a public place like this."

"I know, I just feel like I've lost so much time. I want to be something or get somewhere, and each time I think I'm moving forward, I have to backtrack." She shakes her head and looks down at the floor.

"It is a process, for sure," I tell her, thinking about how much I was told this when I returned.

"The other day, Mom and I were at the post office, and she was helping me get a P.O. Box set up," she says. "The man working there kept looking at me, and I could tell he recognized me. I swear he had a fucking grin on his face. I got so mad, Jenna. When I signed the form, my hands were shaking and when Mom asked me what was wrong, I just ran out of the post office."

"Did you explain it to your mom?" I ask.

"I tried, but I also don't want her to worry. I just got this feeling that the man thought less of me or saw me the way those fucking rapists would look at me or look at us when they were paying to abuse us like they did." She leans her head on my shoulder. "I didn't think it would be so hard, I guess. I'm sorry if I scared you. I know that must have been nerve-racking."

"No apologies needed, Mal. I'm here for you. We will get through this." I hold her hand in mine. "I'm glad you're talking to me about it."

Finally, we get up and leave the store. We go back to the mall office to thank Gus and Janet and to grab the shopping bags I left there. They both look sympathetically at us.

"Thank you," Mallory says softly to both of them. "I'm sorry if I caused an inconvenience or any trouble."

"No need to be sorry at all," Janet says. "We're here to help in any way we can."

It's clear to both of us that they know who Mallory is, and probably me too. Even though Mallory has tried to keep a low profile upon returning, there is still a lot of media coverage about her return, and that also brings back stories about when we were both abducted in Thailand.

On our drive home, Mallory shares some of the terrible situations she experienced after we were separated in Cambodia and the different types of abuse she went through after being traded to someone in Iraq. I feel privileged that I can be there for her to share these experiences with and to talk about them because I know it was hard. Today's events brought up a lot of feelings for both of us.

When we arrive at Mallory's house, I walk her inside. Renee meets us at the door and asks how the shopping trip went. I'm not sure whether she can tell it's been a stressful day. I almost start to tell her, but Mallory beats me to it.

"It was interesting, for sure," Mallory says. "I just haven't quite gotten used to being back in stores and around that many people yet. I'm glad Jenna went with me."

I put my arm around her and squeeze her. "Me too, my friend." Then I grab her hand and Renee's hand. "Well, I'd better get home. Ryan and Thomas wanted to have homemade pizza for supper tonight, so I'm sure they're waiting on me to get everything started." I'm eager to get home and put the memories brought up by the day back into the "history" file in my brain.

I walk out to my car. As I drive away, I become overwhelmed with emotion. I'm drained and feel vulnerable. I haven't allowed myself to go through some of these emotions that I've buried years after I returned home. The uneasiness of everything around me is always there, but I've become good at burying these feelings. I am all too familiar with the thought, *Will I ever be normal again?* Mallory is in the thick of it all right now, and my heart breaks for her. It is hard, and it is sometimes too much.

I turn the corner to get onto the bypass road and head home. The thought of seeing Ryan and Thomas helps me refocus. I take a deep breath and turn my attention to the positive thoughts of pizza toppings.

CHAPTER TWENTY-NINE

Mallory

August 15, 2016

Patricia is staring at me, patiently waiting for a reaction.

I shift in my chair, unable to explain how it makes me feel. The words aren't coming to me, so I look at the bookshelf across the room. There are many psychology books and a few other medical books.

Patricia is a native Californian. From the outside, she looks like what you would expect: tall, tan, fit, blonde hair, blue eyes, and a gleaming smile full of incredibly white teeth. Even her office seems to smell like the beach. It's full of light blues, beige, and ivory tones all blended together to create a very serene place to sit and talk.

She seems put together, always wearing her hair pulled back in a stylish way with casual clothing that still seems business appropriate. She isn't flashy in any way, but she is the type of person who doesn't need to be. She is a natural beauty, but almost keeps that at bay in order to project her intellect.

I've sensed from her that she misses the West Coast. She told me in one of our first visits that she had a hard time adjusting to the Midwest. She moved here with her husband, who is an orthopedic surgeon, and he had the opportunity to go into practice with his brother, so somehow he talked her into making the move. She explained how difficult it was at first to find her place and fit in.

She had a hard time making friends because she was focused on her own career and ambitions. She didn't socialize at the country club or host events for various causes. I'm not sure, but I don't think they have any children. I don't see any photos in her office.

Patricia worked with military patients suffering from PTSD during her residency at UCSD. This is how she came to know Agent Sommers, who recommended her and actually connected us. Once she became an official licensed health practitioner, she continued that work but then volunteered to work with law enforcement with victims suffering with PTSD as a result of terrible crimes, which included sex trafficking. I was surprised at her openness when we first started meeting. She knew I was uncomfortable, so she seemed okay with me asking her questions. I always thought therapists were supposed to keep their life private from patients, but Patricia must have thought differently, which I liked. Knowing all of this about Patricia helped me trust her professionally, but it was still difficult for me to share this information with her.

"Okay," she says. "Let's try this. I am going to say three words, and you pick the one that best describes how this made you feel. Does that sound fair?"

I nod.

"Angry, sad, or jealous?"

The first two make sense, but I didn't expect her to say *jealous*.

"Sad," I reply. "But that isn't it either."

"I know. It's a process." She leans toward me. "Let's try it again. Sad, isolated, or relieved?"

I wonder if there is relief in knowing my mother is seeing another man while my father is living in a home for Alzheimer patients. I think I'm relieved to know she has someone who has been looking out for her, but that isn't my primary feeling either.

"Maybe isolated," I say. "It's hard to think about this and not know where to go or who to talk to about it."

"Have you talked to your mother?"

"I mean, yes, when she told me last night."

"Sure, Mallory. She shared this information with you. But did you have a conversation? Did you ask her questions? Tell me more about that interaction."

I hesitate, remembering my conversation with my mother last night. It was before dinner. I was sitting at the kitchen island while she was preparing a salad. I had taken the opportunity to ask her about information I needed to fill out paperwork for starting classes at Goodwin again.

"Okay, I have my address and social security number," I said, looking down at the form. "Have I read the FERPA policy, check. Have I read the anti-harassment policy, check. Okay, Mom, are you cool with being my emergency contact?"

She shook her head and had a serious expression on her face, but then her mouth cracked into a big grin. She never could keep up on a bit. She would start strong, but she would always end up breaking into a smile or laughter. That was always my thing with Dad. We could riff off each other until we had a full-blown storyline established.

"Okay, well, it says it has to be local, so looks like you're stuck." I reached across the island to grab a tomato slice.

"Silly," she said. "Of course I am your emergency contact. Forever and always." She winked.

"Likewise," I said, and then wondered aloud, "Actually, who is your emergency contact, Mom? I mean, probably not Dad, since he got sick. Who is local that you used before I came home?"

She paused for a moment, and then her voice brightened into a light casualness. "Oh, goodness, look. We're out of peppercorns in the grinder." She went to the pantry to grab more to fill it.

"Mom?" I asked as she busied herself with small preparations for the meal.

"Yes, what?"

"Why are you acting weird?"

"Weird?" She grabbed the colander and rinsed the lettuce in the sink.

I leaned over and turned the water off. "Okay, Mother, what's going on?"

Her face was flushed. Nervously, she wiped her wet hands on her apron and walked around to my side of the island, taking the seat next to me.

"Mal," she said softly, "I need to tell you something."

My skin was tingling. I cocked my head to the side, indicating that I was listening.

"My emergency contact is . . . a friend of mine." She paused. "A male friend of mine."

"What male friend?"

"After your dad went to live at Arbor Ridge . . . well, I have been seeing someone."

I almost laughed, but then realized she was being sincere in telling me this.

"What? I mean, when? What, like seeing another man?" I wasn't sure how to respond to this. My face tightened and I had to look away from her.

"I am so sorry. I didn't tell you because I just didn't want to upset you. There's so much on your plate right now." She reached out to put her hand on my arm, but I pulled away. "You know I am always going to love your father, Mallory."

I stared ahead into the kitchen, slowly nodding. Then I turned and glared at her. "You barely talk about Dad anymore. Now you're telling me you are having an affair?"

Her eyes were watery. "Mallory, it isn't like that. Richard and I met in a support group, and he is a good man." She started to reason, but my head began buzzing as I tried to take in what she was saying. My chest tightened, and I thought my heart was cracking open a bit as I pictured my father and thought about how much this would hurt him.

"Richard who?" I asked, trying to understand.

"Clemson. Richard Clemson. I would really like for the two of you to meet soon."

"Oh yeah?" I got off my stool and started to gather my papers.

"Mallory, please," she said. "Let's discuss this. I want you to know this isn't something—"

"Mom, I don't want to know anything about this right now," I snapped. "I just need to think." Then I retreated down the hallway without another word.

"I understand," I heard her say in a small voice.

I could have handled it differently. I was just caught off guard. The thought of my mom with another man had just never occurred to me as possible.

I shift again in the seat, still a bit uncomfortable and skeptical of Patricia. This is my fifth visit with her, and we've kept things pretty surface level so far. We've talked about how I was recovering physically, the people I've seen since returning home, and some of the expectations I should have. I like her enough, but she seems to want to push me. I don't know if I ever will get past what has happened to me. I am a survivor of human trafficking, and I feel like I have simply accepted this fact. And now I want to move on with my life, but when I say that or behave in that way, it's almost like the people around me are . . . disappointed.

"Disappointed," I blurt out as if there is not a filter between my mind and mouth.

"Okay, that works too." Patricia shakes her head. I can tell she is trying to counsel me with her tried and true methods, but it's hard because I'm not following the protocol. "You are disappointed in your mother?" she continues. "Why do you think you are disappointed?"

"I'm disappointed with the situation, I think, not necessarily with my mom." I sit back a bit and take a deep breath.

Patricia nods for me to continue.

"I just feel like my mom caved, maybe. You know, like she had given up on her own strength and felt she needed to find someone else to lean on, or something." I am disappointed, and I think this is the first time I realize it.

"So, what you're feeling is about your mother? But how does it make you feel as her daughter? Your mother is in a relationship with another man while still married to your ailing father?" She is pushing me again.

"Is that a question or a statement?"

Patricia just looks at me and purses her lips.

"I'm sorry." I sigh. "I know I am not making this easy today."

At that moment, the feeling in the room shifts, and it becomes less tense with my admission of honesty about my behavior. It's like when I was little and I got caught doing something I wasn't supposed to do or telling a fib about something, and once I was caught I was able to relax knowing I had come clean and it was all going to get better from that point.

"Mallory." Patricia's eyes are kind. I can tell she is not just doing a job when she talks with me. She is genuinely interested in helping me adjust to my new reality and deal with my experiences.

I look at the wall where she hung several framed certificates and degrees. This reminds me of her qualifications and that she does know what she's doing. I should consider myself lucky to have a therapist who understands my situation.

"Nobody said it was going to be easy." She smiles, but not enough for me to see her bright teeth.

"I know," I reply. "It has just gotten increasingly confusing the last few weeks, I think."

"How so?" She picks up her notebook.

"I think I'm just feeling a bit lost," I confide in her. "Everyone I know or used to know has their normal daily lives. It's hard to find my place in that, and I don't want to disrupt their lives or force myself into relationships. At first it was good to see people and to reconnect, but now I don't know where I really belong. I need to find a path or my purpose here."

"Mallory . . ." Patricia tosses her hands up, not dramatically, but it is out of character for her.

I smile, feeling like maybe I have done something right.

"This is what I've been waiting for." There's that smile showing her teeth. "And good job. You just bypassed what usually takes a lot longer to identify."

"What do you mean?" I ask curiously.

"We are humans," she says. "We want to feel significant and worthy of the life around us. It is natural for you to struggle with this. However, the fact that you can admit feeling lost and without direction . . . well, that's going to be a big step toward helping you find that path."

"Okay," I respond. "So how do I do it?"

Patricia goes on to explain the importance of knowing and identifying these feelings I've been having. She tells me that it usually takes a patient a lot longer to come to terms with this sense of loss, and it is actually what they call the "vacuum" in her area of practice. A large portion of people who have been victimized and abused like I have get sucked back in, hence the vacuum reference. They return to that life either on purpose, or they are easily targeted and victimized again because it's too hard to get used to a different way of living. It's a long-term condition of being shamed. Humans want to feel needed and to have a purpose. If we are not feeling a sense of those around us needing us, we will gravitate to where we do feel it, and often that is back in the life of being abused and terrorized because at least we know what to expect and what is expected of us in that situation.

"This is real progress," she says. "I want to use our time the best we can today to put some things in place for you to work on."

"Okay."

"Let's explore a couple of the more significant people or situations," she says. "I think your mother and her admission of seeing another man may be one of these, right?"

"My mom just told me about him—about Richard—and I feel like that was a big thing for her, but now it's out there, and she can talk freely about it, but I'm not sure how to respond. I also feel like this is a step for her to go back to her normal life."

"That makes sense." Patricia nods.

"And Jenna . . . I'm not sure what or how to respond to Jenna."

"Your best friend who was also abducted with you?"

"Yes," I continue. "She is amazing in her ability to turn a challenge into something positive, but I'm not as good at that, and I know she is frustrated by this."

"Why do you think she is frustrated?" Patricia asks.

"I think she wants me to be able to talk more about what happened," I say. "And not so much with her, but with others. She is part of a crisis organization and wants me to come and tell my story and talk with other survivors, but I can't do this . . . not yet."

"I can tell you feel strongly about this," Patricia agrees.

"And it just feels . . . I don't know, like fake or cheap." I shake my head.

"Why does it feel that way?"

"I do want to talk about my experience, but I feel like if I can't talk about it with my mom or with Jenna, I shouldn't be sharing it with strangers, you know?"

Patricia nods. "Let's take it slow. Let's also not group people," she advises.

"What do you mean?" I ask.

"Your mom," Patricia says. "Has she asked you about your experiences? Do you feel pressure to share information with her?"

"No." I stop to really think about this. "She hasn't asked me much. I know she's aware, but she doesn't really understand where I was and the things that happened. I think she's just trying to give me space and time."

"What does it change once she knows?" Patricia asks.

"I don't understand," I say. "I mean, I hope it doesn't change anything."

"So, you feel she should know, even though she hasn't asked, and you don't want to do anything to change your relationship at this point. Is that what I understand?"

"I guess."

Patricia sighs. "Mallory . . . here's the real deal. Your mom probably doesn't need to know."

I just look at her. I haven't really thought about this before. I've had this looming cloud of invisible pressure hanging over me and felt obligated to share all the terrible details and facts of my captivity with my mother, but I didn't know how to do it or when.

"You need to trust that your mom will ask you when she wants to know something," Patricia says. "Until then, you can share things when the situation calls for it, or if it seems like the right time, or you don't have to share at all."

"True," I say. I'm starting to see it from a different perspective.

"Jenna might be a different story for you, Mallory."

I'm eager to hear Patricia's view on Jenna's need to push me into support groups and sharing before I'm ready.

"There are a lot of things to work through with Jenna," she says. "I think we need to take this slow and steady. I appreciated what you said to me about feeling the pressure from her and thinking she is frustrated."

"Yes," I say. "I have actually been avoiding her lately because I just don't know how to handle it."

"You and Jenna experienced something together that was horrific."

I swallow the lump in my throat as I imagine the two of us in the beginning of our gap-year journey. We were so fresh-faced and youthful. I long to be back in that time again, or to at least be able to have that feeling of excitement. Now I feel an emptiness and sense of humility.

"I want you to tell Jenna what you told me," says Patricia. "You experienced something together, but you have also had some very different experiences apart. There is also the fact of Ryan and his marriage to Jenna."

"But I'm okay with it, really," I say softly.

"Sure. You are okay with it. You understand it. You have accepted it. But you can still have feelings about it and it is okay to acknowledge those feelings."

"There's just so much there," I say. "I want to be a part of their lives, but I'm afraid if I'm honest it will push her and Ryan away."

"I can understand why you would feel that way." She nods. "Tell me more about that."

"I don't know, really." I sigh and try to relax my shoulders. "It isn't so much that I want to be with Ryan or that I don't want Jenna to be with him. It's more like I miss what could have been. It's something I can't go back and redo or change, so I know I need to come to terms with it somehow. It makes me angry sometimes, and other times I just feel sad, like I really missed out on my chance at happiness."

"That must be hard, Mallory."

"And Jenna has had years to work through a lot of these feelings and triggers of what happened to us. She has been able to get past it. I'm just not ready," I add.

I know Patricia can tell I'm holding something back.

"What are you thinking, Mallory?" she asks.

"Honestly, I don't know how Jenna did it. I mean, I see her, and you would never know what happened to her. Then I feel like everywhere I go, people look at me and see exactly what happened to me. It makes me feel shame, like there is really something wrong with me that I can't ever correct or get away from."

"I think those feelings are okay to have." She nods for me to keep going.

"There have just been some situations where I get . . . I guess, spooked or paranoid." I go on to tell her about the shopping incident with Jenna and a couple of other times when I found myself overwhelmed with anger or doubt.

"So maybe you're feeling a bit of resentment or animosity toward Jenna not just because of Ryan, but also because she seems to have less trauma or negative emotions about her abduction or situation?"

Again, I'm not sure if this is a question or statement.

"Well, yes, I guess. I don't like having those feelings, but I suppose I am feeling a bit hurt over everything that's happening. It just sucks, and it seems really hard to know how to get past some of it. Sometimes it's just easier to be alone than around everyone." I bite my lip, realizing I've just opened myself up with the truth.

"I can't tell you how happy I am to hear you say this." Patricia leans toward me.

I give her a questioning look.

She rubs her palms together. "Mallory, you had such a resigned presence with your return. It's good to know you are experiencing these very real and expected feelings."

"I guess, but it doesn't always feel so good at the moment." I look down at the edge of the seagrass rug. "In fact, it makes me feel like an idiot or a child who is being bullied or scared of the other kids at school."

"That seems like a logical reaction, Mallory." She smiles. "When you were with Jenna shopping, what was her reaction?"

"She felt bad for leaving me alone. I mean, it wasn't her fault, and I hadn't expressed being uncomfortable and really, I thought I was okay." But as the words come out of my mouth, I realize that maybe I did resent that she had left me alone.

"Did the two of you talk about this? Was she able to relate to how you felt?"

"Yes, she was actually really great with it all. We did talk about some of the past."

"That's good," Patricia says. "I think if you explain to Jenna that you just need some time, she'll understand. You need to tell her that. Can you?"

"Yes." I take a deep breath. "I will tell her how I feel. She always means well."

"Good, Mallory." Patricia sits back into her chair a bit.

"So, what's next?" I ask, trying to fill the awkward gap of silence.

"Well, I think talking to your mother about Richard might be a good step. And like I said, talk with Jenna. You don't have to unpack everything from your experiences, but share with her how you need to take it slow and how the process is different for you."

"Okay." I feel good having some idea of what to do next.

"And you mentioned a visit with your father tomorrow," she says.

"Yes." I still haven't visited my father yet since returning, and I'm not sure I can handle it. I don't want to be too emotional and scare him or set him back. "He asked my mom about me, and she had told him I was home a few weeks ago, but he didn't understand. Then last weekend he asked her if I was coming to visit."

"This will be tough, Mallory." Patricia raises an eyebrow. "You can handle it, though. I know you can. The work we have been doing and how well you have been processing and addressing your emotions . . . you are ready."

My eyes fill with tears as I think about my father.

"We will have a lot to talk about next time, won't we?" Patricia smiles and stands up. She walks over to her desk and writes something on the back of her business card, then hands the card to me. "This is my personal cell phone."

I take the card and put it into my purse.

"Please call me if you need to." She looks down at a book on her desk. "We aren't scheduled until next Tuesday, and I have a feeling the week will be eventful for you. I'm here if you just need to talk." She smiles again.

"Thanks, Patricia," I say, knowing that giving me her cell phone number was a big deal. But I also feel she trusts me to not abuse it and that she really is concerned for my well-being.

When I leave her office, my mom is waiting in her blue Toyota Camry. She waves me over.

"Hi, Mom, thanks for picking me up." As I start to open the door, I hesitate. "Mom, do you mind if I walk home?"

She gives me a concerned look but quickly changes it to a smile. This is her new way of responding to me, and I've been getting used to it.

"Sure. You have your phone with you, right?" she says. "Remember, I won't be home for dinner tonight."

This is a carryover from our conversation yesterday about Richard, her new companion. Though talking to Patricia about this helped, I'm still not ready to discuss it with her.

"Yep. No worries, Mom." I smile, pulling my phone from my purse to show her. "Have a nice evening."

She drives off, and I make my way through downtown, stopping at the coffee shop to get an Americano and a blueberry scone. As I walk in, it is a bustle of people, noises, and activity. Although being alone around small crowds of people make me nervous, I am doing better with it. After therapy, I always feel the strongest, as if I've just polished my armor and I'm ready to face my fears.

I decide to keep walking and make my way to the city park a few blocks from the college campus. This park is a great place in Everly Falls, and I used to come here a lot with my father when I was little. He would run through the park while I rode my bicycle next to him. I find a bench overlooking the small pond and watch the ducks gliding across the water.

My thoughts drift to Jenna. We need to talk, and I should tell her how I feel if we are going to continue a friendship. It's going to be tough, and it will bring up memories I'm sure she has forgotten, but we need to at least try. I haven't seen her since the shopping debacle a few weeks before, or Ryan since having dinner at my mom's house. I had canceled our initial plans to meet their son Thomas because I wasn't feeling well. But in hindsight and after talking with Patricia, I know I just need more time to understand this new dynamic. I want to be in their world, but not be that "pathetic" friend who lost out on the life she could have had.

I declined the other offers of dinner at their house and invitations to go to Thomas's ball games or activities, but now I know it's time. If we are going to salvage our relationship, we need to jump in and have a real conversation about everything.

I feel my purse start to vibrate and realize I have a call coming in. I smile when I look at the screen and answer the call.

"Oh, you're clairvoyant," I say.

"Really?" Jenna asks. "What do you mean?"

"I was just thinking about coming to see you."

"It must be that 'best friend' intuition."

I have to wonder if my mother tipped her off that I'm roaming about alone.

"Well, I'm actually planning to come home a little early this afternoon," she says.

"Great." I take a deep breath. "Can we talk?"

CHAPTER THIRTY

Mallory

August 15, 2016

It's late in the afternoon as I park my bike in the driveway of Jenna and Ryan's house. They built a home in a newer subdivision on the other side of Everly Falls about seven miles from my neighborhood, which is centrally located in the middle of town where we all grew up. The yards all have playsets and fuel-efficient cars in the driveways, indicating that this neighborhood is full of young professionals with budding families.

I knock on the front door and hear a deep but familiar bark.

When Jenna comes to the door, I see Carter next to her, and I smile. I didn't even realize that Carter was still around and never thought to ask. He has to be almost ten years old by now. Seeing him reminds me of how young and carefree Ryan and I were when we adopted him. I pet the top of his head around his collar. Indifferently, he turns and trots off like a little old man. He doesn't remember me, I realize, deflating. Jenna is his family now.

I stand and put on a smile, then hug Jenna, and we walk into the living room. Everything is very neutral and orderly, but also airy and open.

"Wow, Jenna," I say looking around, "your home is lovely. Do you guys like the neighborhood?"

"We do," she says. "It took a little bit to fill up with houses. We were the second or third family to build out here, but now it seems to be attracting others. We like having more kids around for Thomas to play with."

We walk into the kitchen area.

"How are you doing?" she asks in a motherly tone.

"You know, it's day by day," I say, deciding to be honest.

She nods and motions for me to sit at the table. She walks over to the cabinet and grabs two glasses.

"Can I get you something to drink? Wine, beer, water . . . juice box?" She giggles as she opens the refrigerator.

"I'll take water, thank you," I say, then after a pause, "but I could also do wine if you are."

"Yes!" she exclaims. Then she walks over to the table with two glasses of fruity-smelling blush wine.

The house is quiet. "Is Thomas still at school?" I ask.

"He had a birthday party after school today. Ryan is picking him up on his way home from work."

"Oh, nice," I reply.

Jenna gets a serious look on her face. "I've been worried about you, Mal, since shopping and then I realized I had forgotten to apologize about my mom when we had dinner. She means well, but she doesn't always say the right thing, you know."

"Oh god, don't be sorry." I smile. "Yes, I know mothers usually don't always say the right thing. Mine just . . ."

I'm not sure if we are at the point that I feel comfortable sharing my mom's love life with Jenna, but Patricia said I need to be honest and real with Jenna.

"My mom told me yesterday that she has been seeing another man," I blurt out. I look at Jenna, trying to gauge if she already knew this.

"I wondered about that," she says. "Actually, my mom had asked me because she said she saw your mother out to dinner a while back with Richard Clemson. She knows him from the VA Bene-fits office."

"Yeah," I say. "That's him. Mom said they met in a support group for spouses of patients with degenerative diseases like Alzheimer's. His wife passed away about a year ago. I think mom said she had Parkinson's."

"Are you upset about your mom seeing him?"

"I'm not sure if upset is the way I feel, but maybe just more concerned and maybe a little sad. I know it would crush my dad, but I also know my dad isn't who he used to be." I surprise myself by admitting this. Maybe none of us are who we used to be.

"Well, Sandra said he is a really nice guy. Have you met him?" she asks.

I smile when Jenna refers to her mom as "Sandra" because this is how she used to refer to her when we were growing up and all through college. I think it stemmed from a time when we were little. We were at some appointment with her mom, and when they called her name, they pronounced it San-dra, and she corrected them, making sure they knew it was Sahn-dra. So then every time Jenna would call her mom by her name in an exaggerated fashion, Sandra would do her best to mispronounce Jenna's name, calling her Gina or Jemma or Jana. It was amusing to watch these continuous, passive-aggressive interactions between them.

"No, I haven't met Richard," I respond. "Like I said, I just learned about it yesterday. Now that I think about it, I did hear her talking to someone a few times on the phone and wondered who it was. I just assumed it was one of my aunts, but it was probably him because she seemed pretty hushed about it."

"Have you seen your dad yet?"

"Tomorrow," I say with a self-conscious smile. "I wanted to go earlier, but it's just a little more difficult than I thought it would be."

"I'm sure." She takes a drink of her wine. Her purse is sitting on the table, and she pulls out some type of pamphlet. "Hey, I also wanted to apologize for being so pushy about you volunteering or figuring out what you're doing next. I'm sure this has all been very difficult."

"Yeah, I appreciate that," I say. Normally, I would have responded with, *It's okay, no worries*, but I am here to be honest, and I also need to be brave. "I actually needed to talk with you about that, Jenna."

"Sure." She sits up straighter and looks excited about what I have to say.

"I can't do it," I say. "I can't talk to other people, or other survivors about what happened to me, to us, until you and I talk about it more."

"What do you mean?" she says with a leery tone.

"I mean that you have had a lot more time than I have to come to terms with what happened to us."

Jenna pushes the pamphlet under her purse. "Yes, but—"

"Wait, please, Jenna," I say, not looking directly at her. "I know what you went through was awful and scary and fucked up, and just because you weren't a victim or prisoner for as long as I was or because you were rescued and I wasn't, it doesn't mean you didn't experience these terrible things." I meet her eyes. "I am not trying to simplify or make your experience any less than what it was, but the one big difference is time."

"Yes," she says. I can tell she's starting to construct a diagram in her mind of what I'm trying to communicate. This is Jenna's way of thinking and talking.

"I think it's easier for you for a lot of reasons," I say. "You have had more time and distance from being abused by those bastards. You have built a life and have a direction and purpose."

She looks away, and I know she's feeling some type of guilt.

"Jenna, I don't say that to make you feel bad. I really don't. I'm saying it to help you see that it's going to take time for me to establish myself and to put some space between who I was and who I am now or who I want to be."

"Sure. Of course it is, and . . . I'm sorry," she says.

"I have tried to act like everything is okay, and like I am super cool with just bouncing back into my life pre-torture, but it's not real, and it's not honest of me."

I am happy with myself for letting go a bit and sharing my real feelings with Jenna.

"What can I do to help?" Jenna asks.

"You just need to give me time, but please don't give up on me, Jenna."

"I would never give up on you, Mallory." She starts to look a bit hurt.

"I know, but I just want you to know it will take a little focus and trial and error for me to figure out what my future holds and where I belong." I shake my head. "The last thing I want to do is be a burden or concern for anyone, but I also need to feel like I belong somewhere."

"What exactly are you saying?" Jenna asks.

"I'm not sure yet." I smile grimly. "I know you want to help, and you want me to have a list of ways you can help me and we can 'solve' the problems around human trafficking together. I know that you see *me* . . . you see *us* as survivors, and you expect me to be like you and use that as a platform to help other people."

"Your story is so powerful, Mallory." She leans in.

"I know you see it that way, but right now I can't use it to help or inspire anyone because I still feel a lot of shame and resentment. I'm not like you, I can't just switch it off to make a profound statement or turn it into activism before I am ready."

"Mallory, it wasn't like that for me at first." She clears her throat. "I was a mess, and—"

"Exactly, I feel like a mess all the time," I interrupt her. "I can't just forget being beaten and raped and . . ." I burst into tears. "All the other women who were just as helpless, some of them were only children, Jenna. Young girls who had no idea what was happening to them."

Jenna is crying with me.

"I'm so confused most of the time. I want to go back to being the naïve, free-spirited person that I was, but I can't. I am so mad at that person because . . . *I was* that person who let this happen to me and to you."

There, I said it. How I really feel. Anger is boiling up inside of me.

"No, Mal . . . no, it wasn't either of our fault." She wipes the tears from her eyes, shaking her head.

"I know that's what we're supposed to think, Jenna, but I am just not there yet. I am recovering physically, but it really hurts inside. And you know I love you and Ryan, but that hurts too. I feel this deep-seated guilt or regret and I hate myself for it."

"I knew there had to be some feelings you still had for Ryan and have been worried about it, to be honest," she said.

"Jenna, it's not that. You and Ryan are married and have a family. I have accepted that, so please don't worry about me harboring feelings or pining for your husband," I say this even though it's possibly a half-truth. I want to get to the friendship part of the conversation more with Jenna.

"I just need you, my best friend, to understand and be there for me now. I can't keep trying to overcome these memories or push them aside. I feel like such a failure for not being able to let it go or to bounce back into the way I used to be," I say.

Jenna watches me without words. I know she is trying to think of the perfect thing to say, but for once, the words aren't coming so easy for her.

"And if I am telling the truth . . ." I inhale deeply and my voice escalates even more, almost to a level where I don't even recognize myself as the person talking. "I am glad you were rescued before me, that I endured more time, more torture, more—"

"No, no, no . . ." Jenna shakes her head. "Mallory, don't say that."

"I have to say it." I look up at the ceiling then back to Jenna. "I am glad you don't have to think about it as much as I do, that you have had more time to forget the hell we went through. Because if it were the other way around, I seriously don't think I could live with myself." My hands clenched the edge of her kitchen table just to stay in my seat. "It was my fault, I should have listened, planned . . . not acted like it didn't matter."

Jenna gets up, walks over, and wraps her arms around me. It's good to connect with her again and for us to talk. She sits back down but pulls her chair closer. This feels like an overdue conversation, and I am starting to feel some stress lift as we speak.

"Trust me, Mal," she says softly. "Not a day or moment goes by where I'm not reminded."

"I know," I choke out. "But you have a life with Ryan and with your son and . . ." I am just about to explain that I can never have children of my own when I hear the front door swing open.

"Mommy!" A young boy comes flying into the kitchen.

Carter barks from the back of the house, and his collar rattles as he rushes into the room.

"Hey, babe," Ryan shouts from the living room.

But I can't take my eyes off the young boy with ominously familiar dark skin and jet-black hair. I see Jenna in his eyes, and he has the goofiest smile with one of his front teeth missing.

Now I understand what she means by being reminded every moment.

The boy is shaking with energy and just wants to burst out talking with her, but stops. He sees me there with his mom and hesitates. Jenna wraps her arms around the boy as he leans close to her with a sense of shyness and curiosity.

"Thomas . . . this is my friend and Daddy's friend, Mallory." She smiles at me. "This is our son, Thomas."

Her eyes sparkle when she looks down at him. Her gaze repositions to me, and it is obvious in this moment that my response to meeting Thomas has been important to Jenna.

"Hello," I say. I'm speaking, but also digesting this situation at the same time. "Thomas, it's so nice to meet you." The realization that Thomas is not biologically Ryan's son lands on me in the most peculiar way.

"Nice to meet you," he says with a little lisp from his missing tooth. He quickly refocuses his attention to Jenna. "Mom . . . Conner's party was the best. We had cotton candy and snow cones *and* ice cream."

Ryan is standing at the entrance to the kitchen. "Hi, Mal," he says.

"Hey," I say. He walks over to the table. The look on his face shows that he senses a conversation interrupted.

"Mom, can I go outside?" Thomas looks at her, waiting for permission.

"Actually," she says, "why don't you and Daddy run back into town and pick up some pizza for dinner?"

"Yeah, buddy," Ryan says, giving Jenna a nod. "Let's go back in. I'll let you pick out all the toppings."

"Ah, Dad. You know you just want muffrooms, and those are gross." We all give a polite chuckle as Thomas's speech is impeded by the missing tooth.

"Well, this time, we can skip the mushrooms. Come on." He starts to walk toward the entrance.

Thomas comes up to me and looks me in the eye. I'm not sure if I'm breathing at this moment. He has the most inquisitive expression, one I've seen on Jenna's face.

"Will you eat pizza with us?" he asks me.

I look at Jenna.

"Mallory, we would love for you to stay for dinner," she says.

"Sure," I quickly respond. I'm just going with it, and I have so many questions swarming in my mind.

As Ryan and Thomas leave, a silence fills the house. Carter saunters into the kitchen and looks up at Jenna. She methodically gets up and starts tending to his food and water.

"He is such a great dog, Mal," she laughs. "He never forgets dinner time, though."

Carter taps his left paw on the top of the dish as she pours it in, and he gobbles up the food. He did that as a puppy too.

"Jenna, how old is Thomas?" I blurt out. I'm looking for confirmation of what I suspect.

Jenna stares at me and doesn't break eye contact. "When I was rescued from Cambodia, I was pregnant. Thomas will turn seven next month."

"Jenna." I'm not sure what else to say.

She smiles.

"Why didn't you tell me before?" I ask.

"Well, when I first saw you, I wasn't sure how, and I just wasn't prepared. I didn't want to make that moment about me. I also wasn't sure if your mom had told you, but I didn't want to ask. Then it didn't seem right at dinner with our moms there."

She walks over to the closet between the kitchen and front room and pulls out a box. She brings it over to the table. It's full of framed photos and small albums.

"I can't imagine our life without him." She starts sorting through some photos. "Here, he is only six months old." It's a picture of Thomas as an infant dressed in overalls.

I put my hand on top of hers. "Jenna, I am so sorry. I had no idea. I just assumed Thomas was . . . well, that you and Ryan . . . you know what I mean."

"I know. But please don't be sorry," she says. "There is no need. It was my choice to have Thomas. It wasn't an easy choice, but it was my choice, and I don't regret it for one second."

I just give her a teary nod, knowing that had to be one very hard decision for Jenna.

"Honestly, he probably saved me, Mallory." She looks at me squarely. "I didn't have time to be mad or angry at what had happened to us. I mean, I was, but I couldn't focus on it or let it consume me. It happened so fast, and I had to be there for this tiny human all the time."

The expression on my face is probably one of shock and I am not sure what to say.

"My first inclination was to . . . to terminate the pregnancy. I couldn't imagine having a baby, but then I remembered the other women who were forced and . . . well, you know." She looks down at the table. "I finally had a choice about my life, so I chose motherhood . . . partly because I didn't think I could live with the other choice and partly because I thought it would be a good way to shift the focus a bit. Mom helped at first, and Ryan was always around and great, but I knew I had to be there for him all the time. So, really, I couldn't think about what I had been through as much as I probably should have."

I smile. She is so strong, and I feel ashamed for doubting her dedication or understanding of what I'm going through.

"He is a great kid . . . so smart. And he is also very kind. I'm so proud of how well he's done so far in school this year." She smiles, and her pride is evident.

"You're a good mother, Jenna." I look through the photos Jenna is pulling out from the box.

"We have probably been too protective of him, but I know he is going to face scrutiny as he gets older." She gets a worried look on her face.

"What do you mean?" I ask.

"People know, Mallory. Eventually, he is going to learn about how he came into this world." She rises up from the table to let Carter out of the patio doors into the backyard.

"We held him back from starting school for a year just so that he could grow a bit more. I don't want him to have any more challenges than what might come."

I stare at a photo of Jenna and Ryan. It looks like it might have been an engagement photo. I hold it up and smile at her, wanting her to know I don't harbor any resentment toward her.

"Ryan is a good dad too," she says. "I'm sure this doesn't surprise you."

"I don't know," I say. "He and his dad never really got along. Has that changed at all?"

"No, not really, but Chuck does adore Thomas. He is a really good grandfather." She shrugs.

"Well, that's good to hear," I say.

"And Moe," she says. "She and Thomas are like two peas in a pod."

We continue looking through photos. Jenna explains how little Thomas was when he was born. She says they attributed this to her body rebuilding itself and supporting a pregnancy all at the same time right after the rescue. Jenna shares some of the milestones of Thomas's life, as well as how she and Ryan got married in a small ceremony when Thomas was only three and a half years old.

It's really good to be in Jenna and Ryan's home. It seems familiar, and I feel welcomed.

Ryan and Thomas eventually return with pizza. We clear the table and all sit around. Thomas entertains us with the different dinosaur facts from one of his favorite books.

I get up to help Jenna clear the table, and Thomas scurries off to get ready for his bath.

"Mallory, how are things going for you?" Ryan asks. "Did you still need help on your driving test?"

"Oh yeah," I say. "I've sort of put it on hold for now. I'm thinking about going back to school, and checking into that has taken up my attention."

"Cool," he says. "Are you still thinking about psychology?"

"Actually, I'm considering teaching," I say.

"Teaching?" Jenna asks. "Well, that is a change. What makes you want to do that?"

"Well, when I was being held in the village, before I escaped I was sort of a teacher. I taught the young boys how to speak English."

"So, you want to be an English teacher?"

"No, but I did like working with the children. I liked the feeling of teaching them something they didn't know." I realize how strange this must sound. "I know it seems weird, but I had to find the good in my situation, and teaching was one thing I looked forward to. I knew I would be able to focus on a task, and for a few hours each day I wasn't in constant fear."

Ryan stands up, and I can tell he isn't comfortable talking about this. "I'm going to go check on the kiddo and get him into the bathtub."

"Okay, thanks, hon," Jenna says as Ryan disappears down the hall. She turns to me. "Up for some fresh air?"

She opens the patio door and we sit together on the porch. As the sun is going down, she tells me about how she was rescued. She talks about how scared she was after we were separated. I share some of my stories of being traded and transported, and I tell her about my escape, or what I remember of it. We don't get into the gritty details, but we do hit some of the main points.

It feels good to talk about it, and I didn't realize how much I needed to share with Jenna until we start talking.

The night has grown darker, and I realize I rode my bike here. "Well, I'd better get going," I say. "Maybe I'll call Mom to see if she could come pick me up."

"Don't be silly," Jenna says. "Ryan can give you a ride home. He can put your bike in the back of his truck."

"Are you sure?"

"Of course," she says.

We go back inside. As I look at the box of photos sitting on a chair by the table, I notice some pictures of Jenna and me from college. I pick them up and look through them.

"Hey, can I borrow these?" I ask. "I don't think I ever saw the pictures from our graduation and the party."

"Absolutely," she says. "In fact, you can keep them. We have them all archived digitally."

"Of course you do," I say laughing.

Ryan emerges from getting Thomas to bed.

"Hey," Jenna says. "Do you mind giving Mal a ride home? She rode her bike."

"Ah, man . . . no way." He smiles in my direction. "Just kidding. I'll go load up your bike."

I give Jenna a hug, a real hug with my best friend. I've waited to have this feeling for a long time.

"We need to do this again," she says. "Seriously, like, at least once a week."

"For sure," I say.

"And I think you will be a great teacher, Mallory." She smiles and rubs my arm.

As Ryan drives me home, we ride in silence for the first few miles.

"Thomas seems like a great kid, Ryan," I finally say.

He smiles. "He's the best. I didn't know what to expect when Jenna told me she was going to have a baby. I never thought much about having kids, you know."

Ryan and I never even had that conversation about kids and family.

"Well, I can't imagine a better person for that little guy to have as a father," I say.

"Thanks, Mal, that means a lot," he says. "I'm sure this has been a lot for you to take in and adjust to."

"Yes, it has." I find myself being very honest with Ryan too. "But I'm getting there."

When we pull up in front of my house, Ryan gets out and pulls my bike from the bed of his truck. I take the box of photos Jenna gave me, and Ryan walks me to the door, pushing the bike beside me. I give him a quick hug.

"Thanks, Ry."

He quickly turns and walks back to his truck.

Smiling, I go inside. My mom isn't home yet, and I just sit on the couch for a few moments by myself feeling like I've made some progress today.

It's been a good evening.

My thoughts continue to drift to Thomas and the fact that Jenna experienced the rapes and abuse just like I did, but she faced the situation of being pregnant. Sitting back, I put my forearm over my face and can't imagine what she must have felt. What would I have done? I will never be sure, but I don't think I would have been as brave to make the same choice as Jenna.

CHAPTER THIRTY-ONE

Ryan

October 19, 2016

"Boom," Mallory says as she puts the car in park and lifts both hands in the air.

"Well done. I guess I'm buying lunch then, huh?" I laugh.

I remember when we were in high school and Mallory used to brag about how well she could parallel park. Her dad taught her how to do this, and he would challenge her to do it in the least amount of moves possible.

Over the last two months, I have been helping her with driving and preparing to take her test for her license. It has been nice spending time with Mallory. I know Jenna wants us all to get to some level of comfort with each other so we can move forward.

It's hard to believe that Mallory has been back for six months. I have a lot of different feelings about it. Jenna has been on edge but also wants to soften that feeling because Mallory is her best friend, and she desperately wants to get back to enjoying that relationship without the doubt and guilt. I want to help her with those feelings, but I finally realize I've been experiencing some different emotions as well.

The guilt and frustrations were buried a long time ago. Building a life with Jenna and Thomas allowed me to focus on something else besides Mallory's absence. My mom was a big part of helping me through it. She was always the person who could see straight through me. She pointed out how much happier and relaxed I had become once Jenna and I started seeing each other in a more intimate relationship.

I figured if my mother could sense a difference, eventually I would be able to feel it, and she was right. Giving my attention to Thomas and Jenna made it easier to focus on the future and push those negative thoughts about Mallory's situation down and out of my mind. I slowly started to regain my desire to advance in my career and to build a home and family. I even started playing softball again on the college's alumni league.

But now, with Mallory back, some of those feelings have been starting to resurface, and the responsibility is starting to impact me. I've been daydreaming and then feeling terrible when I try to imagine how Mallory must have felt when she returned and found out that Jenna had been rescued years ago and that I had married her best friend.

Mallory and I walk through the big swinging doors of Alfred's, a new bistro downtown. The hostess sits us at a table near a window that looks out over the busy street.

"Well, you're doing great," I say. "When is the test?"

"Thanks. You've really helped me remember all these things . . . you know, the technical things I had forgotten. The test is the first thing on Tuesday, so only this weekend to cram," Mallory says.

"Oh wow," I say. "So you're ready for the driving part, but are you ready for the written test?"

"I'm glad you think I'm so ready for the driving part." She laughs. "Remember what a bad test taker I am? It is really the same as it was ten years ago, except for those stupid roundabouts. Who ever thought roundabouts were a good idea?" We both laugh at this.

"Well, if you need to go over the written exam, I can help you out tomorrow afternoon if you want to come by the house."

"Oh gosh, that is nice of you, but I'm meeting with some of the people from my class for a study session tomorrow afternoon." She frames her face with her hands. "Look at me, such a model student."

"How's school going?" I'm curious, as she's been able to go back to add some education classes.

"It's good. It's great, actually." She closes the menu as the waitress approaches.

We both order iced tea and decide to split a club sandwich with a cup of soup each. I grin as I'm reminded of the old Mallory. She always shared whatever I ordered instead of ordering her own entrée.

The restaurant is filling up with business people having power lunches and meet-ups with colleagues. At the table next to us, two men are talking about quotas and an upcoming sales meeting.

"I think I'll get the additional classes I need to add my education minor in only a year." She takes a sip of tea. "With that under my belt, I can apply for my teaching certificate. It does help that the college has been so supportive."

I recall Jenna telling me that the Goodwin Alumni Foundation stepped in to offer Mallory any classes she needed, tuition-free. They were also able to forgive her student loans, which had been outstanding and allowed her to have a clean slate to start from.

"Do you know what subjects or ages you want to teach yet?" I ask.

"I'm not sure, but I do like middle school-aged kids. Maybe it's because they say it's the most difficult. A lot of educators opt to teach high school or elementary because adolescents are hard to deal with. Eventually, I do think I might like to be a school counselor."

The waitress brings over our food and leaves.

"Well, looks like you found a challenge," I say. "But if anyone can do it, you can, Mallory."

"Thanks," she says. "I mean, just think about us at that age. We were so awkward and weird. I think everyone goes through a stage where they're trying to be grown up but they miss the safety of being a kid."

"True." I smile. "Remember Justin Johanson?"

"Oh my gosh. Yes." Mallory laughs. "Wasn't he the boy who always argued with Mr. Denton in PE class?"

"Yeah. Remember he said that being forced to take a shower after gym was a violation of his religious beliefs?"

"Oh yes," says Mallory. "Trust me, I sat by him in algebra class, right after PE, so I was very aware of his anti-showering beliefs."

It's nice to laugh with Mallory again, and it certainly helps me feel better, but there's still something not quite right about it all. I know it's me and the regret I have for not trying harder to find her and save her.

"This is good," I say, "spending time with you."

"It is, Ryan." She isn't looking at me. She has focused her gaze on the traffic outside the window.

"I'm so happy you and Jenna are spending a lot of time together too," I tell her. "That means so much to her. She said you're moving into your new place soon."

"Yes, this weekend actually." She says this with little enthusiasm.

"Do you not want to get your own place yet?" I ask.

"It isn't that." She sighs. "It's just different. I haven't lived on my own, really ever."

"I guess I hadn't thought of that."

"I mean, it is time, and I need to do it." She takes a bite of the sandwich.

"How has living with your mom been going? I bet she's been very protective, huh?" I say, and realize I'm making a lot of assumptions about the situation.

"Yes. My mom has been a bit overcautious of everything I have done since coming home, and I get it." She looks at me. "I just need to take this step and get into my own place. She's helping me even though I have asked her to let me do this on my own."

"I'm sure it makes her feel good to help you, Mal."

I remember back to how hard it was for Renee, especially in the first few years after Mallory and Jenna disappeared.

"Well, let me know if you need help moving, or anything," I add.

"You bet I will." She winks at me. "I mean, who else gets to have a handyman, driving instructor, and former fiancé all wrapped up into one person?"

I'm not sure if I should laugh or not. Her comment seems to be in jest, but sometimes Mallory can share her feelings in a very sarcastic way. I noticed this during our first meeting since her return, and more recently with some of the interactions she's had with Jenna.

"I'm sorry," she says. "I didn't mean that in a hurtful way. I just have to try to make light of things, Ryan. Sometimes when I think too much or try too hard to make everyone around me feel 'normal,' I lose the need to be real and, according to my therapist, that's important."

"I understand," I say, though not fully buying into the approach. "I know it must be hard."

"Really, it isn't as hard as just learning who I am now and how I can move forward."

She really is an amazing person, and I admire her honesty and how she's been dealing with the return home. We've all been able to find a way to make our friendships a priority, and I'm glad for it.

We finish lunch and walk down the street. Mallory tosses me the keys and slips to the passenger's side door. I drop Mallory off on campus so she can get to her class. As she gets out and then opens the back door to grab her bag, she leans in the open window of the passenger's side and says, "Thank you, my friend."

"You're welcome, and good luck with the test."

I watch her walk down the sidewalk connecting to the quad. There is a scratch in my throat, and I feel like running after her in the worst way, but those days are over. It's just the nostalgia of being on campus and actually seeing Mallory again. I pull away and slowly drive away from the college.

When I get home from the office, the smell of chili hits me as I enter. Jenna has made chili several times this fall for dinner.

"Hey, babe," I say and reach into the refrigerator for a beer.

Jenna looks at the beer I have in my hand. "You seem to be drinking more," she says.

"Hi honey, how was your day? I've missed you," I mimic in a dramatic voice. This is my passive-aggressive way to tell Jenna that I don't appreciate her accusatory tone. This has been our go-to communication method in these situations, but lately I've found myself wanting to use it quite often.

"I'm sorry," she says. "How was your day?"

"Good," I say. "I helped Mallory with driving again. Then I spent the rest of the day boarding a new client, which was good. How was your day?"

"That's nice. My day was okay." Jenna takes the lid off the pot of chili and stirs it. "You've been spending a lot of time helping her lately."

"Does that bother you?" I ask bluntly. I'd asked her earlier before helping Mallory. Not sure how to navigate this friendship we're trying to fall back to, I want to be sure Jenna is good with everything.

"No," she says. "I just mean, it's good you have the time to spend with her and help her, you know?"

"Yep," I say and take a swig of beer. "Well, she has the test on

Tuesday, so I've done all I can to help with that." I decide to change the subject. "Where's Thomas?"

Jenna nods toward the patio doors. "He wanted to play outside with the older kids today. I agreed, but told him they could come to our yard this time."

I look outside and see several of the children bundled in coats and standing around the pile of melting snow leftover from when Thomas and I built a couple of snowmen after the first snowfall of the season.

"I like that he's at least outdoors instead of always wanting to play video games," she says.

"This is true." I take another drink of my beer while looking outside.

"Do you mind calling him inside and making sure the other boys head home okay?" she asks. "It's starting to get darker so much faster these days."

"Sure," I say, sliding the door open.

At dinner, we all seem quiet, even Thomas. I smile as I watch him dip the last part of his cinnamon roll into the bowl of chili.

"Dad?" he asks. "Will you come to school next Wednesday to watch me at the spelling show?"

"Of course, buddy. I can't wait to see you become a spelling champion."

Jenna smiles at him. "You mean spelling bee, Thomas. And are you ready?"

"I think so," he says. "The teacher said I need to practice the night before. Did you print my new words, Mom?"

"You know, your mom was always the winner of our spelling bee every year," I say.

"Really, Mom?" Thomas looks at her to confirm.

The last several months have been significant for him. He seems to be becoming a young boy instead of a little boy or toddler. He has stopped calling us "Mommy" and "Daddy" and now it's the shortened, more mature "Mom" and "Dad." He's been picking up on the behaviors of other kids, and it's interesting to watch him grow this way.

Jenna chuckles. "Yes, but my words were much easier way back then, so I know you are an even better speller than I ever was." She stands up and starts to clear the dishes. "Go get in the bathtub, and I'll be in when you're finished to help you practice a few words before bed, okay?"

I pick up the glasses from the table and take them over to the counter.

"What's going on, Ryan?" she asks, looking at me as if she's dissecting my thoughts.

"What do you mean?"

"You seem off, or preoccupied," she says. She starts to load the dishwasher.

"I'm sorry," I say, unsure what else to say and wanting to avoid an argument.

"Is it Mallory?" she blurts out. "Are you regretting our marriage now that she's back?"

I stop what I'm doing and touch her arm. "J, you know I don't regret our marriage. I love you and Thomas more than anything."

"Do I, Ryan? Do I know that?" Jenna asks. She won't make eye contact.

"It's just . . . I don't know," I say, shaking my head. There are a lot of regrets, but those are all about me and what I didn't do a long time ago.

"What, Ryan, what? I can tell there is something gnawing on you, and you don't talk about it with me, so I feel really disconnected." She shuts the door to the dishwasher in a forceful way.

"I know," I say, lowering my head.

Jenna wipes down the kitchen table with a damp rag. She seems very tired and weary, and I can tell she has been thinking about this and worrying about my lack of engagement recently.

I'm not sure how to tell her I just feel bad. The guilt and responsibility I harbored and then hid for so many years was coming back, and it has seemed to be amplified with Mallory in our lives again.

"Well, it's hard for me too," she says, "but I can't just wait for you to figure it out, and neither can Thomas."

"What do you mean?"

"I mean that I don't want you halfway here, and I'm not going to share you emotionally with Mallory, not in that way." She has clearly given this some thought.

"She's your best friend."

"Exactly," Jenna snaps. "And it's hard enough to be with her and try to help her when I constantly feel bad about what happened to her compared to my experience. Then when I put the additional guilt on top with us being together . . ."

"What do you want me to do?" I ask.

She sits down at the table and puts her head in her hands. "Maybe we need space, Ryan."

I'm not sure if I heard this right. "You mean . . . you want me . . . wait, what are you saying, Jenna?"

I'm thrown off guard and didn't expect this. She and Mallory have been reconnecting, and this seemed to have made her happy. I've tried to be a small part of that, but I guess this has not been going as well for Jenna as I thought.

"I don't know," says Jenna.

"I'm going for a drive," I say.

"And there you go. Just leave instead of talking about this with me."

"I don't want to fight about this, Jenna." I grab my keys from the desk along with my jacket.

"I don't want to fight either, but I also don't want us to walk around each other, afraid to talk about what's really going on," she replies.

"What *is* really going on?" I ask.

I hear Thomas's door open in the hallway.

"Mom . . . are you ready?" he yells out from his room.

"Just go, Ryan," Jenna says through gritted teeth.

"I love you, J," I say, but she just walks right past me as if I never said a word.

CHAPTER THIRTY-TWO

Mallory

October 22, 2016

My shower feels invigorating after a day of working in my new condo. It is strange, but comforting, to put on a pair of old, cut-off sweats and a T-shirt from Old Navy. It's so . . . American. I decide to spend the night enjoying my new favorite guilty pleasure: *The Tonight Show*, starring Jimmy Fallon. I really missed television. Although now it's more "streaming" and "on-demand," I find it to be very interesting and informative. I feel like I'm taking a crash course in all things "2016." Jimmy Fallon was on *Saturday Night Live* years ago and now is the host of *The Tonight Show*. It feels good to laugh, especially to laugh by myself without the fear of being punished or scorned. This is something I'm trying to get used to. I still have a sense of being watched or monitored, and I know it will take time.

I uncork a bottle of wine and pour a glass using the stemware my mother gifted me. Most of the stuff in my new apartment has been a gift from my parents through my mom's efforts. I know my mother feels the need to do everything she can to make me feel normal and comfortable. The guilt and anger she feels is still very evident even though she tries not to show it around me. I still pick up on it. She acts overjoyed and elated to be with me, but I know it's hard to not regret the last nine years we've spent apart. Mom blames herself, she blames the government, she blames anyone she can, and I know it's also part of the process. I guess we're both gradually persisting through our own process at our own pace. I know what happened to me. I know I can't change it, and I know it's a part of who I am . . . at least for a while.

Seeing Patricia has been helping a lot. I never realized a therapist could be so . . . well, therapeutic. She seems more like a friend, but I can tell when she listens to me and when she responds to me, she's not doing it lightly. I appreciate that because it means she knows what she's doing as a therapist, but really, I can tell she is a good person. This makes it so much easier to share with her.

I fluff up the throw pillows on the couch and plop down. After five minutes of searching on the TV and navigating through different apps, I find NBC. This new way of watching television is still a bit strange to me. It actually reminds me of my iPod in college.

Just then, there's a knock on my door. It startles me, probably more than it should have since I'm still so uneasy with noises and disruptions. Getting up slowly, I walk to the door, forgetting that I can look at the porch outside through the security system on my new phone. As I approach the door, I consider grabbing my phone but decide to just go old school and look through the peephole. Ryan is standing outside.

Seeing him out there stirs such a weird feeling inside of me, and I can almost sense this from him too, even through the door. I hesitate for what seems to be minutes but is really only seconds.

"Hey there." I open the door and smile. "Come in."

"Hey." He enters, hastily walking several steps into my condo.

I stand with the door open for a few moments, thinking that Jenna might be behind him, but soon it's clear he's alone.

"Are you okay?" I ask, seeing that he is agitated. It makes me feel uneasy seeing him like this.

"Yeah, yeah . . ." He moves into the living room and walks toward the patio doors. "I just need to see you and talk to you, Mallory." He is pacing by the door and looking out over the balcony.

"Is Jenna okay? What's going on?" I decide to try to be calm. "Can I get you something to drink? Water, wine, kombucha ... did I say that right?" I try to lighten the mood.

"No, I'm good. I just needed to see you, to talk to you. Since you got back ... or rescued, or ... you know, I just can't stop feeling like the biggest piece of shit." He finally turns and looks at me. Tears fill his eyes

"No, Ryan, no—"

"Mallory, you have to let me tell you how I feel. I can't pretend that everything is okay now. I haven't been able to work or sleep or even look at Jenna for the past two months."

He walks over to me, and I sit down at the end of the couch to maybe bring down the urgency in the room. He stalls at the other end, but then finally sits down.

"When Jenna told me about her experience and what she had to go through every day ... I wanted to kill someone. It was all I could do to not just lose it. All I could think about was you going through that same experience, and you were still going through it." He looks down at his hands, which he's been wringing together, and takes a deep breath.

He looks straight at me in the most peculiar way like he's getting ready to tell me all the transgressions of the world.

"Mallory ... I wished you dead."

"Ryan ..."

I start to get up from the couch, but he reaches out and puts his hand on my mine.

"No, please hear me out." His gaze becomes softer, and with his touch, I feel his warmth. I know his intention isn't hurtful, but it's uncomfortable to hear him say this. "I couldn't think about you enduring that torture every day, and it ate me up inside to not be able to help you somehow. I remember the day I asked God to let you die . . ."

He is full on sobbing, and I start to feel my throat closing up.

"What are you talking about?" I mutter.

"It was probably about two years after Jenna had been rescued. She had just returned from DC, and I picked her up from the airport in Omaha. She was so upset because it was the day they decided to defund the search missions to try to find you and other missing American women in Southeast Asia." He shakes his head. "She said they had to redirect efforts to more recent trafficking cases, and they didn't have the budget or resources to keep searching."

"Ryan, you don't have to tell me this. I know you, Jenna, my family, everyone did everything they could, and—"

"No, please . . . you have to know that when I dropped her off at home, I drove to the chapel at Goodwin, on campus. Do you remember?"

I nod as I fondly remember the chapel. Attending a service at least five times a semester was required at our private liberal arts college. We all complained about it, but it really did us all good. It made us more understanding, more forgiving, and more hopeful. We always went to the Wednesday evening service and then hit up the local bar scene after, feeling like we were really rebelling against the establishment. But in truth, we just wanted to continue the fellowship of being around each other. Sometimes the professors would even join us. The entire event was somewhat ceremonial, and we often debated the sermon and what Pastor Brennigan was preaching. It just made us better no matter what our beliefs were.

"I wanted to talk to Pastor Brennigan. I needed to hear a voice of reason, but he wasn't there, anywhere. Then I just sat down, sitting there for probably an hour, not knowing what to do," Ryan says. "I remember pulling my phone out of my pocket and dialing your number, just to hear your voice again, even if it was just telling me to leave a message. Jesus, I probably did that a million times up to that point."

I stare at him with a curious gaze, but not wanting to interrupt again. Even though I don't quite understand, whatever he's trying to tell me is very important to him. The heaviness of what he's trying to say is hanging in the space between us.

"When I hung up the phone, I decided the only thing I could do was pray. So I did. I went to the front of the church and kneeled down and went on and on about you and how much I loved you. It seemed like I talked for at least thirty minutes just describing you and us and our life as we had planned it out. Finally, I stopped and thought about when I proposed to you . . . do you remember?"

With tears in my eyes, I nod.

He chuckles even though he's sobbing. "Remember how I got down on my knee and then went on and on and on? Finally, you asked me, 'Is there a question or what?'"

I've thought about that moment so many times over the last decade. It was one of the memories that kept me pushing forward on many days.

"Then I realized I needed to ask God a question." He looks down again, almost ashamed. "I asked God to take you if you were still alive. I couldn't bear the thought of the anguish and treatment I knew you were probably getting from those filthy pricks. I honestly thought you would be better off dead than to be tortured every day like that . . . like Jenna had described."

"Ryan." I'm not sure what to say. I can tell this is painful for him, and he is experiencing a lot of guilt.

"I am so sorry, Mallory. I actually wanted you to die rather than be in that situation without a way to escape or be saved." He is fully weeping. "I asked God, I pleaded with God to take your life so you wouldn't be in danger anymore. That's all I could imagine and every day it got worse."

I scoot a bit closer to him and can feel the heat of his body. Suddenly, I remember the way he always felt when he was emotional. His feelings radiated from him, and this feels very familiar, but still in a distant way. I want to say something to make him feel better, but I don't have the words.

After several moments of silence, we're just looking at each other.

"Mallory, I am so sorry. There isn't anything I can do to change it, but I had to tell you the truth about where my mind was when you were gone." His eyes are searching mine.

I try to give him a soft look—a forgiving look—but the truth is, I don't feel forgiveness. I haven't ever thought there was anything to forgive of Ryan. I spent so much time thinking about the people at home and how they were living their lives while I was being enslaved. It honestly gave me a sense of peace to think of them happy.

In the beginning, I thought a lot about how I had let them all down and how they must have been struggling to find me and Jenna and answers to where we were. I'm not sure at what point of my captivity I let go of that feeling and started imagining them moving on with life, but the picture in my mind did change along the way. It had to or I would have not survived.

"I gave up on you, Mallory," he says softly. "I was too weak to keep hoping and not good enough of a man to know your strength and to have faith that you would survive. It was so selfish of me, and I just had to let you know how much I regret it."

We sit next to each other on the couch for a long time without speaking or looking at one another. There is an emptiness in the moment, a sort of loss but also acceptance.

I already know. I have known it since seeing him and Jenna upon my return, and I want to be angry at him, at both of them, but I can't find that feeling inside of myself. I love both of them so much it hurts. It hurts beyond understanding to see my past and my future being played out in their daily lives, but I've never been able to hold them responsible. I guess that's what time does, and I have played it out in my mind a million different ways. I never did imagine Ryan and Jenna together, but I can't say it's the worst thing. It did sting initially, but it also gave me a different feeling, almost like a purpose.

More time passes as we sit here in silence, and I swear I can hear Ryan's heart beating outside of his body. Finally, I let out a deep sigh. Ryan shifts his focus to stare at me, waiting for a response. I know he wants me to give him some sign of understanding and to signal that I don't blame him. The television screen is still frozen, waiting for me to press play, so I shut it off with the remote. I sit up straight and shift myself to face Ryan.

"When I was being held in Cambodia, I had a . . . I guess I would say, a friend. There was another woman who was held in the same house. Her name was Phalla, and she was younger than I was. She spoke Vietnamese, and we couldn't communicate with words very well, but somehow we found a way to understand each other. It was hard to be a victim, to be at the mercy of the people around me, but eventually I found ways to make it through the days. At night . . . it was really hard. I remember many nights crying so hard I thought I would choke but having to stifle the noise because I didn't want anyone to hear me. If we were caught crying or acting out in any way, they would either beat us or drug us to keep us quiet."

"Please, Mallory, I don't . . ."

I look at him because I want him to just listen.

"I'm sorry. Go on."

"Phalla would often hear me sobbing late at night. Well, I don't know if she heard me or if she just instinctively knew I was crying. She would find her way to wherever I was and just sit with me. Her eyes were always so sweet, and there was a sense about her that made me feel less scared."

I take a sip of my wine and then hold the glass close to my chest as I continue. I relax a bit and lean back into the couch. This memory makes me focus on the wall in front of me instead of looking directly at Ryan.

"One day we were out in the yard bringing in boxes that had arrived on a truck. Phalla and I were there with three other women. One of them was Middle Eastern, but she spoke English. She seemed to be very smart and knew more about what was going on than the rest of us. Phalla was carrying a big box and tripped and fell, and the box toppled over. Smaller boxes flew out of the box, and one of the guards came over. We tried to go to Phalla and help, but the other woman told us to stop. The guard hit Phalla with the end of his rifle. Poor Phalla, she didn't even scream or cry. He then grabbed her and dragged her, and made her pick up each box one at a time and put it back into the bigger box. When she was done, he motioned for one of the other guards to put the box inside the yard. He held Phalla there and made her watch the rest of us finish unloading the truck.

"I kept looking at Phalla as I passed by each time, hoping to catch her eye, but also trying to be careful not to trip. She never looked at me or any of us. She had such emptiness in her eyes as she just stared straight forward. She knew if she looked at us, it would compromise our safety even more.

"The guards made us all go into the room where we slept. Phalla had to stand out in the yard until the sun set. I had the worst feeling in my gut because I knew she would be badly punished. I had planned to sit with her that night when she was allowed back inside, just to comfort her the way she had done with me so many times. As we started to fall asleep that evening, Phalla still hadn't returned.

"Suddenly, there was a gunshot." Tears come to my eyes and my throat tightens again. I focus on the softness of the couch, the fragrance of fall in the air from a window I cracked earlier, the neutral-colored furniture and the walls of my condo. When I'm ready, I look at Ryan. "Phalla never came back. When I heard that gunshot, I looked at the other women. We were all so quiet and still. Several of them had closed their eyes, and I saw the woman who spoke English look at me with relief, then she looked upward as if to God or Allah or whoever with a nod of approval.

"I couldn't ask her then because there was a guard nearby, and if we were caught talking . . . well, you know what would happen. But several days later, the woman and I were at the water hydrant by ourselves. Finally, I had the privacy and courage to ask about that night and what happened to Phalla. She told me that it was a blessing that she had been killed, and I simply could not understand why she would say this. I asked how she could think Phalla being killed was a good thing. At first it made me angry, and I asked how her family and friends would feel knowing that she had died for something so stupid and senseless.

"When I asked her this, she gave me the strangest look as if I shouldn't question it. But then she explained to me that Phalla's family sold her to the illegal brokers when she was only ten years old and that there was no one waiting for her return or praying for her safety anymore. Phalla would never be welcomed back to her family and her land. I remember she put her hand on my shoulder and said something in her native language and then told me not to discuss it again, sort of in a hushed way.

"I remember standing at that hydrant longer than I should have and realizing my situation was so different from Phalla's. I had people who loved me and cared for me. She had brought me such comfort, almost a sense of compassion when there wasn't anyone out there for her. Nobody cared about her . . . not anymore. I was fortunate compared to her because my family and friends would want to see me again, and I had to get back. They had nothing to do with my circumstances, so I had to do whatever I could to stay alive. Imagine the hopelessness Phalla felt knowing that her own family had sold her, had given her to such monsters. It was my life that brought me back to my life."

"I am so sorry, Mallory," Ryan says. "I know I gave up, but I never stopped loving you." He leans in closer. "I will never stop loving you."

"Ryan . . ."

"I know everything is strange and awkward right now, but I want you to give me a chance to make it right." He has a pleading look on his face.

"Ryan, I love you too, and I will always love you." I can sense the direction he's going with the conversation. "And yes, things are strange and awkward for sure . . . and things are not fair, but I can't . . ."

Suddenly, Ryan reaches out and embraces me. Pulling me close, he just holds me. I'm stiff at first, but then in a moment, his warmth, his smell, his energy . . . it becomes the finish line. It is this feeling I'd kept with me for so long. I pull myself into him closer, and we must have stayed like that on the couch for at least ten minutes. I'm overwhelmed with a sense of completion and satisfaction, but I think it's the memories I had carried of Ryan for so long of how my younger self felt with him, in his strength and in his presence. He is so sure of his future and his place in the world.

Ryan is comfortable strength, he is logical and safe. It's the complete opposite of how I am, but I think that's why I've always pushed the limits and could be the laissez-faire friend who went in different directions depending on the day. Having Ryan there and always on the sidelines was the reason I always could take the risks and be carefree. Knowing he was there has made it easier to do crazy things, like take a gap year and backpack through Asia.

This moment we are having right now has been the carrot drawing me forward for the last nine years. It's what drove me to stay positive and to keep trying to escape. Having Ryan and his solid presence show up suddenly brought me to the realization of how much I still love him.

He shifts his position on the couch, which startles me. I've stopped crying and am almost in a state of euphoria just feeling him hold me and hearing his breathing. I start to pull away from him, but he stops me. As we look at each other, I know we are both trying to work through the right and wrong of the situation, but then it's like my craziness won over his rational sense.

Ryan leans in and kisses me. The touch of his lips to mine spark with energy. It's the feeling of his embrace multiplied by a hundred. I didn't think this part of my being would ever be awake again. I've spent so many years being numb and trying not to have these desires.

Suddenly, I find myself kissing him back and we're like two teenagers again, full of emotion and hormones. Not realizing how eager I was to have Ryan touch me and kiss me, my insides are warm, and I haven't felt this sense of comfort or safety since before my capture. I'm on fire inside and need to satisfy that yearning.

Before I know it, my Old Navy T-shirt is on the floor. Ryan is leaning above me on the couch, and I swear I can hear his heart pounding again. He looks down at me with wanting, but also with concern. He doesn't want to trigger anything bad for me or hurt me in any way.

I simply nod and pull him into me. Before I know it, he has scooped me up off my new couch and is carrying me down the hallway of my new condo into my new bedroom.

CHAPTER THIRTY-THREE

Jenna

October 23, 2016

"Come on, come on, Ryan," I say to myself, trying to call him again. There is still no answer. "Where are you?" I say into the phone, leaving him a message for the second time. I check my text messages. He hasn't texted me back.

I'm shaking all over and unsure what to do. My next call is to my mother.

"Hello," she answers.

"Sandra . . . Mom, Thomas is missing."

"Jenna, what are you saying?" She seems to not understand my words, and I can tell I woke her up.

"I woke up and Thomas was not in his bed, and I looked for him all over the house. And Ryan isn't answering his phone." I pause and already know what her next question will be.

"Well, where is Ryan? Is he working on a Saturday? It's too early for work." My mom is always putting the puzzle pieces together. "Maybe Ryan and Thomas went out for something."

"Mom, please, just come over."

The tears have already started, and I am on the verge of completely breaking down. I feel almost paralyzed, as if my whole world is crumbling around me, and now I have to figure out how to explain to my mother that Ryan has been staying at his parents' house for the past several nights.

"I'm on my way," says Sandra. "Call 911."

"I will."

I quickly hang up and do as she instructed, describing Thomas to the dispatcher and giving her our address.

Then Ryan bursts through the front door. "Jenna!" he shouts.

"Ryan." I run to him before he can even get his jacket off.

"He's gone. He's gone." I'm crying. "Why is this happening?"

"Calm down, Jenna." He puts his hands on my shoulders and steadies me. "What happened?"

"I don't know." I'm crying and my words are muffled against his shirt. "He wasn't in his bed when I woke up, and I looked all over the house for him."

"Did you check the basement? The backyard?" he asks.

I nod as he goes down the hall to Thomas's room. He starts opening all the doors and calling out Thomas's name.

Then there is a loud knock on the door. Through the picture window, I see two uniformed officers standing outside.

"Ryan," I call, realizing that I am standing in my pajamas in the living room.

Ryan goes to answer the door, and I go to my bedroom and grab my robe.

"The neighbors," I say as I return to the kitchen where Ryan is talking with the officers, "he plays with the neighbor kids."

"Yes, ma'am," one of them says. "We'll go check with the neighbors now."

"Do you mind if I look through the house?" asks the other officer.

"Of course. Yes, please look everywhere you want," Ryan says, and I nod my head.

"Do you have a picture of Thomas we can see and use?"

I rush over to the mantle and grab the frame with Thomas's recent school picture. I hand it to the officer.

My mother shows up and immediately comes over and embraces me. She puts her arm on Ryan's shoulder and gives him a stern look.

"Can I make coffee?" she asks, not really waiting for an answer before heading into the kitchen.

One officer leaves to knock on the neighbors' doors, and the other starts down the basement steps to look through the house.

I race to the bedroom to quickly throw on some clothes. I am breathing heavily and start to experience a numbness all over my body, and then I feel lightheaded.

I hear the officer open Thomas's bedroom door. There is some commotion, and then I hear it: Thomas's voice.

"Is that a real gun?" my son asks.

I run to his room. Ryan and I stand in the doorway in shock as we watch the officer kneel down and talk to Thomas.

"It sure is, buddy," the officer says. "Are you okay?"

I run to Thomas, grab him, and hold him close.

"Mom, what's wrong?" he asks. "Why is the policeman in my room?"

He pushes himself out of my embrace to run to Ryan and gives him a hug.

"Dad, you're home." He rubs his eyes. Then he walks down the hall to the bathroom.

"He was asleep under his bed, ma'am," says the officer.

"Oh my goodness," I reply. I hadn't even thought to look under his bed.

We apologize to the officers, thanking them for coming so quickly. They each take a cup of coffee to go but assure us that we aren't the only parents who have been through a scare like this. The older officer says he has actually been on several calls where a child has hidden somewhere and then fallen asleep in the house.

After my mom squeezes and hugs Thomas until he can't handle any more, she says her goodbyes, making Thomas promise to not sleep under his bed anymore.

He tells us he was pretending to be a bear and hibernating in a cool, dark place. Although it's reasonable and irresistible to love Thomas's rationale for falling asleep under his bed, I feel that maybe he had also been upset. Maybe he woke up and saw that Ryan wasn't in our bed or even in the house.

"Mom, can I have pancakes for breakfast?" Thomas rubs his eyes, still in his Jurassic Park pajamas.

"Hey, buddy," Ryan says. "How about if I make you pancakes?"

"I can do it," I say to Ryan.

"Please," he says, looking at me with a softness in his eyes. "Jenna, let me make us breakfast."

I toss up my hands and decide to take a shower, needing to feel something calming and soothing. I'm emotionally drained but have an overwhelming sense of relief.

When I get out of the shower, I feel like I've just run a race or finished working out and I'm tired. It's only nine in the morning. I throw on some jeans and a sweatshirt that feels appropriate for a Saturday.

I sit on the edge of the bed, breathing deeply. My hair is dripping, and then I realize I'm also crying. I usually try to regroup and shift my mindset when I feel sad or hopeless, but this morning, I let myself cry. The thought of Thomas missing or being taken from me is my biggest fear, and it has clearly brought up some buried feelings as well as surfacing my vulnerability.

Guilt starts to consume me as I think back to when I learned I was pregnant with Thomas. I remember how sometimes I would resent the tiny human growing inside of me and the part of my life he represented. I never told anyone about those moments, even after he was born, but sometimes I would wonder if I had made the right choice. *Am I being punished for those thoughts now?* After so many years of questioning and slowly becoming the mother that Thomas deserved, I finally thought I had gotten past all the doubt and regret. I knew there were still parts of me that were broken, but

Thomas makes it all work. He makes my life purposeful. He makes me better . . . he makes us all better.

After a few moments, I start to get my wits about me again. I pull the duvet up on the bed and put the pillows in place on the my side to match the other side that Ryan didn't use the night before. The sinking feeling hits me again.

Having Mallory return home has been the best and worst thing all at the same time. It isn't fair for anyone, but I've felt like the status quo has been shifted, and I'm going to be the not-so-lucky involved party.

I can hear Thomas in the kitchen giggling as Ryan quietly roars. This is a favorite activity between the two of them. Thomas will name some prehistoric creature and then Ryan will identify the best roar to go along with it. They haven't done this for a while, and I thought maybe Thomas had grown out of it, but today he seems to be more the toddler rather than the school-aged, independent boy he has quickly evolved into since starting kindergarten.

Ryan and Thomas both look up at me as I enter the kitchen. The smell of pancakes and maple syrup fills the room.

"Dad said we can go to the library this morning. I want to check out the new video game, Ark Park." Thomas put the last bite of his pancake in his mouth.

"Um, I said if it was okay with you." Ryan looks at me.

I pause at first, but then my exhaustion gives in and I decide I don't have a fight in me today.

"Sure, buddy. Why don't we all go?" I kiss Thomas on top of his head, pick up his plate, and carry it to the sink. The aroma of the coffee fills the air as I pour a fresh cup. "Thomas, can you please go to your room and get ready?" I ask. He quickly hops down from his seat. Carter saunters into the kitchen when he hears the chair move. He is checking under Thomas's chair for any potential crumbs. "And don't forget to make your bed."

"I will, Mom," Thomas says, and he rushes out of the kitchen.

"Can we talk, J?" Ryan begins clearing the rest of the dishes from the table.

"I don't know," I say. "Does it really matter at this point?"

"What do you mean?" He refills his cup of coffee and brushes against my arm when he puts the pot back.

"I'm not sure how I feel right now. It has already been a hard day, and it only just started." I am proud of myself for being honest with him.

"I was with Mallory last night." He blurts out as if he is confessing and expecting some type of punishment.

"Yeah?" I look at him as if I already knew this.

"I just want us to be honest with each other, J," he says.

"Well, if I'm being honest, then I should tell you . . ." I am really at a loss for words at this point. I think I've been preparing myself for this since Mallory came home, but I hadn't expected it to come on top of one of the scariest Mom moments I've ever experienced.

Ryan is looking at me, anticipating my rage to take over and for me to be upset with him. He is almost wincing as he waits for me to finish.

"I should tell you that . . . Jesus, Ryan, I don't know. I really just don't know how I feel about any of this anymore." I shrug my shoulders and take a drink of coffee. I walk away from him to the patio doors and look outside at the cloudy sky. "I do know that Thomas needs me, and he needs you too. That is my first priority."

"I know," Ryan says. "And I'm here, Jenna. I'm here and want to be with you and Thomas."

There is a long moment of silence.

"Well, I guess we are going to the library."

As I walk down the hallway, I decide that Ryan can decide what direction he needs to go in. I am exhausted thinking about it over and over in my head and talking about it is pointless to me. I know we are all dealing with an overload of feelings. I need to be concerned with my own reactions and how Thomas is feeling in the middle of our emotional navigation.

When Thomas and I come down the hall to leave for the library, Ryan is standing at the front door.

"Oh good, you guys are ready," he says and smiles at me. "Perfect timing, I have the car all warmed up for us."

CHAPTER THIRTY-FOUR

Mallory

October 25, 2016

As I walk out of the DMV, I'm smiling, feeling like I have just conquered a significant step toward a new life as a woman in her thirties. I am eager to start looking for a car and to be driving again on a regular basis. My mother has been great about transporting me when needed, but I know it's starting to become an inconvenience. She offered to give me my father's old truck until I'm able to afford something new.

I sit on the bench near the courthouse to wait for her to pick me up. The air is crisp this morning and the trees are golden-brown with leaves that drift away and dance around the street. I watch as the traffic slowly makes its way around the brick-paved square of Everly Falls. There is a buzz in the air as people shuffle in and out of the courthouse. Some are in suits, some having serious conversations as they walk in pairs, holding coffees, and carrying papers or briefcases.

As I look down the street, I hear my name from the other direction. Looking to my right, I see Jenna approaching me.

I'm not ready for this, even though I know at some point we are going to have to address our strange situation and the tension between everyone. I really wanted to talk to Patricia about it at my next therapy appointment. From the way she approaches me, I know Jenna knows.

I haven't talked to Ryan since he left me early on Saturday

morning when he got a voicemail from Jenna. He hasn't tried to reach out to me, and I'm glad because I simply don't have any words to talk about what happened. In the moment, it all felt so right. But now that I've had a few days to think about it, it all seems so wrong. How could I have so easily torn apart the life Jenna and Ryan had made together? Thinking back to that night, what felt like a declaration of intimacy now seems so forced and inauthentic, like when people say they want to stay in touch and never do.

Jenna walks up slowly and sits down next to me on the bench. We sit in silence for several minutes.

"He waited, Mallory," she finally says.

"What?" I ask.

"He waited for a long time. He was a wreck," she continues. "All he did was work, and from what I understand, that was going south pretty quickly. He kept to himself and wouldn't even go see his family. He was depressed, and we all were so worried about him."

"Jenna, I don't know . . ."

She takes a deep breath, which makes me stop speaking.

"He loved you . . . still loves you, so much. I know this." She pauses. "When I was rescued, I knew it was even more difficult for him because he had to deal with what I had been through and live with the knowledge that you were still going through the same and possibly worse."

"I'm so sorry, Jenna."

"I know you are. I am too. We're all sorry. I am so tired of everyone being sorry."

She leans forward and stretches her arms, then regains her posture. It's clear she has to talk to me about this and has given it some thought, so I need to give her that space.

"I could deal with you and Ryan getting back together. I could handle it, you know." I can feel her grin slightly even without looking at her. "I always knew he wasn't in love with me the way he was with you all those years ago." She pushes her sunglasses away from her eyes and onto the top of her head.

"I probably wasn't in love with Ryan when we got married either, not like that anyway. It was just an easy thing, I guess. Not easy, but easier than it would have been with someone who wasn't grieving or hurting the way we both were because of what had happened to us, and"—there is a catch in Jenna's voice—"because we thought we had lost you forever."

I want to reach out to her, but I feel like I can't. Not now. Not as the person who caused this hurt for her.

"It's all because of you that we're together. I guess it would only make sense that because of you, we wouldn't be together anymore either." She pauses again. "My heart has been broken before, and I can handle it again. That isn't what I worry about. I am strong, Mallory, you know that. I've lost my father, I've lost you—my best friend—and I've lost myself many times over, in fact." She takes a deep breath. "But what I can't lose is Thomas. That is the heart I don't want to break. That is the heart I have to protect. I don't want him to know loss the way I've known it. I'm his mother. It is my job, and that is the choice I made." Her voice is escalating.

"Jenna," I start to respond, but the words just aren't there.

"It's okay," she says more calmly. "You don't have to tell me we will work it all out and it will be fine. I know families break up all the time, and it isn't the end of the world and sometimes—in fact, often—it's even better in the long run."

She stares off into the distance. "When I decided to have Thomas I had come to terms with the idea of being a single mother. I couldn't ever imagine a man in my life who could deal with the terror of what had happened, or to be a father to Thomas knowing he was the product of that horrible part of my life. I was ashamed of the past, and it has taken me so long to learn how to let go. Whenever I was around Ryan, that shame disappeared. I have grown to love that man, and I know he loves me too, Mallory. He is confused. I am confused." She rubs her eyes. "Fuck . . . everyone in this situation is confused. But one thing I know for sure is that my family is worth fighting for."

I take in what Jenna is saying, trying to find the words to respond. Instead, I just nod as it soaks in. She is so raw right now. She has a plan of what she wants to say, but that doesn't take away from the genuineness of the emotion behind it, and I know that she is holding on by a thin string. The abrasion of her words rubs like sandpaper all over me, exfoliating the surface down to the reality beneath it, seeping underneath my skin and cutting through to my veins.

"I can't force Ryan to be my husband or to stay with me and Thomas. I won't do that. I wouldn't want that because it wouldn't be real, and it wouldn't be right. I also can't be that person who keeps him from you, if that is what the two of you both want.

"But I want you to know, I do love him, Mallory. Like I said, it was different at first, when we got together and even when we first got married. But when I see him as a father and I see him light up when Thomas does something to make him proud, I can tell he belongs right where he is. He came back to life slowly. Our love has been the kind that has evolved and changed, but it is the kind you can rely on and the kind of love that a child needs growing up."

We sit in silence for several minutes.

My mom's car pulls up down the street.

"I know you have to go," says Jenna. "I knew you would be around here this morning, and I just wanted to talk to you and tell you how I was feeling. I want to be angry, Mallory. I want to be upset with him and with you, but I don't even get to do that. I can't blame you or hold you responsible. Maybe I was just the fool who thought we could all be in each other's lives and make it all work somehow. I don't know."

"Jenna," I say, clearing my throat. "You're not a fool. You're right."

"Well, it feels foolish to me for thinking it could all be normal somehow."

"You're right," I say. "I don't know that it will ever be normal, but I know it can't ever be the same as it was years ago. We just aren't the same people."

"No, we aren't." She stands up and looks at me. "I'll leave now. I love my family, Mallory. Ryan and Thomas are my rock. They are how I put myself back together." She pauses. "And I love you too."

I reach up and take her hand as she starts to walk away. She turns and, with an exhausted look on her face, I see her desperateness, almost an expression of surrender. I stand and our eyes meet each other. In our gaze at that brief moment, so many memories, thoughts, and fears pass between the two of us.

Then she pulls her hand away.

As Jenna leaves, clarity suddenly washes over me. For the first time since returning, I realize that sometimes you just can't go back.

I walk down to where my mom is parked.

"How did it go?" she asks as she begins pulling away to drive home.

"You know, it went really well," I respond, still a bit caught off guard by Jenna's presence. I pull on my seatbelt.

"Yay, so you passed," Mom says in full cheerleader mode.

"Yep, I'm official." I hold up the temporary license.

"Was that Jenna I saw? Did she go with you?"

"Uh, no. She just happened to be in the area."

"Well, that's a nice surprise," she says. I can tell by her expression that she notices my flushed complexion but is choosing not to say anything.

I look her in the eyes. "Mom."

"Yes, dear?"

"I'm going to move away."

"What are you talking about? You just moved into your new place." She glances over at me as we drive by the park.

I'm not ready for this conversation either, but I know it has to happen.

"Mallory, I don't know what you're thinking."

"I know it seems crazy," I say, "but I need you to trust me and to know I am doing this only because I have to."

"Where will you go?" She starts to breathe heavily, like she might start crying.

"I'm not sure. I just know that if I'm ever going to be a full and happy person, I need to do this. I know it doesn't make sense, but I can't stay here. I can't be a ghost anymore."

"A ghost?" she says. "That's absurd."

She pulls into the drive of my new condo. I see my dad's old truck in the driveway. Richard had dropped it off earlier.

"Mom," I say, turning toward her. "You have done so much for me. You and I are unbreakable, but I need to create a new life for myself away from here. I wouldn't be able to say that now if it weren't for everything you've done for me."

She puts her hand on top of mine and doesn't say anything else. She knows that what I'm saying is true, and she knows she has to let me go. We are both strong enough to do it because it is our choice to do it. Mom knows she can count on me, especially with my father and when the time comes to make decisions. She knows wherever I am, she will visit me often. But she also knows that if I am ever going to have my freedom, I need to create it for myself.

As I walk into the condo, I feel a new sense of purpose. I feel like I am really moving in the right direction. Looking at the pile of broken-down boxes by the door to my garage makes me give in and smile at the thought of taping them all back up and repacking everything.

Where I'm going, I haven't decided, but I know it's the right decision. Suddenly, I feel that adrenaline rush I felt that day running through the desert. I am taking a risk, but one that will be worth it in the end. This, I know, is the sacrifice I have to make in order to bring peace to the people I love the most.

CHAPTER THIRTY-FIVE

Mallory

October 28, 2016

I hang up the phone with the registrar's office. The arrangements to drop my classes at Goodwin are complete. My hope is to enroll in some type of accelerated program to get my teaching certificate when I settle in the DC area. My aunt lives in nearby Richmond, which is what makes me decide on DC. I have also considered moving to California because I've always felt a sense of comfort and connection with Patricia, my therapist, and I think some of that is due to her being a native Californian. But in the end, I know it will be nice to have family nearby, and it will also make this transition easier on my mother.

When I tell Patricia of my decision to relocate, she is surprisingly supportive. She listens to everything that has happened. She actually tells me she admires my decision and believes it has come from a place of growth, agreeing that going backward isn't the answer for me. She is also pleased that I can continue my therapy with Dr. Kramer, who had helped me upon my return to the US.

I have pretty much finished packing up all the stuff from my condo. It didn't take long, as I really don't have much. All I have left to pack is what is left in my closet. I pull one of the larger wardrobe boxes into my bedroom and start to reconstruct it to pack the few hanging clothes I have. Looking around the bedroom, I can still smell the fresh paint my mom and I had painted through the entire condo less than a month ago.

As I am packing up my clothes, my mind wanders to Ryan. I visited him yesterday to tell him about my decision to leave. At first, I wasn't going to give him any type of explanation or anything. I was just going to drop in and say goodbye to him and Jenna together, but I needed to get some closure on the situation. This was also the advice Patricia gave me when I shared my plans with her.

"Is it because of me?" Ryan asked as he looked up from his desk.

I had stopped into his office. I knew it would likely be the best way to catch him alone.

"No, Ryan," I said. "It's because of me, and I need to have a life that doesn't cause discontent and confusion for everyone."

"Mal, you can't blame yourself for that."

"I know, and I'm not blaming myself. I can't change what happened in the past, Ryan. But I can change what might happen in the future."

"Where will you go?" He seemed caught off guard by my decision, but I did sense a small indication of relief.

"I'm actually moving to DC. Aunt Joan lives close by in Richmond, and I think it might be a place where I can find my future, a purpose in my life. I visited there a lot when I was younger, and I was there right after I returned to the United States. I'm going to give it a chance and see where I land."

"I guess I don't know what to say."

"You don't have to say anything, Ryan." I sat down across from his desk. "This," I motioned with my hand, pointing at him and then myself, "this *thing* between us is not right. Last Saturday was nice, but it was not the reality we both need. I will always love you, Ryan, but I need to let go of what was, and I need you to let it go too."

His posture changed, his shoulders rolling forward and his eyes widening. He swallowed, clenched his lips, and nodded.

"You and Jenna have Thomas. He is a wonderful and beautiful

little boy who needs both of you in his life. Knowing that you three are all together and happy makes me happy too, and I need you to know that and believe that."

"I know. I love that kid, and I love Jenna too," he said and hesitated. "But what we had was special, Mal."

"Yes. It was special . . . at one time. But honestly, Ryan, it has to be over. We aren't those people anymore."

I thought this would be easier, but seeing him still made my heart burn inside my chest. I tried to stay reserved, but it was like trying to stop cracked glass from shattering into tiny pieces.

As I looked into his warm, familiar eyes, I reminded myself of the script I had prepared in my mind. "This isn't easy for any of us. I know you have a lot of guilt and feel responsible in some way, but I need you to know I forgive you. I'm ready to move on. But you need to let me do that."

"Mal . . . " Ryan said, his eyes pleading with me. "What if, I mean, this is a mistake? I made a mistake all those years ago of letting you go, or not trying harder to convince you to let me go with you, or even just trying harder to find you. Will we regret this moment ten years from now?" There was something else in his eyes then, something pulling in the other direction and, as subtle as it was, I realized he wanted my permission, my blessing, to keep loving Jenna and Thomas.

In that very moment, it was like I was on the outside looking at the entire world spinning. I could see the two of us sitting across from one another, discussing the situation. I wanted to be weak and to just give in to my deep desire to have Ryan's unconditional love and attention, but I knew that was the coward's way out. I was strong, so much stronger than I was months ago, or even years ago before it all happened. *I can do this. I have to do this.*

"If you want to show me how much you do care, then all I ask is that you take care of Jenna and Thomas. I love her so much, Ryan, and she needs you. She cares for you, and truly loves you. You have found a way to make a life together, and it is an amazing life you both deserve."

I stood up, and then Ryan came around the desk. As he looked directly at me, I wanted to scream out and just ask him to make all of this go away and take me back to those years so long ago when we would spend Sundays on walks, sipping coffee, and talking about our amazing future together. But then a stronger, more peaceful emotion came over me, and I regained my confidence that this was the right decision.

"Promise me if you need help, or if you need me, you will reach out," he said, looking at me through his puffy eyes.

"You know I will," I promised, but it was only a half-truth.

Ryan pulled me into him. With my head against his chest as we embraced, we stood together for a long time. Finally, I pulled away and turned to leave. For a split second, I thought he started to say my name, but then just cleared his throat. I'm almost glad he didn't manage to get the word out, or I might have been running back to him, or at least would have slipped a glance back at him, and I knew I couldn't. I had to keep moving in the opposite direction.

My eyes were full of tears, and even though my soul was crushed, I was at peace knowing it was the right thing to do. Each step I took, I was closer to leaving the grief of what could have been behind and walking into a future that was mine.

Smiling softly, I return my focus to the box of clothes in front of me. I am actually proud of myself and have a sense of accomplishment from today. I am ready to move on.

I push the box against the wall. I have some college friends who are coming tomorrow to help me load the moving truck. My mom argued with me, wanting to pay to have a professional moving company relocate me, but I told her I could handle it. I did agree to let her and Richard drive out there. Yesterday, they took my dad's old truck and traded it in for a newer car and told me they wouldn't take no for an answer.

Richard selected a Toyota Prius and told me it would be great on gas mileage and easy to park in a city. He is a very practical man, and I'm happy he and my mother have each other. It took a while to warm up to the idea of my mom with anyone other than my dad, but if it had to be someone, I'm glad it's Richard. After meeting him officially, I quickly realized he is kind and very understanding, and there is a sense of calmness about him. And my mother is just as important to him as he is to her. It's good to know she has a person wanting to help her and be there for her just like she has always been that person for other people most of her life.

I'm glad my mother has someone in her life to fill the void left by my dad, a void I never realized was so vast until I finally gathered the courage to visit my father in the care facility.

I certainly hadn't been ready for the emotions of seeing my dad in the advanced stages of this disease. He was not the same person he used to be. I tried talking to him several times when I thought he understood who I was, but when he responded, it was as if he was talking to a stranger. Every now and then on my visits, I would catch him looking at me with a familiar expression, and he would call me "Renee" or think I was someone else. It was heartbreaking, but it was also probably better to not have him know what had happened to me. If he was able to comprehend the truth of my situation, I know it would be worse for him.

This morning, I visited him to say goodbye.

He was sitting in his recliner in his room watching a replay of the Dodgers in a playoff game. He'd always been a baseball fan. When I came into the room, I sat with him and watched as well. He looked at me and just smiled.

"Best season they had, in my opinion," he stated, gesturing vaguely to the game. "Eighty-eight, the year Hershiser broke Drysdale's record of fifty-nine consecutive shut-out innings."

"Yeah, a twenty-year record, right?" I said, nodding. He had told me this story many times, and I watched the grainy replays of that series numerous times with him when I was young.

"The Dodgers won the series that year even though Oakland was favored."

I sat and watched him be completely engrossed in the game. He was as happy as he could be right now, and I had accepted that. But it was still hard.

"I love you, Daddy." I leaned over and hugged him and kissed him on the forehead. This was a bold move because when I had tried this before, he was startled, not realizing who I was.

This time he reached up and patted my arm. "I am proud of you, Malsy."

Tears immediately spilled from my eyes. Hearing him say this brought me back to when I was a little girl when he would cheer me on after learning a new chord on the guitar. He called me Malsy my entire childhood, and when I heard him say it right then, I knew I was making the right decision. I didn't try to push or prolong the situation but just quietly left his room. Knowing that might be the last time my father and I spoke, I was grateful for the moment.

Now, in my old-new apartment, I gather up all of my bedding and put it into plastic bags and then into a big box. I plan to stay at my mother's house tonight so that everything is ready when the crew arrives tomorrow to help me load. As I look up to the top shelf in the closet, I see a box I missed. I open it up and realize it's that box of photos Jenna gave me. I never looked through the photos. Maybe, at the time, I was afraid of how it would make me feel, or maybe it was just my way of keeping the memories in the past, but somehow now it seems like the right time to do it.

There's a photo of the three of us on the green lawn of the quad where we lined up for the graduation ceremony. We all had such a look of innocence. I look at the other people in caps and gowns in the various photos and try to remember their names.

Some of the pictures are from the party after graduation. There are so many people who look familiar, but I can hardly remember anyone. Jenna had written the names on the backs of some of the photos; she has always been really good at knowing who people are. She can probably even remember what classes they took or what their major was.

There is a picture of Ryan with some of the guys he played softball with. They are all standing on the patio, and there are people dancing in the background. That day was one of the best. We were all full of anticipation. A smile crosses my face as I continue looking through all of them. The feeling of nostalgia is nice, but I look at our faces and it seems like a lifetime ago.

Seeing these photos is good for me. Instead of looking at them as something I want back or something I need to remember and get back to, I look at them and just accept them as memories. Six months ago, I wouldn't have been able to do that. Now I am giving myself permission to move on, as Patricia has guided me to do.

Then there is a photo of me and Jenna doing some silly pose with our backs to each other. As I study the people around us in the picture, a rush of adrenaline suddenly hits me as if I'm at the top of a roller coaster, ready to descend fast. Behind us in the photo, I see a man. I've seen him before, and it was not at my graduation. I have seen him since then. I saw him in Cambodia. I blink my eyes and look again. Yes, that's the man.

My heart feels like it's leaping out of my chest. I try to remain calm, but it's all a blur. The next thing I remember is knocking on Jenna's door. I'd ridden my bike as fast as I could over to her house, not even thinking about calling first. There isn't an answer, and then I realize she's probably still at work or maybe with Thomas. The air is cool, and it's late in the day.

And then I hear her voice. "Mallory?" she says.

She is walking around the side of the house with a rake in her hand.

"Oh good," I say. "You're home."

"Are you okay?" By the look on her face and change of posture when she realizes it's me, I can tell she's still carrying some ill feelings. She looks at my bike. "It's kind of cold for a bike ride."

"I'm sorry," I say. "I had to come over right away. Do you remember?" I pull the photo from the pocket of my jacket and hand it to her, trying to catch my breath.

She takes it from my hand and looks at it. Then she looks at me.

"Are you feeling all right? Do you want to come inside, have some water?" Avoiding my eyes, she walks up the steps and opens the front door.

"The picture, Jenna? Him?" I say again.

"Here, come in and let me get you a glass of water."

I follow her into the kitchen, and she sits the photo on the table. Taking a deep breath, I try to calm down, realizing I've caught her unexpectedly.

She brings over two glasses of water and picks up the photo, looking at it again.

"That was a great day, wasn't it?" she says, smiling, tilting her head to the side.

"Jenna, do you recognize him?" I point to the man in the photo.

"I don't." She is shaking her head. "Oh, wait," she says after a pause. "Wasn't that the guy with Sue, or was it Sarah? Do you remember her name?"

"I don't know who he was with, but I remember him." I feel short of breath again and take a drink of water.

"Okay." Jenna just looks at me with a blank, half-concerned look. "Did he go to Goodwin?"

"I think he was in Cambodia, Jenna," I say slowly and gravely so that she understands the situation.

She looks at the photo again, sort of squinting her eyes and shaking her head.

"Mallory, I don't remember him from over there."

"I do," I say. "I remember seeing him in that garage, the one I was in before they took me to another place, when we were separated."

"Oh my god, Mallory." Her grip on the photo tightens and the color drains from her face. "He was the guy who gave us the number . . . the number of the lady, or his cousin, or aunt . . . the taxi driver in Thailand." She stands up.

We are both breathing heavily and pacing around Jenna's kitchen table.

"What do we do?" I ask.

"I don't know." She goes to her purse and grabs a small address book. "I used to have the number of an agent at Homeland Security. I know I have one in my office at work."

"Wait, I have a number for Agent Sommers, the one who helped me when I returned. Should I call her?"

"Yes." Jenna sits down. I can feel her energy change, and just like that, we are on the same team again.

CHAPTER THIRTY-SIX

Jenna

January 10, 2017

Mallory and I wait in the chairs outside of the room where they said Sarah McAllister is giving her statement. It has taken the past two months to track her down and convince her to help us.

I look over at Mallory. I have noticed so many new things about her each time we've gotten together. She's starting to regain that unbridled confidence that I always envied in her growing up. There is a strength I've started to see, and it gives me hope that she will one day find happiness.

To say I'm upset she's moved away wouldn't be fair or honest. There are still many mixed emotions between us, but beneath them is the strong foundation of the bond that has always been between us and will be forever. I understand why she has moved away, and I will always be grateful for her selfless decision to put my family and my happiness before her own. I do want her to find herself and to find peace again, and I'm not sure coming back home to Everly Falls would do that for her. But I do miss her.

Now when we're together, even though much of it has been to build a case with the Department of Homeland Security, I feel a newness to her, a revival of her spirit and being. She sits up straighter and her smile is more genuine, not forced like it seems to have been right after her return. She seems to be doing well in her new life in Washington, DC. She moved into an old restored building close to campus where she is going to start classes in February. She also just started working at the college in the academic counseling office. I got to see her in her new life when I stayed in her apartment last night to prepare for today.

Sarah McAllister had been in our graduating class at Goodwin, and we went through the alumni office to track her down. It wasn't easy. Her address on file took us to a dead end. Then Ryan actually remembered having some classes with her, and he thought she was from a small town in Oklahoma, if his memory served him correctly.

When we gave this information to the agents we were working with, they finally found her. They had been able to locate her mother who still lived there. Sarah was married with a family now and had been living in Oklahoma City for the last eight years. When Agent Sommers told us that Sarah had refused to give them any information about the man in the photo, we didn't know what to do.

They were able to identify the number I had called in Thailand from my cell phone records all those years ago, but it was also a dead end.

Agent Sommers seemed very interested in this case when Mallory and I contacted her. She said because we met this man in America, the Department of Homeland Security was able to possibly extradite him if he was no longer in the States. But the first step was identifying who he was.

"What if I'm wrong?" Mallory asked at one point.

"What do you mean?" I asked.

"Maybe I've convinced myself that he was in Cambodia. What if this is all for nothing?"

"I have never seen you so convinced of anything before," I said.

"True," said Mallory. "I also can't imagine Sarah being so against it if she didn't know he had something to do with it."

When Sarah refused to talk with the agents, Mallory and I decided to try ourselves. At first, the closest we'd gotten was when we called her at work. She hadn't been answering our calls, so we figured out how to reach her. We knew her married name was now Sarah Willamont and she was a real estate agent in Oklahoma City. We finally reached her at her firm one day.

"Sarah, please just give us a moment to explain," Mallory said. I was on the other end of the three-way call.

"No." She had a very upset and hushed tone of voice. "I'm sorry about what happened to the two of you. I truly am, but I'm married and have three children. I'm finally away from all of that. It took me a long time to get away from those jerks, and I'm not looking back."

"Sarah," I said softly, "we understand, but—"

"I said no," she snapped. "That is my past, and I want to leave it there. I can't allow myself to think about it or put my family at risk again. You have no idea how hard it was for me. Please don't contact me again."

At that point, we weren't sure if we could ever get any information from her. Agent Sommers said we could subpoena her for testimony if we could get a judge to agree to it, but that was risky too because she still might not provide information, and then she would be exposing herself and her family.

Mallory agreed to go with me to Oklahoma City and see if we could find her and talk with her in person.

We arrived and drove straight to her office from the airport, but we didn't go in because we weren't sure how to make it seem less like an ambush. Getting her alone was important, so we didn't jeopardize her safety or ours. I had a feeling this really was part of her past and one she hadn't shared with many people.

We decided to find one of the real estate properties she had listed for sale. We went to a coffee shop and used the phone to call and set up an appointment to see the house later that day. As she pulled away from her office in a bright red Lexus, we followed her to the house. We watched from down the block as she got out. Then we noticed she wasn't alone, which was not ideal, but we understood it was probably a policy when showing a house to people for the first time.

"What should we do?" asked Mallory.

"What can we do? I guess we just go in and tell her who we are and what we're doing," I said, adopting the straightforward approach.

Typically, I liked to have more of a plan, but I figured we could not waste the opportunity.

"Okay," she said. "Once we go in, I will try to get the other person with her away long enough for you to talk to her. Do you think you can convince her?"

"I will do my best."

As we walked up to the front door, the older gentleman with Sarah introduced himself to us and opened the door to let us inside.

"I am Conner Blankenship, I work with Mrs. Willamont," he said in a thick Southern accent. "Which one of you pretty ladies is Mrs. Carter?"

A small smile came to my face, thinking back to earlier in the day when Mallory had called to make the appointment and realized she needed a fake name. She'd then evidently thought of the dog we both were fond of and became Mrs. Carter on the spot.

"Oh, that would be me," said Mallory with a dramatic wave of her hand.

We walked into a lavish entryway and saw Sarah, a tall, slender woman, standing by the mantle in the formal living room. She had just turned on the fireplace and was walking over to a set of switches on the wall, flipping on several, including the lights to the very tall Christmas tree in the corner.

As she came in our direction, she halted, recognizing us. We were busted.

I had forgotten how public our faces were because of all the media that surrounded our story, and especially for the people who did actually know us at one time.

I was expecting the worst, but she must have decided to play along, showing us the different rooms in the house and then the backyard. Her nervousness was showing because she rushed through the details and became increasingly agitated.

"And here, let me show you the attached garage." We all followed her through a side entrance and mudroom. "Conner, would you mind shutting all the lights down? I think we will be finished up here soon."

"Yes, ma'am," he said, turning in the other direction.

As we followed her into the garage, she immediately turned to us.

"What the hell are you doing?" she asked. Her face was red with anger. But then it turned into something else, and she started to cry.

"Sarah," said Mallory. "We're sorry, we just really need to talk with you. I promise, we don't want to cause trouble for you at all, but—"

"I said no," she hissed. "You don't understand who you're dealing with. I can't let them back into my life."

"I'm not sure what you mean, Sarah, but we know that whoever it is, they need to be held responsible for what happened to us." I tried to get her to see the sense of duty in all of this.

"Please, Sarah," Mallory said softly. "Can we just go somewhere and talk? We can keep it totally off the record."

She sighed, and I sensed she was considering it.

"We don't want to cause any trouble, but . . . you know what happened to us. Don't you think it's only fair?" I said, presenting the only logical reason I knew.

"Fine," she said.

Sarah agreed to meet us at a local wine bar not far from her office. We showed her the photo, and she confirmed knowing the man in the picture. I wasn't expecting what she told us next.

Sarah explained that she had met him her sophomore year at Goodwin. As far as she could recall, his name was Seni Srisuk. She had answered an ad about a loan forgiveness program and then attended a seminar in Lincoln. Her family struggled financially, and they weren't going to help her pay for college. She was worried she would have to drop out if she didn't find a way to pay for school, so when she saw the seminar, she decided to see what it was all about. He was at the seminar, and when she was leaving, he struck up a conversation with her.

Sarah explained that they went out a few times, and then he started offering to help her pay for her loans. At first she refused him, thinking he was going to force her into some type of shady crime or even sexual favors. Then he explained that he didn't want anything in return except for her to take him places and introduce him to more college kids, especially girls. He wasn't around much, but whenever he was in Lincoln or Omaha, he would let her know and ask to come stay with her and go to parties and clubs as her date.

Each time she did this, he would pay her. At first, she just thought he was a lonely guy and wanted to meet new people. Then one time when he called, she told him that she couldn't meet him because she had other plans. She thought maybe he had decided to leave her alone, but then a week later, her parents called to tell her their home had been vandalized. Sarah didn't put it all together until the next time he called and he said he was sorry to hear about her parents' house.

He became more aggressive and tried to get her to come with him to Thailand several times. She kept refusing but would still bring him to parties or events on campus so that he wouldn't cause any problems for her or her parents. As she explained this to Mallory and me, she was clearly bringing up some sensitive memories.

When Sarah learned about what had happened to us, she knew

it probably had something to do with him. She began crying, and we all sat in silence. My mind was spinning, and I could feel the temperature of my skin rising. Dumbfounded and angry, I had no response.

Mallory, however, seemed to have a calm demeanor as she took this information in. She actually reached out and placed a comforting hand on Sarah's arm, telling her it wasn't her fault.

Mallory continued to ask questions, and Sarah told her that she never saw this man again. Six months after graduation, she got a call from him, and he said that their agreement was over. He also warned her to never tell anyone or she would regret it.

I swallowed hard, never feeling more like a victim or target or marginalized human than I did at that moment.

Mallory was right, Sarah was a victim—or a survivor—in all of this too. I thought of all the women and children I had encountered working on the AG's trafficking task force. Sarah had been a pawn in this dirty crime, and we couldn't blame her or it would derail everything.

If we wanted any chance of figuring out who he was or how he was a part of our abduction, we needed Sarah's help and her testimony. It took a few hours of convincing and, unfortunately, Mallory and I had to share some pretty horrific details of our experience with Sarah, but she finally agreed to testify and help find this man.

Today, we are back in Oklahoma City to support Sarah as she gives a deposition. Agent Sommers has flown in to meet with Sarah and to talk with us about what will happen next.

The door to the conference room opens, and Sarah emerges and stops in front of us.

We all rise to our feet.

"Thank you so much, Sarah," Agent Sommers says and hands Sarah a card. "Don't hesitate to contact me if you remember anything else." Then Agent Sommers heads back into the conference room.

Mallory and I walk Sarah down the hallway toward the exit.

"Sarah, thank you. I know this was very hard for you to do," I say.

She nods and wipes her nose with a tissue. "I'm sorry I didn't do anything sooner. I was so scared and . . . I'm just so sorry."

Mallory reaches out and hugs Sarah. "You are a strong person, Sarah. You were protecting yourself and your family. We are all survivors, and we can only do what we can now."

"Mallory is right," I say, smiling at them. "We have to stick together, and hopefully they can find him and make him pay for what he's done to us and possibly others."

Sarah waves goodbye as she walks through the big, heavy exit door.

CHAPTER THIRTY-SEVEN

Mallory

March 14, 2017

"Cold out there in the capital city, Ms. Shields," Stan says as I walk through the lobby. He's the maintenance guy in my apartment building.

"I see that." I smile. "It makes us appreciate those warm days, Stan."

I close my mailbox, then put the mail into my book bag. When I step outside, the crisp air feels good on my face and in my lungs. As I walk up the sidewalk and across the street to get to campus, I look up to the sky. There are some clouds and a few light snowflakes falling, but the sun is trying to peek through. It makes me think about when I was kept in the village in Iraq and how hot the sun was there. I imagine the women and children in that village and have no idea where they are now. Are they looking up at the stars in the sky, possibly at the same time? Deep inside of me, I hope they have found some element of happiness or peace in their lives.

Each day has brought a sense of calmness and purpose. As much as I want to forget my time as an active victim, I have come to terms with the fact that I am now a survivor. But that doesn't change the fact that I have been a victim who endured a terrible reality. At first, I hated using that word, *victim*, because it can trigger feelings of helplessness for me and others. But it doesn't have the same power anymore, and I know I am so much more than that. What happened to me happened, and I am still working on accepting that. Every day is different, but I do think it's getting better over time. What has been the game changer is realizing I can choose to not let it define who I will be in the future. For so long, I thought I had no choice, but now I know I did. I chose to stay alive. I chose to make the best of the situation in order to someday get back to my life and myself.

Often, I think of the many women and girls I crossed paths with during my time in captivity. They gave me courage, and I feel it's only fair to be grateful for having them at my side during a time that now seems farther and farther away with each step forward. Each day I feel a little more complete, a little more myself.

Living in a new place is daunting, but at the same time, it is refreshing to have this opportunity. I am looking forward to spring in DC. I remember from my childhood how pretty and fragrant the cherry blossoms are. Over the past couple of months, I've met several new people and have started to socialize more. I've joined a bike club and am eager for us to go on longer rides together when the weather turns warmer.

As I get to my classroom, I take off my coat and sit down in my usual seat. I am always early for this class, most days the first one there. Reaching down into my bag, I grab my mail.

There is a card from Jenna and Ryan. Thomas had drawn a picture for me of dinosaurs and snowflakes, and it makes me giggle. His love of dinosaurs reminds me of how committed Ryan is to the things he liked as a kid growing up. Jenna also included a photo of the three of them with Carter standing in the backyard with a snowman in the background. They are holding a sign that says, "Baby Samuelson expected to arrive in August."

I immediately pull out Jenna's letter and read it. This news makes me happy, and I know it means things are as they should be. This will give us a great reason to celebrate when I visit next month.

I have been trying to make it back each month to visit my father, knowing I won't have that opportunity much longer. My mother tells me his responsiveness has been on a big decline, and we are fortunate he has held on for so long. The time away from my family has prepared me for this, but I am also glad I can spend time with him and be there for my mother.

She and Richard enjoy coming to visit me too. We celebrated the holiday in DC with my aunt Joan and her family, who drove up from Richmond the day after to go sledding in Rock Creek Park.

"Did you get the study guide done?" Stacy, my classmate, shuffles in beside me with a loud commotion of papers and books in her hands. This yanks me from my winter wonderland daydream.

"Oh yeah," I say, pulling my laptop from my bag and logging in. "You?"

"Not quite." She sits down and starts typing on her laptop. Like me, she is a non-traditional student. We are both finishing up some extra credits needed to get our teaching certificates.

We have a couple of classes together: Cognitive Learning Theories and Education of the Modern Student. I've enjoyed getting to know her. She is the one who turned me onto the bike club.

Stacy has lived in DC her whole life and is a single mom. Her background and upbringing was rough, and she came to discover college a bit later in life. Stacy has a great outlook, and I appreciate her can-do attitude. Our budding friendship is becoming important to me, and she is great about including me and introducing me to other students. For my birthday, she and her six-year-old daughter Elsie showed up at my apartment with homemade cupcakes to celebrate. Stacy actually brought up the "Teach for America" program last time we got together for drinks and board games with some other people in our program. It was intriguing to me, and I told her I would give it some serious thought.

The professor is finishing his lecture when I feel my phone vibrate in my pocket. It's a missed a call from Agent Sommers. When class is over, I tell Stacy I will catch up with her later that day. Agent Sommers left a message, and I want to hear it as soon as possible.

"Mallory, Agent Brenda Sommers here. I was hoping to catch you, but I needed to let you know . . . we got him. We got the bastard."

My breath catches in my throat.

"He was reentering the US at the Miami International Airport two days ago. He has been apprehended and is being detained for further investigation. We still have a lot to do and more information to uncover, but this is a step in the right direction, and we couldn't have done this without your help. Call me when you can. I knew you would want to know. Please let Jenna know as well. Talk soon."

My feet are unsteady and I sit back down. I could barely focus on most of the voicemail. The only words that have been ringing in my head are, *We got him, we got him, we got him.* After all this time. I have been waiting to hear this news for so long. I didn't even realize how much I needed it. I might have even been waiting to hear those words since I saw him years earlier in Cambodia.

A chill or tingle makes its way throughout my entire body, and I pull out my phone and send a text to Jenna. "Hey there. Great news. They got him. Agent Sommers just called. I will call you later with more details, but this is good news, my friend. BTW—I got your card today and couldn't be happier for baby #2. Can't wait to see you guys next month."

I feel like crying, but there are no tears. I just try to smile at this step toward the reclamation of my life. I knew it would be a long road, and I feel better knowing this man has been taken out of circulation and won't be able to lure any more young people into the awful world of trafficking.

Standing up, I shake out my arms. I pack up my bag, put on my coat, and head out the door. Once outside, I stop to look up at the sky again, feeling the snowflakes fall onto my face, immediately melting. In my mind, the faces of the women I'd been in captivity with appear. I picture Phalla, Fahima, Anke, Boupha, Oliva, CeCe, the British woman, Jenna and all the other faces who have shared the awful, life-altering experience with me. I want them to know somehow that I have found the strength inside myself to continue on, to fight, and to live. It isn't just for me, but for all of us.

I breathe in the crisp winter air, and the sun peaks around a cloud again, bringing warmth to my face.

"Hey, Dickens," I hear a familiar voice across the way.

I turn and see a tall figure coming toward me, and it startles me at first. As my eyes adjust, I realize I've seen him before. It is a friendly face, and I know I'm not afraid of him.

Private Rigden.

"Oh my gosh, how . . . how are you?" I say with a smile. I notice he has a backpack and is dressed in civilian clothing.

"I'm good, ma'am." He smiles. His eyes are so kind and somehow make me feel like the most important person in the world at this moment.

"Mallory," I remind him. "What . . . what are you doing here? I mean, are you a student?"

"That I am," he says. "I started a bit late in the semester, but I'm going to be formally discharged next month, and I wanted to get a head start on classes."

"That is wonderful, Private," I say.

"Please, ma'am . . . Mallory, call me Cash."

"Wow . . . well, congratulations, Cash." I smile and stare up at him, a bit mesmerized by the coincidence of running into him. There is something magnetic about his presence, and I continue staring and realize I'm still smiling.

"I read about . . . I mean, I followed your story."

Blinking and realizing what he just said, I bring myself back to the moment.

"Yes, it was sort of big news, I guess." I feel a tinge of self-consciousness come over me. I think about what a pitiful state I was in the last time he saw me in that base clinic in Iraq. I'm sort of surprised by the fact that he even recognized me.

"I am so sorry for what you endured, Mallory," he says, his eyes expressing a gentle compassion.

This is when other people always look away, or at the ground, when they tell me how sorry they feel for what happened, but Cash keeps looking at me, like he can see into my soul. His focus doesn't waver.

"Uh, well, thanks," I say. "Onward and upward, right?" I try to lighten the conversation.

"I can't believe I ran into you," he says. "You were actually the reason I decided to go for a degree in English Literature."

"No way," I exclaim. "Did you ever finish *Great Expectations* or check out *A Tale of Two Cities?*"

"Ah . . . 'It is a far, far better thing that I do, than I have ever done; it is a far, far better rest I go to than I have ever known.'" We both laugh as he quotes Dickens.

There is a moment of silence that falls between us as we stand on the cold sidewalk looking at each other. Here stands the man who found me on the day I returned to life. He saw me at the confluence of my most vulnerable moment and most empowering moment. His concerned face brings me a sense of peace somehow and ignites my curiosity about him.

"Well, it was so nice running into you, Cash," I say, not wanting to walk away from him. For the first time since my rescue, I feel those butterflies in my stomach that I thought might have died inside of me.

"You too, Mallory." His stare is captivating, and he looks so comfortable in front of me with the snow falling on top of his broad shoulders. He seems much older now, even though he clearly blends into the college student crowd much better than I do.

"Oh, hey . . ." he says abruptly. "I am actually being honored. I mean, it isn't a big thing, but I'm getting a medal for my discharge. It's sort of, well, I guess because of your rescue. There's just a small internal ceremony, but we can invite guests. Would you like to come?"

"Really? I mean yes, I would love to come." I'm flattered he asked me.

We exchange cell phone numbers.

"Cool," he says. "It's at the end of the week, just over the river. I'll text you the details."

"I would really like that, Cash."

"Me too," he says, grinning at me. "Maybe we could catch up after, grab a coffee, and . . . talk about Dickens?"

"Sure," I say. "That sounds perfect."

I walk away, feeling the intensity of Cash's eyes following me. A surge of nervousness comes over me, but in the very best of ways. I inhale deeply, noticing the gradual lightness of my steps, along with the purpose of my forward motion. Finally, I give myself the okay to be happy and hopeful in the moment. As I walk down the street, I imagine myself pulling everything I want closer and closer. I am finding my rhythm, and even alone, there is a sense of belonging that has been absent from my life for the last decade. The awareness of my own emotional strength and capability to shape my future is apparent, not only in my strong posture, but also in my soul… along with an emerging softness or vulnerability, I have longed to give into since returning. The snowflakes continue to gently fall, melting as they meet the ground. The air around me is still cool, but smells faintly of spring with all of the new beginnings and buzz of growth. The satisfaction and contentment of this very moment in time brings a smile to my face—a real, true smile as I continue my walk home.

EPILOGUE
Ruth

July 19, 2007

It was my free period, so I make my way down the hall to the teacher's office. Grabbing a cup of tea, I sit down at the communal table and open up the daily newspaper that always sits in the middle along with take-out menus, conversion charts, and a collection of notepaper and stray pens. I couldn't read anything, but I always enjoyed looking at the photos. If I found anything intriguing, I would ask one of the other teachers to translate.

The tops of my ears get hot, and I tense up when I reach the middle of the paper. Toward the bottom, in a small section, I notice the pictures of two young women. I have seen these women before. I remember them from a few weeks ago outside of the market in Bangkok. Yes, that's right, they were traveling to Chiang Mai. Two young American women. One of them sat with me outside the 7-Eleven; she told me she and her friend had just arrived a week before and were taking a gap year after college graduation. I ask P. Jaeb, one of the local instructors, to tell me what the article says.

After she reads it, she tells me that the women are missing, last seen on June 26. I walk over to the wall with the calendar and count the days back. That was the day I met them. My stomach drops and a slight sense of responsibility comes over me. I can't concentrate in my classes for the rest of the day. During lunch, I tell P. Jaeb of the situation, and she offers to help in any way she can if I want to take information to the police. At the end of the day, I visit the director's office and explain my concern. I ask for the next day off to visit the US Embassy and authorities in Bangkok to share what I know from my quick encounter with these women.

The next morning, P. Jaeb and I are driving in her small sedan over the bumpy roads. We finally hit the asphalt highway and drive thirty minutes into Bangkok. We reach the US Embassy with its high white walls and many small windows placed throughout. I have to wait over thirty minutes to meet with a Consular Officer. P. Jaeb joins me in the case I need any translation or assistance understanding the process.

I show the plainclothes officer the newspaper article and explain meeting and visiting the missing girls weeks ago on the last day they were seen. I share that they were planning to visit Chiang Mai that day and were considering taking the overnight bus upon my recommendation. Again, a pang of guilt runs through me. I describe what I can remember about each of them, what they had purchased, what they were wearing, and where they had been. He jots down some notes and then gives me a card with the Thonglor Police Station address. He says something in Thai to P. Jaeb, who nods.

Twenty minutes later, we are at the police station. It is a stately building with a large sign, gilded with gold with a line of flags behind it. There is another wait to speak with an officer. This time, P. Jaeb translates everything I say, and the uniformed officer records the information on a form. P. Jaeb stands up and I do the same. The officer stands and says something I don't understand, and nods to us.

As we walk out of the station, P. Jaeb explains that they appreciate my information and will add it to the file, but she is shaking her head. I can tell she is concerned, so I inquire. She explains that the officer told her it was possible they were runaways and that they receive over ten thousand calls a year about runaways and missing people, mainly women and children. But he will add it to the other missing person's cases that have been reported. I was hopeful until I learned there are currently over 1,200 active reports in the system.

AUTHOR'S NOTE

While the characters and events found in *Reclamation* are fictional, the premise surrounding the heinous crime of human sex trafficking and enslavement is very real. My goal as the author of this story is to help readers become more aware of the seriousness of sex trafficking by empathizing with the story and experiences of relatable characters.

Human trafficking is a multibillion-dollar industry in the United States. It is one of the largest industries in the world, second only to illegal drug trade. Below are strategies and tips to help you stay safe and alert while traveling.

Statistics and Facts

- In 2016, 3.8 million adults and 1 million children were victims of forced sexual exploitation, according to a 2017 study from the United Nations' International Labour Organization.

- The study also reported more than 70 percent of sex trafficking victims were located in Asia and the Pacific, compared with 14 percent in Europe and Central Asia and 4 percent in the Americas.

- Women and girls, who are disproportionately affected by forced labour, account for 99 percent of victims in the commercial sex industry and 58 percent in other sectors, according to a report by the Global Slavery Index.

- The International Labour Organization estimates annual

profit rates of around $80,000 per victim in developed countries and $55,000 in the Middle East.

- In 2019, there were 118,932 trafficking victims reported worldwide, according to the 2020 Trafficking in Persons Report compiled by the U.S. Department of State.

- Due to the clandestine nature of sex trafficking, gathering statistics can be difficult: "Aggregate data fluctuates from one year to the next due to the hidden nature of trafficking crimes, dynamic global events, shifts in government efforts, and a lack of uniformity in national reporting structures," according to the 2020 Trafficking in Persons Report.

How to Get Involved

Support organizations doing great work in combating sex trafficking and supporting survivors (all with positive ratings on CharityNavigator.org, which vets financial and accountability info)
- Agape International Missions
- UNICEF USA
- Polaris Project
- International Justice Mission

Learn the Signs of a Victim of Trafficking

- Living with employer
- Poor living conditions
- Multiple people in cramped space
- Inability to speak to individual alone
- Answers appear to be scripted and rehearsed
- Employer is holding identity documents
- Signs of physical abuse
- Submissive or fearful

- Unpaid or paid very little
- Under 18 and in prostitution

Use the Human Trafficking Referral Directory to report suspected trafficking behavior, get anti-trafficking resources, and learn how you can be involved in your community.

- Call 1-888-373-7888
- Text "BEFREE" or "HELP" to 233733
- Email help@humantraffickinghotline.org
- Chat at https://humantraffickinghotline.org/chat
- Ask your local, state, and federal elected officials what they are doing to combat human trafficking.
- Become a mentor to a young person or someone in need, since traffickers often target people who lack support systems. The Teammates Mentoring Program or Big Brothers Big Sisters are good organizations to connect with that have local chapters.
- Support companies that use ethical labor practices by referencing ResponsibleSourcingTool.org and the Department of Labor's List of Goods Produced by Child Labor or Forced Labor.

What To Do if You're Traveling

Strategies

1. Know the address and telephone number of the embassy closest to where you are staying. You can find a full listing of US embassies around the world at usembassy.gov.

2. Register with the local US embassy and alert them of your travel plans, and/or share travel details with the

Smart Traveler Enrollment Program (STEP): https://travelregistration.state.gov.

3. Know how to access emergency services in that country. If there is an emergency number (equivalent to 9-1-1 in the US), memorize this number or keep it in a safe place.

4. Take a map of the city you are traveling to and make sure you know how to get from your residence to the bank, embassy or consulate, police department, or hospital in case of emergency.

5. Be wary of strangers and your environment.

   a. Do not give your passport or ID to anyone (even if they require it to hold or rent equipment or vehicles), and keep a copy of your passport information in a safe place.

   b. Don't ever tell a stranger your full name, where you are going, or if you are staying alone. Sex traffickers often come across as harmless and charismatic.

   c. Avoid traveling alone, at night, or on deserted side streets. Travel during the day if possible. Stay alert to your surroundings.

   d. Find a crowded place if you believe you're being followed. Don't hesitate to alert police, friends, and family to your suspicions, and share a physical description of the suspect.

   e. If you walk to your vehicle and there is a pamphlet on the windshield or a ribbon or tie on the side mirror, etc., get in and drive to a safe space before stopping to remove it. This is possibly a decoy to slow you down while in a parking lot.

6. Make sure that you have a means of communication (cell

phone or phone card), access to your bank account, and any medication that you might need with you at all times.

7. Be safe with your online practices.

   a. Be suspicious of strangers who approach you after you've posted something personal on your social media profile and they're suddenly offering you help, advice, money, a place to stay, or a job opportunity.

   b. If you're getting random messages from people on social media, check your privacy settings, turn off your location settings on social media, and only make your posts visible to your friends.

   c. Avoid checking in to places on social media (especially while traveling), although it is important to update friends and family of your whereabouts constantly.

   d. Sex traffickers are often someone victims meet online, or someone they considered a friend. Go with your gut and don't be afraid to say no if you meet someone like this and they want to meet up with you alone.

8. When traveling abroad for volunteer opportunities, do some research beforehand and pick reputable agencies that have strict protocols and thorough supervision.

9. If you've received a work-related travel opportunity that seems suspicious, take the following steps to ensure safety.

   a. Request address information for employment and/or housing.

   b. Request information about travel arrangements and who is expected to pay for travel and any visa or other entry fees.

   c. Make copies of important documents for yourself and

give some to a trusted friend or relative.

d. Have a ticket home in your name and keep it in a safe place.

e. Provide a trusted friend or relative with information about your travel arrangements.

f. Arrange a time to contact a trusted friend or relative to let them know you arrived safely.

g. Have access to a bank account and have a way to maintain control of your own funds.

If Things Go Wrong

1. Take a self-defense class or look up self-defense YouTube videos, and mentally prepare yourself to fight off potential abductors. If you are attacked, make a scene, yell for help, and fight back like your life depends on it.

2. Carry pepper spray with you on your keychain (although, if you're traveling internationally, you'll have to keep it in checked luggage) and use it if someone's being aggressive.

3. If you think you are in immediate danger or have an emergency, call 911 immediately. Another number to contact if you currently feel unsafe is Safe Horizon, 800-621-HOPE (4673).

4. Create and use the Safe Horizon safety plan.

   a. Are there people in your life or in your community who can offer support?

   b. Are there ways to avoid areas or locations that make you feel unsafe?

   c. Where could you go during an emergency?

   d. Are there phone numbers you need to memorize?

e. Do you have children who need to be a part of your safety plan?

f. Do you need a safety plan for work or school?

g. Is your safety plan stored on a computer or smartphone?

5. Learn and use basic phrases in the local language to communicate.

What To Do if you Have a Loved One Who's Traveling Overseas

Strategies

1. Set up safety words with them. Designate words to indicate whether it's safe to talk and they are alone, and when they are not safe.

2. Ask their permission to track their phone via GPS so you know their whereabouts at all times. Most cell phones allow a select few to have access to the owner's location.

3. Learn how to access emergency services in that country. Look up the country's emergency number (if it has one), as well as the address and contact information for the country's embassy or consulate.

4. Designate a regular check-in time with them during their trip.

5. Get a copy of their travel itinerary, with the locations they're planning to travel to and schedule.

6. Compile a list of contact information for anyone they're traveling with. If they're with an organization, make sure you have a list of key contacts for them as well.

7. If possible, make sure they have an international phone plan for their cell carrier.

8. Make sure you both download a reliable messaging app (such as WhatsApp) to keep in contact while they are traveling abroad.

If You're Concerned

1. Call the organizations or contacts they're traveling alongside, or check in with close friends they might be in touch with.

2. Contact the local Embassy or Consulate, or the US State Department Office of Overseas Citizen Services at 888-407-4747 (from the US or Canada).

3. Consider reaching out to international aid organizations.

4. Call the local police in the country where your loved one is staying and find out what they can do to help.

What to Do if you Suspect Someone is Being Trafficked

Strategies

1. Know the signs:

   • An inability to speak to anyone else alone or isn't allowed to speak on their own behalf

   • Scripted or rehearsed answers to questions

   • Being submissive or fearful in public

   • Has tattoos or other markings that could indicate "ownership" by someone else

   • Has a much older sexual or "romantic" partner

2. Make sure you are informed about the prevalence of human trafficking in the country and region you're traveling to with resources such as the Global Slavery Index reports.

3. Don't give money to child beggars who may be the victims of trafficking. This helps the trafficking industry remain profitable. Donate to a reputable charity or local organization instead.

4. Don't support clubs or bars that employ extremely young-looking workers or seem to be engaged in questionable practices.

If you're concerned

1. What to do if you think someone is being trafficked:

   a. Do NOT approach the victim—this would put them in direct danger.

2. If you are in a grounded plane, report to a TSA agent, a customer service agent, or call the Homeland Security Tip Line.

3. If in the air, report to a flight attendant or any flight crew on board.

   a. Call the National Human Trafficking toll-free hotline at 1-888-373-7888. Anti-Trafficking Hotline Advocates are available 24/7 to take reports of potential human trafficking. You could also text the organization at 233733 or chat via www.humantraffickinghotline.org/chat.

4. Report missing children or child pornography to the National Center for Missing and Exploited Children (NCMEC) at 1-800-THE-LOST (843-5678) or through their cyber tip line.

RESOURCES

Bustamante, Clarissa. "Avoiding Sex Trafficking While Traveling." *KNWA* online, November 19, 2018, https://www.nwahomepage.com/news/avoiding-sex-trafficking-while-traveling/.

"How to Spot Trafficking while Traveling," *TVF*, accessed December 15, 2020, https://treasuredvesselsfoundation.org/2019/11/12/how-to-spot-trafficking-while-traveling/.

"Identify Safety Options" *Safe Horizon*, accessed December 15, 2020, https://www.safehorizon.org/our-services/safety-plan/.

"Report Trafficking," *National Human Trafficking Hotline*, accessed December 15, 2020, https://humantraffickinghotline.org/report-trafficking/.

"Safe Foreign Travels: Learn about Human Trafficking," *NCL* online, August 13, 2013, https://nclnet.org/safe_foreign_travels_learn_about_human_trafficking/.

"Safety Planning Information," *National Human Trafficking Hotline*, accessed December 15, 2020, https://humantraffickinghotline.org/faqs/safety-planning-information/.

"Safety Tips to Avoid Sex Traffickers," *Smart Gen Society*, June 13 2018, https://www.smartgensociety.org/blog/article/safety-tips-to-avoid-sex-traffickers/.

U.S. Department of State Bureau of Consular Affairs. *Travel.State. Gov.* Accessed January 14, 2021, https://travel.state.gov/.

"10 Ways to Protect Yourself from Human Trafficking," *Youth Village*, accessed December 15, 2020, https://www.youthvillage.co.za/ 2018/05/10-ways-to-protect-yourself-from-human-trafficking/.

ACKNOWLEDGEMENTS

I want to thank my tribe of supporters, friends, family, and literary experts for going on this journey with me. My friend and spy partner, Susie Bertie, I am grateful for your honesty and gentle nudges in the right direction. Aliese Hoffman, my friend and colleague, thank you for the many hours of review, positive reinforcement, and helping me "get it right." You'll be proud. My dear friend, Amy Peirce, your knowledge, experience, and insight helped me immensely, as well as your continuous encouragement. The three of you provided countless hours of advisement that helped shape this novel. The Book Club members: Cris Wright, Carol Hoffman, Valerie DeJonge, Melissa Hunt, Kim Kern, and Beth Kavan . . . your review gave me the momentum to move forward and allowed me to see the story through a different lens. Thank you to Susan Piver for her Fearlessly Creative retreat at the beautiful Shambhala Mountain Center, an inspirational space to write and share. I also want to thank Melissa Collins, Darcy Koletic, April Myers, and Bree Dority for your reviews and sharing resources and ideas with me. Olivia Ball . . . you inspired this novel and provided sound information to bring it to life. Emily Case, thank you for your literary genius and editorial research skills. Sarah Nottage-Tacey, I appreciate your guidance into finding those feelings and the many porch sessions. Many thanks to my eleventh-hour friend, Amy Loy Herring for her support and feedback. Thank you to Cathy Lang for connecting me to material experts, Diane Blalock, Karen Marks, and Sue Ernst, volunteers for the Agape International Mission (AIM), three of the loveliest humans, who provided motivation, feedback, and invaluable information about the horrific crime and realities of human sex trafficking. Thank you for the work you do to mitigate human trafficking. Many thanks to the publishing team at BQB Publishing: Rebecca Lown for bringing my vision to life with the beautiful book cover, Andrea Vande Vorde for her amazing content editing and helping me reach further as a writer to enhance the story and, of course, Terri Leidich for her guidance, support, and mentorship. Special thanks to my family and friends who always encourage my endeavors, my parents Gary and Barbara Clonch, and my two north stars Wyatt and Madison, forever and always.

ABOUT THE AUTHOR

Lisa Clonch Tschauner is an educator, business consultant, and researcher who has previously written and published nonfiction, business-centric work including *Rule of Thumb: A Guide to Customer Service and Business Relationships.* She is the owner and co-founder of *Open for Business Magazine,* a regional publication. Tschauner is also the founder  of the RE-Write online writing community featuring pieces of prose, poetry, essays, and reflections. *Reclamation* is her debut novel.

In addition to writing, she works in the field of entrepreneurship education and leadership studies. Her education includes degrees in organizational communication and management, and human sciences with a leadership specialization. She conducts observational research through mixed methods including various interview strategies. Tschauner is interested in how the world is changing through the lens of emerging generations and the global influence.

She has attended different writing workshops and seminars. Although more of an academic and nonfiction writer professionally, her personal writing interests include compelling fiction that creates a platform and addresses relevant topics. Tschauner lives in Nebraska and is the mother of two dynamic young adults who inspire and evoke curiosity, leading her to tackle difficult topics that appeal to a wide-range of readers.